W9-BIE-901

Just for the Summer

Also by LAURA VAN WORMER

JURY DUTY
ANY GIVEN MOMENT
BENEDICT CANYON
WEST END
RIVERSIDE DRIVE

Laura Van Wormer

Just for the Summer

MIRA BOOKS

ISBN 1-55166-280-9

JUST FOR THE SUMMER

Printed in U.S.A.

For

Loretta Barrett

and

Dianne Moggy

My heartfelt thanks to my friends Ann Douglas, Carolyn Katz, James Spada and Tom Zito for their unflagging support, and to all the extraordinary, terrific people of MIRA Books worldwide, especially Candy Lee, Amy Moore, Katherine Orr, Randall Toye and Stacy Widdrington.

To my family, as always, my eternal thanks.

And to Chris, all that is good and wonderful, for that is who you are.

Prologue

"You feel *sad?*" the fifty-something partner, Sheila, said loudly to a department secretary. "You should be *mad!* We trained Mary Liz and taught her everything she knows and now she's upped and quit!"

The office party high above Chicago had come to a grinding halt, with partners, traders, analysts, salespeople, clerks and secretaries all turning to look.

"Well, she *is* quitting," Sheila said, addressing the room.

Sheila had been with the firm for thirty-four years and thought young businesswomen today were next to worthless. For years Mary Liz had been an exception in her book, but the moment she had turned in her resignation was the moment Mary Liz had been classified right back into the worthless masses again.

Harold, a "senior" partner—he was only thirty-five—cleared his throat and stepped forward to take charge. "I guess this is as good a time as any to make a toast," he said.

People murmured their encouragement.

Sitting in the corner, watching her, Mary Liz noticed, was the psychic. Somebody had come up with the bright idea of giving her a reading as a going-away present.

"Mary Liz Scott has worked for Reston, Kellaher for over ten years," Harold began. "She came in through our training program, worked in several departments and then was hired in the research department as a junior analyst. While working during the day, she went to school at night and earned an M.B.A. from the University of Chicago." He smiled. "Contrary to any grumbling you may have recently heard—" he gave Sheila a meaningful look "—Mary Liz has taught *us* a lot. She has generated considerable profits for Reston, Kellaher for the last eight consecutive years, and if we credit her with talking us into—when she was still a trainee—getting involved with a certain paging company we all know and love, she has made us considerable money every single year she has been here." His smile expanded. "So thank her for increasing your year-end bonuses every year she's been with us."

There was some applause.

"As a matter of fact," Harold continued, "Mary Liz has already contributed eighteen million to the firm in new business in this quarter alone!"

"My bonus to you, Harold," Mary Liz said over the top of her plastic champagne glass before sipping, making people laugh.

He chuckled and continued. "And while none of us are happy to see her leave, no one can say we will ever regret having had her as a part of our family."

"But only because Mary Liz isn't going to a competitor," Roger from high yield shouted from the back of the room. He made his way to the front. "If she wasn't leaving the business altogether we'd be trying to kill her."

Everyone laughed. But it was true. Retiring, at the age of thirty-two, from investment banking was very different than jumping to another firm.

"I still say you're nuts, Mary Liz," a salesman called. "You made partner, fool! Get paid for all the crap they've put you through!"

When the laughter died down, Sheila snorted. "She's hardly leaving penniless."

The department secretary was still looking distressed. "If Mary Liz wants to have a life," she said, "I don't know why everybody's so upset. Mr. Traplinger did it."

"Mr. Traplinger was forty-six, had a wife and kids and ran for mayor of his town," Sheila told her. "Mary Liz doesn't have any responsibilities and she has absolutely no plans to do anything."

"No plans that I'm willing to discuss," Mary Liz added lamely. Sheila was right, though—she really didn't know what she wanted to do except get out of here. Yes, it was true, in ten years she had amassed quite a bit of money, but she loathed what it had cost her in the process: ten years of virtually no memories of anything but work, and two failed relationships—one long, one short—that only occurred in the first place because she had met the men *at* work, and she had plunged into the relationships because she had known there would be no romantic relationships at all if she didn't follow up on these, even though she knew from the start they were not right.

Not an admirable track record, she didn't think. But that was the point. She hadn't had time to focus properly on anything but her work for ten years.

Roger from high yield climbed onto the conference-room table. "I'd like to make a toast!"

Harold, the senior partner, looked annoyed for having been usurped.

"I want to toast the woman who has been my friend for ten years," Roger said, raising his glass. "Mary Liz is one of the most beautiful women I've ever met—"

"She's still not going to sleep with you," a bond trader cracked, making everone laugh. Roger's infatuation with Mary Liz over the years had not gone by unnoticed.

"Shut up, dog face," Roger growled. "Now, where was I? Ah, yes—to Mary Liz, who is not only a genius—"

"I wouldn't go that far," Sheila protested, making everyone laugh.

"But who is also one of the nicest, kindest, most trustworthy people I've ever met in my life—"

"She's *still* not going to sleep with you!" the trader repeated, prompting laughter all over again.

"I would also like to say," Roger continued, glass high in the air, "that Mary Liz Scott has the best set of coconuts in investment banking!"

The men roared and the women either groaned or remained stonily silent, sadly accustomed to the territory.

"Seriously," Roger said, turning to look at her, "Mary Liz, to you—may your new life be filled with joy. And may you never forget your friends at Reston, Kellaher, who will love and miss you—always."

The sincerity in his voice was touching; everyone murmured, "Hear, hear," and Mary Liz felt her throat tighten with emotion.

"Excuse me? Miss Scott?" the receptionist called from the door. "I'm sorry to interrupt, but Hannah's here to see you."

"Hannah?" Roger said from atop the table. "Who's Hannah?"

"The cleaning lady," said the receptionist.

"Are you friends with the cleaning woman, Mary Liz?" Sheila asked.

"Yes, as a matter of fact," Mary Liz said, walking out of the conference room into the reception area. Hannah was standing just outside the door, in street clothes, and Mary Liz almost didn't recognize her. As Mary Liz closed the conference-room door, Hannah lunged so suddenly at her that Mary Liz nearly fell backward off her high heels.

"God bless, God bless, God bless," Hannah wept into her shoulder.

"Shh, shh, it's okay, Hannah," Mary Liz murmured, patting the woman's back. She looked at the receptionist, who was very wide-eyed indeed. "It's okay, thanks."

After the receptionist left, Mary Liz peeled Hannah off her and held her by the shoulders. "I just didn't want you to worry," she said quietly. "You've got so much on your plate right now and the children deserve a fresh start." At this the cleaning woman wailed again, grabbed Mary Liz and resumed sobbing.

A Bosnian war widow with two children, Hannah had been sponsored to the United States by a local church. She had been given this cleaning job and a little two-bedroom apartment on the South side. The only problem was, Hannah lived in one of the worst public school districts in Chicago and one of her children—children who had already seen and experienced far too much in their short lives—had been beaten up twice already. To make a long story short, Hannah had broken down and cried about it late one night the week before, and Mary Liz had patiently gone through the alternatives—applying to magnet schools (no, the children no English good enough yet), private school (no money!), moving (where?)—and Hannah had spoken wistfully of a parochial school near their apartment....

Mary Liz had gone to that parochial school yesterday to arrange payment for the children's tuition for the next several years, their active enrollment beginning on Monday.

Why not? Mary Liz had no children, and her parents and brothers were all doing well. Why not celebrate the start of her new life with a gift to some children starting theirs?

The conference-room door opened and Sheila peered out. "Mary Liz is out here hugging the cleaning lady," she reported.

Mary Liz stepped back and gave Hannah a warning look. The last thing she wanted was for anyone here to know what she had done. Her multimillionaire partners would kill her for "starting a trend," pointing out that refugee cleaning ladies from Bosnia were not organized charities and thus not even tax deductible.

"Hannah just stopped by to say goodbye," Mary Liz explained to Sheila.

"Yes. I miss," Hannah said solemnly, wiping her tears, but smiling nonetheless.

Miraculously, Sheila seemed to soften. "Well, why don't you bring her in for some cake, Mary Liz? And have her take some of these sandwiches home. They shouldn't go to waste."

And so Hannah, the Bosnian cleaning lady, joined the members of the firm at Mary Liz's going-away party, and sat down to drink lemonade and eat pasta salad and chicken wings—her grateful eyes scarcely ever leaving Mary Liz, which in turn made the soon-to-be-ex investment banker want very much to cry.

It was true—it could be a wonderful life.

The party was over and Mary Liz was stuck with the psychic in her office. At his request, she had come out from behind her desk to sit in a chair opposite him. He had begun their interview by holding her hand for a few moments and then releasing it, explaining that he was just going to let "it" flow through him, that she was to take what was helpful to her and leave the rest. She could ask him questions at any time, he added.

Thus far Mary Liz hadn't asked him a thing. It was too spooky.

"You are about to set out on a grand adventure," he told her. "And it has to do with water. A great deal of water."

"Uh-oh, Lake Michigan's not going to flood again, is it?" she joked stupidly.

He looked at her patiently. "No. That is not it." He smiled. "I feel the sea, an ocean, vast beaches of white sand. Trees." He paused. "It is a very beautiful place."

"I was thinking about going to Hawaii," she acknowledged.

The psychic nodded, looking doubtful though, as if this was not what he saw but was too polite to contradict her again. "I also sense a new love. A real love. A grand love." The psychic met her eyes. "Truly. I sense a man who could be the love of your life."

Mary Liz hated herself for letting her heart start to pound at this.

"He is not married." The psychic's smile thinned. "He has experienced great pain—a tragedy of some sort." Then he squinted suddenly, his smile vanishing altogether. He cocked his head slightly. "Are you starting right into a new career?"

"Not that I know of," she said.

"I believe you are. Soon." Then he looked confused. "I see tremendous wealth, but it is not yours. And then I see—" he gestured, as if to apologize for it not making sense "—I see children. Your children. Down the road. A husband and children."

Mary Liz couldn't help but smile. The thought of children made her happy.

But the psychic's expression had changed again.

"What's the matter?" Mary Liz asked him.

He looked troubled now. Very troubled. "There is danger. A physical threat. Of harm—to you. To others, too. It has to do with this new work you'll be doing."

"Well, if you saw my children," Mary Liz said, "I'm not going to die right away or anything, right?" When he didn't answer her, she repeated, "Right?"

He was studying her carefully. "Be very careful when you start this new career. Be on your guard."

After a moment she said, "What is it you sense, exactly?" When he hesitated, she reminded him, "It's my reading. And I'd like to know."

He was debating, she could tell.

"Tell me," she pressed. "What is it?"

"It's murder," he said.

I

1

No other town, no group of people, no style of living could possibly be as beautiful as East Hampton, Long Island.

Mary Liz Scott had been staying in the caretaker's cottage on the Hoffman estate for almost a month. Her bedroom was small, but lovely, with pale pink and white wallpaper, lots of wood trim, a double bed and matching dresser, and one small armchair covered in the same pink, green and white fabric as the curtains. The second bedroom, even smaller, had been converted into an office, complete with computer desk, file cabinets, photocopying machine and, perhaps most interestingly, a paper shredder.

The kitchen of the cottage was bright and cheery, separated from the living room by only a breakfast bar.

The living room itself was all blue and white chintz, and on the coffee table in front of the overstuffed sofa was a beautiful vase of flowers that changed weekly. There was a fireplace with a brass fender set on the far wall, with a pretty seascape painting over the mantel. On either side were two small windows and then bookshelves, painted white, from floor to ceiling, holding the complete works of Edith Wharton, Henry James and F. Scott Fitzgerald, brass pots of ivy and an assortment of popular fiction and nonfiction. In the magazine rack by one of the wingback chairs were *Vanity Fair, The New Yorker, Golf Digest, Newsweek, Los Angeles, Sailing, Forbes, Martha Stewart Living* and *Architectural Digest.*

Every weekday morning a *Wall Street Journal* appeared at her front door, and seven days a week, the *New York Times.*

This was what it was like to be a guest of one of the wealthier families of East Hampton.

Mary Liz had frankly not expected to like the summer resort town. She thought she'd find it too trendy for her tastes, too Hollywoody and ostentatious. After all, East Hampton had, in the last decade, come to be called Hollywood East, and, heaven only knew, Mary Liz did not think terribly much of that city of excess.

Mary Liz had gotten it all wrong. East Hampton was one of the most beautifully situated places on earth, possessing an abundance of those gifts that are only God-given: vast expanses of wide, white pristine beaches along the breathtaking Atlantic; miles and miles of lush green hills and dales and woods and forests; acre upon acre of farmland, broken only by the occasional horse corral and barn; and dramatic weather ranging from a dry hot sun in a perfectly blue sky, to the darkest gray-black horizon of lashing wind and rain.

Actually, Mary Liz wasn't even technically a guest. They—the real guests—stayed up the hill in the guest house. Mary Liz had only a family connection. She was on the estate to do a favor for her parents and the mistress of the manor, and so she was, at her own request, separated not only from the main residence, but the guest house, as well.

Tonight, however, it was time for Mary Liz to behave like a gracious guest. Her hostess had finally arrived from Los Angeles for "the season," and Mary Liz, whether she liked it or not, was expected to join in the social whirl of the Big House. (Yes, that is what they called it, the Big House, making Mary Liz feel a little like George Raft every time she referred to it.) Tonight was the first dinner party of the season in the Big House, and she had been told it was "cas" (as in "casual") with only the Hoffmans' most intimate friends in attendance.

The telephone in the cottage was ringing. Mary Liz picked up the bedroom extension.

"Mary Liz, darlin'—" It was her hostess, Nancy Hoffman, who also happened to be her godmother. "I just wanted to make sure you had everything you need."

Mary Liz looked at the clock and had to laugh. "You mean, I'm already five minutes late and where am I?"

There was the sound of deep, Southern-belle laughter on the other end of the phone.

"It's almost scary, Aunt Nancy," Mary Liz said, "how much you and Mom are alike in ways."

"I consider that a great compliment, Mary Liz. Anyway, darlin', I've got an awfully nice young man coming I want you to meet, and I promised your mama I'd swing him by your eye to see if you were interested."

"Aunt Nancy!"

"Bye-bye!" she said, hanging up (which sounded more like "Bahbaaa!").

Mary Liz hung up the phone and closed the bedroom door so she could look at herself in the full-length mirror. Hair was so-so. Her hair was brown, but already streaking auburn from the sun and saltwater. It needed a trim, however, and the humidity today was not helping. Her eyes, frankly, looked great tonight, bluer than blue against the tan she had acquired, and with a little eyeliner and mascara… Smile was better than usual with the tan, too.

Her white cotton blouse was boring but flattering, as was her boring cotton print skirt and sandals. The point was, boring but flattering clothes it had to be until she lost the ten pounds she had gained in the last six months of working at Reston, Kellaher.

She pulled her skirt up and turned around. Ugh. The curse of the voluptuous woman, as her mother called it. Her mother's theory was that the body of any large-breasted woman would, after thirty, forever and at every opportunity apply fat intake directly to the hips, abdomen and thighs.

Mary Liz, voluptuous or not (yes, large-breasted, like her mother), knew it was simply a case of eating the wrong food. But then, when one was feeling down, what else tasted good? And so, when she had been depressed back in Chicago, she had turned to the pals of her youth, McDonald's, Domino's, Sara Lee and the like, and now could only pretend to be surprised that she had gained weight. (Actually, she had already taken off three pounds since she had arrived in East Hampton, and thus, in truth, had really gained thirteen pounds before she resigned.)

At any rate, at ten pounds heavier or not, Mary Liz was an extremely lucky young woman. She had been born with good health and good looks and a mother and father and brothers who were absolutely wonderful. She'd also grown up in a well-to-do household where socializing was taught to be fun, table manners were a priority, social etiquette an essential part of one's kit for life and a kind of unrestrained graciousness toward strangers under most any circumstances an absolute must. In other words, her parents had taught Mary Liz how to get along in most every situation.

This did not get rid of her feelings of shyness, however. It only masked her unease, and if and when Mary Liz ever confided in someone that she did feel shy around people, the response was always one of total amazement.

Standing at the foot of the driveway, not far from the stairs of the cottage porch, Mary Liz was feeling shy. Nonetheless, she began the ascent to the Big House. It was an imposing sight up there on the hill. The main body of the house, two stories (with small windows in the attic making it look like three), had been built in 1880 "by some Yankee blackguard who no doubt made his fortune pillaging the South." (This latter description had been provided by Aunt Nancy, whose family had evidently suffered greatly from the Civil War.)

Although the front was built with granite and brick native to the Northeast, the mansion looked more than a little Southern to Mary Liz with its white balustrade and four-pillar front entrance. To the right, extending from the main house, was a long, single-floor wing—containing the kitchen, scullery, pantry, laundry room and maid's quarters—followed by a series of flower gardens, and beyond those, a screen of fir trees hid a tennis court. Two acres of lawn cascaded down the hill in front of the house; to the left was a three-car garage, and just down the hill, also to the left, about two hundred yards from the Big House, was the wood-shingled guest house.

A vehicle was coming up the driveway behind Mary Liz and it slowed when it reached her side. The occupants of the black Infiniti simply stared at her, trying to figure out who she was. Mary Liz smiled. The occupants nodded, but then sped ahead to hurry and park and go into the house before they had to talk to her.

Instead of going to the front door, Mary Liz opted for one in the back. It would be less intimidating to enter the party from the rear. She hoped. She hesitated at the corner of the house, listening to the sounds of the party: murmurs, laughing, the clinking of ice against glasses, snatches of conversation—

"Simply marvelous!"

"Guys were duking it out—"

"I couldn't *imagine*..."

"Twenty yards from the fairway—"

And she could hear the doorbell ringing.

The Hoffmans had remodeled the back of the Big House to take full advantage of the view of the dunes, beach and ocean that lay directly behind the house. The second-floor bedrooms on this side all had private balconies, and the master suite upstairs had an open-air terrace just as enormous as the porch that extended from the living room on the first floor. When there was a hurricane, the housekeeper had explained to Mary Liz, the whole back of the house could be sealed shut with massive wood shutters.

"You haven't seen a pretty blond lady hiding around out here somewhere, have you?" a male voice said from behind Mary Liz, making her jump. It was Bertie, aka Alfred Bertram Hoffman, Aunt Nancy's son, who Mary Liz had met upon Aunt Nancy's arrival. He was blond and blue-eyed like his mother, tall, very nice-looking, about thirty or so. In his navy blue linen blazer, white polo shirt, khakis and loafers without socks, he looked like the quintessential successful young man—except that Bertie Hoffman had never held a proper job, so far as Mary Liz knew. He was Nancy's eldest child. Her younger daughter, Denver, was in Los Angeles, where she starred in a nighttime TV soap on the Fox network.

"From what I've seen," Mary Liz said, "*every* woman in East Hampton is a pretty blond lady—including your mother."

"Ah, yes, but this is mother's best friend I'm looking for," he said, peering behind a bush. "Claire MacClendon. Mother seems to think she might have balked at the last minute and I'm supposed to find her."

"In the bushes?"

"She's an artist," he explained. He looked out across the dunes and then shrugged, turning back to Mary Liz. "Claire's a very wonderful human being, so it's hard sometimes to get her to come to one of Mother's parties." He smiled, showing excellent teeth. "So why are you hiding out back here?"

"I am not hiding," Mary Liz told him.

"Then allow me to escort you in," he said, taking her arm before she could change her mind, and whisking her up the steps.

"Mary Liz, hello, darlin'!" Nancy Hoffman called, stepping out from the living room onto the porch and taking her hand. At fifty-eight, Mary Liz's godmother still had "it," the beauty and vitality that had made her so popular as a debutante years ago. (She and Mary Liz's mother had "come out" together at the Waldorf Astoria Cotillion Ball of 1957.) Looking at Nancy now, it was hard to believe she had been widowed only six months before, when her husband, Alfred, the famous Hollywood movie producer, had died in a plane crash on the West Coast.

Nancy turned to her son. "Any sign of Claire?"

"Her car's here, but I don't know where she is."

"Did you try the cutting garden?"

"Yes."

"Well, she's around somewhere, then," Nancy said cheerfully. To Mary Liz, "Come, my precious goddaughter, and meet everybody."

"Oh, Aunt Nancy," Mary Liz fretted, "I'll never be able to keep all these people straight."

"You'll be seeing them all summer, darlin', so it's hardly a pressing concern. Just smile a little, compliment a lot and they'll love you, guaranteed."

The first guest Mary Liz saw literally took her breath away. She couldn't believe it. It was Sasha Reinhart, the fifty-something mega-pop-star diva.

"Sasha's renting next door," Aunt Nancy explained, introducing Mary Liz.

"How do you do?" Mary Liz managed to say, holding out her hand. She had seen Sasha Reinhart for years in concerts, in movies, and on stage once, too, but never this close. She was lovely, softer in real life, a little shorter, too, but the star possessed a kind of electricity that seemed to make the very air hum around her.

"Hi," the mega-star said, shaking her hand once and dropping it.

Nancy swept Mary Liz along through more introductions.

"Rachelle Zaratan," said the famous clothes designer, extending her hand toward Mary Liz and rolling her r's slightly, sounding a bit like a foreign spy in an old movie. "And this is my husband, Charles Kahn." Rachelle, Nancy explained to Mary Liz, was a very close friend of Sasha's and was responsible for the diva renting in East Hampton this summer.

Next was Randolph Vandergilden, owner of the Eastern Winery, a man about sixty who first looked at Mary Liz's breasts and then positively leered at her as they shook hands.

"Here," Bertie Hoffman said, coming up to her a moment later and handing Mary Liz an icy glass of white wine, "taste Randy's wine." She thanked him, sipped it and froze. It was the most ghastly Chardonnay she had ever tasted in her life.

Bertie was laughing and laughing, and his mother came over, took the glass out of Mary Liz's hand, sniffed it and then shoved it back at her son. "Get Mary Liz a proper glass of wine, if you please, and bring Wendy over to meet her."

She turned back to Mary Liz. "Sadly, Randy is an old friend, Mary Liz, and I'd appreciate it if you told him you've tasted his wine. Now, what you say about it, that I leave to you—but do keep in mind I need to use his winery for an important charity function this summer."

Next she met Claude Lemieux and his wife, Isabel. They were

French expatriates and Mary Liz had read about him in the gossip columns. He was the publisher of the American edition of the women's magazine, *Je Ne Sais Quoi* ("a certain knowingness"), brought over from France five years ago. It was one of the few women's magazines that Mary Liz subscribed to.

"Claude and Alfred were great tennis partners," Aunt Nancy explained.

Next was, "Sinclair Buckley, but call me Buck—everyone does." Buck Buckley was tall, deeply tan, a real man's man, with a hearty handshake and considerable charm. Nancy explained that Buck was chairman of the East End Country Club, of which her husband, Alfred, had been a founding member. Buck had built the club six years ago in answer to the area clubs with waiting lists generations-long.

"Play golf, young lady?" he asked Mary Liz. To Nancy, "You ought to play with her in the ladies' member-guest day next week."

"Good grief," Mary Liz said, fully aware of her beginner's status in the game.

"If I were you," a brunette woman with flashing eyes said, coming up to Mary Liz, "I'd avoid that tournament at all costs."

"Mary Liz, darlin'," Aunt Nancy said, "this is Vanessa Buckley."

"His other half," Vanessa Buckley further qualified, throwing her head in Buck's direction. She was in her forties, very tanned, with long and rather wild dark hair. She also was wearing a revealing halter top and blue-jean skirt. "If you want to play golf, Mary Liz, you come to me. I'll see that you have some fun. Buck's idea of fun is pairing sourpuss semipros with us mere mortals who like to enjoy each other's company on the course."

"My idea is to make you less of a hazard on the course," Buck told his wife good-naturedly. "Excuse me, I've got to go talk to Claude for a minute. Nice to meet you, Mary Liz."

"They take golf so seriously at the club," Vanessa told Mary Liz, "it's just awful. Particularly since so few of the members are any good. It's rather ridiculous, if you ask me. Even at Maidstone I used to see people smile once in a while."

Maidstone was the legendary country club not far from the estate. Mary Liz understood it had been nearly impossible to join for the last fifty years. "You used to belong to Maidstone?"

"Who, me? Sure. Well, because my father did. And his father. And his father," she added. "But then I had trouble getting Buck in—" She made a face and leaned closer. "Just between you and me,

Mary Liz, they said I had brought too many husbands in already who were of questionable character."

Aunt Nancy laughed, and Mary Liz was too polite to ask how many husbands that had been.

"And so when Buck said, 'Screw 'em, I'll build my own country club—'"

"*Who* built their own country club?" a stunning blond woman asked, coming over. "*We* built our own country club. It wasn't just Buck."

"Jeanine!" Aunt Nancy said, sounding pleased and kissing the woman on the cheek. "When did you get in?"

"Yesterday. And I must say, Nance, I think you're absolutely super to include us."

"Mary Liz, I'd like you to meet my daughter-in-law, Jeanine Hoffman. She's Julius's wife."

Julius! Julius Hoffman? Mary Liz thought while shaking the woman's hand. Alfred Hoffman's son from his first marriage, the acting president of Howland Films who had filed a massive lawsuit against Aunt Nancy for control of it? She had invited *him* to dinner?

"So what's your house like this year?" Vanessa Buckley asked Jeanine. All the women thus far had been very pretty, but Jeanine Hoffman was truly exquisite. Mary Liz wondered if she had been a model or an actress.

"Ugh!" Jeanine said. "It's a mess, but the kids are ecstatic. Actually, so am I. I've had enough of the West Coast. Uh-oh," she said, breaking off suddenly. "There's Sasha. What on earth is she doing here?"

"She's renting the house next door," Nancy said.

"Oh, *my*, but you're in for an interesting summer," Jeanine told her. "She's kind of a nut, you know. And she's desperate for friends."

"I think she's very nice," Nancy protested.

"Ask Julius about her last film with Howland," Jeanine suggested. "When she flew in the witch doctor from the rain forest to clear the bad spirits off the set—and then tried to bill Alfred for it."

As they chuckled, a heavyset man came over, slipping a meaty hand around Jeanine's slender shoulders. "Hello, Nancy."

"Hello, Julius," Nancy said, turning her cheek to offer him the chance to kiss it. He did. She smiled and nodded slightly, as if approving of his behavior, and said, "I'd like you to meet my goddaughter, Mary Liz Scott."

"Pleasure," he said, reaching to shake her hand (and giving her a quick once-over in a way that made her feel like punching him. With a wife like that, what was the matter with this guy?).

"Do you play tennis?" Jeanine asked Mary Liz.

"Oh, no, here we go," Julius groaned.

"It's been a while since I played," Mary Liz confessed.

"Perhaps you'll consider warming up with me," Jeanine said.

"In other words," Julius said to Aunt Nancy, "we don't have a court this year and she's going to make a play to take over yours. All I've heard since we've gotten here is, 'How could you rent a house without a tennis court?'"

"Well, Jeanine is welcome to it," Nancy said. "I don't play much anymore and it's a waste not to use it. It's just sitting there. Alfred was the fanatic, as you know, and Bertie's lost interest. So consider yourself Mistress of the Manor Nets this summer, Jeanine."

"Thank you," the exquisite blonde said, kissing her on the cheek. "That's not only generous, Nancy, but extremely gracious of you—considering."

"See, we're suing each other," Julius explained to Mary Liz matter-of-factly. "I think I should be the executor of my father's estate. I'm the president of his studio, Howland Films, let's start with that."

"You're here as family this evening, Julius," Nancy said, bristling slightly. "And as you can see, I've asked several of your father's friends, as well, to make sure they know too that, on a personal level, they're always welcome here. But on a professional level...?" Her eyes narrowed and she placed a lovely manicured finger on his chest. "Just keep it up, Julius, and I'll have you thrown out on your ear. And I don't mean just out of this house."

Julius muttered some sort of unintelligible apology. He was rather like an overgrown schoolboy, Mary Liz thought.

"Really, Nance," he said, "we were very touched and pleased to be asked tonight. Just like when Dad was alive."

"Your father may have passed away, Julius," Nancy told him, "but some things will never change." While Mary Liz was pretty sure this was meant to be a nice thing to say, it came out sounding much more like a threat.

Interesting family. While Aunt Nancy reminded her of her own mother at times, nothing else about this family resembled Mary

Liz's. Of course, her own parents had only been married once, and to each other, and nobody hung out in Hollywood.

"Hello, Jeanine," a voice said, swooping in from behind Mary Liz. It was Bertie again, but this time with a young woman in tow. He kissed Jeanine on the cheek and ignored Julius completely. The latter took one look at Bertie, scowled and walked away. "Jeanine, Mary Liz," Bertie said, "I want you to meet my friend, Wendy Mitchell. Wendy, my godsister—I guess that's what you call it—Mary Liz Scott, and my sister-in-law, Jeanine Hoffman."

"How do you do?" Wendy said politely. She was a tall and very pretty gal, athletic and rather preppie-looking. Mary Liz frankly couldn't imagine Bertie with any other type of woman. Wendy's hair was a windswept brown with blond highlights; she had brown eyes and high cheekbones and, Mary Liz decided, yes, Mary Liz Scott was going to be the plainest woman in East Hampton this summer.

"Are you having a good time?" Nancy asked Wendy. When she murmured yes, Nancy said to Jeanine, "It's not often my Bertie brings home a lady friend, and I must say, Wendy is a very special young lady indeed."

Jeanine smiled, Mary Liz noticed, but her eyes did not. "It's very nice to meet you. Where are you visiting from?"

"New York—Manhattan," Wendy said.

Mary Liz thought she must be about thirty, same as Bertie.

"Originally?"

"Oh, no, originally I'm from Delaware. Just outside of Dover."

"If you young people will excuse me," Aunt Nancy said, "I need to tend to my other guests."

"I need to say hi to a few others, myself, if you'll excuse me," Jeanine said, moving on.

This left Mary Liz alone with Bertie and Wendy. They sure looked the part, these two nice young WASPs, meant to meet, mate and make more of themselves. Mary Liz wasn't jealous; actually, she was just weary and wary of young couples who looked the part, and hoped the relationship between these two perfect-looking people was a lot better than her own had been.

She wondered what Jim and his new wife were doing this summer.

"I'm surprised Mother invited that son of a bitch," Bertie said.

"Which one?" Wendy asked, looking around.

"My half brother, Julius."

"The one who's suing your mom?"

Bertie nodded, sipping his drink. "It wouldn't be so bad if he was a capable guy, but Julius is so stupid! If she lets him have Howland Films, he'll run the thing into the ground. Even Horrible Herbert says Julius is an idiot."

"Who's Horrible Herbert?" Mary Liz said.

"Herb Glidden. He was my dad's money man."

Right. Mary Liz recognized the name because she had been reading through Alfred Hoffman's personal files. Herbert Glidden had raised the money and backing for all of Alfred's movies over the years.

"But your father appointed Julius president of Howland, didn't he?" Wendy asked. "When he was alive?"

"Yeah, but with a small amount of voting stock in the company," Bertie explained. "Dad left him a little, but left the same amount to me and Denver, too. Mother's the one who's got control over the company, and so Mother's the one getting bombarded by Dumbo's lawsuits." He looked at Mary Liz. "And did you hear the law firm that used to represent my father is suing the *entire* estate? Essentially suing the estate they created *for* us?"

"Yes," Mary Liz said, nodding, "my father told me."

"That's right," Bertie said, taking a sip of his drink. "Your father's helping Mother out, isn't he? He's some kind of hotshot lawyer, right?" Mary Liz nodded and he continued. "And did he tell you that Herb Glidden's suing Mom, too?"

"What for?" Wendy asked.

"He's decided *he* wants Howland Films. Mind you, he doesn't know jack shit about making movies, all he ever did was line up investors, but now *he* wants Howland Films." Bertie made a gesture of futility. "And if nothing else is absolutely clear in Dad's will, it's that Howland Films goes to Mother and the children he had with Mother—me and Denver. And there's no way, no *way* we're going to let Horrible Herbert get his hands on Dad's studio. Dad would roll over in his grave."

Mary Liz, having already read the will several times, knew what he said was true.

"Dad's whole life changed for the better after he married Mother," Bertie explained. "And without her, he knew there wouldn't be any Howland Films."

"So who's going to run it?" Mary Liz asked.

"Anyone but Herbert Glidden and that idiot Julius, that's for sure. The only reason Julius even wants it is because no one with a brain in his head would ever offer him a job." He sipped his drink. "As for dealing with Horrible Herbert, I think what Mother needs is an exterminator."

The man who was chairman of the country club, Buck Buckley, was coming back over to them, with another man following behind. "Hey, kids," he said. "Nancy asked me to introduce my houseguest to you guys." He gestured for the younger man to step forward.

Mary Liz's first impression of Buck's friend was favorable. Definitely favorable. He was about thirty-five, around five foot ten, with broad shoulders, light brown hair, and, although he was wearing glasses, she could see that he had a warm set of blue eyes.

"Nancy especially wanted you to meet him, Mary Liz," Buck added, giving her several exaggerated winks.

"Gee, this isn't embarrassing, is it?" Bertie asked the group, making them laugh.

"Schyler Preston," Buck announced, making the presentation.

"And you're Mary Liz Scott," Schyler said, holding out his hand.

"Yes," she said softly. She felt shy again.

They shook. Her impression was still favorable.

"Okay, my part's done," Buck announced, walking off.

"Boy, that Buck is a real social smoothie," Bertie joked.

"Normally, I think he is," Schyler said in his host's defense. "At the club, I mean. Part of the job, I guess."

"So what are you doing at the Buckleys'?" Bertie said. "Not to alarm you, but there are saner people in East Hampton."

"I'm working at the club. At the golf course."

"Are you the new pro?"

"No," Schyler said. "I'm—I don't know what you'd call me, really. I'm not working for Buck, not in the traditional sense. It's more like a trade—I live in their garage apartment for the summer for free, and Buck tells me who to play golf with every morning."

"So you're the summer ringer I heard about," Bertie said. "You must be shit-kicking good then."

Wendy wrinkled her nose at Bertie. "What barn did you grow up in that you use language like that in front of the ladies?"

"I teach school in Virginia," Schyler told Mary Liz. "I've got the summer off. Mrs. Hoffman told me you're taking the summer off, too."

"Yes, although I have some work to do. But I can do it here. I have a little office set up in the caretaker's cottage."

"Hey, Schyler, how about playing some doubles tomorrow?" Bertie asked.

"He's a golfer," Wendy pointed out.

"Look at his build," Bertie said. "He plays everything, I bet."

A hand had grabbed Mary Liz's elbow from the rear and was pulling her away. "Nancy says your wonderful," a melodious voice whispered in her ear, "and that I should talk to you."

Mary Liz turned around. Good grief, it was Sasha Reinhart. Talking to her. Clinging to her arm. "Excuse me?"

"She says you're wonderful," the mega-star diva said more loudly. "That you're a financial genius who's taken early retirement to find a more spiritual path in life."

"Um," Mary Liz stammered, feeling Schyler's eyes on her, "yes, I suppose, but I'm no genius, I assure you. Nor do I intend to join a convent or anything, not that they'd have me."

"Humility," the diva said approvingly. "You must be spiritually inclined. I was hoping to find someone to share spiritual things with this summer." When Mary Liz didn't say anything, she said, "You are, aren't you? Into spiritual matters?"

"Well," Mary Liz said, feeling more uncomfortable by the second, "I say my prayers at night. And I meditate in the morning. Just for a couple of minutes, but I try."

"I knew it!" the diva cried. "Wait a second!" She dashed off.

"Jeanine warned you, Mary Liz," Bertie said, laughing. "I think you've been appropriated as a friend."

"She's Sasha Reinhart, for heaven's sake! What was I supposed to say?"

"Certainly not the truth," Bertie advised. "Because now she's obviously got her heart set on making you pray and meditate with her this summer."

Mary Liz glanced at Schyler, who was smiling at her. In a moment the diva was back, dragging the designer, Rachelle Zaratan, with her by the arm. "Tell her what you told me," she directed Mary Liz.

"I said I say my prayers at night and try to meditate for a few minutes each morning."

"See?" the diva said to the designer. *"She* meditates." To the

group, "I keep telling Rachelle, 'How the hell can you hear the message of the universe if you're always talking?'"

"Oh, pooh," the designer said.

"Oh, pooh on you," the diva said. "See if I ever take you whale watching. You'd probably scare them all away like you did the dolphins in Florida." Suddenly the diva froze, eyes fixed across the room. "Now how did *he* get invited, do you suppose?"

Bertie turned to look. "Holy shit," he said. "What the hell is he doing here?"

Nancy Hoffman, on the other side of the room, was watching as the housekeeper led a man across the living room to her. The party had started to quiet down, and then, a moment later, had fallen completely silent.

All eyes were on Nancy and the man standing in front of her.

"Mrs. Hoffman," the housekeeper said, presenting him. "Mr. Herbert Glidden has arrived."

2

Nancy Hoffman smiled and then, as if it were the most natural thing in the world, stepped forward to kiss Herbert Glidden on both cheeks. Hands still on his shoulders, she turned to say, in a loud voice so all could hear, "Delores, please add another setting to the table," so everyone knew for sure he had not been invited.

The party guests were still silent. Still watching.

"They're scared," Bertie murmured. "Look at them. Buck, Charles, Claude, Randolph—scared to be caught fraternizing with the widow."

People were starting to talk again. Nancy was still talking to Herbert. The magazine publisher, Claude, was walking up to them.

"Why would they be scared to be seen with Aunt Nancy?" Mary Liz asked.

"Because she's his enemy now," Bertie said.

"She certainly doesn't act like it," Wendy observed.

Bertie smiled. "That's Mother. Kill them with kindness." He noticed that his mother and Herbert Glidden were looking in his direction and he took the cue. "He's a bad guy, ladies, avoid him at all costs," he said under his breath. "Excuse me." And he left them to walk over.

Somebody cleared his throat. It was Schyler. Mary Liz had forgotten all about him. "It's none of my business," he said, "but I'd love it if someone would explain to me what's going on."

"That man is suing Mrs. Hoffman," Wendy explained. "He used to find investors for Mr. Hoffman's movies—"

"And where's Mr. Hoffman?"

"He's dead," Mary Liz said. "He died in a plane crash six months ago."

"And so now he wants Mr. Hoffman's studio," Schyler said.

"Right," Wendy said, "Howland Films. Only he never actually worked in the movie industry, knows nothing about it except how to raise money. Mr. Hoffman clearly did not want him to have any part of the company, and so now Mrs. Hoffman is taking him on in court."

"And just now, he crashed Aunt Nancy's party," Mary Liz finished.

"And that guy," Wendy said, pointing at Julius, who was walking over to Nancy, Bertie and Herbert Glidden, "is suing Mrs. Hoffman, too. For the same studio the other guy's suing for, Howland Films. Only this guy, Julius, is Mr. Hoffman's son from his first marriage."

"But he was invited tonight," Mary Liz added. "As family."

"And who is *that?*" Schyler asked, his voice hitting a certain note. He was referring to Jeanine Hoffman, who was following her beefy husband over to Aunt Nancy's side. Of course he would wonder about her, any red-blooded American man would.

"Jeanine Hoffman," Mary Liz answered. "Julius's wife."

"She's very beautiful."

"And she has two children," Wendy said. After a pause, "Amazing what money can buy, isn't it?"

Now Buck Buckley and his wife, Vanessa, were walking over to talk to Aunt Nancy and Herbert Glidden. In fact, Mary Liz realized, everyone was going over to say hello to Glidden. Charles Kahn and his wife, designer Rachelle Zaratan, went over. Then the vintner, Randolph Vandergilden. Finally, even Sasha Reinhart went over, looking as though she had been asked to kiss a snake.

"Well, come on," Schyler said. "Let's go meet this guy."

"No thanks," Mary Liz and Wendy said simultaneously. They looked at each other and laughed.

"I'm going over," he insisted. "It's not often I get to meet a Hollywood mogul."

"Bad guy," Mary Liz corrected. "Bertie said he was a bad guy."

Regardless of whether she wanted to meet him or not, Mary Liz soon found herself face-to-face with him, since Nancy, the ever-dutiful hostess, made sure "Horrible Herbert" Glidden met everyone at the party before they sat down to dinner. He seemed innocuous enough, perhaps even a little charming. He was in his early sixties, had gray hair and a bald spot, was wearing a nice suit, shiny shoes and carried, in fact, a rather quiet way about him.

"Very nice to meet you," Herbert Glidden said to Mary Liz. "I met your parents once years ago. Your father's a hell of a tax lawyer, as I recall, and your mother is a very lovely, very gracious woman."

"India and I were schoolgirls together," Nancy said.

"India?" Bertie said, coming to join the group. "Mary Liz's mother is from India?"

"No, silly darlin', her *name* is India," his mother explained. "It's a very popular name down South."

"Oh, yes, very popular," Bertie said. "Why, there's India Mitchell, the lady who wrote *Gone With the Wind,* India Winfrey, the talk-show host, and, of course, the ever-popular first lady, India Byrd Johnson."

"Been drinking old Randy's wine, or what, Bertie?" Herbert Glidden asked.

"God, it's awful, isn't it?"

Glidden smiled. "Worse. But as your mother will tell you, the winery is such a novelty around here, and the property so beautiful, that it becomes a much sought-after venue for a benefit or two every summer."

"This is true," Nancy said, looking at Glidden with something close to fondness. Fund-raising for worthy causes, Mary Liz knew, was her Aunt Nancy's career.

"Good heavens, Nancy," another woman's voice said, "whatever possessed you to let *him* in here?"

They all turned, and standing there was a fading beauty in her late forties, a soft and lovely blond (yet another!) woman. Her voice was pleasing, but Yankee in enunciation, sharp and clear like Katharine Hepburn's.

"Didn't anyone ever tell you, Herb," the woman said, "that it's impolite to sue the widow of your friend and business partner, and then, to add insult to injury, crash her dinner party?" Still, she gave him a quick peck on the cheek. Clearly, there was history here.

"Well, the lovely Claire," he said. "I'm surprised to see you here. Isn't that your ex-husband's new wife's boss over there? Did I get that right?"

The comment hit its mark, for Claire's eyes flinched in pain and Nancy said, "Herb! Dammit, behave yourself."

He actually laughed. "Oh, you're right," he said, stepping closer to put an arm around Claire, giving her a hug. "I'm sorry, it's just I could see you drawing your gun and I wanted to fire first." He stepped back. "The only reason I'm here is because I can't stand the way things have been. I needed to see Nancy, as the friend she's been—for what? Thirty-two years, Nance? I'm a cad and an emotional coward, Claire, and you hurt my feelings when you came out blasting. I'm sorry."

Silence. Nancy's eyes were on Claire. Mary Liz was looking at Nancy. Claire and Herbert were studying each other like a couple of boxers about to go at it. Suddenly Claire's eyes swept over to Mary Liz. "You must be Mary Liz Scott. You look like your mother. How is India, anyway? I haven't seen her in years."

And so entered Claire MacClendon, the painter from Bridgehampton, who had, she admitted, been hiding in the beach cabana for an hour watching a horse show on ESPN 2.

To say that dinner was a beautiful and strange experience was putting it mildly. The six-foot windows of the dining room looked out over the ocean, to the east, and although it was technically nighttime now, it was still quite light out. At the long, oblong dining table, Mary Liz's place setting was positioned between Julius Hoffman, and Charles Kahn, the designer's husband, but Sasha Reinhart, not the least bit influenced by the intentions of her hostess, forced Julius to switch seats with her. She liked Mary Liz, Sasha announced to the table.

Finally everyone was settled, Nancy at one end of the table, with Herbert Glidden at her right, followed by Jeanine Hoffman, Sasha Reinhart, Mary Liz, Charles Kahn, Vanessa Buckley and Claude Lemieux, and Bertie at the other end of the table. To Bertie's right was Rachelle Zaratan, Randolph Vandergilden, Claire MacClendon, Schyler Preston, Julius Hoffman, Isabel Lemieux, Buck Buckley and then finally Wendy, who was sitting on Nancy's left.

Because it was hot and humid, dinner was the first cold one of the season. Two local girls, hired for the occasion, served cold cucumber soup, followed by a plate of delicate baby asparagus in an unidentifiable but delicious sauce, and then the main course was served, cold lobster with slices of avocado and tomato and hollandaise sauce. Two kinds of tossed salad and warm crusty bread were also offered. How Nancy had handled the white-wine issue, she didn't know, but Mary Liz enjoyed a marvelous Chablis that sure as heck didn't come from Eastern Winery.

Buck, the country club president, seemed to suddenly become a little drunk at his end, and was periodically knocking or dropping a piece of silverware to the floor.

"I'm holding a pagan ritual next weekend," Sasha Reinhart, the diva, was saying to Mary Liz. "Most of the people I know here from Los Angeles are into different spiritual disciplines and so I find that a general pagan ritual is the only way to go."

Mary Liz envisioned cannibals dancing around an iron pot.

"We're going to have a bonfire—"

She knew it.

"And dance and have a special ceremony at midnight. You really must come. I'll have sushi."

"I know you're very popular with our set," Mary Liz overheard Bertie say to Rachelle Zaratan, "but do any normal women buy your clothes?"

"I have two of her suits," Mary Liz volunteered.

"But Mother says you've made millions already," Bertie said, "so you're hardly normal."

Mary Liz hadn't made millions—although she did have well over a million dollars in investments—but that was nothing in this crowd. Mary Liz smiled across the table at the designer. "Your clothes are wonderful. They look great, feel great and last forever. And, best of all, they have a classic look." To Bertie, "They may cost more in the beginning, but the third year you're wearing them and still getting compliments, you realize what a bargain they are in the long run. And yes, normal women do buy and wear Rachelle's clothes."

Rachelle beamed. "Aren't you gene*rr*ous," she said in that accent Mary Liz could not identify. "Thank you."

Sasha elbowed Mary Liz in the side. "What about whales? Are you into whales?"

"I liked Judy Collins's song about them," Mary Liz joked.

"Oh, yes!" Sasha declared. "And I'm going to do one too someday!"

Across from her, although chatting with the painter, Claire MacClendon, Mary Liz could sense that Schyler Preston was watching her.

"I want to do a duet," the diva continued, excited. "In Judy's song, the whale was really just a backup singer—"

"Hey, Schyler!" Buck suddenly yelled from Nancy's end of the table.

He was definitely loaded.

"How do we know each other?" the country club chairman wanted to know. "*You* explain to our fair hostess!"

Schyler looked a wee bit annoyed and glanced down to Vanessa Buckley for help.

"Sky's the summer ringer," Vanessa explained to the table. "We wanted him at the club this summer to bolster the men's A team."

"So you're actually a member?" Mary Liz asked Schyler, well aware that no teacher she knew could afford the fees of East End Country Club.

He looked vaguely uncomfortable. "Of sorts."

"I see," Mary Liz said. "Part of the trade. A place to stay, a club to belong to, in exchange for—well, what you said before."

"Yes."

"But how did you meet Schyler, Vanessa?" Nancy asked. "He teaches way down in Virginia."

"I met Buck at the golf association convention last year," Schyler said. "At the Green Briar."

"Oh, yeah!" Buck declared, laughing about something, and waving the girl with the wine bottle to come over.

"Easy, Buck." This came quietly from across the table—from Herbert Glidden.

Buck looked at Glidden and frowned. And then looked up at the girl. "Get me a friggin' Coke, will you?"

Interesting, Mary Liz thought, the effect Herbert Glidden had on these people.

"I understand you used to be a partner on Wall Street," Charles Kahn, the clothes designer's husband, said next to Mary Liz. He was seated to her right.

"What?" the diva said from her side at the left. "What did he say, Mary Liz?"

Charles leaned forward. "I said, I understand she used to be on Wall Street."

"Not anymore," the diva told him.

"Yes, I know that, Sasha," Charles said.

"It wasn't Wall Street," Mary Liz said, turning to Charles. "I was with Reston, Kellaher, in Chicago."

"What? What did you say?" the diva demanded to know.

The diva then proceeded to make Mary Liz trade seats with her so she could hear Mary Liz as she talked to Charles. This, of course, entailed switching plates, wineglasses, water glasses, napkins, and Mary Liz found herself getting rapidly exhausted, particularly with

Aunt Nancy calling from her end of the table, "We switch for dessert and coffee, Mary Liz, not now!"

"Hi," Jeanine Hoffman said to Mary Liz as she sat down in her new seat.

"Oh no you don't!" Sasha told Jeanine, leaning forward in front of Mary Liz. "We're all set to talk on this side."

Across the table, Mary Liz noticed Schyler's eyes were on her. So were Claire MacClendon's. Were they talking about her?

Probably not, because on a second look, she realized that *everyone* at the table was looking at her—like the ill-mannered woman from the Midwest that she was, who had switched seats in the middle of a dinner party over the protests of their hostess.

"Okay," the diva said, getting Mary Liz to look her way again. "Continue."

The whole table had fallen silent now, waiting to hear whatever riveting tale the ill-mannered woman from the Midwest had to tell.

"You were with Reston, Kellaher, in Chicago," Charles Kahn reminded her. "Excellent firm. And I consider it Wall Street." He looked across the table to his wife. "They underwrote our bond issue."

Mary Liz smiled. "I remember that very well. I was in research there, as an analyst. The analyst in the next office, a good friend, covered the retail area. Jonathan Felder?"

"That was the research guy," Charles confirmed, nodding. "Clay Kirkman headed the deal."

"He's at First Boston now," Mary Liz said.

"I loved him," Rachelle told her. "He was wa*rrr*m and cha*rrr*ming."

"What was your speciality?" Charles asked her.

Specialty or *spe-she-al-i-ty,* as Charles called it? Mary Liz was always put on alert by people who used the latter.

"Communications."

"Really?" This came from down the table. Mary Liz leaned forward to find Herbert Glidden looking at her. "You must have had a claim to fame. What was it?"

Mary Liz nodded. "I got us in early on paging systems and overseas cable."

"No movie companies? No TV?"

"A while back. We had a piece of the Turner business."

"On whose recommendation?"

"Mine," she admitted. "But that's why it's called research. You're supposed to study the industry and see what's most likely to succeed."

"Yes, it is true, that is the way we know it's supposed to be," Claude Lemieux said, "but so often these days you get simple deal-makers, who have no knowledge of the special needs of your business."

"Like the magazine business," Isabel finished for her husband.

Claude was nodding. "Did you ever work on a magazine deal, Mary Liz?" His accent was slight, but still French and romantic.

"We had a piece of some Hachette deals, as a matter of fact." Hachette was an enormous French conglomerate.

"Aren't they behind John-John's magazine?" Jeanine Hoffman asked. "*George?*"

"Yes," Claude said. "They are the main competitors of my old company."

"Of which my father is CEO," Isabel added with a smile.

"What was your last position at Reston, Kellaher?" Herbert Glidden asked Mary Liz.

"She's no longer practicing," Nancy said, making Bertie burst out laughing.

"She's not a doctor, Mother!"

"Mary Liz was a partner," Nancy announced. "And when she quit, it made the *Wall Street Journal.* And she's only thirty-two. Imagine!"

"You're not working now?" Glidden persisted.

"Not this summer," Mary Liz said, feeling uncomfortable again. Everyone was listening. And two of the very people she wished to stay away from, Herbert Glidden and Julius Hoffman, were hearing her professional history. Would they get the connection between her professional training and the fact that her godmother was waist-deep in financial lawsuits over her deceased husband's infinitely complicated estate?

"As I understand it," Claire MacClendon said, jumping in, "this is Mary Liz's first vacation in six years. And that she's toying with the idea of painting—something she left by the wayside on her climb to fame and fortune." Claire smiled at her from across the table and Mary Liz realized Claire was trying to bail her out. Aunt Nancy must have let her in on what she was doing there.

"You've seen the large waterscape in the living room, haven't you, Mary Liz?" Bertie said. "That's Claire's."

Next to Mary Liz, there was a sharp intake of breath. "You're *Claire,*" Sasha said, nodding her head. "Yes, of course, *that* Claire, how foolish of me. I'm sorry, I didn't realize—Hep Morgan has a painting of yours in his house in Malibu. In his dining room. The one of the glen, with the sun coming up."

The painter's smile was a trifle shy now. "Yes."

"I would adore to see your work. I'm just terrible with names. Please, forgive me for not recognizing it."

"Thank you, Ms. Reinhart, that's very flattering."

"Sasha, Sasha," the diva told her. "Perhaps you'll come with Mary Liz and me to see the whales."

"Oh, *God,*" Rachelle Zaratan said.

After the polite laughter died, Herbert Glidden repeated, "What was your last position at Reston, Mary Liz?"

"Um..." She leaned forward to look down the table at him. "I was a partner, as Aunt Nancy said. And analysis was still my thing—communications."

"And what was your last deal?"

"SCA's cable franchises in Eastern Europe and Latin America."

There was a low whistle from Julius Hoffman. "That was a very big deal, wasn't it?"

"Well, our firm is small—my firm was small—and we brought in Merrill Lynch for part of it. It was just too big for us to cover it all."

"Did you get to go to those places?" Jeanine Hoffman asked her.

"Oh, yes," Mary Liz said. "More than I cared to, actually."

"And what was the deal?" Glidden asked.

"A bond issue to finance the laying of new cable and expanding the old. For TV and telephones. And, in some countries, the Internet."

"A monopoly," Vanessa Buckley translated. "Just like my great-grandfather used to have."

"Well, no," Mary Liz said. "It would be like this country before there were phones in residential homes and rural areas. The country could choose to let AT&T wire the country, or have no phones at all."

"We gotta talk, Mary Liz," Julius declared. "We want to get into this kind of thing at Howland."

Bertie snickered.

"So you're very familiar with international financing," Glidden pursued.

"Yes."

Other conversations were springing up around the table, thank heavens.

"Maybe you can do some work for me," Glidden said.

"Not this summer," Aunt Nancy said quickly.

"No, I meant when she was ready to go back to work. Maybe this fall."

"I think I'd like Mary Liz to give me lessons in living!" Sasha announced to all. She raised her wineglass. "Goddesses' speed to Mary Liz, the lucky woman who doesn't have a hundred people living off her income, so she is free to pursue her life and her art!"

"Hear, hear!" Rachelle Zaratan seconded. "Here's to liberation from the *rrr*apacious corporation and it's torturous managers!"

Her husband, Charles, looked at Rachelle in surprise as everyone else at the table hoisted their glass in a toast.

"To Mary Liz's retirement!" Aunt Nancy said.

Herbert Glidden leaned over his plate. "We'll talk, Mary Liz."

"And *we'll* talk," Julius Hoffman promised.

Mary Liz smiled slightly and turned to Sasha. "I can't quite place your friend Rachelle's accent," she said. "What country is she from originally?"

"New York," the diva said.

3

When it was time for dessert and coffee, Nancy had her guests change seats at the dinner table. However, when Buck Buckley, now sitting next to Mary Liz, went to sleep on her shoulder, it put a bit of a damper on the festivities. Schyler got up to take charge of Buck, while Vanessa Buckley said a round of cheery goodbyes, explaining that her husband was on painkillers for a bad tooth and she had told him not to drink on top of them; and Julius Hoffman, nudged by his wife, Jeanine, offered to help Schyler get Buck to the car.

While all the attention was on the Buckleys, Claire MacClendon whispered something in Aunt Nancy's ear, grabbed Mary Liz's arm and led her out the back of the house. When they got down the porch stairs, the painter sighed, "Air." The she turned to Mary Liz. "I told Nancy she had to be careful not to give you an overdose of this crowd, or else you might pack up and go back to Chicago."

"They seemed like a nice enough group."

The painter only laughed and led Mary Liz toward the walkway to the beach. "That marvelous young man was leaving anyway. The teacher, Schyler. He asked me a lot of questions about you." She stopped and turned around. "He said he saw you about a week ago at the movie theater, alone, and tried to get up the nerve to go up and talk to you."

"Really?" She was surprised—and extremely pleased. So she hadn't imagined it. He had liked her right off, too.

They stepped onto the gray, weathered, wooden walkway that extended over the backyard, across the dunes and then broke into a set of stairs down to the beach. Where the lawn met the dunes, there was a cabana house, also in gray weathered wood, which had a sitting area, a toilet, shower, kitchenette and a changing room with beach towels, suits, caps, snorkels, masks, wet suits, kickboards and a variety of other water toys. Mary Liz had been in it several times already.

As they descended to the beach, Mary Liz wondered at how it was yet another glorious night. Dusk was moving in and the ocean was at a low-tide calm. Seagulls were circling, screeching on wing, and then landing and searching the waterline for crabs and clams.

The women slipped off their shoes, left them by the stairs and walked out onto the beach. The sand had cooled, and felt fresh and clean underfoot. Mary Liz followed Claire down to the water and stood next to her on a cliff of sand that the tide had left. "You must think me terribly rude," Claire said, eyes on the water. "Actually, I was rather proud of showing up at all. I saw Claude and Isabel Lemieux get out of their car and I just wanted to die." She glanced at Mary Liz. "Hence why I went to the cabana, to sort out whether or not I could face them at all."

Mary Liz didn't say anything, but when the painter suddenly started walking down the beach, she followed. Claire carried an extra twenty pounds or so (what a novelty out here!), but she was also evidently fit, because Mary Liz was having some trouble keeping up with her on the sand.

"My husband left me for a woman you may have heard of," Claire said. She glanced over. "Cindy Claydon."

"The editor of *Je Ne Sais Quoi.*" Mary Liz had read about her in the gossip columns, too.

"We met Cindy through Claude and Isabel, of course—it *is* his magazine—and normally it doesn't bother me to see them, but Cindy's expecting a baby any minute and I—well, frankly, I am having a hard time." She looked at Mary Liz. "Particularly since they are here in East Hampton this summer."

"Ouch," Mary Liz said.

"Exactly," the painter said, walking on. "She's thirty-six. At fifty-two, that hurts all by itself, forget the baby."

Mary Liz stopped. "Fifty-two? No way."

"You're very kind," Claire said, smiling, "but let's keep walking before I start aging before your eyes like Dorian Gray."

After a few steps, Mary Liz asked, "May I ask how old your former husband is?"

"He'll be sixty this fall."

They walked along in silence for a while, until the facts started adding up in Mary Liz's mind. "Henry," she said, looking at Claire, "MacClendon. He's the architect."

"Yes."

A very famous architect with offices around the world. His specialty was huge new houses with historic features, either Colonial or

Victorian. As a matter of fact, a whole section of Chicago waterfront had recently been revitalized, and Henry MacClendon had designed the corporate offices in the form of Victorian mansions.

"We have two girls," Claire said, "and they are wonderful, if I may say so myself. Madeline and Emily. They're touring Europe this summer with Henry's mother, as we speak."

"How old are they?"

"Twenty-two and nineteen." The painter looked off at the ocean for several moments and then looked back at Mary Liz. "It's very hard for me not to have them around this summer." She smiled. "It's hard *any* time not to have my girls around, but you have to let them grow up. At least that's what they tell me." She chuckled to herself. "I had to sit on my hands last fall so I wouldn't try to physically stop Emily from going away to college."

Mary Liz thought of her mother's own sadness when her younger brother had gone off to school several years ago. But her mother still had her father, and to this day India marveled at how very special that fall had turned out to be for them as a couple. It had reawakened their marriage, startling them with hours and hours of privacy and time together after nearly thirty years of stolen moments when the kids weren't around.

They didn't walk too much farther, for it was getting cooler and damper by the minute. By the time they turned around to head back to the estate, Claire had steered the conversation around to Mary Liz.

"Just so you know," Claire said, "Nancy told me that you're here to inventory Alfred's estate, and that your father's firm is representing Nancy in court this fall."

"How many other people know this, do you suppose?"

"Everybody knows about your father coming to Nancy's rescue, so I imagine they'll guess you're here this summer to help Nancy, too." She laughed. "It was very interesting tonight, to listen to Herb smooth-talk you. I bet he knows, and I bet he knows what a valuable ally you'd be for him. I'd watch out, Mary Liz, if I were you. He's not a particularly nice man."

"How so?"

Claire thought a moment. "He's always been desperate," she finally said.

"He sure didn't look desperate tonight," Mary Liz observed.

"Oh, but that's what makes him dangerous," Claire said. "He

never looks it, but trust me, he *is*—desperate for power, desperate for respect, desperate for acceptance by even those people back there. The men, I mean."

Mary Liz frowned, not understanding why that would be. Her mind skipped ahead to another thought. "Didn't you think it was odd, the way Aunt Nancy welcomed him?"

Claire shook her head. "No. That's Nancy, kill 'em with kindness."

"That's exactly what Bertie said."

"Just be careful, Mary Liz, and I mean of all of them—all the guys at dinner tonight, Herb, Julius, even Claude, Buck, Charles and Randolph. They were Alfred's friends, you know. Heck, they were my friends, too, because they were my husband Henry's friends, and Henry was a great friend of Alfred's. The only one who wasn't a great friend was Herb Glidden. Alfred wouldn't even let him in the house half the time."

"Really?"

"*Really.* And now that Alfred's dead and Herb feels free to crash Nancy's dinner, and all those guys *welcomed* him—" She stopped walking to look at Mary Liz. "I know there's something going on around here, I can feel it, and whatever it is, Nancy won't even suspect it. She's just not the suspicious type. So, please, Mary Liz, watch out for her, will you? Anything strange happens, call me."

"Strange like what?"

"Like tonight," Claire said, "with Herb showing up and the gang welcoming him instead of spitting on him."

Mary Liz shook her head. "I'm sorry, but I still don't understand. Why is this strange?"

"It's strange because Herb Glidden was like a little dog following on Alfred's heels. I don't even know who that man was that crashed the party the way he did tonight, like the conquering hero. Or why everybody was kissing up to him. Oh, well, Sasha—I know she's got to make another movie for Howland this fall, which means dealing with Julius and Herb. But the guys—there's no reason I know of for them to be kowtowing to Herb." She pointed a finger at Mary Liz. "So make no mistake about it, Mary Liz, watch your back with Herb. If Alfred didn't trust him around his own home, I certainly wouldn't, either."

When they reached the Big House, they found that all the guests had gone home. Bertie was upstairs changing, the housekeeper, Delores, told Mary Liz, but Mrs. Hoffman was in the living room. They went in and found Aunt Nancy lying on a chaise lounge with a cold compress over her eyes. Mary Liz had to smile. She was so much like her mother in ways, careening with energy all day—like born-and-bred Southern women always seem to do—effortlessly whirl-winding guests at night, and then, the minute her responsibilities were over, collapsing. She could barely keep her eyes open as Mary Liz and Claire thanked her for the dinner and said good-night.

In the driveway, Claire climbed into an old Wagoneer. "Come over soon. Call first, though, I'm a bear about privacy."

"You're in Bridgehampton?" Mary Liz asked, referring to a town a few miles west.

"Where the real people live." Claire laughed, putting the car into gear.

Mary Liz waved goodbye and walked down the driveway and then across the lawn to the caretaker's cottage. Her cottage.

She went inside, changed into a nightgown and robe, made a cup of tea and came back out to sit in the dark on the front porch. She saw Bertie drive out with Wendy in a BMW convertible. She heard crickets back somewhere behind the hedge. She saw stars against the night sky.

She breathed deeply. The air was sweet, the quiet divine.

"Mary Liz?" a voice said gently.

She was very far away, very deep. The darkness started to clear and she started rising up from wherever she had been. And then she started.

Someone was hanging over her. In the dark.

"It's Sky Preston," he said quietly, touching her arm. "I'm sorry if I startled you."

She cleared her throat, blinking. She was still in the rocker on the porch. "Hi," she whispered. "I fell asleep."

"I was out for a walk and saw that your lights were still on so I thought I'd stop in," he whispered. "And then I saw you out here. I would have left you alone, but you'll get a really bad crick in your neck from this dampness."

"Thanks." Silence. She was really waking up now. "Would you like to come in?"

"Just for a minute." He sounded happy about the invitation.

"You'll have to excuse my attire," she said, slowly standing up. He was right. Her neck was stiff. She moved toward the screen door.

"I'll excuse anything if you'll forgive me for scaring you," Sky replied as he held the door open.

"Have a seat," she said as they entered the room, pointing to one of the wingback chairs. He had changed since dinner and was now dressed in a polo shirt, shorts, running shoes and socks. "Would you like a beer? I've got some Amstel Lite. Or coffee, tea, seltzer—and I've got orange juice."

"A beer would be great," he said, throwing himself down. He looked around. "This is a really nice place."

"Nancy apparently had it redone for my arrival." She was in the kitchen now, talking to him over the breakfast bar as she got his drink.

"You should see my place over Buck's garage." He laughed. "I spent a week scrubbing the walls and floors before I dared to unpack."

"Did he get home okay?"

"Yes. He's fine." He looked around the living room. "There's a guest house on this estate, too, isn't there?"

"Yes, just up the hill."

"So you're considered family, not a guest."

"That's right."

"Didn't you want to be in the Big House? Look out at the ocean?"

"Not particularly," Mary Liz said, coming back into the living room with beer in a glass for him and a glass of seltzer for herself. "Privacy's a luxury I value highly."

"Me, too," he said, accepting the glass from her. "Thank you."

Mary Liz sat down on the couch and pulled her legs up under her, making sure her robe covered all that needed to be covered. "I took a long walk with Claire MacClendon after you left. She likes you."

He held his glass up. "Here's to a great summer for you."

"And you."

After taking a sip of beer, he said, "And I like Claire. She's very attractive, don't you think?"

She liked that, that he could see how beautiful Claire still was at fifty-two and with an extra twenty pounds. And with Jeanine Hoffman sitting at the same table! "Yes, I do." She sipped her drink and then put the glass down on a coaster on the coffee table. "So, what do you teach?"

"History. High-school level."

"I bet you're a good teacher."

"Why?"

"Oh, I don't know." She smiled. "You just seem like a nice person. Smart, patient and, yes, even kind."

He smiled. "Thank you. I hope I'm a good teacher. God knows, there's no money in it. The reward is all in the process itself."

She had been wondering about that. "Do you find it strange being here this summer? Surrounded by all this wealth?"

"Sure, but not because of the wealth. I find it strange because there are some very strange people here, which I'm sure you've noticed. Whether it's because they're wealthy or not, I have no idea. But I am getting kind of a kick out of being surrounded by such beauty, and having such a complete change from my normal work life."

She nodded. "I know what you mean."

"And I'm really glad you're here this summer, Mary Liz."

She told herself not to blush, but the comment caught her completely off guard. "Thank you."

"So, *do* you play golf?"

"I know how, but I'm afraid it wouldn't be very much fun for you."

"But I'm a teacher," he reminded her, smiling, looking into her eyes. "And I love to teach. If the student's into it, of course."

She felt a sense of pleasure sweep through her.

Schyler excused himself and asked if he could use the bathroom. She gave him directions and turned her attention to the picture window, looking up the hill at the Big House. The lights were still on. She wondered where Bertie and Wendy had gone, to a bar, or dancing, a party, or what? Then she wondered what Wendy did for a living, or if she did anything. No, she was pretty sure a woman like that would feel compelled to have a job. Someone between the two of them would have to have a job, but then she supposed that was no longer the case, not with the inheritance that was coming Bertie's way.

"Is the room across the hall your office?" Schyler asked when he came back. "I didn't mean to be nosy, but I couldn't help seeing all the file cabinets, and the computer and everything."

"I'm not formally working this summer, but I still want to keep up."

"And I guess you have your own investments to look after, too." He looked a little sad while saying the last. Mary Liz assumed this was his way of saying, "I guess you're rich, too, at least richer than I'll ever be as a teacher." When she didn't say anything, he came over to stand near her. "It's pretty late. I should go home now."

She took the cue and stood up.

He walked to the front door and she followed. Mary Liz turned on the front-porch light and they went outside.

"One thing, though," he said, turning around suddenly.

He was standing awfully close to her.

"All my good friends call me Sky. I wish you would."

"Sky? Like up there?" She pointed to the night sky.

"Yes."

She smiled. "I would love to. Sky. It's a great name." She tried to think. "Wasn't there a pilot or something—"

"'Sky King.' It was a show in the fifties. I never saw it, but my mom liked it. I asked her why she didn't name me Sky, then, instead of *Schyler*, which I hate, but she said my dad had some uncle who said he'd send me through college if my parents named me Schyler after him. So they did, but the old geezer never did leave us anything in his will. So, there you go. Never name a kid anything except what you want to call him."

"And you don't have any children?"

"No." He shook his head. "And you?"

"No. I've never been married, actually."

"Me, neither," he said. "Almost, once."

She had to laugh a little, it felt so awkward. But it was the kind of information they needed to get out of the way. "Me, too."

"I'd like to get married someday," he said.

It was too much to say that she did, too. Instead, she said softly, "Sky. Yes, I like that name. Very much."

"I'm glad," he said, gazing into her eyes.

They just stood there, looking at each other for several moments.

"Well, I better go," he said without moving—or looking away.

"Thanks for stopping by," she said, swallowing—but not looking away, either.

He said nothing. And then he took a deep breath and smiled. And turned to the stairs. "Thanks for the beer," he called over his shoulder.

"You're welcome. Get home safely."

She heard a quiet chuckle and saw him jog out between the stone pillars of the estate entrance, turning right to run off somewhere in the night.

4

The morning after the dinner party, Saturday, Bertie Hoffman was at Mary Liz's front door begging her to go windsurfing with him. The fact that she didn't know how, and that Bertie expected her to learn in the ocean surf, fazed him not in the least. Wendy, he informed her, had gone the morning before. "Then take Wendy," she told him, yawning, still in her bathrobe. It was just five to nine.

"She got drunk last night," he explained.

"Where did you guys go?"

"Oh, out," he said with a coy smile. "Maybe if you went windsurfing with me this morning you could come out with us next time and find out."

Bertie was wearing bathing trunks—blue and turquoise paisley—and flip-flops. His well-muscled body was tanned and gorgeous. His blond hair was tousled, no doubt from quite a night with Wendy.

Mary Liz wished his mother would make him get a job. It wasn't good to let a man like this go to waste.

"Your mother told me the only reason you ever want anyone to go windsurfing with you is so you can show off. She says you even took a phone out there last summer and called her up to tell her to watch you out the window."

He looked a little crestfallen. "Is that bad, Mary Liz? To want someone to watch? If people weren't meant to watch people windsurfing, why are the sails so beautiful?"

She smiled, shaking her head. The idle rich. "Not this morning, Bertie. But another time, I promise. Really."

"Tomorrow?"

"Well, maybe if it's nice out. Anyway, I've got something on this morning. Hey, I know—why don't you go next door and ask Sasha? If you tell her she might see a whale or something, surely she'll at least sit on the beach and watch you."

His face brightened immediately. "Say, that's an idea. See ya!" He was off like a shot, jogging across the lawn and disappearing through the hedge to the property next door. How he could do so in flip-flops was beyond Mary Liz. Years of practice, she supposed.

She went back inside the cottage, to the office, picked up the coffee cup she had left there and continued reading through one of Alfred Hoffman's personal financial files. She was meeting William Pfeiffer later, a Wall Street attorney (and former protégé of her father's) whose Manhattan office was helping Mary Liz with the inventory of Alfred's estate. Bill had a weekend home in Water Mill, about ten miles west of here, and they had decided to meet face-to-face after talking so much over the telephone. He had asked her if she minded if his little girl was around, and she'd said no, of course not, there wasn't going to be any business conducted—"Was there?"

"No," he'd answered, "not on my end."

"Nor on mine."

"Great. You might even feel like going over to a children's carnival with us."

"Sure."

Mary Liz turned a page.

This was a very interesting file, a personal income tax file, and most anyone could see at a glance that Alfred Hoffman was either a man who was, or had hired, the most sophisticated financial and tax expert around. The fact that this particular tax return was seventy-three pages was a hint. Its contents outlined a massively complicated estate, appearing to tell all to the government, but designed, Mary Liz knew, to point the government in every direction except the ones where there might be some kind of dispute.

Like other entrepreneurial multimillionaires, Alfred Hoffman's company, Howland Films, paid for almost everything in his life. On a personal level, he withdrew a salary from the company and declared that money as his personal income from which he paid family expenses. He paid the expenses of this house, for example, and of the mansion in Beverly Hills; but the company owned and operated the apartment in New York, the apartment in Paris, the fishing lodge north of Vancouver, the villa in Mexico and the condominium in Aspen. His income was considerable, though, and unraveling the shelters and trusts in this estate was going to take some doing, particularly since the lawyer who had created the trusts and shelters, Bernard Braxer, had died in the plane crash with Alfred.

Someone was knocking on the front door of the cottage. Mary Liz had been under the impression that the fashionable elite rarely appeared in public before 10:00 a.m. on weekends, but apparently this was not true in East Hampton. Gathering her robe around her, she went to answer the door.

It was Herbert Glidden. In shorts, a golf shirt and sneakers, holding what appeared to be a nine iron. He smiled. "Sky's giving us a lesson out here. We thought you might like to join us."

When the bewilderment she felt evidently showed on her face, Glidden explained that if one played from the lily pond, down on the southwest corner of the front lawn, up to the third rise, to the left of the house, it was an almost perfect re-creation of the dogleg on the fifteenth hole at the golf course at East End. It was ideal for practice. Alfred had mapped it out five years ago and had played it all the time.

"Good morning!" Sky hailed her. He was coming down the front lawn from the Big House, with Aunt Nancy following in tennis whites.

"Good morning, darlin'!" Nancy said as they approached the cottage.

"Good morning. What a lovely party that was last night, Aunt Nancy. Thanks so much for including me."

Herb Glidden and Sky murmured their agreement. The fact that the person who had crashed the party last night—namely, Herb Glidden—was crashing the estate this morning seemed to escape everyone's notice but Mary Liz's.

"I can only play a little while, Herb," Nancy said. "And I'll have to use your club and putter. Mine are at the clubhouse."

"Do you want to play?" Sky asked Mary Liz.

"I'd love to, but I can't. I've got something on this morning."

"Chuck Scarborough's having a charity tennis tournament at his house in Southampton this morning," Nancy said. "I'm not playing, praise the Lord, but I thought I better at least look the part." They laughed.

"You start with Schyler, then," Herb Glidden said, pushing the nine iron into Nancy's hand. "I want to talk to Mary Liz for a minute." Before anyone could respond, he had taken Mary Liz by the elbow and steered her into the cottage. "I couldn't even sleep last night, I was so gung ho," he told her, closing the front door behind him. "With your credentials, Mary Liz, the things I could accomplish this summer would be phenomenal. I think maybe thirty hours a week would do it—so you can swim and paint and do whatever fun stuff you want." He put his hands up in caution. "No. Don't say no. Hear me out. I know it's your first vacation in years, but this could be the opportunity of a lifetime. I've got to finalize the investors for our movie in the fall, finalize the whole financial plan—stuff I swear to you you'll find fascinating. And I'll pay top dollar. And you'll get to meet lots of movie stars."

By now Mary Liz had crossed her arms protectively over her chest. What the heck was he talking about?

"Ten thousand a week," he said. "For a thirty-hour week. My people ran a check on you last night and you're top-drawer, first-rate."

She was shaking her head. "I couldn't possibly—"

"Fifteen then, and that's it, Mary Liz. Don't say anything. We'll talk later. Fifteen thousand a week, for a thirty-hour week, experience you couldn't get anywhere else, movie stars, trips to Europe if you want, the whole thing. Think about it. That's all I ask, that you think about it."

She nodded. "Okay. I'll think about it."

He looked satisfied with her answer. "So, this is your place for the summer?" he said, looking around. "I remember playing poker down here. Alfred's Friday-night game. Looked a lot different then. Rustic, you know. Nancy must have gotten her paws on it. Ever since she met up with that Martha Stewart..." He was heading for the back hall. "You don't mind if I use your bathroom, do you? Real quick. Before we play?"

The front doorknob rattled. Someone was trying to open the door. It was locked.

"Mary Liz?" her godmother said. "It's Nancy."

Mary Liz opened the door.

"Where is he?" Nancy said in a low voice, pushing her way in.

"The bathroom, I think."

Nancy walked briskly across the living room to the back hall. "The bathroom's here, Herb," she said loudly. And she stood there, in the hallway, until Mary Liz heard the bathroom door close. Then Aunt Nancy came back to her. "He was in the office, looking at the papers on your desk."

Uh-oh. Alfred's income tax return. There went her cover. Now Glidden had to know she was here in connection with the estate.

"I don't want to antagonize Herb any more than I have to," Aunt Nancy said, whispering, "but don't let him in here anymore. Because he will try."

Mary Liz nodded.

There was a quiet knock. "Hey, where is everybody?" Sky asked through the screen door. "Was it something I said?"

"Oh, sweet boy!" Nancy cried, opening the screen door for him. "We're coming."

"Come in, Sky," Mary Liz said. "Can I get you some coffee or something?"

"No, no, no," Nancy said. "We're going to leave you alone, Mary Liz. You get ready for your appointment."

Herbert Glidden appeared in the archway to the hall. "Well, I'm all set," he announced, clapping his hands together and rubbing them. "Let's go, Schyler, I've got a three o'clock tee-time and I've got a lot to do before then."

"Out, out, everyone out," Nancy directed, shooing Herb and Sky out the door. "Mary Liz has places to go and people to see."

Herb left last, pointing at Mary Liz from the doorway. "We'll talk."

Like hell we will, Mary Liz thought, nodding. "Fine. And thank you. It's an interesting proposition."

"You bet."

Mary Liz closed the front door behind Glidden.

His reasons for snooping, Mary Liz thought, were understandable. His reasons for wanting to hire her, obvious. Glidden wanted Mary Liz working for *him,* not in defense of Alfred Hoffman's estate.

Mary Liz had little trouble finding William Pfeiffer's house in Water Mill. Everything near the ocean out here on the east end of Long Island, she realized, was not far from Route 27. It was a charming natural-shingled farmhouse with a lovely white porch. She parked her "summer car," an '88 blue-gray LeBaron convertible, in the gravel driveway and was starting to walk to the front door when there was a high-pitched squeal and a little body came tearing around the corner from the backyard. Seeing Mary Liz, the little girl stopped. She was about five or six. Slipping off the back of her head was an enormous sombrero, just barely holding on by the string tied under the little girl's chin.

Mary Liz smiled and bowed slightly. *"Buenos días, muchacha."*

The little girl remained frozen.

"Mooooooo-cha-cha," Mary Liz said then, sounding a lot like a Mexican cow might.

A smile. A giggle. "Moo," the little girl said back.

Mary Liz stuck out her hand. "How do you do, Miss Moo?"

William Pfeiffer—Mary Liz presumed it was he—was watching them from the backyard. He came forward just as the little girl told Mary Liz that she was a very silly lady and Mary Liz agreed with her. The adults shook hands.

"Live and in person," she said, smiling.

"Live and lovely," he said, smiling back.

"Poppy," his daughter said, "tell her I'm Jenny."

Bill was a very nice man, but a Wall Streeter for sure, even when relaxed, complete with thinning hair, glasses, Lacoste shirt, Banana Republic shorts, Timberland moccasins and cellular phone in his back pocket. He was wonderful with his daughter, though, totally at ease with her, which tipped Mary Liz off that there was more to him than just the cut-and-dried businessman she'd talked to during the week.

Jenny wanted to know when they were going to the carnival, and her father said as soon as he and Mary Liz finished talking. Quite reasonably, Mary Liz thought, Jenny turned to her to ask, "Why aren't you finished talking?"

And so, Mary Liz climbed into her LeBaron and followed Bill's Jeep over the back roads to Southampton.

It was a tiny carnival, designed for children under the age of eight, run by local parents for the benefit of the Children's Leukemia Research Fund. It was held in front of the local elementary school, not far from the center of town. There were several activity and game booths for the children, a ride around the playground on a town fire truck, and one little pony ride in the corner. There were used toys and books for sale, and several booths offering hot dogs, hamburgers, baked goods, ice cream and cotton candy.

The guest of honor, Kenny, was a seven-year-old boy from Riverhead who had been cured of leukemia. The contrast between the vibrant little boy on the makeshift stage and the picture of the pale, bald, smaller child with sunken eyes that he had been, was very moving, and many people, including Mary Liz and Bill, wordlessly went over to the cashier to make a donation.

While Jenny participated in the Space Walk (a kind of gigantic inflatable pillow), the ringtoss and the clothespin drop, and sat on the lap of a clown to get her picture taken, Mary Liz told Bill about the dinner party the night before, about Glidden crashing it, about Julius Hoffman, and what Claire MacClendon had said about how Herbert Glidden used to be a dog at Alfred Hoffman's heels. She saved the worst for last. She told Bill about Glidden getting into her office that morning and seeing Alfred's income tax return on her desk.

"Aunt Nancy said he was reading it."

Bill sighed. "He's going to be a problem, Mary Liz. For God's sake, you can't let him get into your office again."

Little Jenny came up to them. She wanted to try The Maze, a construction of about twenty refrigerator boxes linked together, but it was a little scary, she said, and so Mary Liz crawled through it with her.

"She is an absolute darling," Mary Liz said later, watching as a volunteer plunked Jenny down on the back of the pony.

"She's taken to you, which is unusual," Bill said. "She's had a lot of people coming in and out of her life of late. Nannies, baby-sitters, my wife's—" He stopped himself from saying what it was he had been going to say. "Whatever. Anyway, she usually hangs back a while."

They both waved as Jenny came plodding past them.

"You and Jenny's mother...?" Mary Liz began.

"Are divorced. Just over a year ago." He was obviously still hurting from this. "I tried, that's all I can say. I had no idea our marriage would turn out the way it did." He smiled suddenly. "But look at what I got!" He pointed. "Is that the greatest little girl, or what?"

Mary Liz agreed wholeheartedly, but couldn't help thinking how sad it was that such a young child's family should already be broken up. It baffled her that two people would get married, take vows of eternal commitment, plan to have a child and then split up when she was still so small. Bill was forty-two years old, she knew. Surely he had been old enough to choose a proper partner?

("No wonder you haven't gotten married yet," her friend Sheila would say. "You're a perfectionist." "No," Mary Liz would say, "I'm only determined to give my children what my parents gave me.")

They got onto the subject of her father.

"He's a great man, Mary Liz," Bill said seriously.

"Yes, I know."

"He could be a multimillionaire, you know," Bill told her, "if he'd only take on one or two of those big clients that come to him. You know the kind I mean?"

She laughed. "Oh, yes. But I'm afraid Dad's not big on gangsters, drug dealers and exiled dictators. Anyway, my parents are not exactly suffering." She thought of their home in Winnetka, the condo in Florida, the summerhouse in Canada.

"I'm not sure you're aware of it," Bill said later, as they watched Jenny try her hand at the china-break booth, "but Howland Films was one of the clients your father turned down."

She looked at him in amazement. "He never told me that."

"Not for the reasons you think," he hastened to add. "It was because of the family connection. He said it made him uncomfortable."

Mary Liz asked Bill why he had left her father's firm.

"My wife hated Chicago," he said. "And then I got an offer I couldn't refuse. Two years in London at double my salary—my client was an American expatriate in a truckload of trouble with the IRS *and* the English tax authorities."

"It wasn't Robert Maxwell, was it?" she joked.

"No, but it *was* kind of like that. It was a real mess, but my wife loved London, and we had a proper English nanny who took Jenny to Regent's Park every day."

"So why did you come back?"

He looked pained by this question. "When my wife moved back to New York, she took Jenny."

Mary Liz nodded. "I see."

"So I came back and started my firm," Bill continued. "And then when I heard that your father was taking on the Hoffman estate, I called him, because this is exactly the kind of business I want to do more of. Defense of trusts and estates." He smiled. "You meet a better class of people."

"Something's wrong with the pony!" Jenny cried suddenly, pointing. She dropped her third softball and ran over to the pony ride. Other children were crying the same thing, or just crying. Indeed, as Mary Liz and Bill could see, the little Shetland pony was limping horribly, finally refusing to walk at all. The volunteer holding its reins looked helpless. Then a blond woman, in a smock splattered with brightly colored paints, slipped through the crowd and sidled up next to the pony, murmuring, gently petting it. She moved down to its flank, leaned against the pony and brought up its hoof in her hands to examine the bottom of it. She did something. And then she eased the pony's hoof down, petting its side again. She turned around and held up the tab from an aluminum can. "Wedged in the tender part."

"That's Claire MacClendon!" Mary Liz said.

"Who?"

"Ladies and gentlemen," Claire was saying in a loud voice to the crowd. "The poor little pony has gotten hurt in the line of duty."

There were wails from the children.

"All parents who would like to donate cash so that the poor little pony can go home and rest and feel better should give the donations to this man." She pointed to the volunteer holding the reins. "And for those parents who really, *really* want the pony to get well—"

Children cried, "Yes! Yes!"

"You can write out a check to the Children's Leukemia Research Fund. Kids, you can make a donation, too. Even a nickel will help." As parents (at the wailing insistence of their children) and kids surged forward to drop bills, coins and checks into a hastily obtained hat, Claire walked away.

"Claire, hi!" Mary Liz called.

She turned and her eyes widened in recognition. "Hi!"

"Next time I have a fund-raiser, I'm bringing you." Mary Liz laughed as she and the Pfeiffers walked toward the painter. "Is that blackmail, or what? The poor little pony?"

Claire raised her hands in defense. "Everything I know about fund-raising I learned from your godmother."

"Claire, I'd like you to meet a friend of my father's—and of mine, Bill Pfeiffer. And this is his daughter, Jenny. Bill, this is Claire MacClendon."

He looked astonished. "The painter, Claire MacClendon?" He looked at Mary Liz. "She paints these incredible landscapes—er—" He looked to Claire. "Seascapes?"

Claire nodded, smiling, pleased. "But it's Spin-Art today," she explained, gesturing to her paint-covered smock. "And I've got to get back to my booth."

"Do you have children here?" Bill asked as they walked her over.

Claire threw her head back to laugh. "Good grief, not for years, but thanks for the compliment."

"Poppy," Jenny said, pulling on her father's arm as they reached her booth, "can we do that?"

Claire had three machines that spun a flat plate, over which a piece of paper was laid. When each child's piece of paper began to spin, he or she could squeeze three colors of the nontoxic paints onto the paper. The mess of brilliant colors that resulted delighted all. Jenny donned a smock and started planning her creation, with Claire helping just a little.

Claire was a mother, all right, Mary Liz thought. And she had not lost the knack with small children a bit.

And yet Claire's husband had walked out on her.

And here was Bill, devoted father of a small child, but not devoted enough, evidently, to stay married to the child's mother.

It was a sad world for families, she thought. And she also thought how tremendously lucky she had been.

5

As they approached their cars in the parking lot, Bill insisted Mary Liz follow him to a hardware store to get some kind of temporary alarm for the office in the cottage until Bill arranged for a security system to be installed. "Whether you like it or not, Mary Liz," he said, "there're more people than just Herbert Glidden who would love to get their hands on those papers in the cottage."

"Like who? Julius Hoffman?"

"For starters. Maybe even the other son, Bertram. With the kind of money that's at stake, who knows what he's up to? You can't trust anyone *except* Nancy Hoffman, Mary Liz, and her only because she gets the majority of the estate, the way the will is written now. Most of all, we need to worry about Braxer & Braxer. And they are not a nice group."

Braxer & Braxer was the law firm that had represented Alfred for twenty-six years. Now that their founding partner—Bernard Braxer—was dead, the firm was turning around and suing the Hoffman estate for all kinds of fees and expenses that no one knew anything about.

"Just think how helpful it would be for them if they showed up in court knowing exactly what was in Alfred's estate and we didn't—because all of Alfred's personal files had suddenly disappeared. It's bad enough we don't have access to the papers they've got—I mean, that's why you're here in the first place, Mary Liz, to reconstruct the estate using whatever records Alfred possessed at the time of his death."

He was absolutely right, and so off to the hardware store they went.

"When I install this thing on top of the door," Mary Liz said to the clerk, "and activate it, how do I get out of the room without setting it off?"

"You turn it on while the door is open. The alarm is activated only after the door has been closed," the clerk explained. "Later, when you open the door again, you've got fifteen seconds to punch in the code. If you don't, the alarm will scream its head off for at least three hours—or until the code is punched in properly."

After Bill purchased a miniature wooden rake for Jenny, the trio left the store and the Pfeiffers hurried off because, Jenny announced, she had some important yard work to attend to.

When Mary Liz arrived back at the estate with the alarm, she found a man sitting on her front porch. Beside him was a trolley with six cardboard boxes on it, three to a side. "I'm Jake O'Leary," he said, standing and offering a hand. He was around thirty, very tanned and extremely athletic-looking, to say nothing of just plain good-looking. "I kind of oversee the grounds here, at the manor. In L.A. too—in fact, I just got in. I've been closing up the Beverly Hills property."

He had to be an aspiring actor then. No glorified handyman looked like this.

"Mrs. Hoffman asked me to bring these boxes down to you. They're from Mr. Hoffman's study in California."

"Thank you."

"I knocked and there was no answer, but I thought I'd just wait around a little." He flashed a grin. "It's nice to look at the grounds—and frankly, that's a big hill with these boxes. They weigh a ton. I wasn't looking forward to lugging them back up."

"I'm glad you waited," she said, leaning to look at the labels on the boxes.

"Shall I take them in now?"

"Yes. Thank you. This way," she said, pushing open the front door then stepping back to hold the screen door for him as he picked up a box.

"There's an envelope on the floor," Jake commented on his way in.

Tiffany stationery, she thought, scooping it up. Blue. "Go down that hall," she told Jake. "Last door on the right. It's the office. Put the carton on the floor anywhere." She opened the envelope.

Mary Liz,
Let's talk. Let's play. You choose.
Call me on my personal cellular.
Julius

And then he had scribbled a number.

What the heck was this? Let's talk—okay, she got that part. But let's *play?* She shuddered to think what that might mean. She dropped the note on the table as though it had a spider on it.

When Jake came out for another box, Mary Liz offered him a glass of juice or water or seltzer. He declined. "I've got to get to the tennis court," he explained. "Mrs. Hoffman has friends coming tomorrow to play."

As Mary Liz leaned on the breakfast bar, drinking a glass of seltzer and contemplating the note Julius had left, the telephone rang. She picked up the wall unit. "Hello?"

"Mary Liz, darlin', I swear to heaven I'd forget my name if I didn't have a tag sewn in my clothes. Of course, the tag has someone else's name on it already, like Donna Karan or Rachelle Zaratan, but that's not the point, is it?" Her godmother laughed. "I'm sorry to be calling on such short notice, but I've got three functions tonight and I wondered if you would like to go to any of them. I don't know what your politics are, but there's a Democratic fund-raiser cocktail party—Paul Newman's coming over from Connecticut for it, I think—there's a cocktail-buffet benefit for Body Positive, an organization that helps people recently diagnosed with AIDS—and then there's the dinner-dance benefit for the East Hampton Historical Society."

"Wow," Mary Liz commented.

"Now, I *have* to go to the historical society dance. And Bertie said he and Wendy would be willing to go to the Body Positive buffet. So that leaves the Democratic fund-raiser. But that is a cocktail party and I suppose I *could* swing by there for a quick drink... Yes, I definitely will. Well, then, you see? You don't *have* to go to any of them, Mary Liz, but you *may* go to any you wish. The dinner-dance is black-tie—"

"If it's all right," Mary Liz interrupted, "I'd really rather stay in tonight."

"That's just fine, darlin', then you just do that."

Mary Liz was relieved. She was already getting rapidly peopled-out in the forty-eight hours since the Big House had been officially opened.

"Oh, and something else—Sasha Reinhart came around looking for you today. She wants you to go to an Emily's List fund-raiser tonight. I said I had no idea what your politics are, but I gave her your number, so if she was serious about it, I'm sure she'll call."

Mary Liz glanced at the answering machine. No messages. "Thank you."

"Oh, and tomorrow—oh, I'm sorry, I know you want to have some quiet—I promise I won't be doing this to you all summer—but tomorrow, if you're around, there's a cocktail party in Amagansett that if you attended would be an enormous favor to me. I've got to go into the city and Bertie simply won't give me a definite yes or no and the hostess is a dear friend and it's for a very good cause."

"What's the cause?"

"Um, let me see... Bertha wrote it down here, I think."

Bertha was her part-time social secretary.

"Yes, it's for a battered women's shelter," Aunt Nancy reported.

"In New York?" Mary Liz asked.

She laughed a low, ironic laugh. "Oh, no, darlin', it's for right *here.*"

"Oh. Do they take the children in, too?"

"Yes."

"Consider it done," Mary Liz said. "I will attend."

"Somebody in Los Angeles told me once," Jake said, carrying another box into the house as Mary Liz hung up the phone, "that every year Mrs. Hoffman raises more money for charitable causes than the entire state budget of Montana."

Mary Liz laughed. "My mother said Wyoming."

"Dad, forget it. I'm not going near that guy." Mary Liz had waited until Jake finished moving all of the boxes to place this call to Illinois.

"Just listen to what Glidden has to say," her father, Nelson Scott, said. "You may learn something that will be helpful to your godmother."

"Everyone here, *everyone* has warned me to stay away from Herbert Glidden, and now you're telling me to interview with him for a job."

"What harm could it do?"

"Father," she said, "when you and Mom approached me about inventorying the estate, you said I'd get a wonderful summer vacation out of it, I'd have this wonderful estate to live on and everybody would leave me alone. From what I've seen in the last forty-eight hours, *nobody* is going to leave me alone around here. Aunt Nancy wants to make me into a socialite, Herbert Glidden's already wormed his way into my house and seen Alfred's tax file, that revolting Julius Hoffman is leaving me mash notes under my door and Bertie and his girlfriend expect me to play with them on the beach. *And,* before I forget, *Dad,* you neglected to tell me that *you* once turned down Alfred Hoffman as a client."

Instead of going on the defensive, her father was laughing, which, of course, only annoyed Mary Liz no end. It reminded her of the time when she was little and was trying to learn to play the violin, and how, when she played for her parents, her father had started coughing and had to leave the room. And how she had continued to play for her mother, but then spotted her father through the window, lying on his back outside on the lawn, holding his stomach, choking with laughter. And, as the final blow, how her mother had thought "Twinkle, Twinkle Little Star" was "Silent Night."

Mary Liz had given up the violin.

"Mary Liz, I'm sorry, babe," her father was saying. "I don't mean to laugh, but you make it sound like a P.G. Wodehouse novel there. As for my turning Alfred down, I promise you, kiddo, my reasons were personal, they had nothing to do with his business. I think you'll find things pretty clean in that regard."

"I hope so."

"All I am suggesting is that you listen to what Herbert Glidden has to say, and find out more about how his business runs. If you hear anything unusual, tell Bill Pfeiffer about it and we'll take it from there. The point is, Nancy could use something on this guy to make him back down on his suit."

"Then Glidden has a case?"

Her father sighed. "He has enough resources to tie up Howland Films for years. It's more blackmail than a case. 'Let me buy Howland for cheap, or watch me destroy it.'"

Mary Liz was thinking. "I draw the line at Julius, though, Dad. I'm not going anywhere with him. I'm not even going to call him."

He laughed. "But you could be nice to the wife. She might know something we could use."

She made a face. "I'm not going to be nice to people so I can later stab them in the back!"

"But, Mary Liz, Julius is trying to steal part of the estate from Nancy. If Nancy chooses to let him work at Howland, that's one thing, but to let him steal control of it after Alfred specifically designated it to Nancy, that's a whole other ball game."

True. "Okay, I'll be nice to Jeanine."

Mary Liz got off the phone with her father and started assembling the tools she'd need to install the alarm. She was definitely starting to feel a little paranoid. All she was supposed to do was come here this summer and quietly inventory the estate. The first month had been peaceful. And then the season had started. But no one had told her people would be overrunning her cottage, people who were, coincidentally, suing the estate—like Glidden and Julius Hoffman—or who might be just a little *too* interested in the outcome of Alfred's will—like Bertie and his girlfriend. (Wendy didn't look like a gold digger, but who ever knew until it was too late?)

And then there was Braxer & Braxer to worry about. Who knew who might be an agent for them? Trying to find out what her side knew about the actual contents of the estate. Good grief, she needed to be more careful—even that Jake who had moved the boxes into her office could be working for Braxer & Braxer. What better spy to have than a member of the domestic staff?

She made a note to check on Jake with Aunt Nancy.

And Delores, the housekeeper.

And Bertha, the social secretary.

The gardener, too. Lawn-mowing guys? Cleaning service?

Gee, not too paranoid, was she? Well, better to play it safe.

She brought the tools from the kitchen utilities closet into the office. She smiled at the picture of her family on the desk—her mother, father and brothers, Brendan and Kip. Being the only girl had made up for being the middle child. Dad would have spoiled her if it hadn't been for her mother, Mary Liz was pretty sure. As her mother said, "He just went gaga when he saw you, angel, and I thought, 'Uh-oh, I better watch out or we're going to have a hothouse flower for a daughter.'"

They were quite a couple, her mother and father: her debutante mother, the former India Elizabeth Reynolds of Charleston and The Willows, South Carolina, and Nelson Roderick Scott of Hennick's Trailer Park, Liberty, New York, the only son of the young widow, Patricia, and brother to four sisters. Mother said there was no reason in the world for her to be anything but generous to everyone she met in this life. Mercy, until she kept house and had born children with Nelson, she hadn't done a lick of work unless one considered practicing walking across a room with a book on her head while also holding a dime in her derriere real work....

Her father's story was so very different. Work, work, work, working to pitch in with the family, working for a scholarship to college, where he worked as a busboy in a frat house, a stack-searcher in the library, even a garbage hauler. Law school. More scholarships, more work. Then his first full-time office job in New York, most of his salary going back to Liberty for his sisters. Meeting India at the Harvard Club in New York, thinking he didn't have a chance with her. He did, though. They married on a beautiful Saturday afternoon at The Willows (formerly a plantation, now only a farm), the groom age thirty, and the bride twenty-four, the most dazzling creature he had ever laid eyes on.

The maid of honor had been Aunt Nancy ("another Sugar Magnolia," her mother would laugh), who had been Mother's roommate at Sweet Briar College and with whom she had made her debut in New York that very first fall of freshman year. Aunt Nancy had not met Alfred Hoffman yet. (She had been engaged to a tobacco heir at the time, an engagement her father approved of and she would later break off.)

Mary Liz's parents settled in Chicago, where her father had a big new job. Mother was later Aunt Nancy's matron of honor after she did finally meet, and was quickly swept off her feet by, Alfred Hoffman. Aunt Nancy had later flown to Chicago from Los Angeles (where she had moved with Alfred), to be Mary Liz's godmother at her christening, but the couples rarely saw each other after that. Not until Dad took on a major case in Los Angeles nearly a decade later. For nearly a year he had to commute to Los Angeles, often bringing Mother with him, and, twice, bringing the kids, too.

Those trips to Los Angeles were how Mary Liz remembered her Aunt Nancy. A kind of beautiful fairy princess dashing into the corporate apartment, kissing her, giving her a dress or something and then flying away. Mary Liz never did meet Alfred on those trips (or any other time, for that matter), and had only glimpsed Bertie once, because Bertie had gotten his finger caught in the car door while getting out at the apartment complex and Aunt Nancy had had to take him to the emergency room. Mary Liz hadn't even *seen* Denver that day, because Denver had never even gotten a chance to get out of the back seat of the car.

Mary Liz smiled to herself. And now here she was, all these years later, trying to help out the godmother she did not really even know. But Mother—and Dad, too—had been sympathetic to Nancy's plight. Regardless of the money involved, for a suddenly widowed wife to be betrayed first by the family's own lawyers, then by her husband's primary business associate, and then by her stepson, was an outrage. And thus her parents had moved in to help. And since Mary Liz had quit her job and wasn't doing anything…

So now Mary Liz was a burglar-alarm installer.

It took a couple of hours to get the hang of her new profession. Mary Liz was fairly handy with tools, but impatient, and so she had to do everything twice before getting the alarm to work properly.

Satisfied with her work (but wondering about the lock on the door, which could be opened with the pointed end of a beverage opener), Mary Liz took a long, hot bath, got into her nightie, fixed a salad and cooked a hamburger, and then sat down on the couch in front of the TV to watch reruns of hit shows she could never see when she was working.

At five to nine, someone knocked on her door.

Darn. She had too many lights on in the house to pretend she was asleep. And then in the next moment Mary Liz saw Sasha Reinhart peering in at her through the window, waving, so she could hardly pretend she wasn't home. She got up and answered the door.

"Hi!" the diva said. "Riff's driving me downtown to get a fat-free frozen-fruit ice, wanna come?"

"Who's Riff?"

"My bodyguard," she said. Suddenly she frowned, and started sniffing the air. "Goddess almighty!" she exclaimed. "You haven't been eating *meat*, have you?"

Mary Liz nodded. "A hamburger."

Sasha looked as if she was about to be sick. "Hamburger," she said, shuddering. "You ate of the holy cow."

Mary Liz nodded again. "'Fraid so. And I don't like fat-free frozen-fruit ice," she added, hoping this might further disqualify her for future spur-of-the-moment jaunts. Sasha Reinhart was a superstar, yes, but Mary Liz also suspected she could be a royal pain in the neck. "I only like real ice cream and sugar cones."

The diva frowned again, looked over her shoulder, and then opened the screen door to whisper, "So do I, but it can't get out. I'm not suppose to *do* dairy."

And so, Mary Liz got dressed again and went downtown with Sasha and her bodyguard to get an ice-cream cone, chocolate for her, vanilla and strawberry with chocolate sprinkles for Sasha. It was like any normal evening in any small town, except that they stood in line at the ice-cream parlor behind Mayor Koch and Rosie O'Donnell, the latter of whom was with her little boy.

6

Bertie Hoffman had taken Mary Liz at her word and was parked on her doorstep Sunday morning at nine to go windsurfing. Wendy, he explained, wasn't feeling well this morning and was sleeping in, so it would just be the two of them.

As she was inviting Bertie inside to wait while she put on her suit, the telephone rang. She dashed over to the wall phone in the kitchen and answered it. It was Sky Preston, calling from the golf club, asking if there was any chance she might like to go to a cocktail party in Amagansett with him this evening. It was a benefit for the battered women's shelter. He would have called earlier, but the Buckleys had only just asked him to go.

"As a matter of fact," Mary Liz said, "Aunt Nancy asked me to fill in for her at that same party. But this is great. I'd love to go with you."

"Tell whoever it is," Bertie said over her shoulder into the telephone, "that you have a very important windsurfing lesson."

"Who is that? Bertie?" Sky asked.

"Yes," Mary Liz said, laughing as Bertie yanked like a child on her arm, mouthing, "Come on, come on."

"I'll pick you up around four forty-five, okay?"

"Great," she said. "I look forward to it."

"Me, too."

"Go put on your suit," Bertie instructed as soon as she hung up the phone. "I've got a wet suit for you at the cabana."

"Wet suit?"

"The water's freezing and Mother will kill me if you drown."

Mary Liz changed into her bathing suit, pulled a T-shirt and gym shorts over it and slipped on her Topsiders. She checked that she'd set the alarm on the office door, because she wanted to leave the front door open to air out the living room.

She and Bertie walked together up the lawn of the estate. It was an absolutely gorgeous day, warm, sunny, dry, a few breezes. The ocean, however, when they got to the cabana, looked very rough to Mary Liz.

"I'll get you past the surf and give you a lesson," Bertie said. "There's a sandbar at this tide, so you'll only be in water up to your midthighs."

Yeah, yeah, right.

They went into the cabana, where Bertie tossed her the bottom half of a wet suit. "It's Denver's," he explained, "so it should fit you. I talcked it and everything. I don't think you'll need the upper, but if you want it, it'll be on the beach. Okay?"

It wasn't as hard to get the bottom of the wet suit on as she had first feared. The only problem was, it was bright orange, and while Denver was an actress who was no doubt very thin, Mary Liz clearly was not, and she had no desire to show her thighs off to the world. Bertie did not wear any wet suit at all.

Two windsurfer rigs and a long red surfboard were waiting on the beach. So was Jake, the estate overseer, dressed only in cutoffs and showing spectacular muscles. "Mother insisted on supervision," Bertie explained. "Jake's got his ocean-guard credentials. So do I, but Mother's afraid I'll strand you out there. That's what Jake's surfboard is for. To paddle out and save you." He was laughing and Mary Liz started to hate this whole exercise. Why did she have to do this?

"Why do I have to do this?" she asked.

"So you'll be a more interesting person when you get back to Chicago," Bertie said, fussing with one of the sails. He glanced up. "Mother says you've done nothing but work for ten years." He went back to the sail. "This way, you'll go home with another sport."

"I'm not going back like this," she said, screwing up her face while looking down at the orange wet suit. Here she stood with two Adonises, looking like half an orange idiot. Half an overweight orange idiot.

Jake's eyes, she noticed, were not on her, but on Bertie, and she didn't blame him.

Bertie walked her through the components of the windsurfer. The board, a surfboard, the mast of the sail rising up from it. As she could see, the mast could be lowered away from her, all the way flat, and pulled up by the yardarm all the way vertical. This was how she started and stopped. Raise the sail, start. Drop it, stop.

Did she know how to sail?

"No," she lied, wanting out of this.

"That's probably a plus," he said. "Because a windsurfer has no tiller, or anything. It really is unique and you're going to love it."

Jake carried her windsurfer down to the water for her. Because it was low tide, the surf was almost nonexistent beyond the waves that were crashing on shore. Still, she had to get the windsurfer through the crashing waves. Jake solved that. He simply carried the board through them and plunked it down in the calmer water.

She waded out. Her feet were threatening to cramp already, the water felt so cold.

"Okay," Bertie began. "One of our problems today is that the wind is blowing from west to east, which means you can zoom out into the ocean, but will have trouble getting back in."

"Great," she said, shivering, hands on the windsurfer in front of her.

"Are you cold?" he asked, appearing surprised. "You have the wet suit on."

She gave him a look.

"I'm a good teacher, really."

She continued shivering, imagining that her lips must be turning blue. At least it was too cold for crabs, right? So she need not worry about anything coming up out of the smooth sand beneath her feet and grabbing hold of her. And sharks. Too cold for sharks, right? "By the way, how did Sasha do yesterday?" she asked him. She might as well try getting competitive about it.

"Oh, she didn't go out. Jake rowed her out in the dinghy and she took movies of me."

Darn, she should have thought of that.

"Okay, first thing, we need to get up on the board. It's warm up there," he added as an enticement, patting the surface of his board.

She had no problem pulling herself up so that now she was on her hands and knees on the board. "Okay," Bertie continued. "Now slowly stand up, but make sure to keep the strap to the sail in your hand." Amazingly, she was able to stand. The board was surprisingly stable. It wasn't like a raft or anything, as she had imagined.

"Get your balance, and then slowly try to bring up the sail," Bertie instructed. "As it comes up, you'll be shifting your weight back, to pull, and then bringing your body forward as the sail becomes vertical."

This didn't seem so bad. She got the sail up out of the water, it was coming up nicely and then, she didn't know how, she just lost her balance, let go of the sail and went flying backward into the water.

Yikes! It was freezing!

She shot up out of the water, shaking her hair out of her face and holding herself against the shock of the cold. To his credit, Bertie did not laugh. He simply nodded and said, "You almost had it. That's fabulous for a first-timer. Isn't it, Jake?"

On the shore, Jake nodded.

"Okay, Mary Liz, you'll get it this time," Bertie encouraged her.

She had water in one ear. The salt was stinging her underarms where she had shaved this morning with too dull a razor. Her hair looked like seaweed. And yet, she climbed back on the board. Bertie climbed on his and showed her how it was done. He didn't look very graceful, either, which relieved her slightly. A glance back to shore brought a reassuring nod from Jake. He was ready to save her.

She got up on her feet and was starting to pull the sail up, when there was a horrible electronic screeching sound from shore. Mary Liz dropped the sail to look. Aunt Nancy was waving with both hands from the terrace outside her bedroom. Mary Liz dropped to her hands and knees on the board, and Nancy brought a bullhorn up over the railing. "Mary Liz! There is some kind of alarm going off in the cottage! What should I do?"

Mary Liz dived off the windsurfer and starting swimming in. She could hear Bertie yelling at her, "What are you doing?" When she hit the shore, she asked Jake to get the windsurfer and ran as best she could across the beach. Going up the stairs she felt as if she had two sixty-pound weights strapped to her legs. Panting as though her lungs were about to burst, she nonetheless reached the walkway and made herself jog. Now she could hear the alarm. Either it had malfunctioned, or someone had—

Was leaving the front door open entrapment? she wondered. Had someone wandered into the house looking for her, and gone into the office to see if she was there?

She had left the office door locked. So, if she got there and found the door to the office open, that meant someone had unlocked it and gone in. But if the office door was still locked, it meant the alarm had malfunctioned.

Nancy, Delores and Wendy had picked up the pace behind Mary Liz as she ran down the front lawn. They followed her up the cottage porch stairs, into the living room and down the back hall, holding their hands over their ears. Mary Liz tried the office door and found it unlocked.

Someone had gone in.

Mary Liz went in, closed the door behind her and punched in the code. The noise stopped. When she opened the door, she found Julius Hoffman and Riff, Sasha's bodyguard, standing in the hall, as well.

"What happened?" Julius asked. "I was next-door at Sasha's and heard the noise." He turned to Riff. "Who the hell are you?"

"I'm Ms. Reinhart's bodyguard," the big guy said. "We heard the alarm and she sent me over to investigate."

"If you were over at Sasha's, Julius," Mary Liz said impatiently, "why don't you know who Riff is?"

Everyone looked at Mary Liz. The tone of her voice was not friendly. But she was not feeling friendly. Someone had tried to get into her office while she was out windsurfing.

Julius deliberately gave her the slow once-over, as if she were just so much scum. "Are you hysterical, Mary Liz? Does someone need to slap you?"

Jerk. He was making fun of her, standing here in the damn bottoms of the orange wet suit, with saltwater dripping from her nose and seaweed hair.

"Let's get out of this hallway," Nancy suggested, steering people toward the living room. Mary Liz noticed that her godmother was in a dress and white sandals, while everybody else was in shorts.

"I was walking up to Sasha's house when I heard the alarm," Julius said to Nancy. "I came back down the driveway and ran around to yours, Nance, and came that way."

"I came on the path through the hedge," the bodyguard offered.

"See?" Julius said, turning to Mary Liz. "And why the hell, may I ask, do you have an alarm system no one knows anything about?"

"I knew about it," Nancy said quickly, trying to cover for Mary Liz.

"Well what the hell is it for?" he wanted to know.

"I will go back up to the house, Mrs. Hoffman," Delores said. To Mary Liz, "If you need anything, please let me know."

Mary Liz had grabbed a bath towel on her way to the living room and now wrapped herself in it. Anything for a little dignity. "Thanks, Delores, but I don't think I'll need anything."

"Kids are always breaking in here in the winter," Nancy said.

"What do you *have* in that room that you need an alarm for?" Julius demanded of Mary Liz.

"Did you see anyone leaving the cottage, Aunt Nancy?" Mary Liz said, ignoring Julius.

"No, I don't think so. Wendy? Did you? You were outside."

"No," Wendy said.

"You were outside?" Mary Liz said. "Bertie said you weren't feeling well."

Wendy looked offended by her tone and answered, rather sharply (and looking at Mary Liz as though she suspected Mary Liz might just be so much scum, too), "I was reading in the hammock." The hammock was on the other side of the house, near the cutting gardens.

"So when you came around the side of the house," Mary Liz said, "you must have seen someone coming out of here."

"There is a back door, you know," Julius pointed out.

"I came through the hedge," the bodyguard repeated. "I didn't see anyone."

"But you came later," Julius said.

"How do *you* know he came later?" Mary Liz asked Julius.

Nancy placed a gentle hand on her arm. "It's all right, darlin'."

Julius looked at his stepmother. "What the hell is going on around here?"

"Mary Liz has some very expensive equipment in there," Nancy said, "that's all."

"And you've got two fucking million dollars' worth of art in the living room!" he cried, pointing toward the Big House. "Who the hell's going to break in here on a Sunday morning for some crappy computer equipment?"

"That's just the point," Mary Liz said coldly. "Someone did."

Silence.

"And how did you know, Julius," Mary Liz added, "that it was computer equipment?"

"Fine! Call the fucking police!" Julius thundered. "Track down the scoundrel, hang him from the tree!"

"Fine," Mary Liz said to him. "There'll be fingerprints on the doors, won't there? And you won't mind being dusted, will you, Julius?"

"Now, now," Nancy said, "there's no need for the police, I don't think."

"What's going on?" Bertie asked, bursting in through the front door. He was dripping saltwater, too. Jake stayed outside, peering in through the screen door. Bertie moved quickly to Wendy's side. "Are you okay?"

"Mary Liz thinks we're a bunch of burglars," Wendy explained.

"Mary Liz thinks someone tried to break into her office," Nancy said. "The alarm went off."

"What alarm, Mother? There's no alarm in the cottage."

"Mary Liz put one in."

"What kind of houseguest installs their own alarm?" Bertie asked, turning to look at Mary Liz.

"That's what I said," Julius told him.

"Okay, that's it!" Mary Liz declared. "Everybody out."

"Don't we have to be fingerprinted first?" Julius joked.

"Julius, *out,*" Nancy said. And then in a softer voice, "Thank you for your concern, but everything's under control now. And you, Mr.—" She was addressing Sasha Reinhart's bodyguard.

"Riff."

"Mr. Riff—"

"No, Riff Cahill."

"Mr. Cahill, please thank Sasha for sending you over to help, but everything is fine."

"She's going to want to know if someone broke in," Riff said. "She's a bit concerned about things like that."

"I will talk to Sasha myself," Nancy promised.

"Great!" Mary Liz said, throwing her arms out. "Everyone's in agreement. Nothing happened. Someone walked into the cottage, pried open the lock on my office door, went in and set off the alarm, but nothing happened!"

"She's paranoid," she heard Julius mutter.

Mary Liz glared at him. "Keep it up, guy."

He smiled. "I will, cutie."

"Julius, come on, out," Nancy said, herding everyone out the front door. She waited there for Mary Liz to speak to her.

"I'm positive, Aunt Nancy," Mary Liz said. "Someone tried to get into the office."

"Whoever it was won't try it again," Nancy said. "So, for the moment, why don't we just drop it? It's not worth getting everyone upset over."

No wonder everyone was suing her godmother. She hated confrontation, and people probably figured if they made enough of a disturbance, sooner or later she'd let them have their way just to have it over with.

Mary Liz took a deep breath, starting to calm down. "Okay, whatever you say." But just in case, she thought, she'd get this cottage wired but good, and she'd move the sensitive files up to the vault-room in the Big House.

"Anybody for church?" she heard her godmother ask brightly outside.

7

Julius Hoffman hadn't been gone from Mary Liz's cottage for even an hour before he called to say he was seriously considering filing slander charges against her for the accusations she had made.

"You are such a *jerk!*" Mary Liz blurted out.

"And you are one paranoid bitch, girlie! Why the hell would I want to break into your stupid cottage?"

"You tell me," she dared him.

"I don't know! You're the nut—you tell me." And then there was a pause on his end of the phone, followed by a gravelly sort of laugh. "Ah-ha! I get it. Aunt Nancy's little goddaughter from Chicago isn't here just for a vacation, is she?"

"I've got work to do, so what?" she demanded.

"But not secret high finance, is it? That's why Jake was moving all those boxes to the cottage yesterday, wasn't it? You've got Dad's financial records there, I bet. Maybe even Dad's files that are missing from his office at Howland. You took them—or your father did. You're working for your father, aren't you? On the estate defense."

He had to have figured it out sooner or later, she supposed. It was just that everything was unraveling an awful lot sooner than she had anticipated—like within the last forty-eight hours. And best he believed her father had annexed the business files from Howland instead of Aunt Nancy, who had pulled them herself and shipped them east.

The only thing she could think of to say was, "Watch out, Julius, I'm dangerous to have as an enemy."

He laughed. "Well, at least you're becoming interesting again," and he hung up.

Mary Liz called Bill Pfeiffer immediately to tell him about the break-in, her suspicions about Julius and her most recent conversation with him.

"I'm on my way over," Bill said.

"No, that's not necessary," she said. "But if you can find someone who can put that security system in here ASAP, I'd be eternally grateful. I was thinking of something along the line of a doorknob that will simply electrocute the next intruder."

When she saw her godmother's Jaguar drive up to the manor house, presumably bringing Nancy back from church, Mary Liz dashed up to catch her before she went inside. "A couple of quick questions, Aunt Nancy. First, what's the story with Jake?"

Aunt Nancy seemed very surprised. "Why, darlin', Jake O'Leary's been our property manager for over two years, why?"

"Do you trust him?"

"With my life!" (Which sounded more like, "Wee-yuth mah lauff!") "Why, he's Bertie's best friend in the whole wide world—like brothers those two are, as thick as thieves."

An unfortunate turn of phrase, Mary Liz thought. "And Delores?"

"Goodness itself!" her godmother declared. "She has worked for me for sixteen years." She lowered her voice. "Mary Liz, I'm sorry but you *are* beginning to sound a little paranoid."

"And Bertha?" Mary Liz continued.

"Stop it!" her godmother commanded, stamping her left foot in a mock tantrum.

"And Wendy?"

Surprisingly, instead of becoming angry, Aunt Nancy burst out laughing. "You've got me there, child, but she's the first girl Bertie's brought home in ages, so I'd appreciate it if you weren't too hard on her. But I should tell you that I have it on very good authority she's top-drawer."

"Who's the very good authority?" Mary Liz asked.

"Bertie. He's a terrible snob about some things, you know."

Inwardly Mary Liz groaned, but she thanked her godmother and went back down to the cottage.

Great. She had left the front door unlocked and the alarm off in the office.

She had better get into the swing of things.

By the time Sky arrived at four-forty, Mary Liz *was* in the swing of things, on the portable phone with the security guy Bill Pfeiffer had found. He could come tomorrow at one-thirty. She waved Sky in through the screen door, finalized her date with the technician and hung up.

"Wow, did you get a lot of color this weekend," she said, coming around the breakfast bar. Sky was dressed in one version of the off-the-course golfer's uniform, cheery green cotton slacks, a white shirt and a dark blue linen blazer with the East End Country Club insignia on it. His face and neck were deeply brown, making his eyes even bluer.

"And do you ever look fabulous," he told her, smiling broadly, openly taking her in.

She had made an effort, particularly after her humiliating experiences of the morning, running around in half of an orange wet suit. Actually, her outfit almost matched Sky's. She was wearing a blue, green and white silk wraparound skirt, a white, sleeveless designer blouse that, for some reason, made her look thin in the middle and (sort of) in her upper arms. Sandals were white. Jewelry was silver, which showed off her tan and lit up her eyes: delicate hoop earrings, a choker, a stunning band on her wrist. As for her hair, she'd done her extra-care routine: wash and condition it, dry it upside down, brush it right side up and pull the sides back with an intricately cut silver hair clasp.

He took another step forward and held out his hand. He wanted to shake hands! Smiling, she reached out and took it. And they shook, smiling at each other, Mary Liz reveling in how very pleasant it was to make physical contact with him in such a polite and respectful way.

"May I get you something to drink?" she asked him when the handshake was over.

He looked at his watch. "We really don't have time." He met her eyes, smiling again. "If we want to see everybody who's anybody, Vanessa told me the exact window of time they appear. It's a much smaller window tonight since it's Sunday and a lot of people have to go into Manhattan."

They left the cottage and Mary Liz locked the front door. Outside, parked on the side of the driveway, ready to pull out of the estate, was a pale yellow Mercedes 250 SL convertible with a black top. "Oh, my heavenly day," she said (sounding suspiciously like her mother). "What a gorgeous car." She looked at him. "What kind of teacher did you say you were?"

"The kind who's good with cars." Sky laughed. "No, Mary Liz," he said, guiding her to the car by lightly touching the small of her back, "I'm not secretly rich. No way. However, I do love a good car.

And this is a good car, and it became somewhat more affordable after twenty years."

"It looks brand-new," she murmured, reaching the car and touching the shiny surface.

"Thank you. I've worked on every single part of it and repainted it myself."

He opened the door for her. "Can we put the top down?" The smell of real leather wafted into her face as she slid into the seat.

"Sure. But what about your hair?"

"Oh, right." She remembered, hating her hair.

He squatted to talk to her at eye level. "Tell you what, we do the party and then we'll put the top down. It will be cooler later, anyway."

He got into the car, started it up and turned the air conditioner on low. She was grateful. It was a sure way to preserve her makeup in this heat.

This was very strange for Mary Liz. How long had it been since she cared how she looked? Oh, sure, for business meetings, maybe. But since the whole Jim and Kennedy fiasco a year and a half ago, she hadn't much cared if anyone thought she was attractive. And she had kept herself so busy at work afterward that she could hardly care what she looked like.

Her schedule had been to get up at five, be at her desk by six, work straight through lunch—maybe grabbing a salad or yogurt from the kitchen (the firm encouraged people to work through *every* meal and so kept the kitchen stocked)—maybe getting out of the office around seven. That was a good workday. Most days, though, as a partner, it meant being at O'Hare by 6:00 a.m., flying to somewhere like Denver for a lunch meeting, and then flying down to somewhere like Charlotte for a dinner meeting with a client. Spend the night. Then hightail it in the morning to some godforsaken place somewhere in West Virginia for an afternoon meeting, back to Chicago straight after, hit the office at seven, leave around midnight, be back at seven or eight the next morning with a bag packed to take a flight that night on a thirty-six-hour visit to Europe to pitch to another prospective client.

Glancing over at Sky, she wondered what he would think of how she had spent the recent years of her life. Working, working, arriving at age thirty-two to wonder where her twenties had gone, but still not letting it fully register that her life was slipping away, never stopping to think about it, never stopping, period. And if she did happen to stop—when she finally physically collapsed with some bug she had picked up on the road—she would drown out any knowledge of her passing life with a bottle of NyQuil and a long stretch of sleep. And then, back to running. The phone calls from angry friends who never saw her, never talked to her. Family that wondered how she could be so busy she couldn't travel twenty miles to visit. The weight she'd put on eating junk food while traveling. Anxiety attacks. Insomnia. And then she had finally started hitting the wine bottle every night in an attempt to knock herself to sleep.

Strange, wasn't it? How the moment she had left Chicago she had started to sleep? As if she could only be human if everything was physically taken out of her reach, when she knew for sure there was absolutely nothing else to do.

"Mary Liz?"

She snapped back to the present.

Sky glanced at her. "I asked you, are you sure there's no husband or fiancé or something lurking around? I'm having a hard time believing a woman like you is single."

"No husband, no fiancé," she told him. "Just an ex—" She hastened to add, "Ex-fiancé, not husband. I've never been married."

"Me neither," he said. "But I have an ex, too. Ex-fiancée."

"Golly," Mary Liz said, laughing. "We both sound as though we did away with them."

Sky looked at her and smiled, but didn't say anything more on the subject. They just kept driving east on 27, to Amagansett, which was farther out on the Island. Traffic heading west, toward New York, was heavy already, no doubt in part because the sky had started to cloud over.

How did these people make their money? Mary Liz wondered, walking onto the beachfront property where the party was being held. The house was new, a monstrously large affair on the ocean, complete with tennis court, pool and pool house, the latter two being the location of the party. The landscaping around the pool alone had to have cost a fortune. And the pool itself was custom-built, a long, curving affair that almost looked like a series of ponds. There had to be two hundred people milling about, at least eight in service and a string quartet—in black tie—were over on the grass playing eighteenth-century music, mostly Haydn and Mozart.

She glanced at Sky. He looked utterly at home in this crowd and he was a schoolteacher—what was her problem? Several people waved and said hello to Sky; he knew them from the club, he explained.

They never did find their hosts. They ran into Randolph Vandergilden, the winery owner they had met at the Big House Friday night, who told them the hosts weren't here, they had to be somewhere else.

"They're not at their own party?" Sky asked.

Randolph haw-hawed and slapped Sky on the arm. He had indulged in a few drinks, clearly. "You've got a lot to learn about Hampton society, Sky, I told you." To Mary Liz, "Hell of a player, though, we played nine holes this morning. A lot of fun. Great addition to the community." To Sky, "Very pretty woman, by the way," he said, nodding toward Mary Liz. "Watch out—you don't treat her right, I just might want to," and off he went.

"He's pretty nervy," Mary Liz said, a little wide-eyed.

Sky was chuckling. He took off his glasses and cleaned them with a handkerchief from his trousers pocket. "Buck says Randolph's last wife didn't just leave him—she fled to another country."

"Sky!" a feminine voice called. It was Vanessa Buckley, Buck's wife, waving, bringing someone over. Vanessa was in a sleeveless, low-cut black silk dress, and made Mary Liz feel like Mary Poppins. She might be in her mid-forties, but Vanessa Buckley was one pretty lady who knew how to show off her athletic and shapely body. And was she tanned! Almost as tanned as the back of Sky's neck.

The man she had in tow was Alec Baldwin, the actor. He was very attractive, and very nice and polite to them. Were they from the area? Did they realize how important the shelter was?

"Mary Liz is Nancy Hoffman's goddaughter," Vanessa said.

Oh, well, that explained everything, Alec told them. No one raised more money for good causes than Mrs. Hoffman. She was a legend around here. And then his wife, Kim, came over. Kim Basinger!

Now Mary Liz went from feeling like Mary Poppins to an absolute toad. She had never seen anyone so utterly beautiful in her life.

"How do you do?" the actress said politely, smiling, shaking their hands. And then she told her husband there was someone he had to see. The couple said goodbye and after they left, Mary Liz and Sky looked at each other. "Wow!" Sky finally burst out.

"Down, boy," Vanessa Buckley said, rubbing his back.

Mary Liz was not sure she liked how Vanessa was rubbing Sky's back. She wondered if Sky noticed how Vanessa was looking at him, how intimately she had moved in to touch him.

Rather, maybe the question was, did *she* get it? The message that Vanessa was perhaps trying to send her?

"Is it true, Vanessa," Mary Liz said, "that our hosts aren't here?"

"Yes," she answered, looking around the party. "Helene hates entertaining, so she's never here. I think Bud had some sort of meeting somewhere."

"Oh," Mary Liz said. Silly her, to think people attended their own parties.

Billy Joel, the legendary singer-songwriter, stopped by to say hi to Vanessa. So did John Kennedy, Jr., and his wife, but stayed so briefly Mary Liz barely got a look at them. Then, when Buck Buckley came over to get Sky and Vanessa to schmooze with some key members of the country club, Mary Liz had a wonderful time, simply standing there, sipping wine and appearing to be staring off into space, while in actuality she was eavesdropping on a conversation between some man and—yes—it *was* Martha Stewart. They were talking about the historical society, something about restoring a farm, creating a museum, that regional history desperately needed to be retained for this and future generations.

"Oh, that's Dan Ratiner," Vanessa said, swinging by again minutes later to check on her. She pointed to a bearded man wearing a hat and white suit, and possessing a certain savoir faire. "You know, *Dan's Papers?* The giveaway? Surely you're reading it every week."

She had just started to the other day. She hadn't realized, until Vanessa explained to her now, that *Dan's Papers* was the lifeline of the Hamptons: who was here, who was doing what, where to go to eat, get a massage, or where to, yes, go whale watching.

Oh, hell. Julius Hoffman had arrived and Mary Liz could see he was making his way across the party in her direction. She hastily excused herself from Vanessa, circled behind the bar and went into the pool house. Inside, there was an attractive woman in an apron directing traffic from the kitchenette to the catering crew. "Steve, get out there, take this tray. I don't want the guests coming in here."

The latter comment, Mary Liz assumed, was directed at her. "I just wanted to say the food is wonderful."

"Thank you," the woman said. "Karen, take the potato puffs out of the oven!"

"I saw Martha Stewart sampling everything," Mary Liz added.

Instantly the woman's face transformed. "Really? Could you read her expression?"

"Well, she looked happy." Mary Liz strolled back outside. She saw Julius again and panicked. How to duck him?

She edged her way around the side of the pool house to hide.

"No way in hell, Herb!" an agitated voice said from the back of the pool house. It was a man's voice and Mary Liz assumed he was addressing Herb Glidden. "No more of those invoices! Understand? I've got the damn IRS on my back as it is."

Mary Liz tried to look casual, standing there eavesdropping, one hand holding her elbow as the other held her wineglass near her mouth. The only problem was, this made her appear to be socializing with the pool filter.

There was a low murmur of a male voice in back of the pool house. Glidden's? She thought so.

"You know, Herb," the other man said angrily, "the day's coming I'm just not going to fucking care what you do."

A murmur again.

"An invoice to *who?*" the first man yelled. "No, don't tell me. Jesus, I don't want to know!"

Mary Liz had just turned toward the party, when a man came around the corner of the pool house and stormed his way back into the party. She prepared herself to see Glidden, but no one appeared. So she finally went to take a peek around the corner. No one. Huh.

She moved around to the other side of the pool house, just in time to see Herb Glidden's back as he made his way through the crowd to the bar. Mary Liz stood around for a minute (now appearing to be socializing with the gas grill), and spotted the real estate mogul, Mort Zuckerman. He was talking to—oh, what was his name? The guy who used to run Fox? Diller, Barry Diller.

"Gotcha!" a deep voice said as someone grabbed her elbow from behind.

Oh, Lord, it was Julius.

"Look," he said, breathing a bit heavily in her face—he had thrown back a few, clearly—"I've come to apologize. I was just pissed off you accused me of being in your house. And I'm swearing to you now—" He raised a meaty hand. "I swear to God I did not go in the cottage. It was just as I said, I was going over to Sasha's when I heard the alarm."

Play nice, Mary Liz. "I'm the one who needs to apologize," she said, surprising even herself at how seductive she sounded. *Watch it, girl, don't overdo it.* "I was once robbed in Chicago. They took all my electronic equipment from my apartment. And it was the data on my computer that devastated me, because they took all my discs, too. It took me six months to replicate the data from other sources."

"Why would anyone on the estate want your computers?"

"Oh, I never thought anyone would," she said. "I was just nervous about kids playing around in there, spilling a soft drink, or dripping saltwater."

Julius was staring at something on her chest. "What?" she asked him.

"You have something here," he murmured, stepping close.

Oh, God, what was it? A tick? Mary Liz had been terrified of those from the get-go. Lyme disease was big on Long Island.

But it was not a tick. Incredibly, it was an opportunity for Julius to casually slide his hand down her blouse and under her brassiere cup to hold her breast.

She jumped back and instinctively slapped his face. Not hard, but at least three people heard it and had turned around to look at them.

Julius was laughing. "You fell for the oldest trick in the book!"

The guy was not only a pig, but had the maturity of a thirteen-year-old class creep.

Over his shoulder, however, Mary Liz could see that help was on the way. Jeanine, his wife, was approaching.

"Hello, darling," she said, slipping her arm around Julius's waist and stretching up to kiss him on the cheek. "Hello, Mary Liz, nice party, isn't it?"

"Very," she said.

"I heard you came with Sky."

"Yes."

Jeanine looked across the party. "Vanessa seems to have commandeered him."

Julius burst out laughing. He knew Mary Liz wouldn't publicly humiliate Jeanine.

"Julius," his wife said, "what is your problem?"

"No problem, J-girl," he assured her, kissing the side of her face. "I was just thinking how Vanessa was the only child of a very rich papa who never denied her anything—and how Vanessa's taken that to mean never to deny herself any*one*." To Mary Liz, "I'd get your claws out if I were you, if you want to hang on to that boy."

"Stop it, Julius," Jeanine said, "or Mary Liz won't know that you're joking."

"Who's joking? He's living with her, for crissakes."

"Over the garage," Jeanine said. "Mary Liz, I assure you—"

"Actually," Mary Liz interrupted, "I think Buck commandeered Sky. To do some country club politicking tonight."

"Well, Buck better do something," Julius said, frowning. "Pay a fucking million dollars to join the stupid club, you'd think they could improve your handicap a little."

"A million dollars?" Mary Liz said. "To join East End?"

"I know," Jeanine said, shaking her head. "Unbelievable, isn't it?"

"Hey, look, we wanted to play golf," Julius said. To Jeanine, "What are we supposed to do, wait twenty-five years to join Southampton? Or wait a hundred years and still get turned down from Maidstone because my grandfather came from Eastern Europe?" He took another swallow of his martini. To Mary Liz, "Shit. These guys are so arrogant out here. So Dad and a couple of us said, fine, they won't have us, we won't have them and we'll build the best damn golf course around here. Everybody put in a million—"

Mary Liz was going to say something about Maidstone not liking pigs like Julius—that it had nothing to do with Eastern Europe—but chickened out.

"What's unbelievable," Jeanine told Mary Liz, "is all the foreigners that will pay a million dollars to join a club where they play golf maybe four times a year."

"To do business with us," Julius added. "Fucking great idea. We got like sixty of those guys. And we get tee-times within two hours of whenever we ask."

"How many of those have you had?" Jeanine asked her husband, looking at the empty glass in his hand.

"Not enough if I can still hear you nagging," he answered, moving off in the direction of the bar.

"Thank God he's not driving tonight." She sighed, watching her husband lumber off. "Charles Kahn's giving him a ride." She turned to Mary Liz. "You'd think after Dad getting killed, he'd be nervous about private planes. He says it's not a jet, just a prop, safer than a car in Charles's hands."

"You mean, they're flying?"

"To the marine terminal next to La Guardia. It's less than an hour. Then it's ten minutes into Manhattan. If they drove on a Sunday night like this, it would take maybe five hours."

They were distracted by some murmurs next to them. People were watching as Steven Spielberg and his wife, Kate Capshaw, made their entrance into the pool area.

"About my husband, Mary Liz," Jeanine said, as if they had been talking about this for quite some time and she was now summing up their discussion. "If he annoys you in any way, just say BOO real loud in his ear and he'll run. He can't stand confrontation."

Just like Aunt Nancy. So it ran in the family, even jumping bloodlines.

"Frankly, he's spoiled," Jeanine continued. "All the men in our circle are. But unlike the rest of them, if you say no to Julius, firmly, he'll back off."

And then, as if offering her a bribe, in the next breath Jeanine asked, "Would you like to meet Steven Spielberg?"

For this Mary Liz could be bought, and she allowed herself to be trotted over to meet the brilliant director, producer and storyteller. "Mary Liz is Nancy Hoffman's goddaughter," Jeanine explained, and immediately the director's face lit up.

"Nancy Hoffman does a great deal of good in this world," he said.

Mary Liz wondered if she would ever be important enough to be introduced simply as herself.

The Spielbergs drifted away and Jeanine was talking to someone else, so Mary Liz took the opportunity to approach the bar for a glass of Perrier.

"I see the ringer's deserted you," Randolph Vandergilden hissed into her ear from behind her. "So I've come to move in. Let's see, what is a good line? Come and see my vineyards, oh beautiful lady. Come see how the nectar of the gods is made."

This guy was nuts. All these fascinating people here and she got a pig and a nut to talk to. Mary Liz was getting irritable.

"Shoo, Randy, go hit on someone else," Vanessa Buckley said, slipping between them and actually shoving the vintner away with one hand. He chuckled good-naturedly and moved off. She turned to Mary Liz. "He didn't give you the line about the nectar of the gods, did he?"

Mary Liz laughed, nodding.

"First of all, Randy doesn't really own the vineyard," Vanessa said. "And the way he carries on! You'd think the wine was drinkable! Buck says the only thing it's good for is to kill the dandelions on the golf course."

Mary Liz laughed again. "So who does own the winery?"

"Some Dutch company—that wants to lose a lot of money, I can only assume. I think he has two more years to pull it together, or they sell it or dump it or close it. I sure wish they'd dump Randy. He is such a pompous ass and it's such a beautiful property. There's going to be an outdoor opera there next month, *Aida,* I think. For, uh, let's see—" she screwed up her pretty face "—a home for the opera series perhaps?"

"But your husband likes Randolph, doesn't he?" Mary Liz said, coming back to the vintner.

"Oh, sure, Buck likes him. But you have to understand, Buck likes anyone who'll play cards and smoke cigars and talk golf with him. But it was Alfred, Mary Liz, that my Buck absolutely adored, and other than cards, cigars and golf, they didn't have a thing in common."

"Really?"

"Alfred was an okay golfer, but otherwise, when he wasn't playing cards and smoking cigars with Buck, he was obsessed with tennis, movies and TV—and, well, success. He wanted to be king of the mountain." She smiled to herself. "And Nancy was to be his queen."

She paused, looking into Mary Liz's eyes, and only then did Mary Liz realize that Vanessa was very likely on something. There was a glaze over her eyes and the edges of her speech, usually clipped, were not. Diet pills maybe? Not cocaine—or was it? She didn't think so. No, some kind of pills. A downer. Maybe Valium.

"Actually," Vanessa said, regaining her thoughts, "Nancy was always a queen—who kissed the frog and taught him how to acquire a little class." She smiled to herself again. "When I think of Alfred twenty years ago... Even Bertie, as a child, used to beg his father to lay off the gold jewelry." She sipped her drink. "You wouldn't have known it was the same man at the end. Egad, he used to drive around a shiny gold Rolls-Royce. I give her credit, Nancy really did a remarkable job with him. And he stuck by her, which made it all the more surprising."

"Why?"

"Well, you know, usually, in L.A., if some guy's gone from being a schmuck to the A-list, he gets rid of the wife who knew him as a schmuck. It's harder to forget your past and strut around if you've got someone at home who's always reminding you from where you came."

"Did you ever meet his first wife?"

"Ruth? Oh, God, yes. She stays with Julius sometimes. You cannot get any farther from Nancy on the scale than with Ruthie. Ruthie looks like a tired old washerwoman from zee old country. 'Course, she's got to be almost seventy now. God knows what I'll be like by then. Like a retired madam, I suppose," she added, giggling.

"Never," Mary Liz said graciously. "You'll always be great-looking. It's your spirit."

Vanessa looked surprised. "Why, thank you, sweet girl. No wonder Sky likes you."

Mary Liz raised one eyebrow.

"Oh, *yeah,* he likes you all right," Vanessa confirmed in a thoroughly sexual way. "And if I were you," she whispered, moving closer, "I'd stick very close to him this summer. Very few people are what they seem out here, and a genuinely nice man who's genuinely available is next to nonexistent."

"I see," Mary Liz said, smiling. She was still enjoying the buzz from Vanessa's, "Oh, *yeah*" that Sky liked her.

"I saw you talking to Julius and Jeanine before," Vanessa continued, finishing off the drink in her hand and putting the glass down on the bar. "Now there's a pair."

"He's the lollapalooza in my book," Mary Liz said.

"Granted, the man is a pig," Vanessa said (making Mary Liz laugh). "But Jeanine, Mrs. High and Mighty..." She smiled broadly. "She used to work for Herb Glidden, you know—and not as his social secretary, may I add."

There were sudden murmurs in the crowd, but Mary Liz didn't bother to look at what the hubbub was about. This was far too interesting.

"The only one dumb enough not to know Jeanine was a glorified hooker was Julius," Vanessa continued recklessly. "But what else is new? I mean, for God's sake, the guy ran off to Mexico to marry a sixteen-year-old prostitute the first time. I suppose Alfred thought Jeanine was a tremendous leap forward the second time around."

"Wait a second, Vanessa," Mary Liz finally said. "Before you go any further, you should know that I like Jeanine very much." Truth was, she didn't know her at all, but she did not like what Vanessa was telling her. Whatever her past may have been, Jeanine Hoffman was the mother of two children—and was a good mother, according to Nancy—and deserved to be judged on the merits of her life today. *(But from Herbert Glidden to Julius? Oh, my!)*

"I'm not telling you anything you won't hear from everyone else," Vanessa said, defending herself.

"What about Herb Glidden's wife?" Mary Liz asked. "He's married, isn't he?"

Vanessa rolled her eyes. "Now there's a real case. She hasn't left their house in Beverly Hills since about 1988."

Mary Liz looked at her.

"She's got agoraphobia or something and I think Herb finds it very convenient not to get her help. They stay married, their kid comes to visit, but she never ventures out and he rarely ventures in."

"That's horrible."

Vanessa shrugged. "That's L.A., in my book. That's why I've never liked it."

"Does your husband—does Buck like Herb?"

Vanessa looked at her as though Mary Liz was crazy. "No one *likes* Herb."

"Well, then, why does—" She couldn't finish her question because someone was calling her name.

"Mary Liz!" a woman cried.

It was Sasha Reinhart; it was her entrance to the party that had been making all the buzz. This was, after all, her first time in East Hampton, and so she was a social novelty.

The diva rushed over to grab Mary Liz's arm. "You were broken into this morning?"

"Well, we're not sure—"

"Riff was sure," Sasha said. "I'm thinking I need more security around my place."

"You got robbed?" Vanessa asked Mary Liz. "The Big House?"

"No, it was in the cottage—someone just tried to open a door and set off an alarm."

"Riff said you thought it was Julius," Sasha said rather breathlessly.

"It probably was," Vanessa said, making the women look at her. "He's always trying to jump women when they're asleep."

"Do you think so?" Sasha asked Mary Liz. "Do you think he might break into my house? I've got to make a movie with him this fall!"

"Well, hello there, Vanessa," a masculine voice said. It belonged to a nice-looking man around sixty, in good shape, with a pleasant smile. With a start, Mary Liz recognized him as the man from behind the pool house who had said, "No more invoices!" to Herbert Glidden. On his arm was a woman in her late thirties who was *very* pregnant.

"Henry!" Vanessa cried. "It's been ages!" She threw her arms around him. "And Cindy, don't you look wonderful at this stage," she said, kissing her on the cheek.

"You're a very nice liar," the woman said.

"I almost couldn't get her to come," the man said.

"Henry, Cindy, I want you to meet Sasha Reinhart—"

"We met once," the pregnant woman said, holding her hand out to Sasha, "at the wrap party of your last movie. My magazine, *Je Ne Sais Quoi,* did a story on you."

Sasha's smile vanished and she withdrew her hand. "The article that said, 'Though many may think that Sasha Reinhart is a legendary, but nonetheless over-the-hill diva…'?" Sasha gave a sharp sniff and added, "I think I need to be somewhere else," and walked away.

The man sighed. "Ah, to be married to a member of the press."

"She's always been a bitch," the expectant mother muttered, placing a protective hand over her baby.

"I think the article hurt her feelings," Mary Liz said, prompting the pregnant woman to stare at her as if Mary Liz was some sort of freak.

"Well, anyway," Vanessa said, "Henry, Cindy, I'd like you to meet Nancy Hoffman's goddaughter, Mary Liz Scott. Mary Liz, one of Alfred and Buck's old hole-in-the-wall gang, Henry MacClendon, and his lovely wife, Cindy Claydon."

Mary Liz said a polite how-do-you-do, but her mouth nearly fell open when she realized this was Claire MacClendon's ex-husband. And how he could have left a lovely woman like Claire for this scarecrow was beyond her. (What kind of invoices had Glidden been asking for?) This woman, Cindy, was utterly plastic. She was very pregnant, obviously, but perfectly coiffed, and her very manner of speaking was deeply affected and emotionally detached. Mary Liz had known women like this before. Of course, Cindy Claydon was the editor-in-chief of a fashion magazine, so how could she afford to be any other way than perfectly coiffed, deeply affected and emotionally detached?

The pregnancy, and what it had done to her body, must be killing her, Mary Liz thought.

After making polite chitchat, Mary Liz went off in search of Sasha, but it was too late, the diva was in deep discussion with Steven Spielberg.

"Any hope of getting out of here?" Sky whispered over her shoulder.

"Have you seen Herb Glidden?" she asked him.

"He just left, maybe ten minutes ago." Sky leaned closer. "Everything okay?"

"Oh, yeah, fine." She smiled. "Did you want to leave? Because I'm ready if you are." She had had enough of this crowd for one night.

"Great. And we don't even have to thank our hosts," he commented, casually taking her hand as if it was the most natural thing in the world.

And it felt like it. And they both smiled.

"The only person I wanted to meet and didn't," Mary Liz reported as Sky led her through the crowd, "was Martha Stewart. I eavesdropped on her, but I didn't have the courage to go up to her."

"She left," he reported. He took her glass and put it down, with his own, on a table. Then he took her hand again and they walked up toward the house. "I found out where the money came from for this place," he said. "He's an investment banker for something called United Kingdom Securities. Buck says it's a front for Arab terrorist nations."

This didn't surprise her. She knew of deals done even by Reston, Kellaher, where the company had blithely accepted investment money at face value, doing its best to ignore that the investor might be fronting for someone a lot less savory. There was tons of money waiting to be invested in a stable economy like that of the United States, from vastly unstable empires. And there was always someone willing to act as a front for that nation—or its leader—to invest their money. Of course, there were always special fees added to this kind of deal, the kind that might build pools that looked like a series of ponds....

"Are you interested in that kind of thing?" she asked him. "How people make their money?"

"Sure."

"I guess I am, too," she admitted.

"The big difference between you and me, however," Sky said, swinging her hand as they walked, "is that one of us has already demonstrated she can do it herself."

"It's not as much as you think."

He smiled at her. "I'm not a fortune hunter, Mary Liz."

She smiled and, after a few steps, said, "So what are you hunting for?"

"Brains, beauty, gentleness, loyalty," he listed. "A woman with a heart big enough to love me, and children, too, someday."

Mary Liz was thinking about how effortless he made it sound, meeting someone, falling in love, marrying and having children. It had been her life experience that meeting someone wasn't hard, but falling in love was, thus making the next two steps merely distant dreams.

On the other hand, that psychic in Chicago had said...

In the driveway, standing with the car valets, was Riff, Sasha's bodyguard. Mary Liz said hello and introduced Sky.

"Is everything okay at your place?" Riff asked her. "That was some hoot and holler this morning."

"Everything's fine," she answered.

Sky looked at her, frowning. "What hoot and holler?"

"Oh, it was just an alarm that got tripped in the cottage. I was in the ocean with Bertie and it went off and created quite a ruckus in the neighborhood."

"An alarm got tripped?" Sky said. "Did someone break in?"

Riff said, "Yes," while Mary Liz simultaneously said, "I think it was just an accident."

Riff looked at her. "It didn't look that way to me, and I'm in the business of security."

"Well, let me put it this way," Mary Liz said, "I've had a long talk with the person I believe was in the cottage, and I'm not worried anymore in the least." *Liar!*

One of the valets brought the Mercedes around and they said goodbye to Riff and climbed in. "And nobody saw anything?" Sky asked a moment later, putting the top down on the car, as promised.

"Apparently not," Mary Liz said. "Don't worry about it, Sky. I'm not."

"But why would someone want to break into your cottage?" he persisted.

"I don't think anyone did *break* in," she said. "But a proper security system is being installed tomorrow, so I'll let the East Hampton police worry about it if it happens again."

"Windows up or down?" he asked her.

"Oh, down! The more air the better."

He ran all the windows of the car down and pulled out of the driveway. "Do you suppose someone was trying to make off with your computer equipment?"

She was getting tired of this subject. "I think it was Julius just snooping around."

"Julius Hoffman?" he said, surprised. "Why?"

"I think he likes me," she said, shrugging her shoulders.

"Tell me about it," he murmured.

She leaned toward him. "What's that?"

"He watches you in a certain way."

"Well, he's a pig."

"He's a married man, for Pete's sake."

"To a very beautiful woman," she added.

"I'll say."

"Well, don't be too unenthusiastic, Sky," she said, laughing.

He turned onto the road and the wind started whipping at their hair. "I wish I could have watched you windsurfing this morning."

"Oh, no!" she groaned, clapping a hand over her face. "Thank God you didn't!"

They drove for a while before Sky said, "Why not?"

"I would have felt very uncomfortable, that's all."

"But it's not because you and Bertie..." He let his voice trail off, keeping his eyes on the road.

"Me and Bertie *what?*"

"Nothing." He shrugged.

"Sky. Tell me. Me and Bertie what?"

"Well, I don't know, I just wondered if—" He shrugged again. "I don't know, maybe you like Bertie. I'm sure he likes you."

"Bertie has a girlfriend."

"Right." He nodded and reached into the glove compartment to exchange his glasses for his sunglasses.

"Sky, the only reason I would have been uncomfortable having you watch me this morning was because Bertie made me wear half of an orange wet suit and I kept falling ass over teakettle out there and I looked like a seaweed monster. An orange seaweed monster, thank you, bulging all this way and that." He was laughing. "Really, Sky, it was not a sight I would impose on anyone I wished to impress."

"Impress me, huh?" He glanced over and smiled. "For your information, Ms. Scott, I think you'd be great-looking any which way I could see you."

"Well, in that case," she told him, "I might as well tell you, Mr. Preston, I am not the least bit interested in anyone out here—except, perhaps, a certain schoolteacher and part-time golf-ringer I know." She was embarrassed as soon as she said it. What was going on with her? Oh, that stupid psychic.

8

The only drawback to having the top down in the Mercedes was having to breathe in gas fumes when they got stuck on 27 while trying to get back to East Hampton. "Who *are* all these people?" Mary Liz finally asked, with a Maserati in front of her and a Ford Bronco in back.

"People who have to be at work at 9:00 a.m. on Mondays," Sky said. "If they didn't, they wouldn't be sitting in this traffic." They inched ahead. "I wish I had my map. I know there are back ways to get there."

"Jeanine Hoffman said some people fly. She said Rachelle Zaratan's husband—what's his name?"

"Charles, I think."

"Right. Charles has a plane. He was flying Julius to La Guardia tonight."

"Does he have a jet?"

"No, a regular private plane. You know, with a propeller in front."

"Most of them have jets, or jet props."

"Well, apparently, Charles drives his."

"Flies it himself, you mean?" he said, smiling.

Mary Liz chuckled. "Yes." After several moments, she turned to him again. "Do you think we could go? To the airport? They say on a night like this, you can see people like Billy Joel, Ralph Lauren, William Styron, or Carl Icahn taking off."

"Who wants to see Carl Icahn?" Sky wanted to know.

"I see your point," she said. "But still—I don't know, it just seems like a cool thing to see."

"An odd request for a date," Sky mused, "but your wish is my every command. And afterward, maybe by that time the crowds will be gone and we can get a bite to eat, at Nick & Tony's or something."

"I was thinking of home, actually. I could cook you something."

"Or I could cook you something," he countered. "Although your digs are a lot more glamorous than mine."

"Well, we'll discuss it. I'm not even hungry right now."

"Me, neither. I ate about a hundred hors d'oeuvres. The food at the party was great, I thought."

"Me, too."

They had stopped in the traffic again and Sky was looking at her. Smiling.

"What?" she asked.

"I'm having a wonderful time," he said.

It was almost seven-thirty when they bounced over the ruts into the East Hampton Airport parking lot. Some airport! A hangar and planes! No control tower, no terminal, nothing. They had to park out by the edge of the woods because there was a crowd of adults and children waiting around. Sky and Mary Liz climbed out of the car and headed for the tarmac where some of the jets were parked. On the way, they passed what appeared to be a mechanic in greasy blue overalls.

"Excuse me," Sky said, stopping him. "But is it always like this on Sundays? With all these people standing around?"

"No. One of the commuter planes got hung up at La Guardia and it's screwing everything up."

"Wow, look at that," Mary Liz said, pointing to a jet parked behind Sky. "Whose plane is that?"

The fellow looked. "Oh, that's Mr. Klein's. Calvin Klein. Nice, isn't it? He's leaving later. Well, gotta go."

They walked on, looking around. Walking the tarmac was not terribly different from walking around in a marina to look at the boats that were moored, only these were airships. Some small, others larger, various levels of polish and sophistication. Over by the hangar was a helicopter, a small one. Like the kind used for traffic reports.

"Here comes something," Sky said. In the sky, descending toward them, was the powerful white front light of a plane. It was the missing commuter plane, Mary Liz guessed, maybe an EM-2, which carried something like thirty passengers. She took them for hopper flights all the time.

There were a whole lot more than thirty people hanging around waiting, though.

Suddenly one engine of a jet-prop fired and the right propeller began to turn. Lights came on. There were two men seated in the front.

The plane didn't go anywhere and so Mary Liz and Sky started back to the car.

Walking toward them were two people. One was a man—in slacks, a short-sleeved shirt and carrying a briefcase—who waved. As he came closer, Mary realized it was Herbert Glidden. With him was a woman Mary Liz didn't recognize.

"Need a lift to JFK?" Glidden said.

"You're going all the way to Los Angeles tonight?" Sky asked him.

"I could just be going to New York," Glidden told him.

"No way," Sky said. "JFK means you're boarding a nonstop to L.A."

"A couple of weeks in the Hamptons and he's already a smart-ass," Glidden joked to Mary Liz. "So, Mary Liz, how are you?"

"Great, thanks. I missed you at the party tonight."

"I missed you, too."

She couldn't tell if he was mocking her or not.

The conversation ceased as they watched the commuter airliner land. Mary Liz was right. It was an EM.

Glidden turned to introduce the woman standing behind him. "This is Reesa Kelb. Reesa works for Mortimer Brothers. She and her husband are in East Hampton this summer. Reesa, this is Mary Liz Scott, formerly of Reston, Kellaher—"

"Really?" the woman asked. She was as neat as a pin, in a summer suit, heels and carrying a briefcase. Just the way Mary Liz had looked a few months ago. "What division?"

"Corporate bonds," Mary Liz said, "and some high yield."

"Excuse us a second, will you?" Glidden said to Sky and his companion, pulling Mary Liz away a few steps. Someone called Glidden's name. The stairs of what was evidently his jet-prop had been lowered and a uniformed pilot was waving for him to come. Glidden signaled one minute. "Just so you know," he said to Mary Liz, "as soon as I get into the office tomorrow, I'm firing this broad. That's why I need you. I'm sick of the overhead on Mortimer Brothers. You can do what they do just as easily."

Mary Liz didn't know what to say.

"So when I get back, you and I will sit down and talk." He sighed. "Thirty years I've been financing movies and this idiot's telling me I can't do my next deal without them."

"They are a top firm."

"I don't need a firm. I need you, Mary Liz. Get some other lackey to straighten out Nancy's finances, and let's get you back in the financial pages."

"What if I don't want to get back in the financial pages?" she asked him.

He leaned forward, smiling broadly. "All the better. Certainly it could be worth more to you." He gave her a slap on the arm. "I'll be back in a couple of weeks and we'll finalize it." He held out his hand and she shook it.

"But you haven't told me what it is we'll be doing," she pointed out.

"Making movies, Mary Liz, and making money, big-time." He hailed Sky. "See ya, Sky. Come on, Reesa," he urged. "We gotta plane to catch."

"Nice to meet you," the woman said to Mary Liz as she ran to catch up to the financier.

Mary Liz and Sky watched Glidden and his associate board the plane. Moments later the stairs were pulled up and the shell of the plane was once again smooth and shiny under its flashing lights. There was a small inscription on the side, which Mary Liz only now realized was the Howland Films logo. She wondered how Glidden had gotten use of the plane. Probably part of the deal for financing the company's next film.

Huh. She wondered why he had it and not Julius.

The other prop of Glidden's plane was fired up and the plane started to taxi down the field. It turned, sat and waited. And then, suddenly, its engines roared and it started down the airstrip, in moments effortlessly lifting off the ground and soaring into the darkening sky.

"Oh, *shit,*" said a voice from behind them. "That was Herb's plane, wasn't it?" It was Charles Kahn, the husband of the designer, Rachelle Zaratan.

"I'm afraid so," Mary Liz said.

He made an expression of self-disgust. "I can't believe I missed him."

"He was going to JFK, if that helps," Sky said.

Charles shook his head. "Thanks, but no, that doesn't help." He sounded utterly defeated.

"You're giving Julius Hoffman a ride into town, I hear," Mary Liz said, trying to cheer him up. "I also hear you're quite a pilot."

He smiled slightly. He was a bit on the shy side, Mary Liz realized.

"I better get going," Charles said. "See you next weekend." He walked back to the parking lot where, they could see, he had left his Lexus running and the car door open.

Charles Kahn really wanted to talk to Herbert Glidden, Mary Liz thought. Charles was giving a ride to Julius. Glidden wanted some kind of invoices from Henry MacClendon. Glidden had acknowledged that he knew Mary Liz was working for Aunt Nancy and told her he wanted her to jump ship.

Interesting.

The lights of another private plane came on, and a man, in slacks and a blazer, came striding past them toward it. It was Ron Perelman, Mary Liz recognized, the chairman of Revlon.

By now, the passengers had long deplaned from the commuter airliner, but the crowd of people was still waiting around it. An attendant was standing at the bottom of the stairs to the plane, evidently waiting for something, too.

Something turned out to be actor Brad Pitt, and the crowd began to surge ahead, calling his name.

Ah, East Hampton life.

Mary Liz and Sky ended up going to the grocery store and buying steaks, a can of cooked, sliced potatoes, a big onion and a ready-made Caesar salad. They went to Mary Liz's, where she called the Big House to ask Delores if it would be all right if they used the gas grill outside the guest house.

"I'm sure Mrs. Hoffman would want you to use the one at the cabana," she said. "There are plenty of drinks in the refrigerator and Mr. Bertie and his friend went into Manhattan with Mrs. Hoffman. I think you'll find the cabana very pleasant and very private."

Mary Liz relayed this information to Sky, everything except the last part about the cabana being very private. She was too hungry at the moment to feel very romantic, and the outfit she came back out in—soft, baggy, cotton shorts and a T-shirt—would probably discourage anyone. After all, it was a first date.

Wrong.

"Hey, that's more like it," Sky declared, standing up. He had tossed his blazer over the back of the couch. "There's something about a girl in baggy cotton that I find wildly attractive."

She laughed. He really was too much. But then, she hardly minded. It made her feel attractive.

They brought the bag of food up the driveway. Delores had turned on the outside light of the cabana so they could see their way to get in. Sky admired what they found: the couch, carpet, table and chairs, stereo and TV. "There's something to be said for money, isn't there?"

"Yes, I suppose there is," Mary Liz said, starting to unpack the groceries in the kitchenette.

They both had an icy bottle of St. Paulie's Girl they found in the refrigerator. Sky started the grill while she opened the can of potatoes, drained them, threw them into a skillet with a little butter, a lot of onion and tons of paprika, covered it and let it simmer. She set the table for two. Sky seasoned the steaks and went back outside. The salad was a snap. Mary Liz just threw it in a bowl, opened the pack of croutons and dressing and tossed it. Outside, she heard the sizzle as the steaks hit the hot grill. She lifted the cover on the potatoes, stirred them, put the cover back. She'd prefer to let them cook for a half hour, but they would be okay. She went outside. She loved the smell of meat cooking on a grill; she loved the glow of the grill in the night. "Smells delicious," she said, standing next to him.

Long cooking fork poised in front of him, he turned and smiled. And then he kissed her lightly on the mouth. He smiled. "Sorry. That just slipped out."

"Whoops," she said, leaning forward and kissing him just as lightly on the mouth. "Sorry. That just sort of slipped out, too."

Walking back into the cabana, her body was humming. Nervous. She took a few deep swallows from her glass of beer. She glanced outside. He was taking a few swallows from his bottle of beer. He was nervous, too.

Heck, they had only known each other for two days.

Dinner was delicious. The steak was just how she liked it, medium rare, and Sky liked raw onion with his, too. The potatoes were okay, the Caesar good, the company wonderful. They had another beer.

She felt very comfortable with him. At ease. He seemed to be daydreaming somewhat, though, for every once in a while a little flush would appear on his neck. And nothing would have been said, really, to cause it.

The flush had to be coming from something he was thinking.

A thought that made something flutter a little inside Mary Liz.

Her face was a little sunburned from the fiasco on the beach this morning. Her makeup from the party was half-off and smudged (actually, when it looked best), her hair was one big wild tangle from riding in the car with the top down.

Yes, it was possible she could be attractive like this.

They lingered over their empty plates, sipping beer, talking. Finally, Mary Liz got up to take the plates away; Sky was right behind her, wanting to help. She put the dishes down on the counter, and he put the one he carried down, too. She turned to him and the next thing she knew, she'd slid her arms around his waist and was looking up at him. "I had such a wonderful time tonight. Thank you." She started to pull away, but he pulled her back.

He put his hands on her shoulders. "I haven't met anyone like you for years."

"Oh, yeah?" she said softly, joking. "Who was she?"

"No, you know what I mean," he said, searching her eyes. "How often, after thirty, do you meet someone who only becomes more and more attractive, even when you felt so very attracted to her when you first saw her?"

She knew what he meant. Usually the people she found attractive right off the bat ended up being vastly less so as she got to know them, plainer people often becoming very attractive after a glimpse of their personalities. But with Sky, she had found him enormously attractive in the beginning, and now practically irresistible. She couldn't believe her luck.

His mouth was on hers in a gentle, dry, but long kiss. His arms went around her shoulders and he held her, kissing her still. And then he brought his head up, taking in a breath, looking into her eyes. As if getting permission, he came down again to her mouth, this time holding her more firmly, pulling her close, a hint of his mouth starting to part. He was leaving it up to her. She parted her mouth and his tongue slipped inside and everything lurched between Mary Liz's legs, and the sensation happened again as they slid into what felt like the deepest, most intimate kiss she had ever had. She pressed her hips forward and felt the most wonderful warm, masculine hardness that he had been holding back from her.

Slow down, slow down, she told herself, feeling the ache to make love, the physical ache and desire she hadn't felt in a long time. Just like that. Two days, two kisses, her body wanted him very badly.

Slowly, Sky's tongue retreated, and his hold on her lessened. She relaxed, too. He pulled his mouth away and then hugged her, hard, murmuring, "I don't want to blow this." He stepped back to look at her. She smiled and took the end of her T-shirt to wipe his mouth, knowing full well she was offering a glimpse of her breasts in a lacy brassiere. He saw. And when he looked into her eyes again, he looked genuinely distressed. "Do you understand, Mary Liz, why we can't go fast? Even though, at this moment, I want you more than I've ever desired anyone?"

She swallowed. "Explain it to me."

"We've got to get to know each other. I won't do it any other way. If we ever— Well, if we get to that point, when it's right, when we know each other, I want to do it with genuine feeling. Lust is not enough. Not with you."

She smiled. "Thank you."

"Besides—" he shrugged "—you might not want to."

"Are you mad?" she asked him. "Of course it's mutual, that's why it seems so irresistible." She sighed. "But we are going to resist. Because I want to know *you*, Sky. And I mean know you, not just who you want me to think you are—I want to know the character flaws and everything."

"Character flaws?" he said, head kicking back. "I don't have any character flaws."

"Just like I don't." She laughed, giving him a brief hug.

They did the dishes, feeling close, but definitely cooling off. They decided to take a stroll on the beach to finish the night. It was cool out now, breezy, and Mary Liz wrapped a beach towel around her shoulders to keep warm. Over the towel, Sky put his arm around her shoulders. They walked west along the shore, silent for a long while, and Mary Liz was starting to feel romantic again, when out of the blue, Sky said, "I wish you would stay away from Herbert Glidden."

She awakened from her reverie. "What?"

"Glidden. I wish you'd stay away from him. He's trouble." He looked at her, drawing her a little closer. "And he has obviously taken a shine to you."

"Oh, that. It's just business. He wants me to do some work for him this summer." She felt his body stiffen slightly. "I'm not going to," she said quickly. "But my dad taught me never to reject any business opportunity out of hand. That I should at least listen to what he has to say."

He stopped and turned her around to face him. "Mary Liz, listen to me—don't talk to him, don't listen to him, don't have anything to do with him."

"What? Why?" After a moment, "Sky, what do you know about him?"

He pulled his arm away. "Nothing." He turned to look out at the ocean, shoving his hands into his pants pockets.

She walked around to stand in front of him. "Tell me what you know about Herb Glidden."

"I just know he's not a good guy."

She couldn't see him clearly in the darkness, but she could read his body language well enough to know he was upset. If he was upset, how did he think she felt? He had only known her for a couple of days, had kissed her a couple of times and now was already forbidding her to talk to someone about a job. Well, that answered one question about Sky—why he wasn't married. With control problems like this *already,* what the heck would he be like a few months from now, to say nothing of a year?

"He's very rich," Sky said, "and very powerful. Very powerful," he repeated.

Her temper flared suddenly. "You think someone like Herbert Glidden can sway me one way or the other with his money and power?" she demanded. (It really had been a long day.) "You listen to me, Schyler Preston, I have plenty of money, and plenty of connections. For you to insinuate that Herbert Glidden could do anything for me that I can't do for myself is not only insulting, it's really rather stupid. I don't need him or anyone like him in my life—do you understand? That's why I quit my business. I don't need to involve myself with a guy like that anymore for anything."

"Then why are you?" he asked her. "Why are you interviewing with him?"

She stood there, feeling the cold sand on her feet.

Should she tell him what she was doing here this summer? "Because I might learn something that could help Aunt Nancy in court, with her defense against his suit."

"Don't," he said.

"Sky!"

"Look, I know I don't have any right—"

"You certainly don't," she confirmed. "So, out with it! What do you know about Glidden—and how do you know it?"

He paused. And then, "I've heard things. From Buck, some of the guys at the club."

"What have you heard?"

"That he gets people into stuff they can't get out of."

"Like?"

"I don't know, business stuff. And I don't know, call me old-fashioned, but I don't think you can touch pitch without getting defiled."

"You can't touch pitch without getting defiled?" she said, finding the phrase funny. "Who did you learn that from, Queen Victoria?"

"I'm serious, Mary Liz," he said, taking her hand. "Herbert Glidden could be a very dangerous man and I wish you would stay away from him."

What had the psychic said in Chicago? About danger?

II

9

A week had passed with enormous progress on all fronts.

Bill Pfeiffer's security man had spent all of Monday afternoon installing an alarm system. There were almost no wires involved, but instead a series of electronic motion detectors were placed in the cottage, any of which could be individually turned on or off. If the alarm was activated and a detector tripped, the system would call the East Hampton police unless Mary Liz entered the correct code into one of the control panels.

Mary Liz also had Jake move several boxes of files to the "Safe Room" of the Big House, a room in the basement where Alfred Hoffman had kept some of his collectibles. The room had a solid steel door and concrete walls a foot thick. The boxes she moved contained files from Alfred's office at Howland Films, files Mary Liz was sure Julius, Herbert Glidden and/or Braxer & Braxer would love to see disappear.

Monday evening she also went on the Internet to pull some information together on some of East Hampton's residents who were becoming of increasing interest to her. With the help of a few databases and institutional sources, she accumulated some fairly informative profiles:

Herbert Glidden. Financier, movie industry.

Julius Hoffman. Film-studio president.

Henry MacClendon. Architect.

Charles Kahn. CEO, Rachelle Zaratan Clothing.

Sinclair "Buck" Buckley. Chairman, East End Country Club.

With the exception of Julius, the men were all around the same age—late fifties and early sixties—but other than that, had nothing in common but part-time residence in East Hampton. No school ties, no hometowns, no business.

The only significant connection was Alfred Hoffman. Who was dead.

On Tuesday, it had rained all day and Mary Liz had gotten an enormous amount of work done on the estate inventory, starting at eight in the morning and finishing just after ten that night. Wednesday, however, was whale-watching day with Sasha. Riff, Sasha's bodyguard, drove them out to the harbor in Montauk. As they drove past Amagansett, the road began to climb from sea level, surprising Mary Liz, because the terrain on this part of the Island started to resemble Big Sur in California more than East Hampton. The road began to wind; there were deep green pine trees along the roadside, and rocky cliffs started appearing on her right, dropping into the Atlantic. As they came into Montauk proper, however, the road flattened to sea level again.

Silly Mary Liz had been under the misguided impression they were going out on one of the whale-watching tours. No way, Sasha said. She had chartered a sixty-foot yacht *and* one of the whale-watching tour guides.

The trip turned out to be spectacular. The whales were the most gorgeous creatures, utterly at home and playfully at ease in the rough ocean waters. Sasha, however, missed nearly all of it, because she refused to wear one of the antiseasick patches that Mary Liz, Riff and the captain of the boat all offered her ("Absolutely not," she had said in horror. "It's not organic. I have some root powder that will work just as well."), and so Sasha had spent most of the trip agonizing below decks with a disoriented head and an uncooperative stomach. In the end, however, she finally relented (when Mary Liz swore she thought these particular patches were organic, or at least from California), put on a patch, and within minutes was able to go on deck and catch the last fleeting glimpses of the whales as they headed for deeper waters.

The best part was that Sasha sang a song to the whales as they swam away.

God in heaven, the woman had a beautiful voice; Mary Liz had tears in her eyes by the end. Sasha's voice was that beautiful, the resonance into any person's heart that deep. There was a reason why this woman was a superstar.

Still, as a friend, Mary Liz thought Sasha had a few kinks to work out. While she was extremely giving and generous by nature, twenty-five years of being used by people (for money, jobs or social status) had forced Sasha to largely remove herself *from* people. And thus, when and if she felt safe enough to pursue a friendship with someone, she came to it needy and possessive, unwittingly prepared not only to cling, but to drag her new friend out of their life and into the lonely world of hers. Poor soul.

As soon as Mary Liz got back to the cottage, she started a profile of Claude Lemieux to add to her list of people with mysterious ties to Herbert Glidden. On their ride back home to East Hampton, Sasha had mentioned something rather intriguing to Mary Liz. She had received a call from Claude Lemieux, owner and publisher of *Je Ne Sais Quoi* magazine, apologizing to Sasha for any disservice she felt the magazine had done her in the past.

"Oh, that's nice," Mary Liz had said. "It makes me like Cindy Claydon better. She must have talked to him after she saw you at the cocktail party on Sunday."

"No," Sasha said. "That Cindy Claydon's still a witch—the bad kind." (Sasha had a friend who was a white witch, she had told Mary Liz, which was evidently the good kind.) "I was so pissed off—I told Herb I want the magazine barred from our movie. No ads, no invitation to the premiere, no interviews. And I think Herb thought, 'Uh-oh, the diva's in one of her moods and Alfred isn't here to calm her down—I better do something.'" She leaned conspiratorially toward Mary Liz. "You know how they are. Everything's talent's fault—we're all so moody but brilliant."

"So you think Herb Glidden called Claude Lemieux?" Mary Liz asked her.

"Oh, sure he did—it's not the first time. Those guys have something on."

"What do you mean?"

"I don't know, but something. You can always tell when people have to do business with someone else," Sasha said, "because they get that sickly smile on their face when they're forced to socialize with them. You know, you're good enough to fuck over, but not to be seen with. And Claude always looks like that when he's with Herb. I saw them at a party together in L.A. not long ago."

Later that Wednesday night, after his staff meeting at the club, Sky dropped by the cottage to have ice cream with Mary Liz and watch *Run Silent, Run Deep* on television.

She cared for him. No mistaking it now. They kissed a little and curled up together on the couch while watching the movie. One would have thought they had known each other quite a while.

On Thursday, Mary Liz had another big workday on the estate inventory, starting at eight and finishing at eight, accumulating, she noticed, a fairly large number of leads she wanted Bill Pfeiffer's group to track, leads that might possibly point the way to hidden assets in the estate that Braxer & Braxer knew about but weren't about to share with the widow.

Friday was the Fourth of July, and Aunt Nancy landed back in East Hampton, with Bertie and Wendy in tow. Bertie and Wendy seemed guarded around Mary Liz now. (They couldn't still be upset over the office alarm incident of the weekend before, could they? But it was the only explanation she could think of. She hadn't seen them in days!) Nonetheless, they insisted Mary Liz and Sky come out with them on Bertie's boat to watch the fireworks in Southampton.

They went, and so did Jake, and it was a very quiet, very nice evening. Bertie's boat had a small cabin and head downstairs, so sipping beers did not prove troublesome. By now, Mary Liz and Sky were used to being around each other, to being close, yet not too close, with occasional signs of blossoming affection—a touch of the hand, a long gaze, a secret smile, a whisper in the ear.

What was odd to Mary Liz about that night, though, was there had been little or no sign of affection between Bertie and Wendy. She wondered if the couple had had a fight. In fact, Bertie spoke almost the entire night to Jake, while Wendy uncomfortably tried to talk with Mary Liz and Sky.

"What exactly are you doing down there in the cottage?" Wendy asked her. "Bertie says you're supposed to be helping Mrs. Hoffman with something."

"A few financial things," Mary Liz said, hoping to sound casual. "I'm making some recommendations to her about how to handle certain aspects of the estate."

Sky seemed very interested in this statement. Well, for heaven's sake, if the bad guy—namely, Glidden—knew what she was doing, why couldn't Sky? Besides, the files were safely locked up in the Big House and she had the only set of keys.

"I heard you're inventorying the whole estate Mr. Hoffman left," Wendy said.

"Who told you that?"

Wendy smiled, sipping her wine. There were so many boats moored out for the fireworks, there was plenty of light to see her by. "Jeanine told me. We played tennis. This morning."

Jeanine? How the heck did she know that Mary Liz was inventorying the estate? Did Julius tell her? And if he did, how did he know? From—whom? Could it have been Herb Glidden?

The more she hung around in East Hampton, the more it seemed to Mary Liz that Herb Glidden's suit for control of Howland Films was not entirely unrelated to Julius Hoffman's suit for it. In fact, she was becoming more convinced by the second that Glidden and Julius might be orchestrating their suits against Aunt Nancy, working together to chip away at her.

"Well, let's put it this way," Mary Liz said to Wendy, "if I can do anything to help Aunt Nancy preserve her husband's estate as he intended it to be, I will. After all, my dad's defending it."

"Yes, I know." Wendy was looking at her oddly. "So what's with him?" She was nodding in Sky's direction.

"Pardon me?" Sky said.

Still addressing Mary Liz, "Do you know whose side *he's* on? He could be working for any of them, you know."

"Who's them?" Sky asked.

"Who's them?" Mary Liz repeated.

"Anyone who's unhappy with the division of the property," Wendy said sweetly.

Sky and Mary Liz exchanged looks. "Are you unhappy with the division of the property?" Mary Liz asked her.

"Me? Why should I be?"

"Well, perhaps because you could be the next Mrs. Hoffman," Mary Liz suggested.

Wendy was about to respond when they heard a scuffle and turned to look, just in time to see Jake heave Bertie overboard into the water. As Bertie spluttered to the surface, swearing his head off, Jake shrugged and said, "He's had a few and thinks he can drive the boat."

When they returned to the marina a little after midnight (Jake at the controls), Mary Liz declined a ride back to the estate with Bertie and Jake and Wendy, and went off with Sky for a nightcap.

"Do you find it odd that the hired help threw the heir over the side of the boat tonight?" Sky asked her while they were driving in the car.

"I was just about to say something about it," she admitted. "And there certainly seems to be a lot more going on between Bertie and Jake lately than there is between Bertie and Wendy, don't you think?"

"I've heard more than once at the club that Bertie's gay," Sky said, turning into the parking lot of Riffz, a local club. "But that means nothing out here. Probably hasten a marriage, if anything."

She looked at Sky. "Do you really think Bertie's gay? I wasn't really sure." She laughed to herself as he parked the car. "I was going to ask you if you thought Wendy knows, but I'm sure that one doesn't miss a trick."

"She knows what she wants," Sky agreed. "And my guess is, it's to one day be mistress of the manor."

They went inside and had a drink, and a dance, and another drink, and then, a last dance, slow, warm, wonderful. When Sky took her home, they had trouble parting at the door.

The weekend turned out to be a combination of work and play. Jeanine Hoffman appeared at Mary Liz's door Saturday morning to beg her to hit a few tennis balls with her. Mary Liz threw on some white shorts and a white T-shirt and joined her outside. "I'm really glad you stopped by this morning."

"The kids are up with Nancy," Jeanine said as they made their way across the front lawn to the tennis court. "She's every bit their grandmother, even though they're steps."

Mary Liz tried not to, but all she could think about was how this beautiful mother and wife had once been Herbert Glidden's mistress. "I wanted to ask you, Jeanine," she finally said, "what you think I'm doing here this summer."

Jeanine seemed not at all surprised by the question. "You're trying to inventory Alfred's estate using his personal records."

Mary Liz blinked. "And may I ask how you came to believe this?"

"How I came to believe this?" she repeated, making fun of her. "Well, Mary Liz, how I came to believe this was Julius told me, and I figured Nancy must have told him—and many others, because it's no secret. Everybody in town knows."

Everybody in town? Great.

"And we think you're just great to do it," Jeanine added as they started on the path through the fir trees. "Rumor has it, she's not paying you, either."

"Oh, she's paying me, all right," Mary Liz said, hoping to start this rumor on the circuit (while deliberately neglecting to mention to Jeanine that payment would be in the form of hefty contributions to the charities of her choice: United Way of Chicago, Junior Achievement of Chicago, Police Athletic League of Chicago, Save the Children and a variety of medical research funds.)

"Jeanine," Mary Liz said after a moment, "why does Julius want the studio so badly?"

Jeanine slowed her pace and sighed. She looked over at Mary Liz (who was thinking that the diamonds in Jeanine's ears must be worth twenty-five or thirty thousand dollars—and to play tennis in!). "Julius wants the studio because it's his whole life," she said quietly. "He's desperately hurt and upset Alfred didn't leave control to him—and he wants it. *Needs* it, Mary Liz. To save face, to prove Alfred was wrong. He can and will make Howland Films an even greater independent studio. It wasn't his fault he and his father had a falling-out and Alfred chose to settle the studio on Nancy."

Mary Liz left it at that. She found a racket to use in the tennis shed and went out to try and return the balls Jeanine started belting at her. (Man, was Jeanine good!) While they were playing, Nancy came down from the Big House with Jeanine's children, Kitty and Luke. Kitty, aka Kaitland, was nine, and Luke, seven. Luke was a little blond stick, taking after his mother, but poor Kitty possessed some of the more unfortunate features of her father: his heavy frame, his thick jowls and sloping shoulders. She turned out to be a delightful child, however, and after chatting with her a while, Mary Liz was convinced Kitty's sparkling personality could and would overcome any drawbacks from her looks.

The kids were excited because they were going to camp next week.

(*Camp?* Mary Liz thought. Who would want to go to camp when you had East Hampton?)

Mary Liz worked all afternoon and then met Sky at the country club that evening to have an informal bite to eat with the Buckleys. Mary Liz was coming to like Buck better (probably because he wasn't drinking), and while she liked Vanessa, she couldn't help noticing that, yes, the woman was definitely on some kind of medication. Whether it was medicinal or recreational, she still didn't know—but she did know it couldn't be good to be drinking while taking whatever it was.

After supper, she and Sky went bowling, of all things, where over three games Mary Liz averaged a hundred and fifteen and Sky averaged two hundred and five—and he rarely played. He was, as Bertie had suspected upon meeting him, a gifted athlete.

Mary Liz was driving Sky around in the LeBaron that night—top down—and when she took him home to the Buckleys, he invited her up to see his digs over the garage.

Poor Sky! She could tell the heroic efforts he had made to clean the place up and make it livable. Apparently no one had lived in the apartment over the garage since Vanessa's father died in 1985, and her family no longer kept a full-time chauffeur. (Now, the condition Vanessa's house was in, that was a different story! It was a six-bedroom stone mansion with six fireplaces!) The little apartment was very clean, Sky had seen to that, but there was the matter of a few missing floorboards here and there, which offered an occasional glimpse of the cars below. To compensate, Sky had laid some slats going in the opposite direction, and had thrown a few small rugs down to complete the illusion of a floor. Two of the walls were made of raw plywood sheeting, while the others consisted of the bare wood frame of the garage. There was a little closet with a toilet; there was a tiny hot plate and sink in the corner; and Sky took his showers outside in the stall attached to the back of the main house.

There was a bed, a chair, a card table and a battered dresser. But on the bed was a beautiful cotton quilt and four fluffy pillows, which, not surprisingly, turned out to belong to Sky.

On the wall, he had tacked up a calendar. On the bureau was a group picture that turned out to be his family. There was a pile of books on either side of the bed, and overhead there was a bare bulb on a string.

"They really went out of their way, didn't they?" Mary Liz said.

"Yeah," Sky said with a small chuckle. He walked over and took her in his arms. "I don't live this way at home."

"I didn't imagine that you did," she murmured, kissing him.

"I have a cottage in Virginia. Three-bedroom, not terribly unlike the one you're living in," he continued. "It was the overseer's house to a plantation." He kissed her lightly. "I own it." He kissed her lightly again. "I have a mortgage, a small one." He kissed her lightly yet again. "I have two acres."

It was getting harder and harder not to want to try to seduce Sky. This time, she did, however, succeed in getting him to lie down on the bed with her awhile, to hold each other, but he soon got up, professing to need to use the bathroom. Mary Liz knew better.

He wanted to be a gentleman. So much for her being a lady. What *was* going on with her? This wasn't like her at all.

This bed! she thought, rolling off it. It needed a sheet of plywood under the mattress or something. She lifted the mattress to see what shape the box spring was in.

And there was a gun. A big, black, dull metallic handgun.

Sky came out while she was still looking at it. He looked at her, looked at it, and then looked back to her, easing the mattress out of her hand and letting it fall back down.

"What do you need that for?" she asked him. She hated handguns.

"I have a license for it."

"To do what? Shoot kids at school?"

He shook his head. "I brought it because the Buckleys asked me to. The fact is, Mary Liz, I'm sort of the night security around here, too. One of Vanessa's ex-husbands has been making threats."

"You're a teacher, a golf pro and a security force?" she asked him.

"And an aspiring bowler," he said, smiling hopefully.

She kissed him. "Don't ever ask me to be in a room with that gun again, okay?"

He looked surprised, but said, "Okay."

On Sunday morning, Mary Liz went with Aunt Nancy to the Presbyterian church in town. People always thought that because she was called Mary Liz, she must be Catholic. It used to freak her mother out, who would exclaim, "But lots of Protestant girls have two names, just ask my sister Mary Sue, or my cousin Carrie Liz!"

At any rate, Mary Liz was Episcopalian and this historic church, although a little stark for her tastes, was a pleasure to attend. The American Presbyterian clergyman and father of Harriet Beecher Stowe, Lyman Beecher, had been pastor here around 1800 and Mary Liz could easily visualize what the scene must have been like back then.

Back at the cottage, she did a couple hours of work and then Sky picked her up at two to go sailing with some rich guy from the club. Their idea of sailing far exceeded what Mary Liz had expected (she thought maybe a Blue Jay or Soling), and as they flew through the ocean waves with three sails up and a crew of eight practicing their Olympic drills, Mary Liz spent most of the time holding on, being somewhere between absolutely terrified and completely and utterly thrilled.

When Sky took her home, sunburned and happy, they collapsed on the couch together, too exhausted to do anything. They fell asleep for about an hour. And then they awakened and she and Sky started making out—their lips and cheeks still very salty—but, as usual, he stopped at a certain point and got up to go home.

Life in East Hampton, Mary Liz found, was not hard to take.

10

Mary Liz rolled out of bed and did twenty minutes of stretches and exercises to "The Best of Donna Summer," showered, applied an extra-heavy coating of moisturizer over her sunburn and dressed in baggy shorts and a cotton T-shirt. She made a pot of coffee and brought a cup of it, along with a bowl of cereal, to the office and sat down to work for the next three hours. After making a note to run a check on the names under the Miscellaneous European Expenses that kept turning up in Alfred's personal files (to the tune of a hundred fifty thousand dollars a year), she decided it was time to start scanning his corporate files.

This—the Miscellaneous European Expenses—was a classic lead. Usually such expenses were itemized and partially deducted from someone like Alfred's taxes (invariably there was some tie to the costs of doing business in Europe), but these were not. It was simply an accounting notation for himself concerning his outright expenditures for the year. This signaled only one thing to Mary Liz: these were expenditures Alfred did not want investigated, not by the IRS or anyone else.

If this wasn't a flag that something was up, nothing was. The hundred-fifty-thousand-dollar miscellaneous expenditures could be anything from clothes to the cost of family trips. But if it was, why not itemize them the way he had in every other year? No, more likely, this was money for a mistress, or maybe even some kind of blackmail. Something.

Mary Liz called up to the Big House to find out if it would be all right if she worked in the Safe Room today, and found her godmother in a tremendous state of excitement. "Oh, yes, yes, yes, of *course* you can use the Safe Room, darlin'—you can use the whole blessed estate if you want—Ashley's coming today!"

"Oh, that's great," Mary Liz said politely, not having a clue who Ashley was.

"I'm just leaving to pick her up at the airport. Claire's coming with me. So go ahead, Mary Liz, use whatever you want or need. Delores will be here. Bertie and Wendy have gone off somewhere."

Not long after, Mary Liz saw her godmother's silver Jaguar race down the driveway. She went into the office and grabbed a large L. L. Bean canvas bag and put in her laptop computer, some floppy discs, a four-socket surge protector, a legal pad and a couple of pens and pencils, a napkin, an apple, a plastic squirt bottle of water and a bunch of keys. Hefting the bag, she left the cottage and trudged up the hill.

When she came in through the back of the house, through the kitchen, she found Randolph Vandergilden on the telephone, Delores watching over him with a skeptical eye. "Shit, Bertha, come on, give me a break," he was saying, making Delores flinch at his language. "If I wanted to talk to that asshole, I would. I want you to get Nancy to talk to him."

He was probably talking to Nancy's summer social secretary in New York.

"Let me put it this way," he growled (like many alcoholics, he seemed extremely unhappy and irritable when sober), "either Nancy deals with Glidden on the arrangements or the opera's off." And he slammed the phone down. "Stupid snot-nosed bitch," he told Mary Liz and Delores.

Oh, my. This man really was a mess.

"Herb Glidden is a complete prick. I don't want to talk to him!" he explained. "Pushes me around like the winery's his, goddammit. I'm not going to put up with it anymore!"

Mary Liz couldn't resist. "Why put up with it at all?"

Vandergilden hesitated, as if she had taken him aback. Then he suddenly calmed down and smiled. "We're doing an opera, *Aida*, the details, decorations and things." He turned to Delores. "Thanks, honey," he said, pressing some cash in her hand. "And tell Nancy I came by, will you?"

"I'm sure Bertha will," Mary Liz said, heading for the basement stairs. "See you."

She made a mental note to run a profile on Randolph Vandergilden, too. What was the big deal about his having to talk to Glidden about the arrangements for the opera?

The basement of the Big House was kind of creepy. It was a Victorian stone-and-mortar creation, complete with the floor-to-ceiling beams of the seawall. There was a series of crude stone rooms, one that housed a massive hot-water heater and furnace; one that had a series of circuit-breaker boxes on one wall; another had an elaborate workshop with huge sinks (it used to be the laundry in the old days); and then, behind the steel door near the foot of the stairs, was the Safe Room. The door required two keys, simultaneously turned to the left and right, which then had to be left in place while she pulled down on the steel handle of the door to finally open it.

It was a large windowless room. The walls had some sort of beige material on them, which, Nancy had explained, had to do with maintaining something in the air that helped to preserve paper—or silver nitrate film negatives (Aunt Nancy could never remember which).

In the middle of the room was a large wooden library table, about eight feet by three, with nothing on it. On the left was a variety of small steel doors built into the wall, all with locks. Along the far wall were stacked the packing boxes of office files from Howland Films. There were several freestanding steel file cabinets to the right, empty, keys dangling from the drawers. The air from the vents in the room was cool and dry and Mary Liz wished she had brought a sweater.

She set up her equipment on the library table. And then, not able to resist, Mary Liz started opening the wall vaults to see what was inside. As Aunt Nancy had said, she found books of Alfred's stamp collection, books of Alfred's antique-postcard collection, pull-out drawers that held antique theater posters, and in others, huge metal reels in canisters that were marked as first prints of Alfred's movies. (The original negatives were in archives in Los Angeles.) She had already found the appraisals of Alfred's collections in his files: stamps, $865,000; the postcards, $46,000; and the theater posters, $279,000. One vault door, a square one, about three feet by three could not be opened. Mary Liz didn't have another key, and she made a note to ask Aunt Nancy about it.

Mary Liz went over to start in on the Howland Films files. She was not disappointed. At least not as a spectator. There was a lot more interesting stuff in here than in Alfred's dry financial files. There were memos concerning very famous people. One of the most interesting debated whether or not Howland Films needed to pay hush money to the family of a minor who had been sexually assaulted on a movie set by an employee. If they did, the accountant said, it could be used as a tax deduction as a cost of doing business.

Another memo suggested they hire secretaries as "production assistants," because then they wouldn't be union workers. (Mary Liz's eyebrows went up when she saw that starting secretarial salaries at movie studios in Los Angeles began at around thirty-five thousand dollars a year, the union scale.)

Huh. This was interesting. Howland Films maintained running accounts at three private-detective agencies.

The intercom by the vault door buzzed. "It is Delores!" the housekeeper called. Mary Liz opened the door to find Delores handing her a luncheon tray. "For you." On it was a plate of salad with grilled chicken, crackers, a bottle of Poland Spring Water, a glass of ice, salad dressing, silverware, napkins and salt and pepper.

In the late afternoon Mary Liz went back to the cottage to call Bill Pfeiffer. "I'm faxing this list to you as we speak," she said. "I'll type out formal research requests tomorrow, but I thought you might like to sleep on this tonight."

"Something new?"

"Yes, yearly miscellaneous European maintenance costs of a hundred fifty thousand a year."

"Did he file for a deduction?"

"No, it's an internal accounting note only. It looks as though he has been personally paying for something in France every year. I wondered if you could track the money."

"A hundred fifty thousand a year," Bill repeated. He whistled. "That's a lot of miscellaneous."

"Particularly," Mary Liz added, "when Alfred only stayed at the Howland apartment in Paris when he was in France, the full domestic staff of which Howland Films has listed on their payroll, to say nothing of all the miscellaneous expenses incurred there, from food to flowers to wine."

"What do you think?"

"I'm not sure," she said, looking at her notes. "But he started paying money under this heading the year he shot a movie in France, and it quadrupled three years later, after he filmed another movie there."

"Sounds as though he might have had mistresses," Bill said.

"Or, God forbid, other children," Mary Liz said. "Whatever it is, he didn't feel like advertising it. Could be some kind of off-the-radar investment, I suppose."

"Okay. Anything else?"

"I'm sending you the particulars regarding Alfred's land in Montana. The first parcel's fine, but I can't seem to find any surveyor's reports or accurate measurements on the second. There's also a tax discrepancy on it. I'm hoping your people can figure it out."

"You're faxing me this?"

"It will be in your E-mail in the morning."

"Good."

"There's one more thing, Bill, a question, actually. If I give you a list of all the letterheads I find in the Howland Films files, people and companies Alfred was dealing with, I was wondering if you could run a cross-check for me with any incoming and outgoing payments made in the past two years. In particular, I want to find out if any of those names coincide with any of the investors Herb Glidden lined up for the past two movies, and the one that's coming up this fall."

"Why?"

"I'm curious," she said.

Silence.

And then, "I don't want to try to tell you what to do, Mary Liz," Bill said slowly, "but you're supposed to be doing an inventory of Alfred's estate for assets. Somebody else is doing an audit of Howland Films."

"And I want the results of that audit compared to any names we have on the investors in the movies," she said.

"Why?" he said again.

She was getting a little annoyed. "Why do you want to know?"

"Because, Mary Liz, if you uncover any kind of wrongdoing, it can only hurt the primary heirs, who are our clients, Nancy and her family."

"Who said I was looking for wrongdoing?"

"I'm not dumb, Mary Liz. If Alfred accumulated any assets by double-dealing on billings or anything, I don't want to know about it—and nor do you."

She supposed he was right. Best not to turn over too many rocks. You'd find too much slime underneath. Hollywood was notorious that way.

What she wanted to find out was why Herbert Glidden wanted Howland Films so badly, when he knew nothing about making movies. The only thing she could figure was that he was protecting his interests as the exclusive financier for future movies. Making sure the studio continued to use only him. But why Howland? Surely lots of people in Hollywood needed money to make pictures, and the man who had made those successful movies at Howland was now dead. Why not go with another tried-and-true producer?

Well, maybe Bill was right, her curiosity about Glidden *was*, she supposed, personal. Until, that is, she found another connection with him that in some way could affect the estate. She'd go another route to finding out about his investors for Howland movies.

"You're right," she said to him. "So we'll skip that." She heard some shouting outside the cottage. Laughter. A feminine squeal of glee—and barking. She got off the line with Bill and went out to the front porch. Claire MacClendon was in the process of throwing a tennis ball down the lawn while a black Labrador retriever charged down the hill to retrieve it.

"She's here, she's here!" Aunt Nancy cried, waving her arms. "Look!"

The dog was happily charging up the hill now. But instead of giving the ball back to Claire or giving it to Nancy, the dog circled the women, spotted Mary Liz and came galloping down the lawn toward the cottage.

"Ashley! Ashley!" Nancy called to no avail. The dog was racing, yellow ball in her mouth, ears flying back.

"Well, hello," Mary Liz said, coming down the stairs to greet her. The dog tried to stop in time before crashing into her, an action that tore at the grass. The animal just stood there, panting, smiling, tennis ball in her mouth. Her head was sleek and black, she had beautiful brown eyes, a lovely big black nose and a pink tongue—with purple on it! "Hello, Ashley," Mary Liz said, laughing, squatting to pat her shiny head. She had a little white under her chin. No, she was not a purebred, then, because she certainly wasn't old. "Imagine, I thought you were a person," she murmured, rubbing the dog behind her ears. Ashley dropped the ball in front of her and looked up—and suddenly lunged forward to lick Mary Liz's face.

Nancy and Claire were laughing as they arrived. "Isn't she just wonderful?" Nancy asked. She knelt to one knee to put her arms around the dog and kissed her on the head. "Bertie and I found her in Ireland, on the west coast, near Kinvarra. We nearly hit her with our car but Bertie slammed on the brakes just in time. There was a farmer chasing her, and we couldn't make out what he was saying." She looked at the dog. "And you, you just hid behind me, didn't you? You knew a sucker when you saw one." She looked up at Mary Liz. "He was going to shoot her because she kept killing everybody's chickens."

The dog looked at Mary Liz. "Aye, lassie," Mary Liz said in a very bad brogue, "you were a bad gurl indeed, weren't ya?"

"Poor little lambkin's been in quarantine for six months, haven't we?" Nancy asked the dog.

The phone was ringing in the cottage, and Mary Liz excused herself. She ran in and snapped up the kitchen phone. "Hello?"

"Mary Liz Scott?" a female voice said.

"Speaking."

"This is Herbert Glidden's secretary calling from Los Angeles. I'm calling because Mr. Glidden wanted to set up an appointment with you."

"Oh, right."

"He's going to be back in East Hampton one week from today, Monday the fourteenth. Would it be possible to meet him in the afternoon, say, three o'clock?"

"Where?"

"I believe he'd like to meet at his house. He has an office there."

They wrapped up the details—phone numbers, addresses, etc.—and Mary Liz hurried to get off the phone. While Nancy was calling Ashley's name to no avail, the dog was clawing at the screen door of the cottage to get in.

It wasn't until a moment later Mary Liz remembered how Sky had begged her to have nothing to do with Herbert Glidden. And now she had an official job interview with the guy.

Well, she needed to know what she needed to know, right?

11

Mary Liz was getting a lot of work done on Tuesday. One interesting fact she had not known, which she stumbled across in a manila folder within a Howland Films file—obviously misfiled altogether—was that her godmother had come into quite a bit of money of her own upon the death of her father ten years ago. She had inherited some six and a half million dollars. And, judging from Alfred's earliest personal records and the books of Howland Films, it looked as though the wedding gift of money bestowed on them by Nancy's father—five hundred thousand dollars—had kept them going until Alfred's first big hit, since the small amount he was making at the time from the fledgling studio was going mostly to alimony and child support payments to his first wife, Ruth.

Mary Liz called her mother up. "I had the impression that Alfred was already wealthy when Aunt Nancy married him."

"Well," her mother began, "I think that was the impression Alfred tried to make—on her family, at any rate. Nancy knew—and I knew—he was pretty hard up for cash. Your Aunt Nancy married for love, pure and simple, Mary Liz. What was fortunate is that she did have some money coming to her when she married, money her father couldn't block. It was from her grandmother, I think."

"The wedding-gift money? That wasn't from her father?"

"Heavens, no. He wouldn't even come to the wedding! It was from her grandmother, her father's mother, which made it all the more bitter a pill for him to swallow."

"But why was he so against it?"

"Oh, gosh, Mary Liz, Mr. Bailey was—well, he was a lot of things, most notably, I'm afraid, a bigot."

"You're kidding."

"Oh, no, dear, I'm not. And he just—well, he went wild when his little princess came home and said she wanted to marry a divorced Jewish man from Hollywood. But then Alfred said he would convert, and Mr. Bailey didn't go for that either, but Alfred did convert, became a Christian, and they were married in a church. And everyone came but Mr. Bailey, and I was the matron of honor—six months pregnant with Brendan," she added, "so you can imagine what a nightmare my fitting was."

They laughed.

"Mom, do you know Herbert Glidden?"

"Lordie, yes." She sighed. "Why?"

"He's here sometimes, in East Hampton—right in the middle of everything."

"Your father told me."

"Well?" Mary Liz said. "What's the story?"

"No story, darlin'," she said, making Mary Liz smile at how much she and Aunt Nancy sounded alike when they said that. "Herb's just an old hustler who raised some money for Alfred way back when, and when Alfred's star rose, so did his."

"A hustler?"

"A hustler," her mother confirmed. "Nancy never did like him. Alfred didn't, either, really, but felt obligated to him. I can see why."

"What do you mean, 'obligated'?"

"Obligated. Obligated to friends. Obligated to family. Obligated to his company. Alfred considered Herb an obligation. And Nancy used to say the poor guy had virtually no friends, a basket case for a wife and a namby-pamby for a son. He was always at Alfred's back door, like a kid, begging to be asked in, begging to be asked to play."

"They used to have a big poker game here at the estate," Mary Liz said.

"Al loved cards," her mother said. "I think your father played in his Hollywood game, years ago, when he was commuting to L.A. on the Getty trust. I'm sure Herbert Glidden was not a part of that, though. Alfred was very choosy when it came to who he let into the house."

"When Alfred wasn't here," Mary Liz said, "I heard that Herb would crash the game."

"But I'm talking twenty years ago, angel, and you're talking recent history. Who knows what transpired in between? I certainly wouldn't know."

Was Mary Liz imagining it, or did she hear a note of tension in her mother's voice? As if her mother had heard this thought, she said, "You know how it is, Mary Liz, Winnetka is not Hollywood and we simply drifted apart."

Sky came over around eight-thirty. They just took a walk on the beach tonight, kissing a few times, talking and taking the air, as it were.

"I wondered if you were free Saturday night," he said, swinging hands with her as they walked along the water. "The Buckleys gave me tickets to a benefit that sounded like fun. They have something else to do and can't go."

"What is it?"

"The ARF animal parade and dinner. At the airport, if you can believe. They're setting up grandstands for the parade, and then there's going to be a big spread—barbecue, steamed clams and corn, and salads and stuff."

"What is ARF?"

"Animal Rescue Fund."

"Oh," Mary Liz said, softening immediately. "Yes, I'd love to go. Speaking of which, Nancy rescued a dog from Ireland."

"Ashley. I know," he said. "She brought her to the club this afternoon. A bit of a pain in the neck, actually, since every time someone teed off, the poor dog bolted and nearly hanged herself."

"She is a great dog, though," Mary Liz said. "She came down and sat in the office with me today while Nancy went shopping."

"You spend far too much time inside, young lady," he said, stopping to turn her around toward him. He took her hands. And sighed. "What am I going to do with you, Mary Liz Scott?"

She only smiled, knowing exactly what he was talking about. How long could they go on like this?

"Oh, Sky, hang on—there's a fireworks thing Saturday night," she remembered. "And I told Aunt Nancy I'd go. Actually, I told her I'd ask you, too."

"But that's late," Sky said. "We can go to both. The fireworks couldn't be any sooner than nine-thirty, it's not dark enough until then. Hey, it's not that boys club benefit on the beach, is it?"

"I think so."

He gave a low whistle. "That's two hundred dollars a ticket."

"Well," she said, shrugging, "we've got two at our disposal."

They walked back to the cottage and Mary Liz noticed that the lights of the guest house were on. Bertie and Wendy must be back from wherever they had been.

She and Sky walked back to the cottage, where they curled up to watch the ten o'clock news. Then he went home.

The next morning, Mary Liz spent a couple of hours on the telephone with a researcher from Bill Pfeiffer's firm in New York discussing the Miscellaneous European Expenses lead. Afterward she went up to the Big House to hit the Howland Films files again. This time, though, she brought her document scanner. As a precaution, she thought it would be a good idea to send copies of important documents somewhere she knew they would be safe—namely, to her father's computer at home.

She went into the Big House from the back, through the kitchen, checking in with Delores before going downstairs. She had just turned the second key in the Safe Room door and was pulling the handle of the door down when she heard a sound on the stairs. Startled, she turned around.

"What are you doing?" It was Bertie. He was coming down the stairs—even more tanned than last week—wearing only swim trunks and flip-flops.

"Oh, you're back. Did you have a nice trip?"

"What are you doing?" he repeated, reaching the bottom of the stairs.

"I'm doing a favor for your mother."

"Mother's not here."

"Then she'll tell you what I'm doing when she gets back."

"Even I don't have keys to that room," he said, sounding angry, striding over and making his flip-flops slap. "I'm coming in with you."

"No," Mary Liz told him. "Not unless your mother says you can." This was a pretty stupid statement since Bertie, at six-two, merely had to push her to the side and go in through the unlocked door. "Where is Aunt Nancy?"

"Somewhere, I don't know," he growled.

"Bertie?" came a call from upstairs. It was Wendy.

"In the cellar!" he yelled.

"What's going on?" Wendy asked, coming downstairs. She too was extremely tanned, looking very pretty and slightly wild-looking. Mary Liz realized it was her hair, uncombed for the first time she had seen it. "Oh, it's you," Wendy said, frowning, looking at Mary Liz.

Mary Liz was very confused. "What's the matter?" she asked them.

"As if you don't know," Bertie said.

"What?"

"I'm going in there with you," Bertie said. "I want to know what you're doing."

"You know what I'm doing," she said.

"But for who?"

Mary Liz looked to Wendy for help. "What is it? What's going on?"

"I'm not telling you *anything,*" Wendy said, coming down the rest of the stairs.

Mary Liz took a breath to keep her temper in check. "Aunt Nancy wanted me to look over some papers for her, some financial papers. It's no big deal."

"Then why can't I come in?" Bertie demanded.

Because you and the gold digger are not to be trusted, she thought. She had to make a decision; she chose the path of least resistance. "Fine, Bertie. But please tell your mother I asked you not to come in here until you got her permission." She went into the Safe Room and held the door for Bertie to come through, but when Wendy tried to follow she quickly stepped forward to block her. "Sorry," Mary Liz said, closing the door in Wendy's face and sliding across the iron bar inside.

Bertie looked almost gleeful. "Man, are you in for it now. She will *kill* you."

"Tough," Mary Liz said.

Bertie looked around. "What's in there?" He was pointing to the little vault doors built into the walls.

"Prints of your father's movies, his theatrical poster collection, his postcard collection and his stamp collection."

"Give me the keys," Bertie said, flip-flopping toward her.

"I don't have the keys to those," Mary Liz said. This was true, she had left those keys in the cottage, hidden in a roll of toilet tissue in the linen closet. She held up the keys she had brought. "A key to the Big House, and two for the Safe Room door. That's all I have."

"And what's in there? I don't even remember that."

"That" was the three-by-three vault door in the wall that Mary Liz didn't have the key to. Nancy hadn't given her a key that fit it, and she had meant to ask her about it. "I have no idea," she told him.

"What's this junk?" he asked, kicking a box.

"Just some files of your father's. From Howland Films. Bertie, why are you being so hostile?"

"Wouldn't you like to know," he muttered. He looked at her. "Just remember, Mary Liz, I have my eye on you."

Now she was angry. "Yeah? Well, let me tell you something, Bertie, I've got my eye on *you—and* your so-called gal-pal."

He seemed unsettled by this comment, and actually shivered. But then, it was very cool and dry in here and he was clad in practically nothing but his muscles. He flip-flopped over to the door, slid the bolt over, opened the door and turned around. "Don't fuck with me, Mary Liz, I'm warning you."

Mary Liz locked up the Safe Room and went upstairs to find Delores. She had to find Aunt Nancy.

Delores gave Mary Liz directions on how to find her godmother, and minutes later Mary Liz was zooming along in the LeBaron, looking for a beauty and massage center. She found it, parked and went inside, introducing herself at the front desk and explaining she was looking for Mrs. Hoffman. A messenger was dispatched to verify this with Mrs. Hoffman, and Mary Liz was soon being led by the manager to a private room where Aunt Nancy was having a facial.

She seemed not in the least surprised to see Mary Liz, urged her to sit, and while the attendant—introduced to Mary Liz as Mona—wrapped a steaming cloth around Nancy's face, Mary Liz filled her in on her encounter with Bertie. When she got to the part where she asked what could be causing Bertie's hostility and suspicion (a cagey way of bringing up the topics of hostility and suspicion, two things she herself was starting to feel toward Nancy's son and his girlfriend), Nancy pulled off the cloth and looked at her with dreamy, sleepy eyes, and said in a whisper, "I have no idea. He's a sensitive boy and sometimes imagines slights. But I will tell him exactly what you are doing and why you are doing it—and tell him to leave you alone while you do," and replaced the hot-pack on her face. In a moment Mona replaced it with a new steaming one, and Mary Liz could see that her godmother had fallen asleep.

Mary Liz took the cue, apologized to the attendant for intruding and walked out, not entirely satisfied. Bertie didn't seem the paranoid type. Wendy must have said something to him that made him suddenly distrust her. That, or he was about to try some scam on the estate himself. Mary Liz dearly hoped not. She had liked him.

Just then Sasha appeared in the hall, wrapped in a thick terry-cloth robe. She was being led from one room to another. The diva gleefully grabbed on to her arm, talking a mile a minute, and pulled her into a tiny room containing a lounge, a sink, a chair and a small metal table on wheels.

"I keep calling you but you're never home!" the diva complained, dropping her robe so that she was stark-naked, and flopping down on her back across the lounge. Clearly this was a woman accustomed to being groomed and coiffed by others.

The polite thing, Mary Liz decided, was to maintain eye contact with the superstar while she lay there naked, waiting for whoever Sasha was waiting for. "Why didn't you leave a message on the machine?"

"Oh, I never leave messages," the diva said. "I might change my mind before someone calls back. I like to keep my options open." Her eyes flared. "But I wanted *you* to play with me today. So much so, I went to your cottage last night, around seven, and knocked on the door. But there was no answer."

"That's odd. I was home."

"No, you weren't," the diva insisted.

There was a soft knock on the door and an older woman came in, carrying with her a wooden bowl with a paintbrush in it. "I am Sonja," she announced.

"Hi, Sonja," the diva said, "this is my friend, Mary Liz. Is it all right if she stays?"

"Ya," Sonja said abruptly. "Seet in te chair."

Mary Liz did as she was told.

"Eet es a fool leg?" Sonja asked, checking, stirring her secret potion.

"Ya, full leg," Sasha mimicked, squirming slightly. The diva was on the slight side, around five-four, and thin, but she was over fifty and Mary Liz couldn't believe how lovely her body was. Firm, no cellulite she could see, perfectly shaped breasts. How did she do it?

"Sasha," Mary Liz said, "which house did you knock at?"

"The one at the top of the driveway."

"That's the guest house."

The diva craned her neck to look at her. "I thought that's where we picked you up the other day."

"You picked me up at the caretaker's cottage, remember? At the foot of the driveway?"

"Ready?" Sonja asked Sasha.

"Ya," Sasha told her.

The older woman painted on a thick strip of wax on the diva's lower leg. She waited a moment, took the end of the wax and, with a sharp yank, tore it off Sasha's skin.

"Ow!" Sasha said.

"Eet ees the price of booty." Sonja sighed, painting another slab of wax on Sasha's other leg.

Mary Liz was fascinated. She had heard of leg waxing, of course, but had never had the time or inclination to have it done. A nice, new sharp razor and shaving cream had done just fine—that is, when she had a nice, new sharp razor around. The trick had always been to remember to buy them.

Sonja tore the next slab off and Sasha yelped.

"Actually," the diva said, breathing rather heavily now, "it makes me feel better to know you're in the little house. A couple of times I was going to send Riff over to complain about the noise." She tried to sit up to look at Mary Liz. "There's something strange going on over—"

Sonja pushed Sasha back down flat on the lounge.

"—there." The diva giggled. "Sonja, you should be a wrestler."

"What kind of things?" Mary Liz asked.

"There are always men's voices—"

"That's Bertie. His girlfriend's staying there."

"No, *men's* voices, Mary Liz, at all hours of the night. I don't know what they're doing, but there always seems to be at least two of them in there."

Bertie and Jake perhaps. "I've never heard them," she said truthfully.

Rrrrrrrrip!

"Ooch," the diva said, adding to her vocabulary of pain.

"Over," Sonja commanded.

Sasha turned over on her stomach. No cellulite on the back of her, either. Mary Liz was starting to suspect surgery.

"They always have a window open toward my house," Sasha said, propping herself up on one elbow.

"Down," Sonja commanded, flattening the diva with one hand.

When Mary Liz returned to the estate, she worked in the cottage all afternoon crunching numbers. At around five, Aunt Nancy called from the Big House to say she was going into Manhattan for a couple of nights and wanted to give Delores a day off before the weekend. Would Mary Liz mind terribly if she asked her to take Ashley in with her while she was gone? "She adores you, Mary Liz. I'd feel much better leaving her in the cottage with you."

"It would be a treat," Mary Liz said. And it would be.

"By the way, darlin', I had a long talk with Bertie and set him straight."

Mary Liz doubted it.

"I'm afraid his nose *is* out of joint, and he wouldn't tell me why. At any rate, I told him you have carte blanche around here and to leave you alone." She paused. "Mary Liz, you didn't know Herb Glidden before you got here, did you?"

"Heavens, no!" Mary Liz said. "Why?"

"Bertie just said something odd which made me think he thinks you already knew Herb from somewhere."

"Absolutely not, Aunt Nancy," she swore.

"I thought not. Well, when you get a chance, come up and fetch your new roommate, will you, darlin'?"

Mary Liz dashed up to the Big House and got a handful of lists from Aunt Nancy about the care of Ashley. She needed Jake to carry down to the cottage a huge carton of fresh meats (like people ate!), dry dog food, vitamins and toys.

Ashley was a sweetheart, and there was nothing better than a dog that was both affectionate and athletic. (Nothing better than a man like that, either, she thought, thinking of Sky.) Aunt Nancy was right, Ashley was a lamb, happy to simply snooze at Mary Liz's feet while she worked in the office, knowing, it seemed, that as soon as Mary Liz was through, there would be fun to be had.

At seven o'clock, Ashley had her dinner and her vitamins, and Mary Liz had her dinner and her vitamins. Ashley ate better than she did; she got steak in her dry food and Mary Liz only got low-fat dressing on a crummy-looking chef's salad. Afterward, Mary Liz took her outside to throw a tennis ball for her, throwing closer and closer to the guest house so she could look around. Something was definitely afoot with that Wendy.

No one appeared to be at home. Nancy's Jaguar was gone; the Range Rover was gone (presumably with Bertie and Wendy); and the car Delores used, a Toyota, was gone, as well.

Mary Liz finally went up to the guest house and knocked on the door. She nearly died when Wendy answered it. "Um," she stammered, not knowing what to say, "I wondered if you wanted to come out and play with the dog." Well, that certainly sounded stupid, particularly since this woman apparently considered her an enemy.

Wendy only looked at her. "What?" she finally said.

"I wondered if you wanted to come out and play with us."

"But you hate me," Wendy reminded her.

"Wendy—I don't hate you!"

"Oh yes you do. You yelled at me last Sunday after your break-in and then you slammed the door in my face today."

"Only because you were so hostile to me!" Mary Liz said, defending herself.

"Who wouldn't be?" Wendy glared at her. "You should just pack your things and clear out of here before Bertie loses his temper completely."

"But why?" Mary Liz nearly wailed in frustration, prompting Ashley to whine. "Shh, girl, it's okay," she murmured, bending to pat the dog on the head.

"No, it's not okay," Wendy told the dog. "You should bite her." She looked at Mary Liz. "We know what you're up to, it's only a matter of time before we act. Get your damn priorities straight, Mary Liz. What the hell would your father think?"

She slammed the door and locked it, and would not answer it when Mary Liz began knocking frantically. *What in the world was going on?*

Mary Liz couldn't sleep that night and the dog was restless. It was ten past twelve. Mary Liz threw on some jeans and a sweatshirt, put a leash on Ashley and grabbed the flashlight she kept on the front porch. No need to let the fresh air go to waste.

They walked up the lawn, across the parking area, over the back lawn to the walkway to the beach. The moon was nearly full, casting light whenever there was a break in the clouds. It was spooky. It was beautiful. It was quietly exhilarating walking on the beach.

She unleashed the dog and let her tear around. Then she started walking east, the sand cool and lovely on her feet. The moon came out and lit up the ocean, making the whitecaps appear almost fluorescent, the wet sands of the beach a slippery silver.

There was no doubt about it, East Hampton was one of the most beautiful places on earth. One could practically feel God's presence at moments like this, and Mary Liz wondered if way back when, when Lyman Beecher had been here, if he had walked this beach, too, and felt so at peace, felt so close and blessed by God.

The dog was far behind her, but knew very well where Mary Liz was, because periodically she would charge in her direction, bark once and then go back the other way, wanting Mary Liz to come back.

Mary Liz kept walking, breathing deeply, thinking about how fortunate she was. The only question was, which way after the summer was over? Back to Chicago? To do what? Teach? She had a master's and Northwestern had already approached her about running a graduate seminar in investment banking. Or she could move. Go to Europe for a little while.

Sky.

She wanted to see how the summer went; she wondered how their relationship would go. Would it deepen, strengthen?

She couldn't see why not. They were caught up in each other, that was for sure. They never had a lack of things to talk about, both enjoyed doing just about anything if the other was present, and their views on life—their sense of right and wrong, of values and ethics—were very similar.

The moon went back behind the clouds again and Mary Liz walked on.

It was so strange to have time to think. For years she had not, because if she had, she would have remembered how investment banking had never interested her in the first place (she had achieved a split major in art history and math), how she had joined the trainee program at Reston, Kellaher because she needed a job, and how, after she'd started there, she saw how so many really not very clever people made a million dollars a year. And so she had decided she would make a million or two and be on her way to do what she really wanted to.

Which was... She still didn't know. Not after all these years. A fellow graduate student in the Chicago MBA night program had once asked what she had wanted to be when she was, say, twelve. That, he said, was usually a good indication of what one really wanted to be.

"A detective," she had answered truthfully. "Or an FBI agent. I wanted to track art thieves."

"So what happened?"

"So I interviewed with Reston, Kellaher, and have been there ever since." She remembered feeling a dull pain in the vicinity of her heart as she had said that. Even way back then, some eight or nine years ago.

Funny for her to think this way now, still be at sea about what she might like to do when she grew up.

Maybe she could teach. She could get her certification and teach math. High school. Sky enjoyed it. Maybe she could get a job—

Mary Liz stopped. She heard a noise. And then the moon came out and she didn't know what to do, because less than twenty feet away from her were two naked bodies lying on a blanket. The couple hadn't seen her yet. The woman was on top, kissing her lover passionately, and making some rather provocative noises in her throat. She had a nice body, this woman, and had a tangle of long hair. And was she ever into it.

If Mary Liz moved forward, they would for sure sense her presence. If she went backward, her shadow would fall across them. All she could do was hope they didn't see her and the moon would go back in and she could retreat.

Oh, and the dog! Where was the dog?

Oh, this was awful, she had to get out of here.

The woman had broken off the kiss and had moved up to press her breast into her lover's face. She began to moan, undulating against him.

Come on, moon!

"Yes, *yes,*" the woman was groaning. And then suddenly she rolled down onto the blanket, her back to Mary Liz, but then pulling the man on top of her.

Only it wasn't a man. It was another woman. A slender, obviously deeply aroused woman, who did not see Mary Liz and proceeded to settle into her lover with some seriousness, oblivious to all but the moans of pleasure that resulted.

The moon went in and Mary Liz retreated a few steps, and then turned around and ran. The dog was all the way down at the Hoffmans' beach, lying at the foot of the stairs by Mary Liz's shoes.

Only when they were safely home again and Mary Liz was back in bed, trying to sleep, did the image of those two women reappear in her mind.

Neither of them appeared to have cellulite, either.

Ah, East Hampton.

12

Thursday morning Mary Liz awakened at eight, discovering that teaching Ashley to sleep on the floor by her bed had not been an altogether successful endeavor. The dog was curled up beside her and the retriever's head was tucked under Mary Liz's chin.

"Wake up, little dog," she whispered, prompting Ashley to start licking her chin and making her laugh.

Mary Liz got up, put on a bathing suit and shorts and went straight out to the front porch. She sat down on the stairs to glance over the *Wall Street Journal* while Ashley did her morning business.

It was so strange to be sitting on the sidelines of the communications revolution now. She still knew more about it than most—often even more than the CEOs of the communications companies themselves—but this would only be true for about two months more. By then her data would be hopelessly dated. Still, sitting here, skimming articles in the paper, she knew exactly how the news would play out for each communications company mentioned; who had to downsize, who had to refinance, who had lied to her and other investment bankers about what they were going to do with the money the bankers had raised for them.

But now it had nothing to do with her.

Her life in Chicago seemed like such a long time ago. She remembered it, certainly, but she had a hard time believing that she had really gotten up at 5:00 a.m. every morning and had worked all day, only to end it with some god-awful dinner with clients. Or there had been the four or five cities in three days, holding meetings with clients or doing presentations for clients they wanted, nine times out of ten crossing paths with the big-time competitors like Goldman, Sachs or First Boston.

She well remembered running into Faith Collier from Allied Trust in the Knoxville, Tennessee, airport a little over a year ago. Mary Liz didn't know Faith as much as she knew *of* her, for Collier's brain carried more information about the future of cable TV, satellites, wireless cable, paging and cellular systems than anybody's on Wall Street. Or anybody's in Chicago, for that matter, including Mary

Liz's. That was one of the reasons that Mary Liz had felt so tired. The industry was changing so fast that the demand of the day was—instead of creating sound business deals based on actual products or services—to create sound business deals by luring clients to invest millions upon millions of dollars in what were only *ideas* of products or services that might or might not work sometime in the future. And everybody was competing for the same account.

When Mary Liz had spotted her at the Knoxville airport, Faith had waved, laughed and said, "How many planes did it take *you* to get here?"

"Three," she had answered. "I had a thunderstorm to go around, so I went from Chicago to Dallas, from Dallas to Atlanta, from Atlanta to here."

"Four for me." Faith sighed. "L.A. to Washington, Washington to Charlotte, Charlotte to Atlanta, Atlanta to here." She glanced at her watch and then looked around the terminal. "My meeting's at three and I'm not sure anybody else from my firm made it."

It was in that moment Mary Liz had decided to quit. There was no way she was going to beat out Faith for this account. But that wasn't even it. It was the fact that she knew Faith had to be as exhausted and near brain dead as she was, but Faith looked great—relaxed, confident, blue eyes sparkling, white teeth flashing smiles—while Mary Liz knew she looked like hell.

None of it was fun anymore. And she was fading as a competitor.

Besides, she had completely blown her personal life. She was alone, there was no Jim to discuss work with, no Jim whose body she could feel next to hers when she did get home at night.

She had been so stupid!

She could have settled down permanently with Jim two Christmases ago, he'd wanted to get married, and she had held off for no other reason than she was scared that he would someday bore her. That if she stayed home for some years to have children, and maybe do some part-time work from there, that having Jim as her sole adult companion would drive her to the brink one day and she would have to leave him. And what was the point of getting married unless she wanted to make a family, and there was no way she was going to make a family with someone she was scared she might not be able to stick it out with as the minister said. In sickness and in health, till death do you part. The way her mother and father had.

And then Kennedy Rogers had arrived at Reston, Kellaher in the new year. Former all-American quarterback for the University of Pennsylvania football team, MBA from Wharton, married and divorced once (when young), the man with the looks, the brains, the charm and the oh-so-ever-appealing personality. Mr. Flash and Cash, one of Mary Liz's less admiring colleagues had called him. Ken was an investment banker brought in as a partner from Kidder, Peabody, and he and Mary Liz had been thrown together on a presentation trip to a town near Ketchum, Idaho, where the creator and CEO of a new satellite technology lived. The weather had been terrible and they had spent hours in airports trying to get there, and so when they were finally at least able to fly into Butte, Montana, they had rented a Jeep Cherokee and decided to drive to their destination.

What had impressed Mary Liz most was Ken's indefatigable spirits. In his book, everything was an adventure waiting to happen, and judging from the way he handled the Jeep, he had been out on a lot. Mary Liz kept calling their prospective client on her cellular, to apprise him of their location and to assure him they were going to get there, by hook or by crook. On her fifth call she was delighted to hear that all the other investment banking teams had begged off because of the snow.

It did not occur to Mary Liz that had their vehicle slipped off the road and gotten stuck in the snowdrifts, she would have been outfitted for the tundra in a raincoat and high heels. No, at the time, the trek had been thrilling—radio blasting rock, freewheeling along the empty highways, stopping only to pick up cheeseburgers and French fries.

They had gotten the account, hands down. And to celebrate, Ken had said now they could really kick off their shoes, and he took Mary Liz out in Ketchum for food and lots of drinks and lots of country dancing.

She'd had the time of her life. She loved to dance and Jim hated it, so they rarely did; Jim loved fine food and dining and turned his nose up at noisy bars, which Mary Liz frankly liked on occasion. And Ken was just so *physical.* He never made an improper move or suggestion the entire trip, although after several beers Mary Liz had half wished he would. He made her feel so alive.

It took two months. Even then Mary Liz told herself she was not leaving Jim to be with Ken—although, at this point, she and Ken, on one of their ever-increasingly warm business trips together, had openly discussed what they would do if she weren't attached. Finally she had to tell Jim that she couldn't live with him anymore, because she did not want to marry him. She was sorry, and she was really sorry because she *did* love him, but—*it* just wasn't there.

And so she moved out at the end of February that year and broke his heart. And Ken came over the first night in her new apartment and she had enjoyed the best sex of her life. Free, easy, passionate, he was completely at home, which in turn made her feel the same way. Many nights of the same continued. On their next business trip together, she felt funny about sleeping with him—it was work, after all, and usually she would be working on her laptop in the hotel bed, not on a man—but in the end, she gleefully snuck down the hall to be with him.

And then, in a mere six weeks, it was over. Ken took her to dinner and explained that he and his old girlfriend from New York were getting back together. He was sorry, but Mary Liz understood, didn't she? And they had had such fun together. He was very grateful to her.

There was no old girlfriend from New York. She knew that. It had been getting serious—*she* had been getting serious—and he wanted out before it was too late.

Jim, all along, had been calling once a week to check in. He had no idea she was seeing anyone else. At first his calls annoyed her to no end, making her feel nothing but guilty and angry, but after a while she realized how much she missed talking with him. He knew her so well. And how well she had known him, which, she supposed, had been one of his earliest attractions. With Jim she could count on there not being any surprises.

Well, she had learned her lesson. Three months after her fling with Kennedy ended, last July, she asked Jim to meet her for dinner. It was with a full heart she had gone, to explain what a horrible mistake she had made, that she had thought she was afraid of a commitment like marriage, that's why she had bolted, but now she knew for sure it was Jim she wanted, and Jim with whom she wanted to spend her life.

Unfortunately, Jim had chosen the dinner as the occasion to tell her that although he had felt badly hurt when she'd moved, he had also been surprised to find out, in the end, how relieved he was. That he had always known, in his heart, that Mary Liz had not loved him the way he had hoped his future wife would.

Mary Liz had struggled to object, but he had silenced her.

"You think I'm boring, predictable and not very courageous," he told her. "I've always been like a teddy bear for you, a comfort in the odd moment you're alone and not busy. Or when the whole world seems turned upside down, only then do you seem to put any value on the way I am—and who I am."

Her heart sinking with his every word, she knew that while he was exaggerating, his analysis was somewhere near the truth. But it wasn't that she didn't admire his qualities, it was his lack of initiative and drive and passion for *anything* that had always so frustrated her. She had felt as though every time she had wanted to run, he had yanked her back with a ball and chain. He craved security and there was nothing wrong with that, it was just that his need for it seemed to smother any desire to change, to grow or to move on to anywhere. He would be perfectly happy, she had known, to stay on in the same job he had held for the previous five years—vice president in charge of operations at the commodities exchange—for the rest of his life. He knew his job and did it well. That was enough.

"Hi, Mary Liz," a friendly voice said, snapping her back to the present.

It was Jake. In a pair of bathing trunks. He was a golden brown and Mary Liz wondered again if he wasn't an aspiring actor. Whether he was or not, Mary Liz couldn't blame Bertie if it was true that they were lovers.

"Hi, Jake," she said, waving, noticing that Ashley didn't bark at him, but simply went over, tail wagging, to give him her ball.

He threw it up the lawn toward the Big House. He turned around. "I was wondering if you wanted to take Ashley for a swim. Before everybody else gets up."

"Great idea," she said, tossing the newspaper down and jumping up. Frankly, she was delighted that he didn't seem to hate her, too. Which, on second thought, she supposed, should make her a little suspicious. Was he here as a spy for Bertie? "Let me get a towel—"

"I've got them in the cabana."

"Oh, right. Okay." She accompanied Jake up the hill, with Ashley dancing around them, chatting about how great this or that looked on the property. She finally had to ask him if he had ever thought of acting or modeling. He admitted, somewhat shyly, that he once had, but didn't elaborate.

They went into the cabana and got a couple of towels and Mary

Liz took a bathing cap, but then changed her mind and threw it back in the box. No need to look like her grandmother. "Do you suppose Ashley knows how to play Frisbee?" she asked Jake.

"Everybody knows how to play Frisbee," he assured her.

Well, Ashley didn't. It scared her to death and all she would do in the beginning was run away, barking her head off, keeping her eyes on it so it wouldn't bite her.

And so Mary Liz waded out into the ocean and tossed a tennis ball about ten feet out. Ashley was off like a shot over the waves to get it. She was a great little swimmer. Mary Liz's favorite part, though, was seeing Ashley run in the shallow water, leaping and plunging along like a loping dolphin.

Mary Liz finally dived in, herself, getting her hair wet, and when Ashley swam toward her, she started backstroking out. Jake dived in and swam out to them in a few powerful strokes. If he couldn't get an acting job, Mary Liz thought, he could always be a double for Tarzan. He swam like an angel, the same way Bertie did; they were two men who clearly considered water a second home.

Jake threw the ball back to shore for the dog to fetch. Then he floated on his back the way Mary Liz was. "I know you're helping Mrs. Hoffman," Jake said, closing his eyes against the morning sun.

"You do?" she asked.

"Yes." He opened his eyes and raised his head to look at her. And then he turned toward Ashley, who was swimming back out to them. "Mrs. Hoffman made me promise to help you in any way I can."

"That's nice," she said, closing her eyes against the sun, too. It was hot already. "I appreciate it. Particularly since Bertie seems to have gone off the deep end. You don't happen to know why he and Wendy are so upset with me, do you?"

He didn't answer for a moment. Ashley had reached him and he was treading water, trying to wrest the ball from her. He finally got it and threw it back on the beach. "I think it has something to do with Mr. Glidden."

She opened one eye. "What?"

"I didn't say I could explain it. I just think it has something to do with him."

"Jake," Mary Liz said sternly, breaking her floating position to tread water, too. "Explain."

"Good girl," he told Ashley, petting the dog as she brought the ball back to him. He rose out of the water to throw it back on the beach. "I think we better go in. Look how low in the water she is."

He was right. Despite her spirit, the poor dog was exhausted. "She's been cooped up for six months in quarantine," Mary Liz said, doing a breaststroke in. "I had a leash on her last night and she seemed perfectly at home with it, which seemed rather odd to me for a dog who used to run free in the fields of Ireland."

"They would have had to keep her on a leash in quarantine," he agreed.

When they reached shore, Mary Liz turned to him. Water was streaming down Jake's gorgeous body and blue-green trunks. He slicked his hair back off his face with both hands and dropped them.

"Okay, Jake, time to explain. What about Glidden?"

"He's a major sleaze," he said. "Out in L.A. everybody knows it. People might have thought he was okay before Mr. Hoffman died, but not now, not after going after Mrs. Hoffman in court for what everyone knows isn't his. Bertie thinks you have something to do with him."

"That's ridiculous," she said. "And you can tell him that I said so. Come on, Ashley!" she snapped at the dog, who happily ignored her.

"Wait, Mary Liz—listen," Jake said. "Everyone's under a lot of stress here. Please don't write Bertie off. He's very protective of his mother."

"I hope to God he is," she said. "Because you can also tell him, Jake, that if he's up to anything on the estate that is *not* in his mother's best interests, I will see him behind bars. And that's a promise." She started to walk away, but stopped and turned around, pointing her finger at Jake. "And be sure to tell Wendy that goes for her, too. Perhaps doubly so."

Bill Pfeiffer called in the afternoon. "Those miscellaneous European expenses are turning out to be very interesting, Mary Liz. We've tracked the payouts to two people—a Yvonne Bonet in Paris and Elienne Bresseau, also in Paris, on behalf of a minor named Marc Bresseau, age ten."

Mary Liz sighed. She had been afraid of this. She was either going to have to send someone or go to Paris herself to check this out. If Yvonne and Elienne turned out to be mistresses of the late producer, which now it appeared they could be, and the boy was his, the child would have a claim on the estate—which meant Mary Liz would have to tell Aunt Nancy that her husband had been cheating on her and, worse yet, had started another family.

Or maybe she wouldn't have to tell her. Maybe Bill Pfeiffer could dress it up as something else, set up a trust for the child and say it was...

No, she'd have to tell Aunt Nancy. Or ask her mother to. Nancy would have to know if Alfred had fathered another child.

But maybe he hadn't! Maybe this was something else entirely. Maybe they were... *What?*

"What bothers me about this," Bill Pfeiffer was saying, "is that if this is what I suspect it is, that old Alfred had a couple of mistresses and a kid tucked away over there—"

Mary Liz felt her heart sink. So he had concluded the same thing she had.

"Braxer & Braxer might have hammered out a legal agreement between Alfred and these women to protect his estate, but Braxer & Braxer's never going to tell us about it. If anything, they'll use the knowledge as blackmail against the Hoffmans to settle their suit."

Mary Liz shrugged. "Well, I'll just have to hightail it over there and find out what's what."

"I wish you would," Bill said. "It's not going to be very good publicity for the Alfred Hoffman Memorial Foundation if it gets out that the husband Mrs. Hoffman is trying to lionize was cheating on her all these years."

"Bill, do me a favor, will you?" Mary Liz said. "Keep this under your hat until I personally find out what it's all about? There's no need to tell Dad yet. Not until we know for sure. My parents and Aunt Nancy are pretty good friends."

"I hear you," Bill assured her.

Mary Liz hung up. Her worst fear about inventorying the estate could be coming true. Digging into Alfred Hoffman's past could reveal a man far different than the one her aunt Nancy had been devoted to. For her godmother's sake, she hoped not.

She spent the rest of the afternoon on the porch, throwing the ball for Ashley and mulling things over. The only person she saw was the gardener, who remarked that it looked like rain.

13

The inventory of the estate was coming along nicely. Bill Pfeiffer's researcher called on Friday afternoon to say it looked as though at least one of Mary Liz's leads was turning up some hidden assets. It appeared that Alfred Hoffman had some kind of overseas investment, a large one they had not known about. The researcher just wanted to let her know the good news; he would work straight through the weekend to nail it down.

Mary Liz was delighted. If she ended up having to give Aunt Nancy any less than good news about her husband, it would be nice at least to turn up some more assets for the estate.

Someone knocked on the cottage front door around four o'clock and both Mary Liz and the dog were startled. Ashley went charging out of the office to the door, Mary Liz following.

"Oh, you silly dog!" Aunt Nancy was saying through the screen door. "Don't you even recognize me?"

Ashley stopped barking and pushed her nose against the screen.

"You're back!" Mary Liz called.

"Barely," Nancy said, coming in and smothering Ashley with hugs as if the dog were a small child. "Imagine, we left Manhattan at eleven-thirty and have only arrived now. Four and a half hours! The traffic gets worse and worse. I think I'm going to start flying." And then she grimaced slightly, probably thinking of her husband.

Aunt Nancy had not only come down to pick up Ashley (who, loyally, did not appear eager to leave the cottage, causing a pang in Mary Liz's heart), but also to beg Mary Liz to fill in at her social engagements that night: a cocktail and dinner benefit for the Red Cross in Wainscott, an East Hampton gallery showing to benefit the Strang Cancer Prevention Center and an art auction to benefit AIDS research in Southampton. "What I would suggest," she said, "is that you attend the gallery first at around six, the dinner at seven-fifteen and then get to the auction by nine. I've made notes on what I want you to bid on, and for how much."

Mary Liz inwardly groaned. How would she find all of these places? Who would she talk to? And an auction!

"Claire's going to pick you up at five forty-five," Nancy added. "This is, if you will do this for me." She waited.

What could Mary Liz say? "Sure, I'll do it for you."

"Thank you, darlin'. I hope you didn't have plans for tonight."

"No, not tonight." This was true. She and Sky were going out again tomorrow.

"It wouldn't be so important," her godmother said, "except that I've got a luncheon to throw tomorrow for the board of the hospice and I'm absolutely exhausted."

"No, it's fine," Mary Liz said, meaning it. "I like Claire a lot. I'm sure it will be fun."

With Ashley gone, the cottage felt impossibly lonely. Mary Liz checked the time and realized that if she hurried, she had time for a quick swim. She threw on a suit and Topsiders and hurried to the beach, where she found Wendy (looking gorgeous in a black bikini) and Bertie (looking gorgeous in one of his ten thousand pairs of bathing trunks) sitting in low beach chairs, drinking water out of squirt bottles, talking to Jeanine Hoffman, who was standing over them in a tennis dress (looking, of course, gorgeous, period). The threesome turned to look at her as she approached, making her feel hideously self-conscious.

"Hi," Mary Liz said.

"Hi," Jeanine said.

Bertie and Wendy only stared at her.

Mary Liz looked at Bertie. "Now what?"

Without a word, Bertie got up and walked toward the house. A second later, Wendy followed him.

Mary Liz looked at Jeanine. "And why are *you* looking at me so strangely? Will you please tell me what it is I've done?"

"I'm sorry," Jeanine said, lowering her head, "but I just can't get involved in this." And she walked away, too!

God forbid anyone would tell her what was going on. To heck with them, she thought. Since she had cleared the beach, she might as well get her swim.

She walked down to the waterline and kicked off her shoes. It was high tide, and the waves were breaking on shore. After feeling the water for a moment, she dashed between the waves, and dived in. Cold. No, refreshing. She loved how the water felt streaming over her scalp, her arms, her legs, all of her getting wet, cleansed, after sitting around in the office all day. Surfacing, she wished she had brought a cap, for her hair was all over the place, and, better yet, goggles, so she could do some good old-fashioned Australian crawl without salt burning her eyes. Well, there was always the backstroke, which she resorted to so she could see and still feel the pull of her muscles.

How she loved to swim outside! Lake Michigan had a short season, but back in Illinois she took complete advantage of it on weekends, switching to a pool at her health club in Chicago to do laps in the fall, winter and spring.

Ironically, Lake Michigan often had bigger waves than she'd encountered here.

She swam a ways out and floated, resting, basking in the sunshine, acutely aware that she was not enjoying the swim the way she should be.

Why were Bertie and Wendy so angry with her?

"This Hampton's outfit is so old," Claire MacClendon told Mary Liz as they bounced around in Claire's old wood-paneled Wagoneer, "I'm thinking about donating it to the historical society." She was wearing a soft, white cotton shift, with pretty pastel designs quilted into it. The shift had a square cut in the front, which showed Claire's ample breasts to advantage, whose purpose, Claire explained, was to draw attention away from her ampleness of another kind. "Actually," she said a moment later, shifting gears, "in a couple more years, I can donate me, the car *and* the dress."

"I think all three are classic and lovely," Mary Liz told her. And it was true. Claire would always be beautiful, no matter how much weight she gained, the dress was simple and expensive and becoming, and the Wagoneer, well, what could one say except how classic could it be to have a top-of-the-line, four-wheel-drive vehicle over twenty years old and in mint condition? The three put together were very much Claire: durable, lovely and top-drawer.

"I don't usually go to a lot of parties, as you know," Claire continued, "but tonight I made an exception. The artist whose work is being shown is a friend, I've been a tremendous supporter of the Red Cross over the years and I donated a painting to the AIDS auction so I'm curious about how it goes. It's a very different painting than what I normally do, but I've worked like a slave on it and I think it's good."

On Aunt Nancy's behalf, Mary Liz was supposed to make an

opening bid of five thousand dollars for Claire's painting and go as high as fifteen thousand. Mary Liz was trying to figure out Claire's pay scale as an artist. Claire said it took her at least a month to find a subject, sketch it out, paint it and revise. So if she sold one painting a month, that would be—picking the higher end of the range Nancy gave her—in ten months, a hundred fifty thousand a year. Claire owned her house, studio and car outright, and she knew Henry had paid for all of the girls' education expenses.

For an abandoned housewife and mother of two, Claire had done pretty darn wonderfully.

The East Hampton gallery where they were going first was just off Main Street. They were early and could still park nearby. Later, Claire said, it would be a mob scene. It was not an overly large studio, just a square, wood-floored room, about thirty feet by fifteen, with a small office and bathroom off the back. The painter whose work was on display here, a woman named Syd Lyberg, came flying across the gallery to embrace Claire. Claire introduced Mary Liz, and Syd brought them over to the refreshment table in the corner, pushing a plastic glass of white wine into each of their hands.

Syd Lyberg painted in acrylics, and while there were two still lifes in the show, she preferred landscapes. The glitch was (in Mary Liz's opinion) that she used only neon colors, so that suns were blinding, trees were fluorescent and the whole scene was like something off a sixties acid-rock album. The price? On a modestly outrageous painting, eighteen by twenty-four, fourteen hundred dollars. "Ten percent of the proceeds go to the Strang Cancer Prevention Center," a voice smoothly whispered in her ear. He introduced himself as the gallery owner.

"And what about the proceeds of the tickets?" Mary Liz asked. The one Nancy had given her had a price of twenty-five dollars printed on it.

"After expenses, all of it goes to the clinic."

Mary Liz took another sip of her wine—which was excellent. Too excellent for a fund-raiser, she thought. She thought the point was to raise money, not spend it on expensive wines.

When Claire came over to her, Mary Liz whispered, "Can I just make a straight donation to the clinic? I mean, and not offend your friend?"

"Of course. She won't be offended. She was a protégée of mine, you know, way back when." Claire leaned closer. "She does her real work under another name. She's just cashing in on a trend with this junk, to support herself with the other. It's like ghostwriting. The gallery owner tells her what to paint, sometimes with specific buyers and color schemes in mind."

"What's her other name?"

"Her other name is her real name—Michelle White."

Mary Liz's eyebrows soared. "From Michelle White to Syd Lyberg?"

Claire shrugged. "Whatever works. She's got to live."

Mary Liz wrote out a personal check to Strang Clinic, hoping this would make up for the expensive wine and cheese they were serving, and they climbed back into the Wagoneer for the next "do," the Red Cross cocktail and dinner benefit in Wainscott, the tiny village just before Bridgehampton. They turned onto a back road, winding around and around, finally emerging at a charming farmhouse where the lawn had been set up for a party. And some party: there were three yellow-and-white-striped open-air tents, with uniformed caterers with silver trays bearing food and drink. Under one tent was a five-piece musical ensemble and dance floor; another held the next long, lavish tables of food being prepared and served by uniformed attendants, and in the last, there was a series of gorgeously appointed dining tables, all with flowers and candles, linen, crystal and real silver.

No way was Mary Liz writing a check here to make up for the expenses.

Thank heavens for Claire. She knew half the people there and introduced Mary Liz simply as—shockingly—her friend Mary Liz Scott, explaining only to their host and hostess that Mary Liz was Nancy Hoffman's goddaughter and was substituting for Nancy tonight, who was not feeling well. No, nothing serious.

Mary met the novelist Kurt Vonnegut, and Jill Krementz, the photographer. (Of course, she met "normal" socialites, too, whose names meant nothing to her.) She met the journalist and biographer, Shana Alexander, and then Rona Jaffe, the author of two of her favorite novels, *Class Reunion* and *The Cousins*. She met the grande dame of New York radio, Joan Hamburg. They were all very nice to her, although they had no idea who the heck she was except that she was a friend of Claire's. And then, while standing around with Claire, who was chatting with the national-news anchor, Peter Jennings, and a local New York anchor, Bill Beutel, Mary Liz nearly choked because of someone she saw.

"Oh my God," she said. "Claire," she whispered, grabbing her arm, "you don't know Lauren Bacall, do you?"

Claire smiled and led Mary Liz over to introduce her to the legendary actress. "I just—I don't even know what to say to you," Mary Liz stammered, "except that you're wonderful and I love you. Your work, I mean—no, fact is, I love you."

The actress looked at Claire and winked. "You should bring more of your friends more often, Claire."

When they moved away, Claire was laughing at her. "Imagine, a big shot like you gushing and gawking like a schoolgirl."

"Come on, it's Lauren Bacall, for heaven's sake! Sue me, I'm human." She smiled. "Wait until I tell my mother—"

There was some murmuring from behind them and Mary Liz suddenly felt two hands on her shoulders. "You told me you were staying in today," Sasha Reinhart growled in her ear.

"Sasha," Mary Liz said, whirling, "I swear, I'm only here because Aunt Nancy asked me to fill in for her at the last minute. She wasn't feeling up to it."

The diva crossed her arms over her chest, squinting at her, as if to decide whether or not to accept this explanation.

"It's true, Sasha," Claire said, stepping forward. "Otherwise there's no way Mary Liz would have come. And don't you look beautiful," she added.

The diva smiled, pleased, and touched at her hair. Tonight it was swept up, with a big white lily in it, making Mary Liz think of Billie Holiday (which, she guessed, was the point).

"And what do you think of her dress?" Rachelle Zaratan asked, stepping up to the group. She herself was very demurely dressed in a white silk shift and sandals. "Though admittedly, it takes a sensational body to wear it."

"Why, thank you, Rachelle," the diva said. She was decked out in a little black number, cotton, a very short sleeveless dress with an intricate design cut out of the top that showed just about everything of Sasha's except the nipples of her breasts.

Mary Liz and Claire murmured how great they thought the dress was, and Claire, when no one else was looking, rolled her eyes at Mary Liz as much as to say, Can you imagine ever wanting to wear such a thing?

"So when are you coming over?" Sasha demanded. "You're right next door, a whole week has gone by and not a peep."

"What she means is," Rachelle added, "what is the matter with you? The whole world wants to be with her except you."

The diva made a face at her friend. "We're great friends, Mary Liz and me."

Mary Liz nodded. "Yes, that's true."

"And Rachelle is jealous," the diva explained to Mary Liz. "And because Rachelle doesn't have any friends, she always tells me she's my only *true* friend."

"Sasha!" the designer protested.

"Well, it's true, you don't have any friends. You don't have any time! All this woman does is work. If you didn't need me to wear your clothes all the time, Rachelle, I'd never see you."

"Sasha." This time the designer sounded truly hurt.

The diva frowned. "You silly dope, I love you!" she said, handing her glass to Mary Liz so she could hug the designer.

A photographer snapped a picture and Sasha's temper flared. "Oh, come on! If you're going to sneak a shot, you get Rachelle, Mary Liz Scott and Claire MacClendon all together in it! Come on, girls." And Sasha lined them up, sliding her arm around Rachelle and Mary Liz, Claire standing on the end. "Mary Liz, put those glasses down or everyone will say you're a drunk."

The photographer took the picture, apologized to Mary Liz but asked her who she was. "No one," Mary Liz said cheerfully.

"She's a rich investment banker who retired at thirty- two!" Sasha said. "And she's Nancy Hoffman's goddaughter, so you better print that picture if you know what's good for you."

Their hostess then arrived to drag Sasha off somewhere. Claire, Mary Liz was somewhat shocked to find, had moved off to the side to talk to her former husband, Henry McClendon. She didn't see the new wife, Cindy Claydon, anywhere around.

"So," Rachelle said to her, "I hear you'll be working with Sasha this fall."

Mary Liz brought her head back. "Excuse me?"

"On the movie. Herb Glidden just told me you're going to be a producer and handle the financing."

"Herb told you *what?*"

"That you're working for him," the designer said. "He's right over there, just flew in." She pointed.

Sure enough, Herbert Glidden was standing near the bar, talking to Julius and Jeanine Hoffman.

Well, well, well, this was turning out to be quite a night. Mary Liz looked around for Claire, but she was still engrossed in her conversation with her ex.

"I'll go with you to talk to him," Rachelle offered. "I'm not scared of him."

Mary Liz looked at her. "I'm not scared of talking to Glidden, I'm scared I'll kill him in front of too many witnesses."

"You and everyone else," Rachelle said, sipping her drink. "My Charles hates his guts, but with Alfred gone, Herb is a very unpredictable man—and no one wants to be on his bad side."

"But *why*, Rachelle?" Mary Liz said. "Your husband doesn't work with him or anything. I mean, you guys don't even live in L.A., do you?"

"True. We only know him from here. Through Alfred."

"Then why do you have anything to do with him? I don't get it."

Mary Liz wasn't kidding. She had combed the profiles of Alfred's poker group—the same men who had some relationship going with Glidden that no one would admit to—and couldn't find anything to link them, not education, not professions, not colleagues.

Charles Kahn: NYU, CEO, Rachelle Zaratan Clothing.

Henry MacClendon: Cornell, chairman, Henry MacClendon Architects.

Claude Lemieux: Cambridge, publisher and owner, *Je Ne Sais Quoi*.

Randolph Vandergilden: Princeton, vintner, Eastern Winery.

Sinclair "Buck" Buckley: two years UCLA, Founder, East End Country Club.

All they had in common was East Hampton and knowing Alfred Hoffman. As for Julius Hoffman, his link to Glidden was long and solid at Howland Films—and now they were supposed to be in competition, with both men suing Aunt Nancy for control of the company.

Rachelle was shaking her head at Mary Liz. "In case you have not noticed, these men—our men—are not the most secure in the world. My Charles works for me, Vanessa has all the money in the Buckley household, Claude has a magazine, but only through the break of marrying a magazine magnate's daughter—namely, Isabel—Randolph's just an old alkie who ran through his inheritance and is trying to hang on to a winery that he doesn't even own." She flipped her head in Claire's direction. "And Henry, that fool, still doesn't get it—what Claire inspired in him. He ran off with that young Cindy and now he's finished. Hasn't had an original thought since." She looked at Mary Liz. "You do know that, don't you? That Henry has not designed anything since he left Claire?"

"I had no idea."

"No, and now he's just an old man trying to be young again, riding on his assistant's skills to imitate his old and best work." She lofted her eyebrows, eyes still on Henry. "He must know it by now. And he must be desperate for Claire."

Mary Liz finished the last of her seltzer. "But they all seem like very capable, very nice men. Like your husband."

"Yes, and perhaps in way over their heads," Rachelle said, staring off at the sunset. She brought her eyes back. "You see, Alfred made them feel—hopeful. Inspired. After they watched his ascent, saw the wives, the business setbacks, the new starts and the reign of undeniable success that was genuinely his." She smiled. "But Herb, he makes them feel insecure. I know he does Charles. Terribly so. Because Herb does his best to make them feel insecure, constantly reminding them of painful things, mistakes, situations. And that, Mary Liz, is what makes Herb Glidden feel like a big man." She looked over at him and narrowed her eyes. "He is a goddamn son of a bitch." The latter was said in a good old New Yorkese, and the designer did not sound vaguely foreign anymore at all.

"Then why do you continue to socialize with him? Why don't you cut him dead?"

Rachelle smiled slightly. "Because this is East Hampton, Mary Liz, and here you keep your friends close, but your enemies closer. We've all come too far to let a loose cannon take shots at us."

Glidden had spotted Mary Liz and was waving.

"Go on, go pet the shark," Rachelle said.

Mary Liz walked over, swiping a glass of white wine off a waiter's tray and taking a gulp on the way. Glidden kissed her on the cheek and took her arm. Julius smiled mysteriously and nodded, while Jeanine simply looked pained.

"I hear you're going to work for Herb," Julius said. In that moment, Mary Liz realized that Julius's smile had been promising no less than murder.

"Don't count on it," Mary Liz said sharply, turning to Glidden.

"So this is what you do? Tell people I'm working for you, when I haven't even interviewed for a job yet?"

"What?" Jeanine Hoffman said, looking suddenly alert.

"It's just a matter of working out the details, Mary Liz," Glidden assured her, smiling.

"Working out the details? How about telling me what the job is?" Mary Liz turned to the Hoffmans. "I'm sorry, but he's seriously misled you."

"So you're *not* working for Herb?" Jeanine asked. She whirled angrily. "Herb, what the hell is going on? Why did you tell—"

"Monday," he said firmly, shutting Jeanine up. "I will explain everything to you on Monday."

Amazing. With one word, *"Monday,"* he was supposed to stop them all from discussing the fact that he had lied to them. What was weirder still was that Mary Liz didn't want to argue here, either. Glidden was obviously playing some kind of hand and she wanted time to figure out what was in it.

Glidden had turned to Mary Liz. "I'd like you to meet my son." A gawky young man, dark-haired, smiling shyly, stepped forward. "Alex, I want you to meet Mary Liz Scott. She was Uncle Alfred's goddaughter."

This was not true. While Aunt Nancy was her godmother, Mary Liz had never even met Alfred, not even when she was a baby.

Alex shook her hand; he was nervous, sweating.

"Alex is finishing his MBA at Stanford," his father explained.

"Great school," Mary Liz complimented him. "What are you interested in?"

"Movies, of course!" his father said, laughing.

Mary Liz looked at Alex and raised her eyebrows. "Movies?"

"Business side," Alex mumbled, looking down into the beer in his hand.

Poor kid. He was a social retard. Well, if his father was half as influential as Rachelle said, it wouldn't matter. Everyone would be too scared to trip the kid up.

"Here for the weekend?" Mary Liz asked him.

He nodded. "Yeah."

"Play tennis?"

He nodded. "Yeah."

Mary Liz looked at Jeanine Hoffman. "Any chance you and a partner would like to take on Alex and me?"

Alex seemed shocked—and grateful—when Mary Liz shot down Herb's immediate suggestion that they play with him instead of his son. "Come on, Dad," Mary Liz told him, "let Alex have an hour off."

"Claude and I were going to play tomorrow morning anyway," Jeanine said. "Around nine-thirty."

Mary Liz looked to Alex. He nodded. "It's done then," she said. Good. Maybe she could learn something about Glidden from the kid.

The group chatted on, but Mary Liz and Alex merely listened, and because he did, Mary Liz's opinion of him began to change. In a world where everyone was talking all the time, the ability to listen could serve him well. It had served Mary Liz well in meetings within her firm. If nothing else, people respected the quiet ones, assuming—and correctly in her case—that if she had something worthwhile to say, she would say it, and so when she did open her mouth, she commanded attention. (This was only after two years of mistakes, speaking up when one of her colleagues cited incorrect information—which happened all the time—which would sidetrack the meeting while obstinate Mary Liz refused to let the meeting continue until everyone understood that what he or she had said was wrong and why. This, in turn, had sidetracked her career in the beginning, labeling her as "not a team player.")

Watching and listening to this group in front of her was beginning to amaze Mary Liz. She thought about Herb Glidden's wife, unable to leave their home in L.A. She thought about Julius pawing her breast at that cocktail party. She thought about Jeanine having been Glidden's mistress before she married Julius. Only Rachelle Zaratan (who had come up to join them), the New Yorker with the fake foreign accent, seemed to be without secrets. She'd had the talent and drive and the all-consuming desire to become a famous and successful designer, and her friendship with Sasha Reinhart was based on the fact they were two highly creative, high-powered women somewhat trapped by their own success.

Claire came over to Mary Liz to plead sudden exhaustion. She didn't want to eat, she didn't want to go to the auction, she simply wanted to go home.

"Hello, Claire," Herb Glidden said.

"Hello," she said without looking at him.

"Talking to the ex, huh?" Herb continued. "I wouldn't if I were you. Henry's not very pleasant these days. I suppose it's the baby coming and all."

"Drop dead, Herb," Claire said matter-of-factly.

Mary Liz thought of the exchange she had overheard between Henry MacClendon and Glidden at the Amagansett party two weeks ago, about Henry declaring there would be no more invoices and then, evidently, caving in to whatever it was that Glidden had wanted. She still couldn't figure out what an invoice would be for. Henry was not, she had found out since then, doing any work for him—or for Howland Films.

"Is that young Alex I see?" Claire asked, pushing past the father to shake hands with the son. "Nice to see you."

"Hi," Alex said stiffly.

"Excuse us, please," Claire said then, pulling Mary Liz away. "Listen, Mary Liz, I'm sorry, but I really don't feel terribly well. I want to go home."

"What a wonderful surprise," a voice suddenly said from next to Mary Liz.

She turned and was surprised to see Bill Pfeiffer. "Hi," Mary Liz said, happy that *she* finally knew someone the others didn't.

"It's Claire, isn't it?" Bill said, reaching past Mary Liz to offer his hand to her.

"Yes. I'm sorry—" the painter faltered.

"Bill Pfeiffer. I met you with Mary Liz at the leukemia benefit—the carnival?"

"Ah! Yes! Your daughter, Jenny, I remember," Claire said, smiling.

"Are you having a good time?" he asked Mary Liz.

"Actually," Claire said, "I drove Mary Liz here, and I was just explaining to her that I'm not feeling terribly well."

"That's too bad," he said.

"You're not by chance going to the art auction in Southampton tonight, are you?" Claire asked him.

"No, I'm afraid not. I've got to show up at a friend's thing in Bridgehampton." He checked his watch. "Soon."

"Bridgehampton. It's not the pirate party, is it?" the artist asked.

"As a matter of fact, it is."

"Roscoe's?"

He beamed. "Yeah!"

"Well, I live right down the road from Roscoe," Claire said. "Do you think it might be possible to give me a ride home when you're ready to go?" She turned to Mary Liz. "That way, you can take my car to the auction. And take it home."

Before Mary Liz agreed, Bill announced he was ready to go now. Claire scribbled directions to the auction on a cocktail napkin and handed her the keys to the Wagoneer. "I'll pick the car up tomorrow. Sorry to desert you."

"Be talking to you!" Bill said, leading Claire from the party.

Sasha came scooting over. "Are you going somewhere?"

"Oh, the art auction in Southampton." She held up the napkin. "I've got directions."

"The AIDS thing. Rachelle—Rachelle?" She looked over her shoulder, sighed heavily, went over to grab the designer and drag her over. "Do you want to go to the art auction in Southampton?"

"The AIDS thing? Sure, but Charles won't and we're in his car, remember."

"I've got a car," Mary Liz said. "A cool car, we can go anywhere, it's an old Wagoneer."

"Then it's settled," Sasha said. "Tell Charles we're outta here, it's ladies' night out."

The diva and the designer were very funny and excellent company. The only drawback was their fame, particularly Sasha's, and although the staid old-time residents of Southampton (there was formidable high society in this town) would scarcely look at her for fear of invading her privacy, the tourists and vacationers happily mobbed her for an autograph in the municipal lot where they parked. The mob followed them right up to the doors of the art museum where, at last, Sasha signed a couple more autographs and left them. Tickets for the auction were two hundred and fifty dollars each; Mary Liz had Nancy's, and gave Rachelle Claire's ticket, and the benefit people took one look at Sasha and said she was happily welcome for nothing.

There was wine and cheese and coffee and tea available on a table inside, and there were folding chairs set up in the front gallery. The auction block was on the stair under the archway leading into the second gallery, and the bidding had just begun. Mary Liz grabbed a napkin and some cheese (for she hadn't yet eaten dinner), and as they took seats in the back, Sasha whispered did Mary Liz know how much fat was in that piece of cheese.

When a "Syd Lyberg" painting came up for sale—whose show Mary Liz had just attended earlier in the evening—Mary Liz nearly burst out laughing, particularly when Sasha proceeded to say something about the neon of life and bid a thousand dollars for it. It ended up selling for fifteen hundred, and the diva let it go, saying she didn't need the orange in it to match her "orange room" in Malibu that much.

It was a lively little auction, and there were two assistants sitting at tables on either side of the auctioneer taking telephone bids. Claire's painting was the last in the catalog—clearly the high point of the auction—and as they sat through the sale of the other paintings and a couple of sculptures, Mary Liz was often amazed at what people paid for what looked to her to be, well, half-assed efforts. (But that's what they got for charity auctions, didn't they? Donations of the least saleable works of a known artist?)

When it came time for Claire's painting to be placed on the easel, however, Mary Liz felt her heart skip, and heard others in the crowd murmur appreciatively. This painting was no toss-away for charity. It was not overly large, perhaps eighteen by twenty-four, but completely took over the room. It was a dramatic seascape, at dusk, just as a thunderstorm was lifting. It was dark, but charged with energy, and very, very beautiful. It was much like a person's soul, Mary Liz thought, when one felt as though the darkness and fury and pain would go on forever, but then suddenly, when it lifted, even just for a moment, the faith returned that the sun would come up again.

Glancing over at Rachelle and Sasha, she could see they were affected by the work, too.

"This is the last painting," the auctioneer said, "and may I tactfully suggest, the most remarkable of the group. As many of you must know, Claire MacClendon is a local artist, living full-time in Bridgehampton for the past four years. Prior to that, Ms. MacClendon divided her time between Manhattan and Bridgehampton, and credits living in New York with inspiring an even greater awe of the land and sea than she might otherwise possess."

Sasha was nodding.

"Her preference is for watercolor, but, as you can see, for this particular painting she chose oils, combining the detail of Turner with the romantic sweep of the Hudson Valley School, using light and reflection—and the lack of light—to full advantage. This is truly a rare painting, the only one of its kind the painter has ever attempted.

And, as you can see for yourselves, it is a most excellent one. Ms. MacClendon has had showings of her work in New York City, Los Angeles, San Francisco, Washington, D.C., and London, England, and has been profiled in numerous periodicals, including *Redbook*, *Je Ne Sais Quoi*, and *Town and Country*. We would like to open the bidding at three thousand dollars."

The three thousand jumped to four, and Mary Liz found herself calling, "Five!," startling her companions. Sasha bid six. Rachelle six-five. A man in the front bid seven, Mary Liz eight, a woman on the telephone signaled nine, Sasha ten, Rachelle jumped to twelve, and Mary Liz to fifteen, causing Sasha to elbow her. "Slow down! Slow down!" she hissed.

The man in the front went to sixteen, another man, in the middle of the group, went to eighteen, the woman on the phone to twenty. After a slight pause, Rachelle went to twenty-one, and there was silence.

"Do I hear twenty-two?" the auctioneer asked.

"Twenty-five," a voice boomed from behind them. The three women turned and found Herbert Glidden smiling at them.

Sasha raised her hand. "Twenty-seven, five."

"Thirty," Glidden said.

Now the entire room was murmuring.

"I have thirty thousand dollars for the one-of-a-kind Claire MacClendon painting," the auctioneer said, beaming. "Going once, going twice—"

"Thirty-five thousand!" Mary Liz called, standing up and feeling very close to throwing up. She looked back at Glidden, who smiled, cocking his head to the side, thinking. Then he looked at the auctioneer and shook his head.

"I have thirty-five thousand dollars." Silence. "Going once, going twice..."

Everyone held their breath.

"Sold," the auctioneer said, slamming the gavel down and pointing to Mary Liz, "to the lady in the back row."

Everybody turned around to look at her and Mary Liz smiled. She couldn't help it. There was no way in hell she would have let Herbert Glidden have that painting.

14

The phone rang the next morning at eight o'clock and Mary Liz fumbled to find it. "I'll honor your bid, Mary Liz, darlin', but for heaven's sake, I said to go up to fifteen," said the voice. "Not that I don't think a painting of Claire's is worth thirty-five..."

"The painting's for me, Aunt Nancy," Mary Liz croaked, reaching for the squirt bottle of water she had the sense to bring to bed last night. "I bought it for me." And then Sasha and Rachelle had "bought" her a million drinks at Sasha's house. The last thing she remembered was doing the fox-trot on the front lawn with Riff, Sasha's bodyguard, while Sasha sang "I Could Have Danced All Night," and Rachelle banged out an accompaniment with the handle of a croquet mallet on the metal fuel-holder of a lighted lawn torch.

No, that wasn't all; she remembered diving into Sasha's pool with her clothes on, a memory confirmed by the fact that the back of her head was still damp and her hair reeked of chlorine.

"*You* bought it!" her godmother exclaimed.

"I had to have it," Mary Liz said. "It's a remarkable work, Aunt Nancy, it's not like anything she's done. And it, well, I just really loved it. I saw it and felt deeply moved, knew I had to have it, and then Herbert Glidden joined the bidding and I couldn't bear to let him have it."

Her godmother laughed and laughed. "Oh, how wonderful! Though you may have to wait until you're sixty to make your money back on it."

"I really don't care," Mary Liz said, blinking at the ceiling. "It's mine now. And it will always be in my family. Always. Wait until you see it."

Wait until I *see it,* she thought. *Thirty-five thousand dollars!* Good grief. She was starting to live and act as if she belonged in East Hampton.

After a glass of Alka-Seltzer, a shower and a glass of milk, Mary Liz tried to slip on a tennis dress that had been hanging in her closet in

Chicago for years. It was a no go. She could barely get it down over her hips, and when she finally did, looked like a sweet Italian sausage waiting to be skinned and cooked. She rustled around in the bureau and came up with her white gym shorts and a white T-shirt (she had been trained too well as a child, she still felt compelled to wear white on the courts), put on some cross-trainers and walked across the front lawn to the tennis court.

It had been so long since she had played regularly, the oversize racquets still looked mightily stupid to Mary Liz. Like clown shoes. Nonetheless, in the shed she found the Head racquet— 4 1/2 grip— she had used the other day, grabbed a bucket of balls, opened the gate and went out onto the court. It was green clay, beautifully maintained by Jake (who had to sweep, water and roll it almost every day), and was surrounded by evergreen trees as a natural windbreak. The Hoffmans had a tennis cannon under cover, but also a low backboard on one end of the court. This was what Mary Liz headed for to warm up.

Oversize racquets sure looked stupid, but there was no question why the sport had turned to them. The "forgiveness" area in a racquet this size had to be twice as large as in the old. In other words, with one of her old racquets she would miss-hit a ball, but this racquet would "forgive" it and make it a winner.

They still looked like clown shoes to her, though.

She was sweating already. She took a white hair band out of her pocket and pushed her hair back. Then she carried the bucket of balls to the end of the court and started belting serves. This had always been the best part of her game, the movement of bringing the racquet up and over the ball feeling as familiar as riding a bike.

Not bad, she thought.

"Want me to hit a few with you?" It was Jake, in shorts and a T-shirt and low Converse tennis shoes.

"Thanks, but no thanks, Jake, I'm in a weakened condition this morning. I was just going to drink ten gallons of water and rest until my game arrives." She walked around the net and started bouncing balls up with her racket and putting them in the bucket. Jake was walking the court, surveying it, checking the net. Then he went to the shed to get a line sweeper and came back out to wheel the clay off the tapes that defined the boundaries. Mary Liz went over to the water cooler under the shed awning and began drinking water.

She felt like death. If dehydration didn't get her this morning, the pounding in her head would.

Minutes later Jeanine appeared with Claude Lemieux. Jeanine was in a white tennis dress, he was in pale blue shorts and a yellow shirt. While she went off to talk to Jake about the court, Mary Liz chatted with Claude about the weather. "It's supposed to rain this evening," he told her. "And Isabel, my wife, wants to trot her little dog around in a parade."

His French accent was very slight, but nonetheless there, making the magazine publisher sound very cultured and worldly, which Mary Liz did not doubt for a moment he was.

"It's not the ARF benefit, is it?" she asked him. "The parade? At the airport?"

He smiled. He was not an overtly good-looking man, and a bit on the small side, wiry, but there was something very attractive about him. Probably the accent and worldliness again, as if he were far too polite to make Mary Liz feel like anything but the smartest and most attractive woman in the world.

Mary Liz thought of what Rachelle Zaratan had said last night about Alfred Hoffman's poker group, of which Claude had been a member, and how insecure they all were. It was extremely hard for Mary Liz to imagine the man in front of her ever feeling that way, even if he had gotten his professional start through his wife's father.

"Yes," he told her. "The ARF *do*." He shook his head, smiling up at the sky, and then brought his head down to look at Mary Liz. "She made a costume. The dog is going to be a ballerina."

"What kind of dog?"

"Toy poodle. Spoiled rotten."

"Well, the court's all set," Jeanine said, coming back to them. "All we need is Alan."

"Alex," Mary Liz corrected.

"And what ever possessed you to invite him?" Jeanine asked her. "And basically telling Herb to shove it—"

"She did?" Claude asked, openly surprised.

"Well, not like that," Mary Liz protested.

"You should have been there, Claude," Jeanine told him, smiling. "Mary Liz asked Alex to play, and then asked if I could get a partner, and Herb immediately invited himself—you know how he is—and Mary Liz just looked at him and said, 'No. I want to play tennis with your son. Come on, *Dad,* give the kid an hour off.'" She laughed at the memory.

Claude smiled during this rendition, but then excused himself to get some water.

"Look at that," Jeanine marveled under her breath, eyes on Claude. "We've made him nervous. I wonder what Herb's got on him."

"What makes you say that?"

"Because he's scared of him. *Look* at Claude. I bet he wishes like hell he wasn't playing tennis with you—she who dared to defy Herb publicly."

"Oh, that's ridiculous," Mary Liz said.

"So you think," Jeanine said, turning to face her. "Didn't yesterday teach you anything? And by the way, I'm sorry about walking out on you on the beach yesterday, but after Julius told me that you were working for Herb, I just felt sick."

"But I'm not!"

"I know that now, Mary Liz, but yesterday he very clearly and deliberately told Julius you were working for him."

"Jeanine, the man is a liar. It's true I have a meeting with him on Monday, to discuss the possibility of—"

"Ah, that must be it," Jeanine said quietly. "Just because he wants you, he's already telling everybody you're coming. That sounds like him." She thought for a moment and then looked at Mary Liz again. "Either he's confident of hiring you—"

Mary Liz raised her hand in oath. "I swear to you, I am not going to work for Herbert Glidden. I only wanted to hear what he had to say. I didn't even know what the job was!"

"But ultimately that wouldn't matter, would it?" Jeanine said. "So long as everyone perceived you as changing sides, going from helping Nancy on the estate to working for the guy who is suing her."

"Julius is suing her, as well," Mary Liz pointed out.

"And that's why Julius was so angry when Herb told him you were working for him. It's one thing to stand up for what you think is right in business, but screwing Nancy when she's down is another."

Mary Liz was shaking her head. "This whole thing is absolutely outrageous." She glanced over at Claude, who, for an awfully long time now, had been reading a notice posted on the bulletin board of the shed.

Jeanine cleared her throat. "Just understand this, Mary Liz," she said, practically pointing her finger in Mary Liz's face, "Nancy is Julius's friend. More than friend. She's family. Really. Truly. If and when Julius gets Howland Films, Nancy and the others will get every cent they're entitled to. All he wants is the chance to run it, and considering that his father made him president of it, that doesn't seem like too much to ask. And it was Nancy who prompted the suit, telling Julius she might want Bertie to run Howland—"

"Bertie!"

"Exactly," Jeanine said.

"But she only said that because Julius sued her!" Mary Liz said.

"But Julius only sued her because he knew she might not let him run the company!"

"Girls, girls, please," a voice said, coming up the path. "No fighting over who gets to play with me."

Jeanine stiffened immediately and all three of them looked over. It was not Alex, but Herb Glidden coming up the trail, dressed in a black-and-white-swirled tennis shirt, black shorts, white socks and tennis shoes. "Alex couldn't come, Jeannie, so you're going to have to refigure the odds—"

Mary Liz noticed how Jeanine flinched when he called her Jeannie.

"—because Mary Liz and I are unbeatable," he finished.

"The only problem is," Mary Liz said, "that I'm not playing with you. I'm playing with Claude."

"What a mistake," Glidden said. "Five bucks says we'll wipe the court with you."

They walked onto the court and without much ado, began to play. Mary Liz was so angry with the man she could scarcely concentrate, but she was determined to keep her temper in check until they met on Monday, at which time she hoped to understand the other, bigger game he was playing.

She and Claude were beaten 6–3, 6–4, and Mary Liz had to cough up five dollars to Glidden, which she promised to give him at their meeting on Monday.

"Oh," he said, amused, "so you're still coming, are you?"

"Of course I'm coming," she replied, "because you have a *lot* of explaining to do."

He didn't bat an eyelash. He only smiled and said he was looking forward to it.

Mary Liz went back to the cottage, showered and passed out on her bed until nearly two o'clock, when she was awakened by knocking on the front door. She slipped on a robe and made her way out to answer it.

She was feeling much better.

"Bertie," she said, looking out. "And Wendy. What a surprise. Please come in. I was just getting up from a nap. Have a seat. What can I get you? If I don't eat something, I'm going to expire."

Miraculously, Bertie had a shirt on over his bathing trunks this afternoon. He threw himself down on the couch, and Wendy sat in one of the wingback chairs. "I heard you got smashed over at Sasha's last night," Bertie said.

Rather than argue, Mary Liz merely said yes. She asked them again if she could get them something and they finally accepted: seltzer for Wendy, orange juice for Bertie, seltzer and a banana for herself. Once they were all settled, Mary Liz said, "I hope you're here to tell me why you loathe and despise me."

Wendy and Bertie exchanged looks.

"I know I've been a bit secretive here in the cottage, and perhaps even a bit unfriendly when I felt you were snooping—" Mary Liz began.

"Tell me about it," Bertie said.

"But that's hardly reason to declare war against me," Mary Liz finished. "That is, unless you were about to make a play against the estate yourself. In that case, I can see why the two of you would want me out of the way."

Bertie and Wendy looked genuinely shocked. *"Me?"* Bertie finally managed to say, struggling to his feet. *"You're* the one working for Herb Glidden, and I ought to rip your fucking throat out."

Mary Liz nearly choked on her banana. Managing to swallow, she picked up her glass of seltzer to wash the rest down. "Oh, so that's it."

"Yes, that's it!" Bertie shouted. "Jeanine told me yesterday. And Julius got it straight from Herb."

Mary Liz was shaking her head. "But it's not true—"

"Don't try to deny it, Mary Liz," Wendy said accusingly. "We *know* about your secret meetings with him."

"My *what?*"

"In your cottage, at the airport, and then you saw him last night, and again this morning. And you have a secret meeting scheduled at his house on Monday—"

"Secret meeting? There's no secret meeting!"

"How dare you do this to my mother!" Bertie shrieked, threatening to jump her.

Now Mary Liz jumped up. "I don't know what you're talking about, Bertie!"

"How many files have you destroyed in that shredder in your office?" Wendy demanded.

"How much is he paying you?" Bertie demanded.

Mary Liz was dumbfounded. Finally she found her voice. "Look, Bertie, the only person I am working for is your mother."

"Yeah, right." He laughed a bitter little laugh. "And Mother is not terribly pleased with you right now. She's talking about having you arrested."

"Don't be ridiculous, Bertie. I only just talked to her this morning."

"Right," Bertie said. "Before Herb stopped by after your tennis game to let Mother in on the score."

Mary Liz just didn't get it. "Will someone *please* tell me what is going on?"

"He told Mother you were working for him and that she might as well settle the suit, because he has everything he needs now to win the suit—and he got what he needed from you!"

"That's a complete and total lie!" Mary Liz shouted, chucking her banana peel down on the magazine.

"Mother's so hysterical, she's over at Claire's," Bertie said, sounding near tears.

"That's it! I'm going to kill that son of a bitch!" Mary Liz cried, storming into the kitchen. She flipped open her address book and punched in some numbers. "I am not working for him!" she yelled at Bertie and Wendy. "Do you hear me? The only reason I ever agreed to even talk to him in the first place was to see if I could find out anything that would help your mother! In court! Get it?"

"Notice that she keeps Glidden's number in her book," Wendy said to Bertie.

"Sod off, Wendy!" she snapped. "You don't know what you're talking about!"

A male voice answered the telephone. "Hello?"

"Glidden?" she demanded.

"You must want my father."

"Alex?"

"Yeah."

"Mary Liz Scott. Where were you this morning? You were supposed to play tennis with us, not your father." She glanced over to see that they had heard this.

"Dad told me he was going."

"And so you just let him?"

"He pays my tuition," came the answer.

Mary Liz took a breath, trying to relax a little. "Well, Alex, would you please leave a message for him? And please, write this down, word for word. And promise that you, personally, will not be offended? Because I like you, Alex. But I've got to tell you, your father is one for the books."

"Yeah, I know." Pause. "'Kay, what's the message?"

"The message is, 'You should pray I will only kill you.'"

Alex laughed.

Mary Liz hung up and took a deep breath. It was childish to leave a message like that, but she was so darn mad. She had to find Aunt Nancy and talk to her. Jeanine was absolutely right. Herbert Glidden was out to create chaos within the ranks. By the time she straightened everything out, she wondered if anyone connected to the estate would ever trust her.

She searched through her address book again and dialed once more. "Claire? It's Mary Liz Scott. Is Aunt Nancy there?"

"Mary Liz, I've got to tell you," Claire was saying, "I am shocked at you."

"Claire, I am not working for Herbert Glidden!"

"He says you are, and understandably Nancy's beside herself."

"*Who* are you going to believe?" she demanded. "You're going to take his word over mine?"

"Why would he lie?"

"*Why would he lie?*" Mary Liz shrieked, composure utterly gone. "He would lie to get Aunt Nancy hysterical and have me thrown off the estate, and then move in for the kill, that's why! My father would freak out at her accusing me, she'd fire him and Glidden would have her right where he wants her—vulnerable, without key information, scared of more confrontation."

"Oh," said the painter quietly. She covered the phone and was talking to someone, presumably Aunt Nancy. "Hang on, Mary Liz," she said. "I think you better repeat all this to Nancy. She's been crying her eyes out all afternoon."

"Oh my God," Mary Liz said.

When Nancy came on, Mary Liz hurried through her explanation and became aware of how large Bertie's and Wendy's eyes were becoming in her living room. She finished by saying, "Aunt Nancy, I'm going to have Dad call you himself. He was the one who wanted me to hear what Glidden had to say about a job, but it was only to see if I could find something out about his business that might in some way help us in defending the estate."

"I believe you, I believe you," Aunt Nancy was saying. And then there was a wail and a new set of tears. "I'm so sorry I didn't believe in you, Mary Liz! It's just he was gloating so, standing there in the foyer, proudly announcing that you were working for him, that you had destroyed papers for him—"

"Aunt Nancy, listen to me," Mary Liz said. "This is why he did it. To create chaos. What's important now is that we all understand exactly what is going on and turn the tables on him." She paused for effect. "It's time to mow him down—and I will be most delighted to be the person to do it."

"I feel like such a fool, Mary Liz. But he sounded so convincing and I just fell apart. I couldn't imagine having to face the suits alone."

"And you won't have to."

When she got off the phone, she looked at Bertie. "So, are you clear on this? That I'm here trying to complete an inventory of the estate so my father can not only get these stupid suits dismissed, but see that you get everything you're entitled to?"

Bertie sat back down. After a moment, so did Mary Liz.

"I thought you were double-crossing Mother," he said weakly. He looked to Wendy. "All the signs were there, weren't they?" He looked back to Mary Liz. "It didn't seem possible you would be doing all this work for nothing."

"Your mother is—"

"Giving charitable donations, I know," Bertie said. "But the suits are worth millions and millions to Glidden—to say nothing of Braxer & Braxer." He paused. "You're really doing this for Mother?"

"For my parents, really," Mary Liz answered. "They've never asked me to do anything like this before—nothing, ever—so I knew your mother must really need the support."

Bertie sat back against the couch, shaking his head, and they were all quiet for a while.

"So you understand all the estate stuff?" Wendy finally said. "The contracts, the deals, the investors, moneys, company versus personal assets, all that?"

"Yes."

Bertie looked at Mary Liz. "I'm so sorry, Mary Liz. I didn't know."

"I know you didn't," Mary Liz said quietly, reaching for her seltzer. She took a sip. "So what's the story with you two? And don't tell me you're boyfriend and girlfriend."

They exchanged looks, and then Bertie said, "You have to promise not to tell Mother. She's so happy to think I have a girlfriend."

This was true. Pathetically true. Aunt Nancy was hoping for an engagement announcement any day now.

"I can promise," Mary Liz said, "as long as you two don't do anything that could endanger Aunt Nancy, or in any way threaten her interests."

"But that's just the point!" Bertie cried. "I've been trying to *protect* Mother! She's far too trusting, and you've seen for yourself, it seems like every piece of shit in East Hampton comes through this house, and I can't watch everything and everybody by myself."

"I'm a private detective," Wendy explained.

Mary Liz was surprised—Wendy looked so much the part of the high-powered WASP debutante ready to marry money—and she started to laugh. "I thought you were a gold digger."

"*What?*" And then Wendy and Bertie started to laugh, too. When she settled down, Wendy continued, "I specialize in family security. Families like the Hoffmans."

"You mean rich families."

"Rich or high-society, or both."

Mary Liz caught the distinction.

"This is my first time working in the Hamptons. My base is in New York, in Manhattan, but the last three summers I've gone with families to their summer homes. Newport, last year. Martha's Vineyard the year before. Newport the first year, too."

"Doing?"

"Posing as a friend of the family's, but actually keeping an eye on the children, or a single child, or maybe one of the spouses, the servants, or security in general. My clients are almost always people who are nervous about kidnappings." She smiled. "By the way, Mary Liz, it was I who broke into your office."

Mary Liz's mouth opened to protest.

"I had to know what was going on in that office," Wendy explained.

"So *that's* what all that windsurfing nonsense was about, Bertie! To get me out of here so she could break in?" Mary Liz thought about biffing Bertie one with a pillow from the couch, but then had another thought that distracted her from doing it.

Julius Hoffman had been telling the truth that day. He hadn't broken into her office. So it was possible he was telling the truth about other things, too.

Julius was quickly falling behind the pack. Whatever was afoot around here, Mary Liz was almost positive now that he was not a part of it.

15

"My morning game wasn't bad," Sky called from the living room as Mary Liz finished putting on her makeup in the bathroom. "But this afternoon Buck made me play with some German guys who didn't speak any English."

"What were they doing here?" Mary Liz said, trying to get a small clump of mascara off her lash with a Q-tip.

"They're some of those international members who come once a year."

This makeup was going to have to do, Mary Liz decided, looking at herself in the mirror. And what did one wear, exactly, to an animal parade and barbecue? She hoped she had guessed right and was wearing one of the many cotton skirts her mother had made her pack ("Trust me, Mary Liz, I *know*,"), a pale and dark blue number, short, with a pale blue sleeveless cotton blouse. She wore small, solid silver earrings, a single silver bangle, a delicate silver necklace around her neck and blue sandals (that belonged to her mother).

It was not particularly Mary Liz, but it was the way India Reynolds Scott's daughter from Winnetka should probably dress.

Whatever.

"Wow, you look sensational," Sky said when she came out.

"Not too suburban?"

"What do you mean?"

She smiled. "Never mind," she said, going to the kitchen. "How are you doing on that Pepsi?"

"I'm fine," he assured her, following her to the kitchen and sitting down on a breakfast stool to watch her pour a glass of seltzer. He was looking very handsome tonight, in gray Dockers and a gray and white polo shirt. His tan was getting beyond tropical proportions.

She leaned on the counter and sipped seltzer, smiling at him. "What happened to your glasses?"

"Are they still crooked?" he asked, taking them off to look at them.

"Well, just a little."

He fussed with them, trying to bend them back into shape without breaking them. "Buck sat on them yesterday in the clubhouse. I've got contacts with me, but they've been killing my eyes lately."

When he put them back on, they still looked a tad crooked, but Mary Liz didn't want to curse him with self-consciousness. "That looks fine now." She sipped her seltzer again. "Now, Mr. Preston, I need to ask you a question."

"Ask away."

"Have you heard anything about me around the club lately?"

"I heard you bought a painting for thirty-five thousand dollars last night."

She blushed. She couldn't help it. For heaven's sake, Sky was a teacher and didn't take home that much money in a year. It must have seemed to him an inconceivable waste and indulgence.

"I'm afraid I got carried away," she muttered into her glass.

"It was for charity," he reminded her. "And it was painted by Claire."

She looked up, appreciative of the rationale. He smiled. "And since you probably made half a million dollars last year," he added, "I think you're entitled. You don't live very ostentatiously for a big-shot financier. You drive an '88 LeBaron."

Actually, she had made just over seven hundred and fifty thousand last year, and would continue to over the next three years, which were the terms of selling out her partnership at Reston, Kellaher. It was an astronomical amount of money, but low by industry standards. Had she hopped around instead of staying at one firm, it would have been a great deal more.

But who cared now? She made the money, handed over around a third of it in the form of taxes, gave fifty thousand dollars to a variety of charities in anonymous gifts every year, paid her living expenses and otherwise socked it away with the dream of having a life one day. She knew that she would always have that money to help any of her family should they ever need it, or keep for her own immediate family should she ever have children.

"I also have a year-old Camry in the garage in Chicago," she admitted.

"Mary Liz," Sky said, suddenly serious, "there *is* something else I heard, something we need to talk about. And I've been dreading it all afternoon." He paused. "About you working for Herbert Glidden."

"Well, dread it no more, because I'm not," she said. "It's a flat-out, total, one-hundred-percent lie." Angry all over again, she put her glass in the sink and tried to walk out of the kitchen, but Sky caught her arm.

He was such a handsome man. Such a nice man. She had an overwhelming urge to sink into his arms and ask him to please just go club Glidden over the head for her. She wondered why she felt this way, wondered why she felt she could trust him. She still scarcely knew him, and yet… And yet she did.

"Glidden told me himself," he said quietly.

"And he's lying," she told him. "He's doing it to cause trouble. He wants the Hoffmans to get rid of me. He thinks, and correctly so, that if he provokes Aunt Nancy into getting rid of me and my father, he'll be able to just roll her over in court and get Howland Films."

Sky was frowning, as if he didn't get it. He probably didn't. Normal people didn't operate the way Glidden did.

"He's been running around telling everyone that not only am I working for him, but he told Aunt Nancy, only this morning, to her face, that I've been destroying estate documents on his behalf."

Sky's frown deepened.

"Which," she added, "is not only a lie, but couldn't happen if the guy offered me a billion dollars. Poor Aunt Nancy believed him at first and nearly went off the deep end, and I thought Bertie was going to—" She looked at him. "Are you following this at all?"

He nodded. "Unfortunately, yes."

"Tell me exactly what Glidden told you."

"You're not going to like it."

"Word for word."

"Word for word." Sky closed his eyes. "He came into the clubhouse this afternoon around three to buy some balls. I was in the back, helping set up some tee-times, and he came back to chat. When we were alone, he kind of elbowed me and said, 'I hear you're doing my girl.'"

She felt her face grow warm.

"And I said, 'You sure got that wrong, Herb, I don't even know your wife.'"

Mary Liz laughed.

"And so he said, 'I'm referring to Mary Liz. She's working for *me*. And you're right, she's not my girl, not in that sense, but she does work for me and I want to underscore that fact to you.'"

"I said, 'Why?' and he said, 'So she doesn't get any grief from you about moving to Los Angeles.'"

"Moving to Los Angeles!" she cried, throwing her hands up in frustration. "This guy is off his rocker! Sky, I swear to you, the only connection I have with this man is that I had an appointment with him on Monday to *discuss* a job offer. I never even considered, not for a second, taking it."

"But why are you talking to him?"

She sighed. And then took his hands into hers. "I know you warned me to stay away from him—"

"You bet I did. This guy is bad news, Mary Liz."

"I know, I know. But Sky, my father thought I might be able to learn more about how Glidden's business runs, maybe get a lead on something my father could use to help Aunt Nancy's cause."

Sky was shaking his head. "Mary Liz, please, cut the line now. He is not someone to fool with."

"Don't worry," she assured him. "The line is cut." After a moment she said, playing the coquette, "So, Mr. Preston, you actually thought I might be working for Glidden?"

"I was sure there was an explanation," he said.

"Oh, yeah? Like what?"

"Like what you just told me," he said, sliding his arms around her.

Sky was looking at her with a kind of intensity she had not seen before, and her heart told her she might be witnessing a man falling in love with her. The danger signals started flashing in her head, signaling wildly that she should not go any further into this relationship until she was sure that seeing Sky after this summer was something she wanted.

But you don't even know him, she told herself.

But I do, another part of her said.

No, the first part said. *That's infatuation. That's what always happens in the beginning.*

No, the second part said. *What always happens in the beginning is you think, this guy is not for me, and then you go ahead and get involved with him because you think he* should *be for you. That's not what's going on here. Since the moment you met this man, every instinct you possess has been telling you to wake up, Mary Liz, and pay attention. This is a wonderful person, and he represents almost everything you admire and respect.*

"What's wrong?" he murmured.

"I wish we had known each other longer," she finally said.

"Oh, God." He sighed, hugging her. "Me, too. Like ten years ago, so we could be celebrating our wedding anniversary tonight."

She gave a little laugh into his shoulder and looked up. "Our wedding anniversary?"

He kissed her deeply, and Mary Liz could feel a marked difference. Whatever was transpiring between them tonight, it was making Sky start to lose his cool. She gently pulled back. And smiled at the lipstick she had left on his mouth. And chin. And neck.

"Lipstick?" he asked.

She nodded, touching his face with her finger.

"Come look in the mirror at you, Clownie," he said, taking her by the hand to the bathroom.

She laughed when she looked in the mirror. She did look like a clown. "What kind of lipstick is this?" she wondered aloud, taking a Kleenex to wipe it off.

He cleaned the lipstick off himself, too.

They stood there then, looking in the mirror at themselves, he standing behind her, hands on her shoulders. He took a deep breath and then let it out slowly. "This is getting very serious very fast, Mary Liz."

She nodded. "I know."

"Does it scare you?"

She thought a moment. "A little. Until I remember it's you."

"You're smart and beautiful and funny—and most of all, you're *kind,* Mary Liz Scott. Regardless of how much money you make, or the circles you travel in, you will always be that way. A beautiful woman with a vast and generous heart."

She felt like crying.

The animal parade benefit was a complete delight. The airport hangar was decorated in animal themes, and buffet tables were laid out, waiting for the barbecue to begin, and tables and chairs were set up, with two bars, as well. Just outside the hangar a grandstand of sorts had been put up, and a parade pathway was roped off with garlands of artificial flowers.

The chaos was wonderful, the air full of barking and meows and squawks and hisses coming from the preparation area behind the hangar. The parade participants could be heard but not seen. There were probably five hundred adults and children waiting to watch.

The first person Mary Liz spotted was Herbert Glidden. This was pretty easy since the group around him—Buck Buckley, Claude Lemieux and Charles Kahn—were all staring at her. Glidden approached her and Mary Liz felt Sky tense up beside her.

"That was some message you left for me today," Glidden said.

"I'm still trying to figure out if you're stupid like a fox or just a complete psycho," Mary Liz said amiably, surprising Glidden by suddenly kissing him on the cheek. "Watch out, though, Mr. Glidden, because I meant what I said. You fuck with Aunt Nancy anymore and I will see you suffer. Big-time. Enjoy the parade." She took Sky's arm (who was about as wide-eyed as he could be) and strolled over to Buck, Claude and Charles.

"Did he tell you the big news?" she asked them. "That I'm going to nail his ass to the wall if he messes with me or Aunt Nancy again?"

They were all in shock, and when Glidden approached, their eyes all skirted over to him.

"Enjoy the parade," she said gaily, pulling Sky with her.

"Holy crow," Sky muttered. "I'm not sure that was such a smart thing to do."

She looked at him. "You think that was an idle threat? Let me tell you something, Sky, I would never say something like that unless, A, I meant it, and B, I had a darn good idea of what rocks to look under to get the goods on that guy."

He took her hand. "That's what worries me."

"Sky, for tonight, forget it. Let's have some fun. I've had enough of that creep for one day."

Making their way through the crowd, they spotted the lieutenant governor, Betsy McCoy Ross. Then Sky pointed out Calvin Klein, just as he noticed Rachelle and Sasha watching the designer, whispering, no doubt, about the man.

"Hey, it's Ginger Rogers," Sasha called out, spotting Mary Liz and elbowing Rachelle. "I think my bodyguard's smitten with you."

"Did you feel as awful as I did this morning?" Rachelle asked Mary Liz.

"You slept in a lounge chair, Rachelle, you *should* feel awful," Sasha said.

Mary Liz turned to Sky. "We were out rather late last night."

"You should see her dance," Sasha told him.

"Across the lawn," Rachelle embellished. "In the dead of night."

"We had a few," Mary Liz explained. She turned to Sasha. "What were those drinks, anyway? I could still taste them this morning."

"Bitter almonds," Sasha said.

"Bitter almonds is the smell of arsenic," Sky informed her.

"I mean toasted almonds," the diva said.

"I think it's close to the same thing," Mary Liz said, holding a hand to her head.

"It was Mary Liz's thirty-five-thousand-dollar painting that got us rolling," Rachelle explained to Sky.

"When she beat out Herb," Sasha told him. "So we were celebrating."

Sky looked at her. "You were bidding against Glidden?"

She nodded.

"And me," Sasha said.

"And me," Rachelle said.

"By the way," Sasha said, "why didn't you tell me you're working on my film this fall?"

"I'm not."

"But Herb said—"

"Herb has lost his mind," Mary Liz said.

"Darn!" the diva said. "I was looking forward to it."

"Told you," Rachelle said to her friend. "She wouldn't have anything to do with the likes of him."

Mary Liz and Sky had to move on to find a spot to watch the parade, because Sasha and Rachelle got to stand in a special viewing area roped off for VIPs and celebrities. They saw the actress, Kathleen Turner, accompanied by a man and child, heading toward it. And then they saw the star of "All My Children," Susan Lucci, and her family heading for the area. Up on the top row of the grandstand they saw Bertie and Wendy and Jake waving at them, calling for them to come up and join them. They shook their heads, no, and motioned that they were going to the head of the parade where they could see better. Mary Liz bumped into someone and hastily excused herself, finding herself face-to-face with Tom Cruise. The actor murmured it was okay, and moved past her.

They found a position on the parade route, at ground level, right next to one of the garland borders.

"Did I tell you that Glidden usurped his kid's tennis game this morning?" she said. And then she told Sky how she had met Alex at the party last night, and how they were to play tennis with Jeanine and Claude, but how Glidden had shown up instead.

"How old is he?"

"Alex? Oh, around twenty-three, I'd say."

"Oh. When you said 'kid,' I thought you meant a twelve-year-old."

"He might as well be. I asked him this morning on the phone why he let his father take his game, and he said his father paid his tuition."

"He's still in college?"

"Getting his MBA."

Sky nodded, thinking.

"What?" Mary Liz asked him. "Come on, I hear those wheels turning."

"I was thinking how Glidden knows enough to keep his son away from you."

Away from her. Yes. Of course. Maybe she should try to stop by and see Alex sometime, sometime when his father wasn't there.

The master of ceremonies came out to welcome them to the event. (He was apparently somebody of local fame, for Mary Liz hadn't a clue who he was and everyone was giving him the big bravo.)

Sky casually put his arm around Mary Liz and kept it there.

They heard the reasons for the benefit, about the wonder and companionship of animals, about how much money this event would raise and where it would go, and how people should feel free to write checks throughout the evening (laughter). And before the actual parade started, he wanted to introduce a few animals currently up for adoption, ones who had been rescued from the streets, the wilderness or from the cruelty of sick owners. Out came a little sheltie, as cute as could be, like a miniature collie, and everyone oohed and aahed. "I want her!" cried one woman.

It was explained that she should go to the desk at the hangar to begin the screening process. The next animal was carried up by a young man; it was a pretty little calico cat. More oohs and aahs.

The next was a mutt, a pretty mix of what looked to be golden retriever and German shepherd. As if to prove how good the dog was with children, it was being led by a little girl.

And then the emcee said many other animals were available for adoption and people could see them over by the ARF van on the opposite side of the hangar.

Everyone applauded.

Then a John Philip Sousa march was cranked up over the loudspeakers and the parade began. It was one of the cutest and most hysterical things Mary Liz had ever seen in her life. At the head of the parade was Vanessa Buckley, leading a huge Great Dane wearing racing goggles, an aviator's hat and a white silk scarf.

"Oh," Sky groaned, "poor Spike. Look at him. You can't do that to a dignified dog."

Everyone around them, however, was delighted with his costume and was cheering and applauding.

The next out was Isabel Lemieux, leading one of the smallest dogs Mary Liz had ever seen, a white toy poodle who—as Claude had forewarned her this morning—was wearing a sheer pink leotard, pink taffeta tutu and little silk booties on her back feet. When Isabel stopped and the dog stood up on her hind legs, the crowd went wild with applause and cheers. Dog after dog was trotted out—a terrier Conehead (as in "Saturday Night Live"); a German shepherd movie star with sunglasses and a rhinestone coat; a pretty mutt suited up in a saddle and fake bridle; two huskies pulling a child along in a Radio Flyer, wearing paper antlers on their heads. Then a big rabbit came out on a leash, with its owner carrying a sign that read: I Am Really A Saint Bernard." A bird cage was carried by a man, containing a parrot who whistled and then screeched, "Vote for me! Vote for me!" A little boy in a cat costume walked along with a fishbowl (sloshing the water out of it) with two goldfish in it.

On and on they came: an iguana led on a leash, wearing sunglasses and a straw hat; a cat carried with a hat and little blond wig on its head; a long snake curled around a boy's arm (inspiring shrieks and screams). And then more dogs came by: an African ridgeback wearing war paint and an Indian headdress; a wirehaired Jack Russell wearing a baby's dress and bonnet, a pacifier strung around its neck; two golden retrievers pulling a wagon, made up to look like a dogsled, that had a cat sitting in it; and then a familiar black shape came around the corner of the building....

"It's Ashley!" Mary Liz said excitedly to Sky.

Yes, indeed. But the poor dog looked very depressed, having to wear a blue bandanna tied over her head, a black patch over one eye (with a hole cut out so she could see), a belt with a cardboard cutlass and little cloth booties. She was slinking along, arching her back as if to try to slide out of the costume, occasionally stopping to shake a paw or two to get those stupid booties off. Nancy was leading her along, coaxing and encouraging her, and the poor thing, tail between her legs, made tentative little spurts of progress.

"Bravo!" Mary Liz said, clapping.

Suddenly Ashley's head snapped up in her direction; she saw Mary Liz and made a break for it, pulling Nancy nearly backward to the ground and yanking the leash out of her hand. Ashley the Pirate, like a true swashbuckler, tore off the parade route and jumped the garland of flowers to land on Mary Liz's chest. Mary Liz had no choice but to try to catch the fifty-pound-plus animal, which in turn sent her rolling onto the ground with Ashley gleefully licking her face. Mary Liz sat up, holding Ashley—who persisted in licking her face—and the crowd cheered.

"I had a feeling she was just being a good sport," Nancy later confessed, loading Ashley—now gloriously free of that stupid outfit—in the back of the Range Rover and closing the hatch.

"Come on, Mother, we'll take her home and give her a bone," Bertie said from the driver's-seat window. Wendy and Jake were sitting in the back seat. Bertie looked at Mary Liz and smiled. She felt sure they were going to be great pals now. "You guys are coming to the fireworks tonight, aren't you?"

"Absolutely," Sky said.

"We'll bring beach chairs for you," Bertie promised. "See ya. Remember, nine-thirty sharp, fireworks at nine forty-five."

Watching the Range Rover pull away, Sky sighed and shook his head. "It's going to be awfully hard to keep me down on the farm after this."

They went back to the hangar to get some dinner. It was a bit of a madhouse and the lines at the buffet tables were long. Sasha and Rachelle were already finishing at their table—clearly, they had some sort of VIP line for food, too—and couldn't believe Mary Liz and Sky hadn't eaten.

"Is Glidden still around?" Sky asked, looking around.

"The guys are showing off their planes," Rachelle said. "You know, mine's bigger than yours."

As if this reminded her, the diva announced, "I need a boyfriend."

"And I need food," Mary Liz said. She looked at Sky. "Can't we go somewhere for a burger and a shake?"

"You got it."

"Great." Mary Liz looked at the women. "Are you going to the fireworks tonight?"

Rachelle nodded. "Yes."

"We'll be there, too. See you there."

As they walked away, they heard Rachelle say, "If I were you, Sasha, I would pay a little more attention to that gorgeous Riff under your roof."

"Sky," Mary Liz said as they drove out of the airport, "would you mind very much if we swung by Glidden's house for a minute?"

"What the heck for?"

"I thought I'd just stop in and see the kid, Alex."

"Mary Liz," he said warningly.

"I just want to talk to him."

"About what?"

"I don't know, about his father. Maybe he'll tell me something. Besides, I'd love to see Glidden's face when he gets home and finds out I've been there."

"This is a dangerous game to play, Mary Liz."

She looked at him. "It's not a game. It's real life, Sky. Just ten minutes, that's all I want."

Sky glanced over. "Are you sure?"

"Yes."

He sighed. "Okay, I'll take you. But not for long. I don't want to be there when Glidden gets back."

When they reached his house, Mary Liz said, "If you want, you can park up the street. Just in case."

"No way," he said. "There's no way I'm leaving you here."

Glidden rented the same house every year, a four-bedroom wood and glass house on the beach. It was very modest compared to the Hoffmans', and, unlike the Big House, he had neighbors close on both sides. There were no lawns, really, to speak of, either, just a series of serious oceanfront homes that were crowded together, lovely, and costing a bundle. Aunt Nancy had told her that a house like this would probably rent for about forty thousand for the season or twenty-five thousand for a single month. The house had a large wraparound deck in back. It was from there Mary Liz could hear music, and so she made her way around the home.

Alex was sitting on the deck, working on a large wooden model of a clipper ship. It was no easy task. The boat itself was a skeleton now, and he was gluing and bending individual wood strips to make the frame. The picture on the cover of the box showed the intricate rigging and detail in the finished model.

He was listening to an instrumental of a forties song, "One O'clock Jump," if she recognized it correctly.

"Alex?"

He looked up, surprised. "Hi."

"I was in the neighborhood and I thought I'd just stop by and see if you wanted to go to some fireworks tonight."

He smiled slightly, bashful. "I can't, sorry. I'd like to, but I've got stuff to do."

Mary Liz walked up the steps to the deck. "Ah, come on, it'll be fun. My friend Sky and I are going and we'll sit with Aunt Nancy—Mrs. Hoffman."

"I call her Aunt Nancy, too," he said.

"So come on, why not? Aunt Nancy would love to see you."

"I've got to go back to the West Coast tomorrow."

"Really? That's too bad."

He didn't say anything, but looked down at his model.

"How will you get that home?" she asked.

"I'll carry it."

He seemed positively morose now.

"Alex," Mary Liz said softly, kneeling to look at him eye level in his chair. "Is something wrong? Is there something I can do?"

He shook his head. "No."

"Is it your father?"

"No. He's the same."

"The same?"

He met her eyes for the first time. "I hate him. He's a bastard. To my mom, to me—but I don't care about me." Now the words were tumbling out. "I'm getting out of here. I don't know why the hell I came in the first place."

"'Cause your dad pays your tuition," Mary Liz said gently, trying to lighten things up.

Slowly and deliberately, he said, "Fuck him." He looked back at his model. "You better get out of here. Before he gets home." He glanced over. "In case you haven't noticed, he's paranoid about anybody talking to us."

"Us?"

"Me or mom."

"Why?"

"You better go."

He wasn't telling. Well, she had to try one more tack. "Listen, Alex, your father wants me to work with him on his next movie with Howland Films."

"He doesn't do films. He couldn't give a shit about movies. All he cares about is money and power and staying alive."

"Staying alive?"

He pushed his chair back and stood up. "You've got to get out of here."

"Can I talk to you again?"

He shook his head. "You've gotta go."

He was scared now, looking over his shoulder as if Glidden was about to appear at any moment.

"But, Alex," she said, standing up, "tell me why I shouldn't work with your father. He's one of the biggest names in Hollywood and he's offering me a lot of money."

"Just don't," he said, backing toward the house.

"But why?"

"You'll regret it."

"But why?"

"Don't do it," Alex warned, and he closed the sliding glass door, locked it and pulled the floor-length drapes closed.

Mary Liz sighed and walked across the deck and down the stairs. Obviously the son was disturbed—mentally or emotionally, maybe both—and scared to death of his father. It was so sad.

She was making her way around the side of the house when she heard the sound of a window being opened. "Mary Liz," Alex whispered.

She couldn't tell which window his voice was coming from. She couldn't see through the screens. "Yes?" she whispered back.

"Uncle Alfred. Dad didn't do it, but it was because of him."

"Your uncle Alfred's plane crash was an accident," Mary Liz whispered.

"I don't think so."

"Alex," she said in her normal voice. "What do you know?"

"Just don't do it. Stay away from my father."

"Well?" Sky asked her as she climbed into the car.

"He was there. He doesn't want to come, though. He's flying back to the West Coast tomorrow."

Sky drove along for a while. "Did you ask him anything?"

"About what?"

"You know, about his father."

"I asked him if I should work for him."

"What did he say?"

"Not to."

After a while, Sky asked, "Anything else?"

"No." Mary Liz shifted in her seat to look at him. "How about that burger? I'm starving."

16

After cheeseburgers and chocolate shakes ("Ah, fat and happy," Mary Liz said, sighing), Sky drove them to the Simpsons' house, which turned out to be only four houses west of the Hoffman estate. Those who had come to actually sit on the Simpsons' beach had paid two hundred dollars a ticket to benefit medical research for multiple sclerosis. The fireworks themselves had been donated by a wealthy local (so what else was new?) family whose son had designed the show. He had apprenticed with the Grucci family for years, the same family who designed and orchestrated the Macy's fireworks.

The house was not overly large, but the grounds were sensational. There were police officers directing traffic. Sky presented the tickets and one of the young valets took the Mercedes to park it.

There must have been forty torches lit on the beach, giving the festivities a warm, flickering glow. The water was dotted with the lights of boats anchored to watch the fireworks for free. A crowd of about two hundred was on the beach already, sitting on blankets and in beach chairs or milling about to chat. The actual silos for the fireworks were set up on the next beach, aiming out toward the ocean. Also parked on the beach next door was an ambulance and a four-wheel-drive fire rescue truck.

This was not a wine-and-cheese benefit. Every cent from ticket sales went into the fund. So everyone had coolers with them, and the Hoffman family had practically set up a compound, from where Bertie and Jake were passing out supplies to anyone who wanted them: iced bottles of Amstel Lite, iced bottles of fruity wine spritzers, iced bottles of Arizona Ice Tea, iced bottles of Poland Spring Water, bags of freshly made local pretzels, potato chips, Cape Cod cheddar-cheese popcorn and, in yet another cooler, Popsicles and Good Humor bars.

Delores was there as one of the family, dressed in slacks, blouse and cardigan, sitting right next to Aunt Nancy. Claire MacClendon was sitting on the other side of Nancy, talking to her, and surrounding them in chairs and on blankets were Sasha, Rachelle and Charles

Kahn, Buck and Vanessa Buckley, Isabel and Claude Lemieux and the vintner, Randolph Vandergilden.

While Sky went off to compliment Isabel and Vanessa on their dogs' performances in the parade, Mary Liz went over to squat between Aunt Nancy and Claire. Claire smiled gratefully. "I was just trying to get Nancy to snap out of her funk."

"What's the matter?" Her godmother didn't look very good.

"I'm just not feeling well," Nancy said quietly.

"I'm sorry. Well, just let us know if you want to go home," Mary Liz said. "Sky and I will take you any time."

Her godmother smiled appreciatively. And then she reached out to take Mary Liz's hand. "I am so very fond of you, Mary Liz, you know that, don't you?"

"Yes," she said, glancing at Claire before she leaned forward to give her godmother a hug. Mary Liz frowned. She could feel that her godmother was practically trembling. She leaned back on her haunches. "Are you sure you don't want me to take you home?"

"No, darlin', thank you. It's better that I'm here."

Claire followed her back to the seat Bertie had set up for Mary Liz. "I don't know what's gotten into her."

"It's not post-shock or something from this morning, is it?" Mary Liz asked her. "She was pretty upset."

"I shouldn't think so," Claire said. "Hey, by the way, thanks for the compliment last night!"

"Oh, the painting."

"That's right, *Oh, the painting.* Mary Liz, are you out of your mind? You shouldn't have paid more than twenty thousand for it. That's what the gallery would have sold it for in New York."

Mary Liz smiled. "No, I'm not out of my mind. I absolutely fell in love with it, Scout's honor."

"I heard Herb drove up the bidding," the painter said. "Now, that wouldn't have had anything to do with your bid, would it? Although, I must confess, the idea of him owning it made me feel nauseated."

"To be honest," Mary Liz told her, "I bought it for my children. And my children's children. And I know it will be worth far, far more down the road."

"Actually, you may be right about that," Claire said. "It is a one-of-a-kind for me." She smiled shyly. "I painted it when I finally thought I could bear the fact that Henry had left." She turned around. "Anyone seen Herb around? I nearly forgot, I want to punch him in the nose."

"I saw him at the animal parade," Sasha called. "He said he was coming."

"I think I saw him," Isabel Lemieux said. "In a pink shirt?"

"Isn't he with Henry?" Rachelle said. "I saw Henry around here somewhere."

"I think I saw him with the Hoffmans," Charles Kahn said. "On the other side of the beach. Down by the water over there."

"Well, when any of you do see him," Claire said, "let me know. I've got a bone to pick with him."

"Who doesn't?" Vanessa Buckley asked. She turned all the way around in her chair. "I must tell you, Mary Liz, that I'm very relieved to hear you're not working for him."

"Claire?" Nancy said, standing and looking up toward the house. "Is that your friend? There's a man up there with a child and he seems to be searching for someone."

Claire turned around, which made Mary Liz look. "Yes, I think it is. Excuse me." She walked up the beach.

Mary Liz blinked several times and looked again. She could swear it was Bill Pfeiffer and his little girl. Yes, when they walked toward them with Claire, she could see that it was. "Bill, hi," she said.

"Bill was so nice to give me a ride home from the party last night," Claire said to the group, "I asked him if he'd like to come tonight, and bring his little girl."

"My name's Jenny and I'm not little, Spin-Art Lady," the little girl told her.

They all laughed. Claire explained the circumstances under which she had first met Jenny, and then made introductions all around. Bertie got the newcomers some refreshments—an Amstel Lite and a Popsicle—and they settled in next to Claire.

Almost all of the torchlights were being capped on the beach, quieting the crowd. A single whirlybird firework was lit on the next beach, spinning multicolored sparks off a pole, which signaled the beginning of the fireworks. People on shore began to applaud and those on the boats honked their horns. Mary Liz and Sky crawled over to sit on a beach blanket to watch the fireworks, Mary Liz comfortably curled under his arm.

The fireworks were super, better than the ones on the Fourth of

July, beginning small and working their way up to multiple sky-rockets exploding in three, four, five bursts of color. And then there were the big boomers, the sound slugging them all in the chest, and causing a few children to cry out. When the next rocket lit up the sky, Mary Liz looked and saw that Jenny had crawled into her father's lap and had her hands over her ears. Claire reached over to stroke the child's hair once, and then leaned over to say something to her.

Bill was forty-two, Mary Liz knew. Claire was fifty-two. Might something happen between them?

Oh, she hoped so. She got up on one elbow, kissed Sky's cheek and then settled back down next to him again. He held her with both arms now and Mary Liz couldn't care less who saw him do it.

"It's going to take a while for everyone to clear out," Sky said to Mary Liz while they helped load the last of the camp in the back of the Range Rover. "Maybe we should go for a walk on the beach or something until it clears out."

"Sure," Mary Liz said.

"Hey, Sky?" Vanessa said, coming over to them. "Would you mind if I caught a ride home with you? My errant husband has gone off with the boys for a night on the town."

"Sure, I just have to drop off Mary Liz," he said.

"Mary Liz can come with us," Bertie said, closing the hatch. "Mom's already gone ahead with Claire."

Feeling dreadfully disappointed, Mary Liz listened as it was arranged that she would go home with Bertie, Wendy and Jake, and Sky and Vanessa would go home to her place.

"I'll call you in the morning," Sky said, giving her a kiss on the cheek.

"Okay." She smiled. "Thank you for such a great night."

He leaned forward and said, "Thank you for being you," and kissed her lightly on the mouth.

"Come on, Romeo," Vanessa said, pulling him toward the valet.

Mary Liz climbed into the back of the Range Rover next to Jake. "He's a good-looking guy, that Sky," he commented.

Mary Liz didn't know what was wrong with her. After letting herself into the cottage and turning off the alarm system, she felt so let down, so disappointed, so lonely for Sky she felt close to crying. It was ridiculous.

Absolutely ridiculous.

Shaking it off, she went into the bedroom and undressed. Then she went to the bathroom to shower, put on some moisturizer, brush her teeth and floss. She went into the kitchen to get a cold glass of water, brought it to the bedroom with her and put it on the bedside table. She closed the curtains, activated the alarm system in the living room, kitchen and office, climbed into bed, said her prayers and reached for a book.

And then it hit her.

Alex Glidden had practically accused his father of causing Alfred Hoffman's death.

There was a tapping at her window and Mary Liz nearly jumped out of her skin. God, who the heck was this? At her window!

She went over and flung open the curtains. It was Sky! He gestured for her to open the window, which she did after turning off the security system. He had his finger over his mouth. And then he whispered, "When we got home, Vanessa got a call. They're having some sort of party next door, in the guest house."

"I wasn't invited."

"Me, neither. So I parked up the street and ran back. They're all sitting out on the front porch and I didn't want them to see me."

"Why not?"

He shrugged. "I don't know. I just didn't feel like having everybody watch us."

She laughed quietly. "Would you like to come inside?"

"Yes, very much," he whispered. He paused, lowering his head. "When Vanessa dragged me off tonight, I got so depressed."

"So did I," she told him. "Come around to the back."

She went to the kitchen, moving only by the cottage night-lights that always came on once it got dark. She opened the kitchen door. Sky slipped in, closed the door behind him and they just stood there for a moment.

"Oh, Mary Liz," he murmured, holding her tight, gently rocking. He was soaked with perspiration.

They stood there like that for a long time, so that when they did finally part, Mary Liz felt slightly damp, too. "How about something to drink?"

"No, thanks." He hesitated. "What I really need is a shower. I'm a mess."

"I'll get you some towels," she said matter-of-factly, walking into the living room, turning on a lamp, and continuing toward the bathroom. "Toss out your clothes and I'll give them a quick wash and put them in the dryer. There's a terry-cloth robe that should fit." She hoped her voice did not betray her, that it sounded casual and nonimportant, and that she was not aroused, obsessed now with the idea of him being naked in her house, in her robe.

This was not like her.

"Are you sure it's all right?" Sky asked her, following. "It's just that I feel so scrungy, like something you should leave outside overnight."

She pushed him into the bathroom with a towel and got his clothes in exchange. She checked the pants; just Dockers, no reason why she couldn't wash them. She went back to the kitchen and tossed everything into the washer, noticing in particular that he wore Jockey shorts.

Stop it, Mary Liz.

Now someone was knocking on her front door. What was it with this place? And she was in a nightie and Sky had her robe in the bathroom. To heck with it, she'd answer the door in her nightie and hide herself behind the front door as best she could.

It was Bertie. In bathing trunks, no shirt and flip-flops.

"We're having a little party at the guest house. Why don't you put on your swimsuit and come over? Then we'd have enough for volleyball on the beach. At least have a bonfire."

"Thanks awfully, Bertie, but I'm afraid I'm out for the count."

"Sasha's coming over with that bodyguard guy. And you could call Sky and ask him, couldn't you? Come on, Mary Liz."

The water in the shower stopped and she prayed Sky didn't come out. In a loud voice she said, "I'm sorry, Bertie, but I'm just too tired. I'd be grouchy and rude and fall asleep."

He looked at her oddly, no doubt wondering why she was practically shouting. "Okay," he said softly. "But just so you know you were invited."

"Thanks, Bertie." She opened the screen door to kiss him on the cheek.

He smiled, said, "I've got to go check on Mother," and then leaped off the porch to go running up the lawn.

She closed and locked the front door. Then she walked to the back hall, where the bathroom door opened, letting out steam. Sky was wearing her robe, toweling his hair dry. "Who was that?"

"Bertie. I was invited to the party, after all, and he wanted me to call you up and invite you, too."

He brought the towel down from his head. "Why do you suppose Vanessa wanted to go?"

She shrugged. "She's been married four times, maybe she's shopping for a fifth." She smiled. "Of course, if that were the case, I should think she would have merely headed straight for her garage apartment."

He pushed the wet towel into her face. "Hey, I'm an upright sort of guy."

Laughing, she backed out of the bathroom. "Come on, come have a soda or a beer or something."

They both opted for seltzer over ice and settled down on the couch, facing each other, sipping their drinks. The buzzer went off for the washer and Mary Liz got up to toss his clothes in the dryer.

"I feel so much better," Sky told her when she sat down. "What is it about hot showers?"

"Renewal."

"Yes." He held up his glass. "To renewal."

They clinked glasses and drank. He reached over to put his glass down on the coffee table and reached to take her free hand. She glanced down, aware of his bare muscular legs, aware that all she had to do was flip back the robe and she could see all there was to see. When she brought her eyes up, she found his eyes on her breasts; his eyes darted back up to her face. "Sorry," he said, giving her hand a squeeze. "I only just now realized you're in a nightgown."

They sat there, stretching for conversation. Suddenly things seemed awkward and strange.

She yawned.

"I'll go as soon as my clothes are dry enough," he promised.

"No, it's just that I'm tired, suddenly. I was up very late last night—"

"Hanging out with the A-list, baby," he said, winking.

"Sasha's really so nice. But she's so lonely, too. When she's not working, she's got virtually nothing to do."

"She must have hobbies. And she's pretty close to Rachelle, isn't she?" He laughed. "'Rachelle,' I say, as if I'm on a first-name basis with all famous clothes designers. I should have gone right up to Calvin Klein at the parade tonight and said, 'Hey, Cal, how ya doing?'"

"But that's what happens here," Mary Liz said. "It becomes the norm. I went into the Bridgehampton library the other day and saw Don Hewitt—the '60 Minutes' producer?—and almost said, 'Hi, how are you? I'm Nancy Hoffman's goddaughter.'"

They laughed.

"She sure does raise a lot of money around here," Sky said.

"I hope she's okay," Mary Liz said absently. "She didn't look well tonight. I hope she's not coming down with something. She's got her big dinner dance coming up."

"I'd imagine this summer is triggering a lot of memories for her," Sky said. "It must be hard, seeing all their friends, and knowing that her husband's gone. Forever."

They sat in silence for a while, Sky still holding her hand.

"Sky—"

He looked almost startled.

"Why aren't you married?"

"Why aren't you?"

"Touché," she said. She got up to refill their glasses and said, while doing so, "I wanted to tell you about that." And she proceeded, for the next half hour, to explain how she had lived with and left Jim, how she had flung herself at Ken, how Ken had broken up with her, how she had gone back to Jim last summer, only to find he had come to find he felt better off without her.

"And where's Jim now?"

"Married already."

"And what's she like, the wife?"

"Very pretty, very devoted."

"Does she work?"

Mary Liz nodded, sipping her seltzer. "She's a sales rep for a drug company. She's planning to quit, however, as soon as she gets pregnant—which they hope is soon." She shrugged. "I think it's great, actually. I'm even a little jealous."

"That she got him?"

She looked at him in surprise. "Oh, gosh, no! I meant about trying to have a baby."

"Oh. And what about the other guy, Ken?"

She made a face. "I was a complete and utter fool. I just couldn't see it for what it was."

"And what was that?" He was holding her hand very tightly.

"A high. It was—he was—so completely different than Jim."

"And what about me?"

She met his eyes. "Oh, Sky, you have no idea. Meeting you has been the best and worst thing that's ever happened to me." It looked as though he had winced at the word *worst*. "From the very beginning I knew you were, well, just wonderful. I don't think I even believed guys like you existed." She sighed, trying to choose her words carefully. "What the worst thing about it is, I simply don't know if I'm up to someone like you."

"What are you talking about?" he said, looking bewildered.

"I just don't know yet if this is real for me, or whether I'm only infatuated. I mean, I know I feel very differently about you—than I have about any other man in my life—enough so, there is no way I want to encourage you unless I know I can go through with this."

He gave a little laugh. "I didn't ask you to marry me."

"You know what I mean, Sky. I don't know what's happened to you in the past, but I sense there is a great deal of hurt there. I don't want to let you down."

He got impatient suddenly, letting go of her hand and shifting his position. "Let me get this straight—you're scared you can't fall in love with me."

"No." Pause. "Actually, that's not it."

"Then what is it?"

"I'm scared I'm not the kind of person who can make a lifelong commitment."

"So don't!" he declared. "Stay in the present, stop projecting—no wonder you're freaking out. I would, too, if I tried to plan the rest of my life after a few dates."

He was right. And she wasn't sure why she was saying these things.

"By the way," she said, getting up from the couch, "you haven't seen this." She carefully pulled her nightie up so he could see the scar on her left hip. "Do you know what that is?"

"It looks like a grazing scar from a bullet," he said.

She stared at him. "Now, how did you know that?"

He shrugged. "It just looks like one."

"Were you in the service?"

"No."

"Well, anyway," she said, dropping her nightie, "that's where my brother Brendan accidentally shot me when I was a kid."

"Oh, I see. That's why..."

She nodded. "Exactly. Brendan had found my father's gun up at our summerhouse, and we were just playing around. I was fine, I mean I just had to go to the doctor's with Mom, but our poor dog died. The bullet hit the poor little guy in the head. At least he didn't suffer." The memory instantly made her want to cry. It had been so awful. Brendan had been hysterical. None of them had ever really gotten over it.

Sky held his hand out to her. She took it and he pulled her down toward the couch to sit on his lap. "I'm sorry," he murmured, putting his arms around her.

"That's why I hate handguns. Every time I hear a story about a kid and a gun, I get crazy."

They were quiet a while, holding each other, nuzzling.

"Now it's my turn," Sky suddenly said, easing Mary Liz off him and onto the couch. "I've got something very serious I have to talk to you about. And if you're angry that I didn't tell you before, I'll understand."

The tone of his voice scared her.

He was looking down at her hand, which he held in his. He brought his eyes up. "I was in love with a girl named Kate. I met her just after she got out of college. We dated a long time, moved in together and were going to get married."

"How old were you? When you got engaged?"

"Twenty-seven. She was twenty-five." He cleared his voice. "Anyway, we were living in Washington, and Kate got sick. We thought it was just a cold she couldn't shake, or a bad strain of flu. It dragged on and on and then her doctor suggested testing for AIDS and we both thought it was ridiculous, but then..." He blew air out of his cheeks and looked away. "The test came back positive."

"Oh, Sky, I'm so sorry."

"And it turned out, that—well, she had had this ski accident when she was in high school. Broke her leg and tore out all the ligaments in one knee, and she had to have surgery. The operation took a lot longer than they had anticipated and she had been losing a lot of blood, so they gave her a transfusion. It wasn't much, maybe a pint." He shut his eyes, pressing his mouth in a hard line.

"I'm so sorry," Mary Liz murmured. She had done the math in her head. The operation must have been around 1980 or so, before they had known—

"Even just eight years ago, when they told us she had it, that she had already gone from HIV to AIDS," he continued, blinking rapidly, "they didn't know what to do, how to stop it." He turned to Mary Liz. "And we tried—we tried everything. Kate's parents flew her to every hospital where there was any new treatment available. That is, until she was too sick to travel."

"How long did it go on?"

"Not long. Eleven months." He looked at her. His eyes were brimming with tears. "I stayed. I didn't want to, believe me—oh, God, Mary Liz, she was so sick, so helpless. And I loved her. And she was just wasting away, only about eighty pounds at the end, and yet she was always so full of hope, her eyes so trusting, she kept saying, 'Don't worry, Sky, they'll find something—'"

She took him in her arms and pressed his face against her shoulder.

They didn't talk for a long while. And then Sky got up and went into the bathroom, where she heard him blowing his nose. He came back after a while, sat down and finished what he had to say. "We had been sleeping together for three years, Mary Liz, and I tested negative for the virus. I felt so awful, so guilty, while she was lying there, dying—"

Mary Liz nodded. "Survivor's guilt. It's a tough one."

"I'm still testing negative," he told her. "But they say you can't know absolutely for sure for ten years."

"Sky," she said, interrupting him, "*I* could test negative today, but what would that mean? Who's to say I haven't come into contact with the virus in the last ten years?"

He was looking at her funny. "What are you saying?"

"I'm saying that I hold the same risk for you as you do for me. I've been tested and I'm negative, and you've been tested repeatedly and are still negative. What's incredibly important here is that you sat down and told me all this before we ever had sex. I hate to say it, but I can't think of many men who would have done the same in your circumstances, certainly not after eight years."

"God, I hope not." He stood up. "I better go."

"No," she said, going to him. "Stay. At least, let me show you something."

She took his hand and led him to her bedroom, sat him down on the bed, kissed him on the forehead and then went to the closet to find her cosmetics case. She set it down on the bed, opened it, pulled the lining back, withdrawing the items that were in there and laying them on the bed next to Sky: the plastic case that held her diaphragm, a tube of spermicide and a box of condoms.

She tossed the cosmetics case into the closet and came back to sit down. "So what does this make me? Bringing these here this summer, when I didn't know a soul?"

"Smart," he said. "God only knows what's floating around out here."

"Exactly." She took his chin and turned his face toward her. "I didn't bring them because I was planning on having sex. I brought protection because I am a sexual being, like most human beings are, and if for some strange reason I should have been so moved by someone that I would want to make love with him, you can see I am not inclined to take risks."

Sky didn't say anything, but only looked at her.

"And nor are you," she said. "And that's just the point. I'm falling for you, Preston. Big-time."

His eyes lit up. "Really?"

"Yes," she said. "And that's why I want to make love with you. Tonight. I know it's soon, but this is what I want to do."

He searched her eyes, looking as though he might want to cry. He reached to take her hand. "I'm falling in love with you, Mary Liz. I can wait."

"But I can't," she said, leaning forward to kiss his ear.

Oh, they were in for some lulus of arguments ahead, she knew; they were both independent, opinionated and old enough to know they were set in their ways. For heaven's sake, he was a schoolteacher living in suburban Virginia, and she was a high-finance type living in Chicago proper. *Obviously* there were going to have to be adjustments made. And they would take their time.

But not with making love.

"Stop thinking and simply feel," she whispered, kissing his ear again.

"Oh, I am," he assured her.

He said it in such a way as to make her draw back to look at him.

His eyes moved down to his lap and he gave a helpless little shrug.

He was feeling, all right. The robe was raised like a tent in his lap.

The place between Mary Liz's legs was damp. She looked back up at him, catching her breath.

"I want you so badly," he whispered, slipping a hand on her waist and moving forward to give her a long, searching kiss. His hand started to inch up over her nightie, finally brushing softly over her breast. It came back to settle, then, to hold her breast, and she felt his whole body go hard.

They parted for a moment; Mary Liz took his glasses off and put them on the night table. Then she came back to kiss him, and put his hand back on her breast.

They fell back on the bed, sliding farther up so as to be able to lie down across it together.

He took her in his arms, kissing her deeply, allowing his entire body to press against hers. Through the thin nightie, she felt his chest, and felt his muscles hard against her. And yes, then, finally, she felt it through the robe, pressing against her inner thigh. His hand breezed over her leg, sliding the nightie up, and then his hand slid up, under the flimsy material to touch her breasts, lightly at first, and then with more passion. "We've got to get this off," he breathed into her mouth, referring to the nightgown, as they parted for a moment.

"Let me help," she whispered, smiling, assisting him in getting the nightie up over her hips, over her breasts and, finally, over her head. She tossed it on the floor.

He was looking at her body, breathing heavily, rubbing his palm lightly over her stomach. "You are so beautiful."

"Come here," she murmured, pulling him back down on her to kiss again. While he explored her breasts, and chest, and stomach, and thighs with his hands, she gradually worked the robe's terry-cloth belt undone, sliding her hands underneath to feel his chest. It was muscular; it had hair, some, but not too much. "We have to get this off," she whispered, mocking him, softly laughing.

"Let me help," he echoed, moving to pull it off. He tossed it on the floor, too, and rolled back to her.

What she felt on her thigh surprised her. And thrilled her.

They went on exploring until Mary Liz knew she had to get up. "I'm sorry," she whispered. "I've got to put my diaphragm in."

"No problem," he whispered.

Two minutes later, she was back.

Sky was lying on his back, hands behind his head, eyes closed.

He was gorgeous, lying there, and between her legs Mary Liz had begun to ache.

"Hi," she whispered, sliding back on the bed.

He opened his eyes, smiling. He turned on his side, propping himself up on his elbow. "Have you any idea how beautiful you are?" he asked, stroking her hair.

"I was about to say the same thing to you."

He smiled. Looked at her mouth. And kissed her. "Where were we?"

"We were skipping right to the end," she said, curling up to reach the box of condoms. It was opened. She looked at him.

He smiled again and withdrew a foil packet from behind his back. She snapped it out of his hand. "We can always go back later to study the terrain in detail," she said, ripping the foil open, "but I've never gotten this part right and I have a feeling now I will." She gently pushed him onto his back. Catching her breath, she reached down to touch him. He was very erect, and deeply red, almost purple, but his skin was soft, the rounded end like velvet. She put the condom on him, leaving a little space, and slowly unrolled it, working to cover his width, working her way down over all of him.

There.

She looked up.

He looked as though he was in pain. He reached for her, pulling her up, then reached behind himself to snag a pillow, and then, easing her hips up with one hand, he slid the pillow under her with the other. Then he scooted up between her legs, taking hold of both her hands. "All right?"

"Please."

He released her hands and, holding himself up on one arm, lowered himself slowly down. With his free hand, he was gently rubbing himself between her legs, making sure he was in the right place, making sure also that Mary Liz was quietly groaning with pleasure. It was so—so *right,* and God, it felt so good.

He pushed himself in just a little, holding himself up on two arms now, and slowly, very gently, started to make his way in. An inch, an inch and a half, two inches, two and a half, three, three and a half, and then, as if he couldn't help it, he lay on top of her, sinking the rest of him into her and making her gasp.

"Are you all right?" he said, startled.

"Oh, God, yes," she breathed.

"I'm not hurting you?"

"No," she whispered, sliding her hands onto his lower back. "Sky, you feel wonderful."

He started to move, slowly, and continued that way for some time. But then his speed started to change, and so did his movement. He was pushing harder, a little faster, and his breath in her ear was ragged. But not from being tired. "I gotta do math," he panted. "I gotta do math. I gotta hold on. I'm not sure I can."

The thought that he was about to come sent her flying to freedom. Way down deep in her, a surge of feeling ballooned, and then billowed up, overwhelming her whole body, and she thought, *Oh my God, feel this,* and then out loud she gasped and her body convulsed and she whimpered—she couldn't help it—her body had locked into position, unable to move, and Sky started to whimper, too, working harder because her body was locked so tightly against him and then she cried something, getting sucked under the huge wave of sensation, and her whole body then started to vibrate and shake.

He pushed and moved and thrust maybe three times more before he cried out—holding her so hard she thought he might crush her—and then collapsed.

He pulled himself out of her and moved a little to the side so as not to have all his weight on her. They were both perspiring heavily, trying to catch their breath.

"Oh, my," Mary Liz finally said, flinging her arm to cover her face.

Sky dropped the side of his face on her shoulder.

She unfurled her arm from her face and struggled to maneuver it around him. "Oh, Sky," she said on a sigh, contented.

He kissed her ear and whispered, "I'll never let you go."

17

Mary Liz slept like a rock until the telephone began to ring at eight-thirty the next morning. She looked next to her; Sky had left but there was a note. She picked up the phone, and then picked up the note. "Hello?"

"Mary Liz, this is Delores speaking. Mrs. Hoffman asked me to call you and ask if you might join her for breakfast, upstairs, on her terrace, at around nine o'clock. She said she was sorry to disturb you, but that it was very important."

Mary Liz was scarcely paying attention. She had read Sky's note three times already.

Mary Liz,
I love you.
Sky

"Mary Liz?" Delores said.

Her heart was pounding. "What? Yes, of course I'll come." She looked at the clock. "Let me just shower and throw on some clothes."

She hung up and rolled onto her back. Smiling. At the ceiling. Wishing she could just lie here, reveling in the scent of them.

Sky.

She got up and did little leaps all the way to the bathroom. *Sky!*

Mary Liz went in through the kitchen, where Delores took her breakfast order: poached eggs, bacon and an English muffin. She was famished. She went upstairs (humming, no less) and padded her way down the thick carpeting that led to Aunt Nancy's suite. The door was open, but she knocked anyway. Immediately Ashley started barking and tore around the door. Just as quickly, she stopped, wagged her tail and tried to jump up to say hi.

"Down, girl," Mary Liz whispered. "We don't jump on people."

"Is that you, Mary Liz?" Nancy called.

"Yes." She went out to the terrace, where Aunt Nancy, still in her dressing gown, was sitting under the awning, reading the paper, sipping coffee. "Thank you for coming up."

Mary Liz kissed her on the cheek and sat down. "Delores is making me breakfast."

"Good." Nancy put the paper down in the chair beside her. "Two things. First. The key you asked for—for the square door in the Safe Room...?"

She remembered. "Oh, right."

"We don't seem to have it anywhere. Not here, not in our safe-deposit boxes, and it's beyond Jake's ability to get it open. He's arranged for a specialist from the manufacturer to come Tuesday. You'll have to check with him about the exact time."

"That would be great," she said, something outside catching her eye.

"Second," her godmother said, "and this is rather serious, I'm afraid." She followed Mary Liz's eyes. "What is it? What do you see?"

"I'm not sure. Something's drifting in."

"Where?"

She pointed. "Way out, a couple hundred yards."

"I don't see anything."

"It looks like—" She squinted, trying to clear her eyes, and looked again. "Oh my God," she cried, feeling her stomach lurch. "Oh my God." She ran for the bedroom door, prompting Ashley to start barking.

Nancy grabbed the dog's collar. "What is it?"

"Someone's in trouble!"

As Mary Liz hurried down the stairs, she heard Aunt Nancy screaming, "Bertie! Bertie! Wake up!"

"Someone's drowning!" Mary Liz said to Delores, pushing her aside and running out the kitchen door. She flew across the porch, down the stairs, across the lawn to the walkway and down the stairs to the beach. When she hit the beach, she ran, stopping only at the water's edge to whip off her shoes.

Yes, the person was still there.

She sloshed her way in through the low tide, waded out to the sandbar, ran across it and then dived into deep water beyond. She swam fast and then stopped, treading water, trying to see where the swimmer was. The waves were rough and she was bobbing up and down. She heard something and looked back. Bertie was plunging in off the sandbar behind her. She swam out farther, toward a flash of blue and white, her fear starting to turn to dread.

She reached the body. It was a man. Obviously dead. In plaid trunks, facedown, in the water. Still, she tried to turn him over.

Dead weight. There was reason why they called it that.

Bertie got there, and the two of them, bobbing in the rough water, succeeded in flipping the body over. Bertie cupped the man's chin and started dragging him to shore.

Jake was running across the beach, Nancy and Delores behind him. As Mary Liz and Bertie reached the sandbar, Jake had splashed his way there, too, and the three of them took hold of the man's body and rushed it onto the beach, where Jake immediately dropped to his knees and started CPR.

After a minute, Bertie put a hand on Jake's shoulder. "Give it up, Jake, he's been dead awhile."

Jake sat up. The dead man's face had a massive purple bruise across the side of his forehead, temple and cheek, and there was a strange smattering of bruising across his chest and stomach; his tan was that of a golfer's, arms and legs brown, but the rest of his body was maidenly white.

The body was Herbert Glidden's.

18

By afternoon, chaos at the Big House had settled into an atmosphere of dull anxiety. The East Hampton police had arrived quickly, as did an ambulance, but at one-thirty the body was still on the estate, waiting for the county coroner.

The tide had started to come in, so the police had to move the body fifty feet up the beach as it was. And then the scorching sun had started to rise in the sky, threatening to hasten the decomposition of the body, and they decided to move the body up to the cabana. When the temperature hit ninety-one degrees, Jake hauled up an air conditioner from the basement to help cool the cabana off.

The New York press had started arriving (NBC by helicopter, a vacationing WCBS-TV reporter with a home video camera by boat, *Newsday* by foot through the bushes) and some New York state troopers arrived to help keep them off the estate. Because Herbert Glidden had been a California resident, two FBI agents came out to the house, as well.

At the Big House, the phone had been ringing off the hook. One call—which Nancy had on the speakerphone in the living room—was from an agent from ICA who summered in East Hampton. Did Nancy think this could be a good true-crime story? (In other words, since the murder happened around her house, didn't she agree that the murderer was much more likely to be a *somebody* as opposed to a *nobody?*)

"No one has suggested Herb was murdered," Nancy said calmly, "but I will make it a point to tell the police that you did." She hung up and turned to look at the group assembled: Bertie, Wendy, Mary Liz (settled on the floor, sitting back against the couch, Ashley's head resting on her thigh) and Claire MacClendon. In the study was Carlson Lieber, a criminal lawyer, whom Nancy had summoned to hang out in case of who knew what.

They had all talked to a local detective, then to a state trooper and then with the FBI agents. Yes, they had all seen Herb Glidden at the animal parade benefit at the airport last night, all, that is, except Claire because she hadn't gone. And then Glidden had been seen at the fireworks, sitting on the other side of the beach with Julius and Jeanine Hoffman, they thought. That was the last they had seen of him. Until this morning.

"The coroner's still in the cabana with the body," Jake reported, entering from the dining room. "Alex Glidden identified him. They think they'll be out within the hour."

"Any news?" Bertie asked.

"Not that they're saying," Jake said, sitting cross-legged on the floor. "They're just repeating what we thought. That it looks like he was swimming last night and got racked up on one of the jetties."

"What jetty?" Bertie said. "And the current's wrong to bring him from the closest one. No, it's a lot more likely someone smashed him in the head with a baseball bat."

"Bertie!" Nancy said, looking pale.

"Well, it's true, Mother, everybody hated him."

"It's all right," Claire murmured to Nancy, putting a hand around her shoulders. She looked at Bertie. "He could have swum into a tree trunk or a board. They wash in all the time."

"Or maybe he fell off a pleasure boat," Mary Liz said, "or was on a surfboard, a windsurfer, or in a rowboat, it could have been a lot of things."

"Herbert Glidden surfing," Bertie said. "Right."

"Well, he obviously felt like swimming last night," Wendy said. "He stripped to his boxers and went in."

That was something they had realized on the beach, that his plaid bathing trunks were actually only cotton boxer shorts. He must have stripped down and gone into the water. But from where? His house? It was pretty far.

"We'll all know soon enough," Nancy said, rising. "If you'll excuse me, I'm going to go upstairs. Claire, if you'd be an angel—"

"I'll handle the police, don't you worry. Get some rest."

"You're a lifesaver," Nancy said. "Are you staying? Tonight?"

"Yes, Nancy, I will."

Nancy had stopped on her way to the front hall, and was looking out the front picture window now, getting a faraway look in her eyes. "It's so strange, isn't it? Last summer we were all here..." She lowered her head for a few moments. "First Alfred and now Herb." Her head came up. "Oh, I don't know, maybe it isn't so strange." She moved out of the room.

Mary Liz jumped up, startling them all, including the dog. "Come on, Ashley," she directed. "Come on. You need to go upstairs and keep Aunt Nancy company."

Jake stayed in the Big House in case the police needed anything. Bertie, Mary Liz and Wendy were walking over to the guest house when they saw the body, in a body bag, being carried up from the cabana. Two attendants loaded it into the back of the ambulance at the head of the driveway. A police officer signaled to Bertie and he jogged over. They discussed something, looked at the Big House once and then shook hands. Bertie came back. "They're going to leave a couple of officers here to keep gawkers away," he reported. "And the coroner says the cause of death was drowning, although they're going ahead and doing an autopsy."

The inside of the guest house was even more formal than Mary Liz's cottage, and probably cleaner, she guessed, since she knew it had biweekly maid service. Mary Liz had drawn the line at having a weekly maid visit; yes, at home, it was true, she had a gal who came in once a week to clean, but here, when she was working right there in the cottage, it would have made her feel obscene. So the cottage was clean, but not like this.

Standing there, Mary Liz realized she was still in some kind of shock, under some kind of veil of denial.

She remembered how Glidden's dead flesh had felt in her hands as she tried to pull him in.

Wendy threw herself down in a chair, Bertie onto the couch. "Sit down," Wendy said.

"I don't know," Mary Liz said slowly. "I don't feel terribly well. I think I want to go to the cottage and lie down."

"We'll come get you if anything happens," Bertie promised.

"Thanks." She turned and went to the door.

"Mary Liz?" Wendy jumped up to come over to her. "If you need anything, call me, okay? If you'd just like to have someone else in the house. Or maybe you'd like to stay here tonight."

"I'll be okay," she said, touching her arm in gratitude, "but thanks."

There were two messages on her answering machine. One from her parents, and one from Bill Pfeiffer.

She dialed the number of Sky's cellular. It rang and rang, but there was no answer.

She called her parents and told them what she knew about Glidden's death, and told them, about ten times, not to worry, she was fine.

Then she dialed Bill Pfeiffer.

"I debated whether or not to call you," he said. "You've had quite a day."

"How did you hear?"

"Claire. She called earlier. We were supposed to go somewhere for lunch."

So they did like each other. Good for them.

"Last night I checked my office E-mail, because one of the kids in research was following up on something in the office yesterday. He called you, didn't he?"

"Yes, on Friday, he said one of my leads was panning out."

"Sure is," he said. "He worked on it all day yesterday." There was the rustle of papers. "I know this is a horrible time for you, Mary Liz, but then I thought maybe this would take your mind off things. I thought maybe I could fax you what I've got."

"Please do." She sighed, feeling utterly uninspired.

She went into the office to make sure the fax machine was on, and back into the kitchen to make a pot of coffee. Then, knowing her stomach would probably not be able to take the acid, she nixed the coffee and simply poured herself some water and put ice in it. She looked at the kitchen wall phone a minute, and then went over to it. She dialed Sky's number again. No answer. She looked up the Buckleys' home number and dialed.

"Hello?"

"Buck?"

"Yes."

"It's Mary Liz Scott."

There was a moment of hesitation and finally he said, "I'm so sorry you had to find him. It must have been a terrible shock."

"Thank you," she said. "Listen, Buck, I'm sorry to disturb you, but I'm trying to reach Sky and there's no answer on his cellular. Is he at the club, do you know?"

There was another moment of hesitation. "Actually, Mary Liz, Sky had an emergency at home and had to leave."

And he hadn't called her?

"He'll probably call you any minute," Buck hastened to add.

"Is someone sick?"

"He didn't say. He only said he had to leave and that he'd let us know as soon as he knew when he was coming back."

She felt a surge of relief. "Oh, so he's coming back."

"Oh, yeah," Buck said enthusiastically. "As soon as he can."

She hung up the phone, took her ice water and made her way to the office. The pages that were coming out of her fax machine turned out to be very interesting reading. And Bill was right. It did take her mind off things.

At five o'clock, Mary Liz, showered and dressed in clean shorts and blouse, knocked on the guest-house door. Wendy opened it and smiled. "You look so much better. Do you feel better?"

"Yes, indeed I do," she said, coming in.

Bertie was watching a ball game on television. "Hi," he said without looking away from the screen.

"Would you like a drink?" Wendy asked her.

"A beer would be wonderful," Mary Liz said. She sat on the other end of the couch from Bertie.

"Oh, brother!" he exclaimed as a Dodger was struck out by a Mets pitcher. He flicked the game off with his remote control and tossed the control on the coffee table. He looked at Mary Liz. "You do look better."

She nodded. "And I've got something important to talk over with you."

"Is it all right if I sit in?" Wendy asked, handing her the beer.

"As long as it's all right with Bertie."

"Fine with me."

The three settled in; Mary Liz took a long draft of her beer. It tasted great. "To begin with, Bertie—" she put her glass down on a coaster "—I've found some hidden assets your father had."

"Hidden," Bertie repeated.

"Hidden," Mary Liz confirmed. "Meaning that the IRS knows nothing of them. Now, whether your father should have paid taxes on them, I'm not sure yet. But I'm also not sure if he ever withdrew any income from those assets, if he had simply tucked them away for a rainy day."

"What kind of assets are we talking about?"

"It's a small film company in Amsterdam, but it also has a substantial video production and distribution company attached."

"Are you sure?" Bertie asked. "Dad always said he missed the boat on video."

"Oh, I'm very sure your father owned it. And get this, I'm also absolutely sure he and Bernard Braxer founded the company *together* in 1968."

"Dad's lawyer?" Bertie said. "Bernard Braxer was his partner?"

"Yes," Mary Liz said. "And their ownership was very cleverly concealed through a series of holding companies, that's why we're having such trouble finding—" She shook her head. "Look, you don't need to know that part. The important thing is, your father and Bernard Braxer were *joint tenants,* meaning that if one of them died, the other would get all of it—one hundred percent of the Amsterdam film company. But since they both died in the crash, it should be split fifty-fifty between their estates. The catch is, Braxer & Braxer handled all the documentation and contracts, your father kept no record of it at all. We have every reason to believe Braxer & Braxer intends to sit on that documentation, not say a word about it, and simply try and keep the whole thing for themselves."

Bertie's mouth dropped open.

"But if Mr. Hoffman kept no records," Wendy said, "how did you find out about this?"

Mary Liz smiled. "It was a fluke, believe me. But that's often the only way to find assets like this. To pick up on any chance mention of anything and run a tracer. Remember that guy you met at the fireworks last night? Bill Pfeiffer?"

"The guy with Claire," Bertie said.

"He's a lawyer, in finance, and his firm's been doing the research for me on things like this. Only this turned out to be something, while the others haven't yet. Anyway, I noticed your father made a note to himself in his income tax file of 1995 to tell Braxer he wanted to get out of Dag Gisteren. I didn't know if it was a stock, or a piece of real estate or what, so I ran a tracer on Dag Gisteren, and, seven holding companies later, found out it was an Amsterdam film company that your father and Braxer owned together."

Bertie was looking incredulous. "And the lawyers were just going to keep it? And not say anything?"

She nodded.

"How much are we talking about?" Wendy asked.

"Bertie's father's half? Anywhere between ten and twenty million. I simply won't know until I fly over and look at the whole operation firsthand. The tricky thing is, Bertie, the first thing I have to do is determine if there are any illegal aspects to the ownership. Because if there are, I'm going to suggest we keep quiet and let Braxer take the company for themselves—and after they do, *then* blow the whistle on them, leaving your family completely out of it." She took a swig of beer and continued.

"But, if the ownership turns out to be legitimate—and we're not going to have any problems with the IRS—then Bill and my dad say we'll have a way to prove that Braxer & Braxer is attempting to defraud the estate, and get their suit against your mother dismissed."

Bertie's face brightened. "Hey, that would be great."

"*If* the ownership is legal," Wendy reminded him. She looked to Mary Liz. "But if it's not legal, if there are problems, then we are to know nothing about it. Correct?"

"Correct."

"In that case," Wendy said, picking up the book on the coffee table and opening it, "I better erase this." Inside was a microcassette recorder.

"Wendy!" Mary Liz objected.

"He's my client," she said, nodding in Bertie's direction. "I have an obligation to protect him."

Mary Liz smiled, shaking her head.

"How much of this have you told Mother?" Bertie wanted to know.

"Only that I'm investigating the possibility of assets in foreign countries," she said. "Until I know what's what,"—*like whether or not your father had another son*—"I see no reason to burden her with this."

He nodded. Then he lofted an eyebrow, looking at her in the oddest way.

"What?"

He smiled. "I was just thinking what a great person you turned out to be."

"Thanks." She meant it. "Anyway, Bertie, the reason I'm telling you all this is because my father and I feel that at least one of the heirs needs to know what is going on." She smiled. "And you have been selected. So if it's all right by you, we'd like to keep you up to date on everything we do from here on in."

Mary Liz might as well have told Bertie he had been elected president of the United States, his surprise and elation was so instantaneous. "Really?" he said, eyes bright, "you want to talk to me?"

III

19

It was the wee hours of Monday morning and Mary Liz had not gotten more than three hours of sleep.

She hadn't heard from Sky and she kept thinking about Herb Glidden's body—what it had felt and looked like, and during what little sleep she did get, she was tormented by twisted nightmares of plane crashes and zombies.

At five-thirty she gave up and got up, put on her bathing suit and went to the beach. The sun was just coming up, and though it was surprisingly chilly after yesterday's heat, the day was absolutely gorgeous.

And then she started thinking about Glidden's body again. And then about Alfred Hoffman and Bernard Braxer, how the pilot had been making the critical climb out of Palm Springs with them on board, trying to get up and over the mountains, when the plane hit a bad downward draft simultaneously with the right engine stalling. The plane had dipped sharply to the right, the wing clipped the top of the mountain and they had gone cartwheeling down the other side. The plane broke up, the fuel tank exploded and the pilot and the copilot and the passengers were killed.

Dead, dead. Everybody dead.

Standing at the water's edge, she thought of Glidden's body again and thought what a fool she would be to go swimming without a partner.

Once more she thought of how Glidden's flesh had felt, and then she had to leave the beach altogether.

Dead.

She had prayed and prayed for most of her waking moments last night, not only for Glidden's soul, but for the recovery of her own. She felt as though she had glimpsed not only death, but the sure outcome of a man who had lived his life as though there would never be any consequences. And Mary Liz was not just thinking of his terrible death—no one should have to die like that, drowning—but of what Glidden was facing now, now that he was no longer a rich and powerful man, but merely a simple soul in search of a merciful God.

She believed that. With all her heart. And that's why she had stared at some of her colleagues at Reston, Kellaher in astonishment when they had done something less than ethical (and, boy oh boy, how some of them had), wondering, didn't they know that ducking the detection of the Securities Exchange Commission would do them no good in the end, that the consequences of unethical behavior was inevitable? That one day every single one of them would be held accountable for the actions of a lifetime?

When Mary Liz reached the top of the stairs from the beach, she smiled; Ashley was running around in the backyard and Aunt Nancy, in her dressing gown, was out there playing with her.

She must be feeling better, Mary Liz thought, walking over. Ashley saw her and came bounding across the lawn. Mary Liz bent down to say hi. "Hello, girl!" As usual, Ashley tried to lick her face off, but this time, at least, she didn't jump up.

"She's starting to obey," Aunt Nancy said. "At least sometimes."

Mary Liz laughed, gave the dog a final pat and straightened up. "Good morning."

"Good morning," her godmother said. And then Aunt Nancy's face took on a serious expression. "Darlin' Mary Liz," she said sadly, "come inside with me. There's something I need to show you."

Feeling apprehensive, Mary Liz followed her godmother into the house and upstairs to her room. Aunt Nancy led her to the sitting room and directed her to take a chair. Ashley settled in at her feet, resting her chin on Mary Liz's foot.

Nancy opened her secretary, withdrew an envelope and handed it to Mary Liz. "Herb gave this to me Saturday morning. When he told me you were working for him. I didn't even look at it until later. Until yesterday morning. That's why I had asked you to come up. But then..."

Then Mary Liz had seen the body in the ocean.

She looked down at the envelope; it was a plain legal one, with no writing on it. Mary Liz slid out a sheet of paper and unfolded it.

It was a photocopy of a college-yearbook page. Looking at the first entry, she realized it was a law-school yearbook.

"Stephen Pembroke," Aunt Nancy said.

She looked down, found the name—
It was Sky. In the picture.

STEPHEN M. PEMBROKE
Juris Doctor

Mary Liz looked at her godmother.
"Herb said Sky was working for him, too. That he's a lawyer, a finance lawyer."
Mary Liz looked down at the yearbook again. Stephen Pembroke? "Glidden lied about me, I'm sure he was lying about Sky, as well."
"Even so, Mary Liz, I think you need to ask Sky about this." She pointed to the paper in her hands. "Particularly about that."
This was a nice way of saying, Mary Liz, who the hell are you dating?
Mary Liz thanked her godmother, asked if she could have this, the yearbook copy, and made her way back down to the cottage. She did not believe for a second that Sky had been working for Glidden, but she also had no idea who Stephen Pembroke was.
She tried Sky's cellular number. No answer.
She looked at the clock; she'd wait a while and then call the Buckleys again.

When the phone finally did ring at the cottage, it was the police. They wanted to know if Mary Liz could come down to the station and answer some questions.
"I think I've told you everything I know," she said.
"Yes, Miss Scott, but now we are investigating a murder."
She wished this news surprised her.
"And we'd really appreciate if you came down today."
She promised to appear that afternoon and then called Wendy in the guest house. "The police want me to come down and answer some questions. They say Glidden was murdered."
"I know," Wendy said. "They called me, too. Bertie's already at the station. Carlson Lieber, that lawyer of Mrs. Hoffman's, found out Glidden's body was loaded with barbiturates when he drowned—sometime between one and three Sunday morning."
Sky had been in bed beside her then. Yes. They had still been up, still making love. Well, that was one worry down. "How do they know it was murder?"
"Lieber said somebody clubbed him over the head with a tool of some kind and the barbiturates had been injected," Wendy said.
"Oh."

To be drugged and drowned, how awful.

She and Wendy drove to the police station together. As they were going in, Alex Glidden was coming out with a man in a suit who was probably a lawyer.

"Alex," Mary Liz said, stopping him. "I'm so sorry. Truly."

Alex looked at her. "Why?"

She knew what he meant, but she also knew what he had to be going through. Before she quite realized what she was doing, she found herself giving the young man a tremendous hug. "Be strong for your mother, okay?"

He nodded grimly and walked away, the other man following.

"I guess you don't realize," Wendy said, watching him walk away, "that he's probably the murderer."

Mary Liz looked at her.

"He probably did it when Glidden came home from the fireworks. Hit him over the head, shot him full of drugs and tossed him into the ocean."

The worst thing was, Wendy could be right. She hoped not. Alex Glidden had enough of a battle to face in himself.

The police took Wendy in first and talked to her for nearly an hour and a half. Then another detective arrived, before Wendy was through, and he ushered Mary Liz into an office. He explained that he needed to ask her some questions, instructed her to answer them as best she could, and asked did she mind if he taped their conversation? Mary Liz said, no, not at all. And then she remembered what her father had always told her about answering lawyers' questions—answer what she was specifically being asked and add no more. She wondered if this applied to law enforcement, too.

When he asked her about Saturday night, she told him, yes, she had seen and spoken to Herbert Glidden at the animal parade. Yes, it was true, she had been very angry with him. Because he had gone around lying to everyone that she was working for him. No, of course she wasn't, she loathed the man. That's right, she had recently resigned from her job at Reston, Kellaher. She was here to do a family favor, to help her godmother inventory her deceased husband's estate.

No, she had never met or talked to Glidden before she met him at Nancy Hoffman's dinner party. Yes, he had financed Alfred's movies. No, he did not work for Howland Films. Yes, that's right,

Glidden had been suing the estate in an effort to take over the studio. No, she didn't know why.

Why did he want to hire her? She supposed Glidden admired the international work she had done as an investment banker. No, he first mentioned it at that same dinner party. Yes, the next morning he said he had run a check on her.

No, she didn't think he ever really thought she'd work for him. Right, so when he knew that for sure, he started telling people she was. To get the Hoffmans upset, to make Aunt Nancy think she was being betrayed and push her to get rid of her, and maybe her father, too, leaving her godmother wide open to harass. She didn't know for sure, but assumed Glidden felt that in that situation he could make Aunt Nancy give up and sell him the studio.

At the fireworks? Yes, she had known he'd been there, although she hadn't seen him herself. Someone said he was with Julius and Jeanine Hoffman. Yes, Sasha Reinhart had been there. Right, she has a movie with Howland Films this fall.

No, to her knowledge, her father had not seen Glidden in years. Yes, there was a lawyer in New York helping. Bill Pfeiffer. Yes, she would give him his number. No, he had never even met Glidden, as far as she knew.

Bertie? He had seemed absolutely fine to her. Yes, he stopped by the cottage around midnight to invite her up for a party. In the guest house. Yes, where Wendy Mitchell was staying. Who? Oh, Jake—he was a sort of overseer, for all the Hoffman properties, she thought. He had an apartment over the garage.

Vanessa Buckley? She had no idea why Vanessa was at Bertie's party. No, she didn't think there was anything between her and Bertie. Jake? No, she didn't think so.

That's right, she didn't go to the party, she stayed at the cottage. Uh… Well, yes, she did have someone with her. Sky Preston. He was staying with the Buckleys. Um, well, actually, yes, she did know he had parked up the street. Because he didn't want anyone to know he was at her house. For gossip reasons.

No, he wasn't married. No, he wasn't involved with Vanessa Buckley! It was because he's a gentleman. No, really, that's the way he is.

No, she didn't know where Sky was at the moment. No, she hadn't talked to him. Oh, yes, he had been there, with her, all night.

Absolutely. No, it wasn't the kind of evening she would forget. (She smiled despite herself.)

Oh, the message I left with Alex. Yes, I guess I did say he would be lucky if I only killed him. Yes, I was very angry! But no, absolutely not, I had absolutely nothing to do with what happened to the poor man.

No, she had no objections to being fingerprinted, but as a securities analyst her fingerprints were already on file. Was she a suspect? No? Because of her alibi? (Her alibi of sleeping with a man who had disappeared right after the murder? she thought. What kind of alibi was *that?*)

No, she had no idea who might have murdered him, they'd have to ask the people who knew him best. Oh, the Buckleys, Claude and Isabel Lemieux, Randolph Vandergilden, Henry MacClendon, Charles Kahn... They played poker with him or something. No, for years, she thought. Yes, Julius played in the game, too. Yes, but Julius knew Herb extremely well from working at Howland Films. No animosity she knew of, except they both wanted the studio.

Bertie? He was very irritated with Glidden for suing his mother, but not *that* irritated.

By the time the detective let Mary Liz go, she was a nervous wreck. She went outside to find that Wendy wasn't much better. Comparing notes in the car, it was clear the police didn't have a clue who had killed Glidden.

"What a wonderful surprise," Claire MacClendon said when Mary Liz arrived on her doorstep. "You're just what the doctor ordered—a distraction."

"Right back at you," Mary Liz said, accepting Claire's brief hug.

It was long after dinner and dusk was descending. Claire gave her a quick tour of the yard (big, with woods in back), her gardens and her studio. The latter was shingled in cedar with enormous windows and skylights, while the main house was more turn-of-the-century, with smaller windows and white sashes. "It's supposed to look old," Claire said to Mary Liz. "Henry designed it and we only built it nineteen years ago."

It was not an overly large house. It had a living room, kitchen, bedroom and bath downstairs, and two bedrooms and a bath on the second floor. On the far side of the house was a huge screened-in porch where Claire evidently lived on summer nights. It was to this "room" she took Mary Liz, offering her a cup of coffee, and she was obviously pleased when Mary Liz remarked on the incredibly wonderful scent coming from Claire's gardens.

They settled in with their coffee, and whether it was Claire's mood—which was thoughtful—or the death of Herbert Glidden, Claire was nostalgic tonight, and once she got started on the subject of "The Gang," it was hard to stop her.

And so Mary Liz didn't try to, but happily sat back, put her feet up on an ottoman, sipped her coffee and let the painter take her back to another world.

"I was so nervous yesterday that Herb's death might start unraveling Nancy," Claire said. "There are *decades* of memories there, you know. And I can't say that Herb's death left me unshaken, either. It's all so intertwined with Nancy's past with Alfred."

"When did you first meet the Hoffmans?"

"Oh, I was young then—in comparison to now, at any rate. Henry and I had been building this very house, a lot of it with our own two hands. Nancy was the one who contacted us. She said she had heard that Henry was a very clever architect, and wondered if he would come over and look at the big old white elephant they had just bought in East Hampton. See if he had any ideas."

Claire remembered so very well, and so ably described to Mary Liz, turning into the driveway of the manor for the first time, and how overgrown with weeds and wild roses and trees it had been. The roof of the caretaker's cottage by the front gate had completely collapsed, and the guest house was boarded up, with brambles and bushes growing over the porch. The Hoffmans were Hollywood people; she and Henry had both known that and they were very nervous. While Henry was doing okay, he was still, at that point, at forty-one, working for someone else, and was anxious to break out on his own. But he had two little girls, one four and one only a year old, and an ailing grandmother he supported. And so no matter how run-down the manor was, the MacClendons had known that any work he did there would be seen by the crème de la crème of society and might, in the end, offer a way out of his firm.

How different East Hampton had been back then! The big farms were still there, the big estates, the nice homes and yards of the year-round people. What were missing in those days were the condos and the traffic and about five thousand weird-looking new summerhouses.

Bridgehampton, good grief, it had been like a farming village, but even back then it had been a retreat for writers and artists. Claire remembered so well once seeing James Jones, Irwin Shaw, William Styron and Truman Capote standing together on a shady corner of Main Street, and stopping the car to try to explain to little Madeline why it was important she remember that image for the rest of her life.

That day they had first gone to the manor, Alfred hadn't been there. It was Nancy who'd greeted them, and from the first she and Claire hit it off. Denver, the Hoffmans' daughter, who was all of about five at the time, happily took charge of Madeline to play with, and their nanny, an older woman Denver called My-Mimi, My-Mimi, gladly took baby Emily into her arms so that Claire could accompany her husband on the tour of the estate.

Henry's passion as an architect was revising the principles of historic American architecture to incorporate the innovations of new building materials. The plan he ended up designing for the Big House was typical of him. He recommended the restoration of the turn-of-the-century front, and that the addition Nancy wanted be built in a way that made it appear to be an original part of the house. The plan also called for a complete renovation of the back of the mansion, so as to bring as much light and air as possible into the dank old place. The landscaping design Henry developed with a local was superb. But the real genius was in Henry's plans for the execution of these grand designs: it was a ten-year plan, specifically created so the Hoffmans would never miss a day of summer, and, should the Hoffmans ever suffer a financial reversal, they could simply stop the development at various stages and still have a magnificent house and property.

Before the renovation even started, when it was all still only plans, the Hoffmans had taken the series of blueprints back to Beverly Hills to study, and not long after, Henry's phone began ringing off the hook. Everybody in Los Angeles, it seemed, wanted a ten-year plan for their property. They wanted to know what they could do as their fortunes rose, and they wanted to know exactly what they would have—and how impressive it would be—if their fortunes never increased after stage one.

And so, with three such contracts in hand nineteen years ago, Henry MacClendon had gone out on his own. And that was when he began to be away for long periods of time, at a mansion in Malibu, a palace in the Hollywood Hills, even an estate renovation in France.

During that very first visit, though, while her husband was crawling around in the attic and basement of the Big House, Nancy and Claire had sat outside on the rickety porch and drunk lemonade. Nancy was irresistible in those days, even more so than today, because back then less had happened to her and she still possessed that kind of "oh-gosh" Southern-belle quality that Claire would later see her lose.

It had also been that first day, on the rickety back porch of the Big House, that Claire first met Herb Glidden. A car had torn up the driveway and Nancy had called to the driver from the porch, and a much younger Herb Glidden had dashed up the back stairs, panting, "Where's Al?"

"He's deep-sea fishing," Nancy said. "Herb, I'd like you to meet—"

"We've got to radio him or something!" he said excitedly. "I've got it, Nancy!"

Nancy turned to Claire. "Herb has been after Alfred to let him co-produce a film."

"Fifteen million dollars!" Herb cried, doing a little jig and nearly falling when he hit a bad floorboard.

Both Henry MacClendon and Herbert Glidden's careers were about to take off. Henry was getting his contracts for private homes, Herb had gotten fifteen million dollars to finance Alfred's feature film starring a relatively unknown singer from the New York theater world, Sasha Reinhart. Who could have known the public would go in droves—many more than once—to see her in a movie?

Claire became Nancy Hoffman's favorite on the East End. Every summer when Nancy arrived, Claire was the first person she called. And after Henry's work took off, not only were the MacClendons invited to the Hoffmans all the time, but the MacClendons were invited to parties by all sorts of rich and important people they had never met. And then when the money started coming in, the MacClendons became regulars at the high-price benefits, as well, all of which—the parties and the benefits—Claire frankly hated to attend ("Why can't we just write them a check and cook outside with the girls?"), but attended anyway because she knew how important the contacts were for Henry's business.

Were those happy summers? Claire used to think so, but she wondered about it sometimes now. There were happy times, many happy times, but every time she really thought about those happy times, she could scarcely remember Henry even being there: the cookouts at their house or the Hoffmans'; letting the kids sleep outside in a tent; the girls dressing up like cheerleaders for Bertie's baseball games; Denver and Madeline riding in horse shows; taking all the children fishing, or sailing, or playing Scrabble with them on the back porch of the Big House, or working on the giant jigsaw puzzle Nancy always left in progress all summer long on a table in their playroom.

Claire could not remember Henry there. As a matter of fact, she couldn't remember Alfred being there, either. Or if she did, it was a memory of the men standing outside in a haze of cigar smoke, or sneaking down to the renovated cottage to play poker with the gang.

The gang. Oh, how young they had all been! None of them could possibly still drink like that (as evidenced by the one who hadn't slowed down at all, Randolph—who might have stayed sober after rehab if he hadn't taken over that dreadful winery). The old gang: Alfred and Nancy, Henry and Claire, Randolph and Marie (who left Randolph and headed for Europe about six years ago). There was Alfred's divorced (and penniless) golfing pal from California, Buck Buckley, who came to visit about ten years ago and got hooked up with the young heiress, Vanessa Walker (or had it been Driscoll then?), thrice married already and choosing Buck as her fourth. There was Alfred's stockbroker, Charles Kahn and his wife, Rachelle, and she remembered so well when Rachelle's dress-design business started to take off and Charles quit the Street to run it. And then the latecomers to the group arrived, maybe six years ago, the Lemieuxes, Claude and Isabel, fresh from Paris. She was sort of a mindless drag, but Claude and Alfred got on famously as winning partners on the tennis court.

But Herb Glidden had never been included if the Hoffmans could help it. It wasn't that Nancy found him common (How could she? When it had taken all this time to get the gold jewelry off Alfred and make him stop flashing his bucks?), it was that having Herb around put Alfred in a terrible mood. Over and over again Nancy would talk to him about it, why did he do business with Herb if he so disliked him, and Alfred would say he didn't dislike him, he just couldn't stand him in his house. He was a social climber, a clinger-on, and Alfred hated it.

(He hated it, Claire thought, because he must have seen in Herb a lot of what he himself used to be. And like Alfred, Herb was rapidly learning, dropping his questionable manners and taste and adopting those that were expected in high social circles. Herb even took elocution lessons in L.A., Alfred, drunk one night, had told everybody.)

The gang. Once a week there was a poker game in the cottage. The regulars were Alfred, Henry, Randolph, Buck, Charles and later Claude, but when Alfred was out of town, which he often was, Julius was supposed to substitute. But somehow Herb Glidden always seemed to push himself into the game. Henry told Claire that the one time Herb showed up as a substitute for Buck, Alfred had nearly walked out on the game. But this was the way Alfred was around Herb Glidden. He practically humiliated the guy every time he showed his face in East Hampton. And yet Herb always took it, and always doggedly resumed trying to be included.

They were a strange pair, those two. Alfred and Herb. And now they were both dead.

The knocking at the front door of Claire's house persisted. Claire and Mary Liz looked at each other. Claire looked at her watch. "It's late," she said, rising from her chair. "Who could it be?"

The person knocked again, harder.

"I hope it's not about one of the children," Claire said suddenly, rushing into the living room.

Mary Liz heard the front door open and Claire say, "Henry! What is it? What's happened? It's not the girls, is it?"

"No, no, nothing like that," Henry said.

There was a moment of silence, and then Mary Liz heard Claire say, "You scared the hell out of me. I thought something had happened to one of the girls."

"I'm sorry," he said.

There was silence again. "Henry, what is it, what's wrong? You look terrible." And then, "Oh, no, something hasn't happened to the baby, has it? Or to Cindy?"

"No." He cleared his throat. "She just delivered a little boy. Tonight. I just came from the hospital."

"And the baby's okay? Come in, come on, I'll fix you something to eat."

"I'm sorry to bother you," he said quietly. Mary Liz imagined he was following her to the kitchen. "I didn't know where else to go. I was in Washington when I got the call, and I flew back and she was in full-fledged labor."

"And the baby's all right?" Claire asked again.

"Oh, yes, he's fine. Six and half pounds. Screamed his lungs out. Cindy's fine, too."

"A boy. I'm glad for you, Henry. You always wanted a little boy."

It was silent again for several moments and then Mary Liz heard Claire whisper, "What is it? What's wrong?"

She swore she could hear Henry MacClendon sobbing.

"What is it?" Claire whispered again.

"I want to be with you," he said, starting to sob harder.

Mary Liz wondered if she should just slip out the porch door and go home. Leave them alone. She decided she'd wait three minutes more and then—

"I'm sorry, Henry," Claire murmured, "but you have to leave. You have to go home and rest." Pause. "Cindy and the baby need you. You know that."

He blew his nose.

Silence.

Mary Liz heard the door open and then close. Outside, Henry had started up his car and was pulling out.

Mary Liz just sat there, waiting.

Fifteen minutes later, Claire came back out on the porch. Her eyes were red and her face blotchy. She looked at Mary Liz. "So who says there're no surprises left in the world?"

20

"Research tells me you just put in a request to profile a firm called Dunlau Gunney in Dublin," Bill Pfeiffer said to Mary Liz Tuesday morning.

"Yes."

"Why?"

Mary Liz frowned at the phone in her hand before returning it to her ear. "Because I want a profile of Dunlau Gunney."

"And I'm asking you why and what it has to do with the Hoffman estate." He sounded as annoyed as she felt.

Mary Liz had found this name in Alfred's business diary and had been pondering it. He had evidently jotted it down this past January while filming in Ireland. This was the trip that Nancy and Bertie had accompanied him on (the one where they had rescued Ashley while tracking ancestors on the west coast).

There was no record of any connection between this investment firm and Alfred, none that Mary Liz could find, but it made her curious that Alfred would have written down the name so carefully. And so, on a hunch, at lunchtime she had called Herbert Glidden's office in L.A. and reached his personal secretary. Holding the phone away from her mouth, she said, "Hellooo! I am calling froom Dooblin," and pretended she worked for Dunlau Gunney. The secretary hesitated only a moment and then offered the sad news that Mr. Glidden had passed away in a swimming accident over the weekend. Then she offered Mary Liz the telephone number of the law firm who was handling all inquiries. "Dooo they have our files? Will they know what I'm calling about?" Mary Liz asked.

"They have your files," the secretary admitted.

"And what be the firm's name?" Mary Liz said, stretching her luck (her brogue was really bad).

"Kleighorn & Myers. They're here in L.A. and are handling Mr. Glidden's estate."

The call confirmed that Herb Glidden had a connection with this investment firm, and it was clear that Alfred Hoffman, while in Dublin, had intended to go there, or call them, or check on them, or something. He had scribbled three other names on that diary page, one that turned out to be an independent investment banker in Paris, the second a commercial bank in Brussels, and the third a commodities broker in Amsterdam. Not wanting to go off half-cocked, Mary Liz wanted a profile on the Irish investment house to see what turned up before investigating the others.

But this was hardly reason for Bill Pfeiffer to be so annoyed with her.

"I'm sorry to get so upset," Bill was saying, "but dammit, Mary Liz, my firm bills at three-fifty an hour, and I can't bill your father for this stuff. It has nothing to do with the estate, as far as I can see."

Mary Liz hesitated. She could argue with him about it, or she could simply back down and go another route. She opted for the latter. She wanted to keep her father out of this, anyway. He'd be upset if he knew she was sniffing around Glidden's past when the man had just been murdered.

She sighed heavily into the phone. "You're right. I apologize. I was just curious. I knew Alfred had been filming in Ireland in January, and I just wondered if he had done any business with Dunlau Gunney while he was there."

"There's no sign that he did, is there?"

"Well, no," she lied.

"Then where did you get the name from?"

Come on, think of something.

"Actually, it was for Bertie. He's thinking about making a film there—he went with his father last time, you know, to Dublin—and he asked me if I knew anybody who might have some investors that'd be interested. A friend mentioned the firm to me but I wasn't familiar with it."

"Tell Bertie then," Bill said, "if he really wants us to look into it, we will, but that I will bill him directly—at three hundred and fifty dollars an hour."

"I'll tell him. Sorry, I wasn't thinking. Shred and toss the request, I've got someone I should have hooked him up with in the beginning. Oh, by the way," she added, moving things along, "Dad's pushed the papers through, so I can sit down with the film guys in Amsterdam next week. And while I'm there, I guess, go on to Paris and check out those miscellaneous European expenses—those women and the boy."

"Very good. We may be able to wrap this up pretty quick, then."

"Hope so."

As soon as Mary Liz got off with Bill, she dialed her father and waited for his assistant to get him on the line.

"Hi," he said. "How are you feeling?"

"Much better, Dad, thanks. Listen, I was wondering when I could expect the papers for Amsterdam?"

"Are you sure you don't want me to go with you?"

Absolutely not, she thought. Because she had already determined there were going to be one or two things she'd do while she was over there off the radar. She assured him there was no need for him to come. He said the papers would be FedExed and be in her hands Saturday at the latest.

"Great, I can fly out of here on Sunday," she said, making a note. "Dad, by the way, does Bill Pfeiffer work for me, or do I work for him?"

"He works for me and you report to me, so it's a stalemate. Why?"

"Just wondered."

"You haven't had a disagreement, have you?"

"No. I just wondered if I was in the position to be able to overturn his veto if I wanted."

"Through me you can. Always, babe."

Shortly after Mary Liz hung up, someone knocked on the cottage door. It was a young woman in a uniform who worked for something called RFT. "Mary Liz Scott?"

"Yes."

"Would you sign here, please?" The girl pushed a clipboard at her and Mary Liz signed on the very first line. "Thank you." And then she handed Mary Liz an envelope and walked off to her Jeep.

Mary Liz closed the door. The envelope had nothing on it, no return address, nothing. She used a knife in the kitchen to slit it open. There was a small piece of paper inside, partly torn, upon which someone had hastily scribbled:

House, phone, fax, computer bugged.
1-800-555-4949

She went back to the door; the Jeep was gone.

She reread the note and went up to the guest house and knocked on the door. She motioned for Wendy to come out on the front lawn.

When they were away from that house, Mary Liz said, "I just got this." She handed her the note, which Wendy read. "I have no idea who it's from. Some fake deliveryperson just made me sign for it, if you can believe."

Wendy looked at her. "We need to sweep the cottage, then. The guest house, too, to say nothing of the Big House."

"Do you know somebody who could do it?"

She nodded. "Yes. Someone excellent. From the city. I can probably get him out here tomorrow."

"Good."

"Who do you think it is?"

"I have no idea. And I have no idea why anybody would—" She cringed. "Unless it's Braxer & Braxer, trying to find out what we know." She clutched her head as if she had been hit. "The phone, the fax, the computer—dammit! If it's them, they know everything I know now!" She held her head again, ready to scream. "Oh, God, please, tell me I didn't give them the whole thing."

"But it might not be them," Wendy reminded her.

"Who else could it be?"

"Well, there's Glidden. And he's dead now."

True.

"Or Julius."

Mary Liz shook her head. "Somehow I don't think so. Glidden or Braxer & Braxer, I should think."

"And maybe you're not bugged at all. All we've got is this—and it sure looks fishy to me. Look at the scrawl. And what's that number?"

"I don't know, I haven't called—my phone's bugged, remember?"

"Yeah, well, mine may be, too, so if I were you, Mary Liz, I'd find a pay phone."

Mary Liz drove into town, feeling more like a spy every minute. She'd had the presence of mind to bring quarters for the telephone so none of her calls would appear on her credit card.

Yes, she was paranoid. Who wouldn't be?

God. Wonder if it was true? That someone had bugged the cottage?

First she made a call to Chicago, reaching an old friend and colleague who was working in research at an investment bank. Her request was an in-depth profile on each of the four names Alfred Hoffman had jotted down in his diary: Dunlau Gunney, Eeghlenburger, Banque de Veurne, and Jacques Gorce.

While Mary Liz complied with the operator and fed more quarters into the telephone, Marla Maples Trump walked by with a little girl. What a town.

"I'll get you everything I can find, Mary Liz," Betsy promised from her office.

"All I can say is thank you."

"How do you want me to get the information to you? On-line?"

"No!" Mary Liz nearly shouted. "I mean, no, Betsy. Federal Express, if you could, I have a charge number to use. Send it to me here, at this address."

After hanging up with Betsy, she took a deep breath, looked at the number on the paper again and dialed it. It was toll-free.

"Rapid Fire Transit," a male voice said.

"Oh," Mary Liz said.

"Hello? May I help you?" the man said.

"I, um, not long ago, you people delivered a package to my house. And this number was on the note inside."

"What's your name?"

"Mary Liz Scott."

"And your mother's maiden name?"

She squinted at that one. "What is this, some kind of credit-card scam?"

"No," the man said simply.

"I am not going to tell you my mother's maiden name," she told him.

A sigh. "Okay, then tell me the first name of your last boyfriend."

"My *what?*"

"Then give me his nickname, I don't care," the guy said. "If you want to get your message, you're going to have to tell me, and I don't know how else to prove to you this is no credit-card scam."

"Wait a minute," Mary Liz said, turning her back to the teenager who was waiting to use the phone, "I'll tell you his nickname, but you tell me his last name."

"I don't have his last name," the man said. "Only the first."

"Okay," Mary Liz said. "His nickname was Ken."

"Short for Kennedy."

"That's correct."

"Okay, Ms. Scott, hang on, this may take a while."

Mary Liz turned to the teenager. "I'm so sorry, but this is going to take longer than I thought."

"So what am I supposed to do?" the boy asked. "I'm supposed to call my mother."

Mary Liz handed him a five-dollar bill. "Find another pay phone."

He took off and she turned back around, waiting. And waiting. Maybe five minutes went by and then there was a clicking noise and suddenly she heard Sky's voice say, "Hello?" It was very faint. And then the first man's voice said, "Go ahead, she's clear."

"Hello? Mary Liz?"

"Sky, where are you? Are you okay?"

"I had an emergency. I had to leave. I couldn't call until today and I don't have long. Mary Liz, you've got to pull back on anything you're doing that's in any way connected to Glidden."

"What is going on, Sky? You must have something to do with—"

"Just listen to me, please! Don't do anything about Glidden. Don't say anything about Glidden. Don't say it, don't write it, don't even think about it—you're being watched, you're being monitored. Just back off! Do you understand? I can't tell you any more—"

The line started to break up.

"Sky?"

"I love you," he said, the line crackling terribly. "Promise me, Mary—"

The line went dead. And then a moment later, there was a dial tone.

Mary Liz pushed the receiver down and redialed the number. There was a funny electronic sound and then a recording that said that it was not a working 800 number.

She called again. And got the same recording.

But he had reached her. And warned her. And told her that he loved her.

But who the hell was he? She had forgotten to ask.

When she got back to the estate, Mary Liz found the master locksmith from the vault manufacturer waiting for her. She walked him up to the Big House, introduced him to Delores and told Ashley not to bite him, and then, with Ashley, accompanied him downstairs to watch as he worked on the three-foot-by-three-foot vault no one had keys to.

After about forty minutes, the door opened, revealing a file cabinet inside that was crammed with manila folders. With her heart quickening, Mary Liz quickly signed all the necessary paperwork and locked the Safe-Room door behind her to see him out. As soon as he drove away, she and Ashley dashed back downstairs, and she locked the door behind them.

Maybe these files would explain everything.

The drawer in the vault slid out easily and her hands were almost trembling. These could tell her everything she needed to know. This vault could contain all the secrets, of the estate, of Alfred's relationship with Herbert Glidden, what Braxer & Braxer knew; she might walk out of here knowing all.

She pulled out a bunch of folders in front and brought them over to the table. She sat down and drew the first one to her. "Adams, Lucinda," it said on the tab. The name was hand-written. In Alfred's handwriting.

She opened the file.

A photo was stapled to the left-hand leaf. It was of a pretty young woman, dressed in an inexpensive evening gown. Whoever had been in the picture with her had been cut out. The right side of the folder had notes written on it, also in Alfred's hand. The buzzer on the Safe-Room intercom door buzzed and Mary Liz's heart stopped. "It's me, Mary Liz!"

Aunt Nancy.

"Coming!" she called.

Mary Liz quickly emptied one of the Howland Films cardboard file-storage boxes and transferred the files from the vault into it. Then she stuffed some Howland files into the vault, replaced the lid on the storage box, put it down with the other Howland files boxes and went to the door. She opened it.

"There you are," Nancy said to Ashley, bending to pet her. "It's your dinnertime, silly girl." She looked at Mary Liz. "Did the technician get the vault open?"

"Yes."

"What in heaven's name was in there?" Nancy said, moving past Mary Liz to look. She examined some of the files, frowning. "These are just more Howland files."

"I'm afraid so," Mary Liz acknowledged, "but I'll go through them carefully. It looks like your husband just wanted to keep a duplicate file here on certain projects."

"Or Alfred shoved these in here because he couldn't stand to see it empty after spending so much money to install it." She sighed. "That would be just like him. Well..." She looked over at the dog and raised her eyebrows. Ashley was over by the Howland boxes, sniffing at the box where Mary Liz had put the files from the vault. "Come on, beautiful silly creature," Aunt Nancy said, walking to the door and holding it open. "Dinner!" Finally the dog tore herself away from the box and followed her mistress.

Phew.

Mary Liz slid the bolt across the door. And then she went over to get the box of files on the floor and drag it over to the table.

Adams, Lucinda

3/89 Waitress in backwater café Route 101. Stopped in limo. Surprised by beauty. Ordered food, ate at counter, talked to her about movies. Asked ever ride in stretch? Said no, eyes shining, clearly interested. Took a break, picked her up in back, driver went in circle. Sucked Buster. Really good. So much for innocence.

Picked up later and went to motel. Two hours. Gave her normal and then let me give it in the ass. Fun. Gave her some bucks. Gave me her prom picture! Nice kid. Sixteen, she said.

Talk about surprises. This was going to be an inventory of a different kind. For sure.

21

"I've got good news and I've got bad news," the electronics expert said Wednesday afternoon as he met Wendy, Mary Liz and Bertie in the middle of the front lawn. The three had just come from the tennis court where Jake had run them all around in a lively match. Jake said they needed to be run around, that they all looked stressed-out.

And they were. Bertie had just come from his fifth interview with the police.

"Good news first, if you please, Liam," Wendy said. She had brought him out from New York to sweep the property for listening devices.

"Good news is," Liam began, "the grounds themselves are clean. The cabana's clean. The Big House is clean. And the guest house is clean."

"Thank God," Bertie said.

Liam turned to Mary Liz. "But the cottage, I'm afraid, is wired for sound, I mean figuratively and literally."

Mary Liz started to feel sick. She hadn't been paranoid for nothing. She should have been *more* paranoid. From the start. Since the day she got here.

"I think what's best is I take you in and point out what I've found. If you don't want me to disconnect or disturb what's set up in there, we have to be careful, though."

"Boy, it's hot!" Mary Liz declared, coming in the front door of the cottage. "What do you guys want to drink?" And then she and Wendy and Bertie proceeded to try to act and sound normal as Liam walked over and pointed to the small chandelier of lights that hung from the kitchen ceiling, to the top of a lamp in the living room, and then took them into her office where Liam pointed to the Scotch-tape holder on the desk.

They continued to talk and made a show of going out on the front porch—where Liam pointed to the bottom of the porch swing—and then the group loudly decided to go next door to the guest house for some cold beers.

When they were at the side of the house, Liam pointed to some metal conduits that went inside the house.

When they reached the living room of the guest house, Mary Liz found herself wanting to cry. "Who is doing this, Liam? Do you have any idea?"

"This much I can tell you. We've definitely got two different parties listening in, possibly three. My best guess is three."

They all looked at him in horror.

He nodded. "The bug in the kitchen lights and the one that's screwed into the lamp in the living room—that's the same guy. Or gal. Someone else, I believe, put the bug down in the well of your Scotch-tape holder in the office and planted the bug on the porch.

"What kind are they?" Wendy asked.

"Microphones and transmitters."

"So where are the receivers?" Wendy asked.

"My guess is, the receivers are very close by, being monitored live, or being recorded on laser disc in a stash somewhere.

"Then outside," Liam continued, "on the access pipe for the phone lines into the house, inside that little metal box, someone's put in a tri-splitter, diverting the phone, fax and computer."

"Splitting them off to where?" Wendy said, frustrated.

"I can't track it, not without the phone company."

Mary Liz sighed, collapsing on the sofa and rubbing her eyes. She had spent hours going through Alfred Hoffman's secret files last night, which had served only to haunt her with more nightmarish visions and deprive her of yet more sleep.

"What do you want to do, Mary Liz?" Wendy asked her.

"Leave them, I guess, for the moment," she said. "But Liam, for heaven's sake, leave me your card. I may change my mind."

"Oh, and one other thing," Liam added, pulling something out of his shirt pocket and holding it up. It looked like an elaborate, black rubber dart, "I found this outside—"

"Oh, that's mine," Wendy said, swiping it out of his hand. "Forget about that one."

"Wendy!" Mary Liz said.

"It was from a long time ago, when you first came. It fell off the window and I couldn't find it. That was *ages* ago."

"At least two weeks," Bertie confirmed.

Mary Liz looked at Liam. "Leave me your bill before you go, okay?"

"No," Bertie said, shaking his head. "This one's on me. As your host."

"My host," Mary Liz repeated, getting up from the chair. "Well, dear host, I have some thinking to do. So I'm going to lie down in my bug-infested cottage and think things through. I'll let you know what's what before I leave for Europe." She turned to Liam, "The bedroom and the bathroom are *not* bugged, is that correct?"

"They are not bugged."

She went down to her bug-infested cottage, which *felt* as if it was bug-infested (the real kind, making her look over her shoulder and under her pillow every five minutes), and thanked the heavens she could at least stretch out on the bed without worrying about radio waves penetrating her brain.

She needed to think.

She needed to make a decision about the right thing to do.

About a lot of things.

It was nearly 1:00 a.m. when Mary Liz, sitting down in the Safe Room of the Big House, looked at her watch. Her neck was stiff, her back was practically locked and she could no longer ignore the state of her bladder. She got up, stretched, unbolted the door and took care to lock it behind her. She went upstairs to use the powder room off the kitchen, got a glass of milk from the Hoffmans' refrigerator (her stomach was killing her; it knotted and cramped whenever she concentrated too hard for too long), and she was about to take her drink back downstairs when she heard voices in the study. Bertie and Wendy were still up. She started down the hall to say hello, and to let them know she was there, when she heard Bertie, who sounded extremely upset, say, "I can't believe you could think that!"

"I don't think anything," Wendy said quietly. "I'm merely asking you. To make sure. And keep your voice down, you'll wake up the whole house."

"Fuck you, Wendy."

"Bertie, look at it from my point of view. Your mother told you something that night that set you off, and the last time I saw you, you said you were going to shut Glidden up for good. You disappear, the police say you were seen taking the boat out of the marina—"

"I went out to cool off."

"Or you could have gone to Glidden's beach, knocked him over the head, filled him full of drugs and then dumped him in the ocean."

"Right, so he'd wash up on *our* beach. What kind of idiot do you think I am?"

"You're keeping something from me, Bertie," Wendy said. "I know you, and I know you're not telling me something about that night. And since you, of all people, are supposed to trust me, why shouldn't I think you had something to do with it?"

"If I wanted to murder Glidden, I wouldn't have done it myself," Bertie said. "And I would have had it done on the West Coast, and probably the same way Glidden had my father killed."

The way Glidden had his father killed?

"Which is yet another motive for you to kill him."

There was silence for several moments.

"You hired me to do a job, Bertie. And you won't trust me to do it." Pause. "I thought you trusted me."

"It has nothing to do with all of this," Bertie said.

"You're lying. And I want to know why."

There was a pause, and then Bertie said, "I can't."

"Fine. I quit."

There was the squeak of leather and Mary Liz started, knowing that Wendy had probably stood up and was preparing to leave. She backed down the hall.

"Wendy, *please.*" Bertie sounded agonized.

What should she do? Make noise and come down the hall? Or walk in and simply ask them what this is all about?

"Wendy," Bertie said in a hoarse voice, "if I tell you what Mother told me that night, you have to swear on your life that you'll never tell Mary Liz."

There was a long silence. "I can't promise that, Bertie."

Pause. "Then I can't tell you."

"Then just tell me this, on your *mother's* life, Bertie, did you have anything to do with Glidden's murder?"

"I swear on my mother's life, no."

Still carrying the glass of milk, Mary Liz went back down the hall and downstairs to the basement. When she reached the table in the Safe Room, door secured behind her, she found that her hands were shaking.

You have to swear on your life that you'll never tell Mary Liz.

What could it possibly be about?

She took a large swallow of milk, put the glass down and then put her head down on her arms.

It was getting to be too much. She was on overload. Never in her life had she experienced multiple kinds of shocks like this, and not normal life shocks, but weird, twisted, fantastic shocks: Sky at an 800 number that disappears; three different parties bugging her cottage; a guy who wants to hire her is drugged and drowned; Aunt Nancy tells Bertie something about Glidden that Bertie would do anything to keep Mary Liz from finding out about.

And this. These files Alfred had locked away. She brought her head up, face screwing up in distaste and revulsion.

It would kill Aunt Nancy if she ever saw these files. And no doubt many lives would be destroyed should any of them ever reach the light of day.

On her legal pad she had listed the names of the two hundred and seventy-six women who had a file in here, and any information that could help Mary Liz locate them if she needed to. For a couple of them, she hadn't had to jot down any information because she knew exactly where to find them.

Here. In East Hampton.

It was bad enough realizing that Alfred Hoffman was a sexual sicko, obsessed with chronicling his every sexual conquest. And, judging from the condition of the files, he had thumbed through them again and again, trying to relive each experience.

He seemed to favor two kinds of women: women who knew his wife and underage girls.

Reinhart, Sasha

9/79 The great prima donna herself! On her knees in my hotel room, sucking Buster like her life depended on it. Swallowed it, too! All for a little more blow to get her through shooting. Sings better than she sucks, but nice wide-open throat. Never watch her sing the same way again!

Mary Liz checked the date again. Thank God Sasha had gotten over her drug habit, for she was not mentioned again in the files.

Driscoll, Vanessa

7/85. Had dinner party here. Took Vanessa to show new cabana. Got inside, could see she was game. Told her I found her sexiest woman in E.H. More than any actress. Or model. Put her hand on Buster. Knows what she's doing! Very hot. Wet. Spread her on the table and did it there, clothes on. Five minutes, tops, and we were back. Perfect host. Caught eye in dinner. She excused herself. Found her in upstairs bathroom. Fucked her again on sink. Back three minutes for dessert. Very hot. Thought Claire smelled her on me. Looked at me funny. Really good fuck. Want to do again.

There was no further mention of Vanessa, so maybe she had come to her senses. Or met Buck.

And then the worst, the very worst. The file with a picture of a teenager, cut out of a group shot.

MacClendon, Madeline

8/89 Gorgeous. Snuck her booze at parents' party, went with me to get ice. Talked on way. Asked if she had boyfriend. Yes. How much did she do with him? She said, nothing, Mom would kill her. (Yes, good old Claire, ever-faithful watchdog of the Wife.) Explained lots to do without doing that. Parked in way back of Pete's Deli, back by trees. Whipped out Buster and showed her. She stared. Never saw one before, she said. Told her to touch it. Took her hand and put it on Buster. Told her only get pregnant if put between her legs. She could just rub it, nicely, and no one would know. She could do it to her boyfriend. It would make him very happy. Took hand away and said she better not, but still staring. Told her to touch it, and watch what happens, how happy it makes it. Buster swelling gigantic, dying to come. Guiding her hand, up and down, up and down. Watched her face, totally absorbed in Buster. Had to keep guiding hand, she was too tipsy to concentrate. Buster straining. Took out handkerchief at last moment. Buster pumped all over her hand. So good. So very good.

Wiped her hand, had her wipe Buster, said that's all to it. Not to tell. Don't worry, she giggled, she wouldn't. Went in store like nothing happened and got ice. On way home she fell asleep.

What had Madeline been, *fifteen?* The sick, filthy son of a bitch! The child of his wife's best friend?

That's it, she had made her decision.

It was 4:00 a.m.

Mary Liz stuffed the files back into the box and put a lid on it. The box weighed a ton, but she was determined to make just one trip. And so, while staggering under its weight, she lugged the box out of the Safe Room and put it on the stairs while she locked up. Then she lifted it for six stairs, stopped to rest, and then made it to the top, where she rested again. She didn't know how many times she had to stop and rest while trying to get the box out the back door of the Big House, across the back lawn and then down the driveway.

Other than her breath, the only sounds she could hear were those of crickets.

Finally she made it into the cottage. She turned off the alarm, turned on the lights, locked the door and drew the curtains over the windows.

To heck with the people listening in on her cottage. Let them try to figure out what was going on.

She moved the fire screen and opened the flue of the fireplace. She read the directions on one of the DuraFlame logs that had been sitting there forever in the wood box, set it up in the grate and lit it. The flame caught and the artificial log was soon burning very well. She went to drag the box over and then sat cross-legged on the floor, starting to feed files into the fire.

It was hard work. First she had to strip the photo and burn that. Alfred had written pages about some of the women, and so those pages had to be burned, too. Then she had to rip up the manila folder to get that going. Regardless of what she did, unless she burned everything piece by piece, the files only seemed to want to stick together and smother themselves out.

And she had two hundred and seventy-six to burn.

Ten minutes later someone was knocking on the front door of the cottage.

Now what?

The person knocked again.

Mary Liz got up and went to the door to look out. Jake. She opened the front door a crack. She put a finger over her mouth to hush him, slipped out onto the porch and waved for him to follow her out onto the lawn.

She was soaking wet with perspiration and had black soot all over her hands and arms and, she bet, her face. Thankfully, it was still dark. She looked back at the house. There was enough early light in the sky that heavy black smoke could be seen rising from the cottage chimney.

"I heard your house is bugged," Jake said quietly, "but what's going on in there?"

"I decided to have a fire," Mary Liz said, wanting to laugh out loud then, partly from exhaustion and partly because it was about eighty degrees out and she knew what she looked like and the whole thing was absolutely insane.

"Mrs. Hoffman told me I am to trust you completely," he said seriously.

"Yes," she confirmed.

"But I have to make sure you're not destroying any important documents. I saw you lugging that box down from the Big House."

"Oh, Jake," she groaned. "You could have helped me. I practically threw my back out."

"What are you burning in there?" he persisted.

"Something that will destroy my godmother if she ever sees it, something that would break Bertie's heart. I'll show you."

She went in the cottage and got a file on some girl in Georgia she was sure Jake wouldn't know, grabbed a flashlight and came back outside. She handed the file to him and clicked on the flashlight. "Open it."

Jake opened the manila folder, looked at the picture of the teenager in her high-school baton-twirling uniform and white marching boots. Then he looked at the hand-written narrative on the other side which began: *Major majorette fuck! Out of the blue! I get a knock on my motel door in this miserable little town and there she was, asking if it was true, was I a big Hollywood producer…*

Jake read on, his face writhing in disgust when, Mary Liz was pretty sure, he reached the part about the girl coming back the next night and how Alfred had used the baton on her.

"Oh, Jesus, Mary, Mother of God," he said under his breath, closing the folder and shoving it back at her.

"I've got over two hundred and fifty like this left to burn," she said.

Jake had taken a few steps away, and with his hands on his hips, was looking up at the sky.

Mary Liz walked over. "Will you help me?"

He turned around to look at her. "God bless you. Of course I will."

They went into the cottage and Mary Liz turned on the stereo radio. Silently she showed Jake how she was burning them. He stopped her then, and motioned for her to get up and follow him. He picked up the carton and led her back to the office. She turned on the light as he set the box down on the floor and pointed to the paper shredder.

Of course. They would burn much better that way.

Jake pointed to her and then to the box, and then to himself and toward the direction of the living room.

She got it. She'd shred, he'd take the basket of scrap out and burn it. That way, only she would ever know who was in these files.

She smiled. He was a great guy, Jake. And if what she suspected was true, she thought Bertie was a very lucky man indeed.

She turned on the clock radio in the study, to the same station as in the living room, grabbed the staple remover and set to work.

22

Thursday ended up being a wasted day. Mary Liz and Jake had finished shredding and burning the files at around seven-thirty in the morning and then Mary Liz had shut off her phone and hit the sack, not to awaken until nearly four that afternoon, when Bertie asked her to go windsurfing. After giving him the eye—like, *What, you want to break into my cottage again?*—he said, no, really, he thought she'd be pretty good at it.

But Mary Liz doubted she would ever be able to get back into the ocean. Not on that beach. Not any time soon. Bertie said he understood and then had another idea, an idea that turned out to be brilliant. He took her to a friend's stable near Montauk, where he borrowed a horse for him to ride bareback, and saddled another horse Western—a smaller, older, utterly tame little beast named Cupcake—and took Mary Liz riding down the trail to the beach. Bertie galloped and Mary Liz only plodded along (Cupcake's preferred speed, a kind of swaying walk), but the wind and the water and the sky put the "i" back in *life* for her.

That night Mary Liz had dinner at the Big House, alone with Aunt Nancy, to explain to her the possibility of Alfred having more assets in Europe, and about the trip she was taking next week to investigate. Beyond that, she did not tell her much; there was no reason to.

Amazingly, she had gone to bed at nine-thirty that night and slept through until nine the next morning when Federal Express arrived at her door with a package from Chicago.

Mary Liz signed for it, made herself some coffee, and then went out on the front porch to sit on the stairs and skim the reports from her colleague in Chicago. Dunlau Gunney, the investment banking firm in Dublin; Eeghlenburger, the commodities broker in Amsterdam; Banque de Veurne, the commercial bank in Brussels; and Jacques Gorce, the independent investment banker in Paris—there were profiles here on all four.

Aunt Nancy drove down the driveway and waved. She was in good spirits these days, largely because the acceptance rate for her big *do* on Saturday night was extremely high. It would be the first annual Alfred Hoffman Memorial Foundation Dinner Dance.

Merciful heaven, it was a good thing he was dead because the man should have been shot.

Mary Liz went in to her bedroom, grabbed a pencil, flopped down on her unmade bed and started to read. Betsy had done extremely well by her. The numbers were there on the companies, the history was there—including personal details of the top executive or executives—and, best of all, Betsy had written question marks at certain places, flagging things that didn't quite add up. Her marks, Mary Liz realized, indicated places where there well might be a front being used for clients who wished to remain anonymous.

Looking at the reports, Mary Liz couldn't help remembering the time when her boss—years ago, when she had just started in business—had told her Reston, Kellaher had landed a bunch of South American clients who wanted to invest in American companies that did business with South American companies, and that every Reston employee should be looking for deal opportunities. Mary Liz had done a little checking on these prospective clients and found that not one but *all* of these investors had Swiss bank accounts. She had gone straight to her boss to tell him, confidentially, that as far as she could tell, Reston, Kellaher was being offered entrance into a classic cocaine-cartel money-laundering operation.

"I have no idea what you're talking about," her boss had said evenly.

"Oh, my dad runs into it all the time," she had said proudly, little twenty-two-year-old innocent that she had been. "Let's say you're in Brazil and you've got ten million illegal dollars in cash and you can only deposit it at a bank that asks no questions. Otherwise, the bank would alert the authorities. No matter what Switzerland says to the contrary, it's still a world leader in such banks. So our Brazilian cocaine dealer deposits the ten million in a Swiss bank, and the bank then issues a 'clean' check to us in the States, which we use, in turn, to buy, say, a coffee-importing firm.

"Time goes by, and because the coffee importer employs Americans and dutifully pays all its corporate taxes, there's no reason for the feds to harass them about their books. And since nobody is scrutinizing their books, for at least a couple of years no one notices that the American importing firm is paying double or triple or even four times more for its coffee from Brazil than anyone else does. And that, by doing so, the American firm is sending some legitimate money back to Brazil, but also tons of *illegal* money from cash drug sales in the United States. In other words, what on paper looks like a cash payment from a coffee vendor is, in fact, the returns from, say, their street-crack sales division in South Chicago.

"And so," she finished grandly, "the only way you can catch these guys is to tag them right where we are now. They've gotten money out of the United States, but need a bigger laundering operation. So what we need to do is call in the authorities and let them work with us. If it turns out the money's clean, we still make our commission, if it isn't, we get a big gold star from the feds."

Needless to say, Mary Liz had been quickly transferred to another division and no one ever invited her to work with investments coming from Swiss banks again, or the Cayman Islands, or anywhere else that might spark her imagination. If she was so good at speculation, she was told, then she should start researching and speculating about the future of media and advise their investment bankers accordingly. Which she had. After all, Reston, Kellaher—at least most of the company—was more ethical than most firms. Not wanting to see illegal sources of money was the favorite pastime of Wall Street. No one actually *laundered* money for bad guys, they maintained; if millions and millions of dollars appeared to be clean, then it was clean, right? Until someone stepped in and proved otherwise.

The more Mary Liz read in these profiles, the more determined she became to drop by these firms while she was in Europe. Why had Alfred jotted down these names? Had he talked to them? Was he planning something with them? Had he already invested with them—or, had they invested with him in some way?

She twiddled her pencil, thinking. Before leaving for Europe, she would need someone acting as her secretary, someone to confirm appointments, to construct a front for her with these firms. Wendy. She'd ask Wendy.

And what about Sky? Aunt Nancy said Buck had told her that Sky had to go home for a family emergency. Nancy then told Mary Liz she hoped everything was all right, particularly since Buck had said it was Sky's mother who was sick, and then, in the same conversation, said it was Sky's father who was sick, then quickly explaining that they were both sick, see?, that's why Sky had to leave in such a hurry. (Her godmother looked at Mary Liz as if to say, "Do you know who your beau is yet, darlin'?")

She could run a check on the name Stephen Pembroke through Wendy. No. She decided against it. She would trust him. (Whoever he was.)

Now, about Wendy acting as her secretary. Mary Liz dropped her pencil and got up and got dressed. She grabbed a legal pad and some pencils from the office, activated the cottage alarm and locked the front door. Outside, Ashley came barreling up onto the porch and nearly knocked her over. Jake waved from up by the Big House and put two fingers in his mouth to whistle. Ashley responded by joyfully barking at Mary Liz and then dashing around to hide behind the cottage. Mary Liz went back there and then Ashley ran around to the front of the cottage and charged up the lawn to Jake.

"A delayed response, but she obeyed!" Mary Liz called to Jake, laughing.

She made her way to the guest house and heard a radio playing on the back deck. She walked around; Wendy had evidently been sunbathing. A towel was draped across a lounge chair, a bottle of water was sitting on the deck next to it, and, of course, the radio was playing.

Mary Liz skipped up the stairs and headed for the screen door to the kitchen. She had just been about to call inside when she heard a moan. The kind that could not be mistaken for another.

She didn't want to look, but her eyes moved before her brain could stop them, and she saw what she saw. Numb, she backed away, and as quietly as possible, went back down the stairs of the deck.

Only at the corner of the house did she start to breathe again. She stood there, unable to move, breathing through her mouth, trying to digest what she'd witnessed.

She had never seen two women together like that before. Not even on the beach that night. Now she knew who they were, and she had come upon them again, only this time they had been rendered completely vulnerable; dear God, right there in the kitchen, with the door open? What could they have been thinking?

They had been thinking they were dying to make love, she decided, walking back to the cottage.

Wendy and Vanessa Buckley.

23

On Saturday evening, Mary Liz, Wendy and Jake were being driven in a limousine to the first annual Alfred Hoffman Memorial Foundation Dinner Dance. Bertie was behind them in another limousine, serving as his mother's escort until they arrived at that gala, at which time he would return to Wendy's side and Nancy would pair off with Buck, her acting host.

Mary Liz had thought she would never be able to look Wendy straight in the eye again, but found instead it was almost impossible not to look at her. With her eyes shining, her hair soft and luxurious, down around her shoulders, and that brilliant smile of hers against a deep tan, anyone would stare at Wendy. She was very beautiful tonight. She was dressed in an extremely demure (but nonetheless slinky, and she had the body to wear it) blue-gray silk evening dress, and two long strands of real (and what looked to be old, as in inherited-old) pearls, the latter establishing her as a definite descendant of something or someone perhaps even vaguely royal.

Jake, who was to be Mary Liz's escort for the evening, was unbelievably handsome in his white dinner jacket, black tie, black slacks and highly polished black dress shoes.

So that was the gig in the guest house this summer, Mary Liz figured, Wendy and Vanessa, Bertie and Jake.

East Hampton would never cease to amaze her.

Mary Liz must have looked very preoccupied because Wendy asked her twice in the car if she was all right. "You look so pretty," Wendy told her. "It would be a shame if you didn't feel that way." Then Wendy burst out laughing. "I'm sorry, that's what my grandmother would always say to me when I was sulking."

Mary Liz smiled. "I'm not sulking."

"But you're not very happy, either."

"I'm only distracted," Mary Liz said.

"We're *all* distracted," Jake said. "And Wendy's right, you do look very beautiful tonight, Mary Liz."

She did not feel like it. And yet, she knew the cocktail dress she had had her mother send her from Chicago, though white, managed to cover a multitude of sins, and, against her coloring, was really quite flattering. And her hair had turned out rather well tonight, because Delores had come down to the cottage and blow-dried it, skillfully using a round brush to give it body, just the way Mary Liz's very expensive hairdresser always begged her to do it (but to no avail because Mary Liz's left hand was utterly skill-less, not even fit to hold the dryer, much less handle the brush in anything but a fatal maneuver).

When Mary Liz had emerged from the cottage, carrying the genuine 1920s white beaded evening clutch purse Wendy had loaned her, the gardener had been working out front. He had glanced up from the flower bed, looked down and then looked back up at her, got up from his knees, took off his baseball cap and held it over his heart. "Excuse me," he said, bowing slightly, "but you are drop-dead gorgeous, Miss Scott."

She missed Sky terribly and wondered where he was, what he was doing.

She also envied him for not having to attend this dinner dance, this dreadful farce in memory of the muck and mire of a thing called Alfred Hoffman. She'd be lucky if she didn't choke during the tribute.

Wendy held her hand out. "Let me check your purse." Mary Liz handed it over. Wendy opened it, rewound the microrecorder and held it to her ear. "Okay, that's good," she said a minute later, snapping the purse shut and handing it back. "Just remember not to move it after you put it on the table, or rustle your napkin against it—and remember, latch side up. Or out, if you're standing."

Then Wendy opened her clutch purse to check hers. She had told Mary Liz she had five such purses; she went to formal functions a lot in her line of work.

The decorations at the East End Country Club were magnificent. Aunt Nancy had personally paid for an "event" designer, and together they had planned to convert the clubhouse and grounds into an old-time movie studio, complete with mock studio gates at the entrance.

It was five after six. The three were deposited at the front door of the club and were directed through to the rose-garden terrace outside, where well over one hundred guests had already assembled for the cocktail party.

The mechanics of the fund-raiser were these: A huge mailing of invitations was sent out for the cocktail party and black-tie dinner dance to be held at the East End Country Club. There would be plenty of food and drink. The Peter Duchin Orchestra would be playing. And then, on the inside of the invitation, celebrity after celebrity was named as a sponsor of the event.

Now, whether any of these celebrities were actually coming or not, Mary Liz didn't know, but the names had enough voltage to make most people want to go, if for no other reason than to look at them in person. And the trick was, tickets for only the cocktail party were fifty dollars, and tickets for the cocktail party and the dinner dance were five hundred dollars. What would happen—at least how it had happened in Aunt Nancy's experience—is they would draw at least a couple hundred celebrity gawkers for the cocktail party, and with only an hour and a half to eat and drink while running around to find the celebrities, the benefit would clear another nine thousand dollars from them. It would also, Nancy hoped, send them running to rave to their friends about what a worthy cause the Alfred Hoffman Memorial Fund was.

Most of the five-hundred-dollar ticket holders wouldn't show up until eight, after the cocktail partyers were safely gone.

The 1939 yellow Bentley that Aunt Nancy had hired for the occasion must have arrived in front of the club, because the orchestra struck up the music. A minute later, Nancy, Bertie, Julius and Jeanine Hoffman appeared on the threshold of the terrace, where Buck Buckley introduced them and the guests began to applaud.

The rose garden was lovely. The benches, tables and chairs that were normally out there had been replaced with art-deco ones, and there were life-size stand-ups of movie stars from the Golden Age, every one of them glamorous in black-tie finery: Clark Gable, Jean Harlow, Cary Grant, Mae West, Gary Cooper, Bette Davis and many others.

The cocktail-party guests were definitely not A-list, Mary Liz could plainly see. Nor B, or, quite possibly, C, since all but about fifteen men had ignored the "Ties and jackets are suggested for the gentlemen attending the cocktail party only" on their tickets, but had chosen instead to wear jeans and khakis and, in one case, shorts. These were the celebrity seekers, walking around, staring intently, trying to determine whether anybody was Anybody. One woman rushed up to Wendy and asked if she was related to Charlotte Rampling, whom she looked so much like. Wendy smiled and said, no, she was sorry—but her mother was a district attorney in Dover, that was pretty cool, wasn't it? Did her mother know Charlotte Rampling? the woman wanted to know. Wendy was sorry, but no, she didn't think so. Not unless the actress had murdered someone in Dover lately. (The woman frowned at her and stomped off, evidently unable to tolerate such sacrilege.)

"We have to give them somebody soon, Mother," Mary Liz heard Bertie say.

"Don't worry, darlin'," Nancy said. "Sasha swore she would be here at six-fifteen—" Just then, they could hear some sort of commotion in the clubhouse. "See? She's here. And she's staying the whole time. I've got five undercover security in the crowd to keep people in line. And then, in about ten minutes, I've got Dick and Stephanie coming, Martha and Kathleen at six-forty, Kim and Alec and Ralph and Rachelle at six-fifty, and, let's see, Tony, Jason and Betty at seven. And at seven-thirty we clear them out."

The way the celebrity thing worked, Bertie explained to Mary Liz—as they watched Sasha clutch Riff in terror as the crowd rushed her—is that in exchange for their making appearances with the public (which was, truly, not only tiring, but often vaguely alarming because of the ferocity of their fans' adoration), Nancy would put her considerable social muscle into supporting any fund-raiser that the celebrities wished to promote in the future. All of it, Bertie said, produced good money for good causes.

And just as her Aunt Nancy had promised Bertie, Dick Cavett arrived promptly at 6:25, followed a moment later by Stephanie Powers; Martha Stewart and Kathleen Turner made almost simultaneous entrances at 6:40; Kim Basinger and Alec Baldwin arrived at 6:50, and, within three minutes, Ralph Lauren and Rachelle Zaratan, as well; and finally, at seven o'clock sharp, Tony Randall, Jason Robards and Betty Buckley made their appearances.

The cocktail party went off without a hitch. The celebrities were generous with their time and attention, and the gawkers went away gratified. They had been to a genuine A-list party, they thought, which they could tell their friends and family about for years to come.

At about seven forty-five, cars started arriving with the five-hundred-dollar-a-head dinner-dance people. Some of the cocktail people waited around out front, on either side of the front door of the club, to see who was attending. They were not disappointed. The men were dashing and handsome and distinguished in their fancy dress, and the women radiantly alluring. Billy Joel, Steven Spielberg, Brooke Shields and Lauren Bacall were all loudly applauded, and although the crowd didn't really recognize the writers—Michael M. Thomas, E. L. Doctorow, George Plimpton, Ben Bradley and Sally Quinn, Rona Jaffe and Peter Mathiessen—they sensed they were Somebodies and applauded them, as well. Perhaps the biggest moment was when Lee Radziwell Ross disembarked from a car with her husband, and a respectful hush fell over the crowd. The moment was only marred by the man in the shorts calling, "Hey, where's your niece and nephew?"

The best fund-raisers, Bertie explained, pried donations of good food and drink out of people, plus a great place to have it. Otherwise, if it was a nice party and nothing was donated, there would be little left over for the cause. ("You haven't lived until you've been to one of Mother's chicken-wing, day-old bread-and-beer blasts when times get tough," Bertie said, laughing.)

For this supremely romantic and elegantly appointed dinner dance, they were paying nothing for the use of the club (hence Buck's role of host to Nancy's role of hostess); nothing for the decorations; next to nothing for hors d'oeuvres, which had been prepared by local caterers (who were reimbursed for basic cost of the food); and three famous East Hampton restaurants had sent over their chefs to prepare the food donated by a number of fine-food stores in Manhattan. Desserts had also been donated, and every generous person and establishment was very gratefully acknowledged in the glossy booklet about the foundation that each guest would leave with.

In a kind of tragic irony, the biggest expenses for the benefit—the hard liquor, the car valets, the rest-room attendants, the bartenders, serving staff and cleanup crews—had all been paid for by Herbert Glidden.

Randolph Vandergilden had offered to donate white wine, but (thank heavens), so had some of the finest area vineyards: The Lenz, Duck Walk, Palmer, and The Bridgehampton Winery. It had been a rotten trick, Mary Liz thought (but it *was* for a good cause), that the bartenders had been told to pour only Vandergilden wine at the cocktail party ("unless, of course, the guest is in black tie"), trusting that none of them would notice anything wrong with it.

In the end, the cost of the dinner dance was roughly forty-five dollars a head. Ticket sales had exceeded three hundred, though only two hundred and six were expected to actually attend. Deduct maybe twenty tickets that were gratis to certain celebrities. And then there were the cocktail-party ticket returns. Presuming it all went off well, the foundation would clear over one hundred thousand dollars, and that didn't include what they had saved on the guests who had bought tickets but had not RSVPed to come.

When Mary Liz saw Claire MacClendon arrive, she knew something major had happened since she had seen her last—something for the better. Claire looked absolutely knock-out beautiful and positively aglow, and moments later Mary Liz realized there was no doubt about it, it had something to do with Bill Pfeiffer who was at her side.

"Hello, Mary Liz," Bill said to her, holding out his hand and kissing her on the cheek. He looked extremely attractive in his white dinner jacket. "You look very beautiful tonight," he added.

"And so do you," Mary Liz told him, kissing him back. "Though I think you're escorting the most beautiful lady in the place."

Claire gave her a hug. "Thanks, Mary Liz, but I've got to tell you—" She took a step back. "You should have seen me way back when!"

"No way," Bill said, smiling and taking her hand. "I prefer the here and now."

Yep. No doubt about it. These two were *together.*

"I'm sorry Sky's not here tonight," Claire said. "Is everything okay with his family now?"

"He'll be back when he can," Mary Liz said. She gestured to Jake. "But I get this charming gentleman as my escort until he does return."

Jake smiled and stood at her side.

"We're starting to lead people into dinner," Nancy said, breezing by. This was their cue to move.

The grand ballroom was spilling over with flowers. Around the room there were life-size cutout pictures of couples eating at tables in movies: Katharine Hepburn and Cary Grant, Jimmy Stewart and Donna Reed, Greta Garbo and Fredric March, Bette Davis and Leslie Howard, and one that made everyone laugh out loud when they saw it, Elizabeth Taylor, Richard Burton, Sandy Dennis and George

Segal carrying on over the dinner table in a scene from *Who's Afraid of Virginia Woolf?*

The tables for the guests were round ones of ten, set with white linens, silver settings, bone china, crystal glasses, silver candlesticks and gorgeous centerpieces of low-cut flowers. The head table was presided over by the hosts, Nancy and the president of the club, Buck Buckley. Bertie and Wendy, Julius and Jeanine Hoffman, Claire MacClendon and Bill Pfeiffer, and the husband and wife who would be dual caretakers of the foundation also sat at that table.

At Mary Liz's table, she had Jake, Sasha Reinhart, Rachelle Zaratan and Charles Kahn, Claude and Isabel Lemieux, Vanessa Buckley and Randolph Vandergilden. There was an empty seat with the placard, "Henry MacClendon," and just as the salad was being served, he appeared. "The baby," he explained, sliding into his seat. He looked over at the next table, at Claire, specifically, several times, Mary Liz noticed, but Claire did not pay him the slightest bit of attention, even when Nancy Hoffman waved hello to him.

By the time the main course arrived, Mary Liz's table had already consumed an unbelievable amount of wine. Everyone at the table was clearly there *only* out of respect for Nancy, and since it was mostly a group of old friends, they had decided to get drunk and make the best of it. And the more they drank, the more references were made to Herbert Glidden's death, until, toward the end of the dinner, the table was openly devoted to discussing it. The only one who didn't join in was Vanessa Buckley, who sat glassy-eyed and vaguely smiling, eyes almost constantly on the next table. On Wendy, Mary Liz thought.

"I went to the police station for questioning today," Charles Kahn said.

"He wasn't even in the state when it happened!" Rachelle exclaimed.

"I was asleep in Pittsburgh by then," he said. "And then they had the nerve to ask me if I would mind if they checked with the airport to verify my arrival."

"He flew," Rachelle explained.

"I wish I had a good alibi," Randolph Vandergilden groaned. "I got so pissed that night I couldn't even remember where I was."

"You were with us," Claude reminded him. "You, me and Buck."

"Drunk as skunks," Isabel said in her French accent. "I made Claude sleep on the porch. He reeked of cheap gin."

"I never had any gin," Claude said.

"You had gin that night in Barcelona," his wife said.

"Fifteen years ago!" He turned to the group. "America changes women, have you noticed? She used to be so nice."

"Don't feel bad about the police, Randy," Sasha said cheerfully. "They even think I might have murdered him. They think I met him down at the beach for a midnight rendezvous and hit him over the head and shot him full of drugs and threw him in the water."

"You're five foot four, for heaven's sake," Rachelle said. "And what? A hundred and ten pounds?"

"A hundred and five, thank you," Sasha corrected her. "Anyway, they think I told Riff to do it." She laughed. "They think Riff is my lover."

"Isn't he yet?" Rachelle said.

The diva threw a piece of roll across the table at her friend.

"No food fights," Bertie called from the other table.

"Yeah, well, I'd like to be a fly on the wall when they question Julius tomorrow," Randolph said. "Everybody's told the police they last saw Herb with him."

"And Jeanine," Claude added.

"Now, there's a murderer if I ever saw one," Henry said sarcastically, speaking for the first time. "Jeanine Hoffman, mother and murderer."

"And *professional,* shall we say?" Isabel said.

"She could have done it," Claude insisted. "With or without Julius. You know how she feels—rather—felt about Herb."

"That's ridiculous," Henry said.

"The police don't think so," Isabel said. "They brought her in this afternoon for questioning, too."

"And they've asked you to come down, too," Claude pointed out. "Ah! Now, there's a thought. Isabel hobbling out on the beach in her high heels and clobbering Herb over the head with her pocketbook."

"Claude," Isabel said, "try not to be an ass."

Everyone seemed irritable now and the wine was flowing faster and faster, the waiter barely able to keep up with the draining of glasses.

"What I don't understand is why we all have to go to the police station," Randolph said. "Aren't they supposed to come around to our houses to question us?"

"Sometimes they prefer to question people out of their homes," Jake said politely. "They prefer to talk to them outside their fortresses, away from their wealth and power, hoping it will reduce their resistance to answering questions. Particularly if the questions are personal."

Randolph was staring at him. "Who the hell are you?"

"My date," Mary Liz said. "Jake O'Leary."

Isabel leaned over to whisper something in Randolph's ear that made him narrow his eyes at Jake. "Jesus, we're eating with the groundskeeper?"

Mary Liz had half a mind to walk over and slap them both across the face.

"They didn't make Nancy go down to the station," Rachelle pointed out.

"Who'd have the nerve to ask her?" Isabel said. "It'd be like asking the Queen if she minded stopping by the Old Bailey for a chat."

"The thing is, you know," Sasha said, "that anybody could have murdered Herb. Everybody had a problem with him, one way or another." She turned to Mary Liz. "I heard you went to Glidden's house that night."

Every head turned in Mary Liz's direction. "Yes," she acknowledged. "As I explained to the police, I stopped to see if Alex wanted to come to the fireworks with me and Sky."

"Ohhh, Sky!" Randolph suddenly roared. "Herb dies, Sky disappears—" He snapped his fingers. "The butler didn't do it, the teacher did!"

Vanessa unsteadily moved her gaze to Vandergilden. "Sky did not murder Herb. His mother's sick."

"Buck said it was the father," Isabel said.

"I thought it was the mother *and* the father," Sasha said.

"You know," Rachelle said, "in New York, I've heard rumors that Herb's death was a mob hit."

"Everyone in the garment industry thinks everything is a mob hit," Charles said wearily to his wife.

"No, I am serious, Charles," Rachelle insisted. "They say it was all of his funny investors, all those mystery financiers he represented."

"They've always said in L.A. he was money-laundering," Sasha said. "But then, what studio isn't?"

"He wasn't a studio," Mary Liz pointed out.

"He might as well have been," Rachelle said. "Alfred always took his money for Howland Films, the two were in each other's pocket forever."

"Alfred had nothing to do with it," Charles said, sounding angry.

"How could he have nothing to do with it," Rachelle wanted to know, "if he always took the money?"

"You don't know anything about it!" Charles snapped.

"Here, here," Claude said, applauding.

Rachelle looked as though she might give both of them an obscene gesture.

Randolph sighed. "First Al, now Herb."

"Herb Glidden is no loss," Henry said in a voice that made them all look at him. "Come on, admit it," he demanded. "Everybody's *relieved* he's dead. The man was a walking plague."

"So why did you suffer his company?" Mary Liz asked.

Henry frowned at her. "What?"

"If you thought he was the plague, why did you hang out with him? Like at the cocktail party in Amagansett?"

She thought Henry might have a stroke, he seemed so stricken. Henry's eyes darted over to Claude, and then to Randolph, and finally, to Charles.

"I already told you why, Mary Liz," Rachelle loudly complained. "Because this is East Hampton. You *have* to swim through the scum once in a while."

At this comment, people at the next table frowned at Rachelle.

"I only meant," Henry said to Mary Liz, "that Herb was one thing, and Alfred was a great man and a great friend—to us all."

Some friend, Mary Liz thought. *The guy molested your daughter, Henry.*

"I think Randy meant being shocked by them both dying," Claude said. "That our mortality is staring at us all. Let's face it, we're not as young as we used to be."

"Mortality?" Henry said. "Dying in a plane crash and getting murdered are hardly natural causes!"

"Oh, I keep forgetting," Randolph said to the group, barely suppressing a burp behind his napkin, "that our Henry is the father of a newborn babe. One shouldn't remind him that he'll be in an old folks home by the time the kid goes to college."

"I am a good father," Henry nearly shouted, standing up. Evidently Randolph had struck a nerve. "And my son will have the best, just like my girls have and always will!"

"Okay, okay," Randolph said. "Calm down, Henry, you're among friends here. Maybe I'm just a little jealous, that's all. I don't have any kids, no one to carry on for me." He paused, sighing with a resigned smile. "And no one to care if I live or die."

Henry looked undecided. People at other tables were looking at him. Finally he shook out his napkin and sat down again. The waiter came around and refilled his wineglass.

"There hasn't been a murder in East Hampton," Rachelle said, sounding as though she were reminiscing about a pleasant memory, "since that art guy tied up and tortured that kid and chopped him up and dumped him in a field."

"Not during dinner, please," Sasha pleaded.

"And *he* was at *your* party," Randolph said, laughing, pointing to Rachelle. "Remember?"

"Who was at our party?" Charles asked. "The chopped-up guy?"

"The murderer," Randolph said. "Remember? He was an art dealer or something? Part of the dirty-Crisco set?"

"Dirty-Crisco set?" Isabel said, frowning.

"I'll explain it to you later," Claude promised.

"It was a fund-raiser, Randy," Rachelle protested. "I was hardly in control of who bought tickets."

"Who else, besides me," Vanessa said loudly, "thinks it's very likely that Herb's murderer is at *this* fund-raiser?"

Silence at the table.

"I'd hardly think so," Henry finally said. "It's sounds as though it was a professional job."

"Oh, I don't know," Vanessa said coyly. "You guys are all pretty smart. In fact, I'll put good money on it that the murderer is sitting either at this table or Nancy's. You all hated him. Why not admit it?"

"Admit that we murdered him?" Rachelle asked.

"That you hated him. That all you men wished him dead," Vanessa said. "I know Buck did."

"Why would Buck wish him dead?" Mary Liz asked her.

Vanessa shrugged and waved her hand. "If I knew the answer to that, Buck would have had a backbone, as least where Herb was concerned." She polished off her glass of wine, something she didn't need. Her eyes were even glassier and her movements badly off. "All of you," she added. "Buck, Henry, Charles, Claude—oh, God, and *you*, Randy, more than anybody. You all hated him and I *know* it had to have something to do with money since that's all you guys ever care to talk about."

"Go fuck yourself, Vanessa," Randolph growled. "As if half the town isn't already."

Vanessa threw the water in her goblet at him, splashing nearly everyone at the table in the process. At the next table, Wendy was up like a shot, Buck following unsteadily behind her. Wendy went over to Vanessa and squatted, whispering something to her. Buck stood over the table—where everyone was blotting water off themselves with their napkins—and asked, "Is there a problem here?"

"Yeah," Randolph said. "Vanessa's a problem. Always has been, always will be. Tell her to shut the fuck up."

Buck glared at him, his face darkening. "Maybe we need to get some fresh air, Randy."

Wendy was already steering Vanessa away from the table and out of the ballroom.

"No thanks," Randolph said. "I don't need to play Mr. Macho with you, Buck. You broke my goddamn tooth last time."

"Then why don't you try behaving?" Buck said. "For Nancy's sake?"

Randolph waved his napkin in the air, indicating the incident was now over.

"This is the most depressing dinner I've ever been to in my life," Sasha announced as Buck returned to his table.

"Yeah, well," Randolph shot across the table, "you should have been there the night Henry ran away with that girl and we all had to sit there and eat with Claire."

Henry threw his napkin on the table and left the room. Buck came back to the table, looking at Randolph. "Problem?"

"No problem," Randolph said. "The problems have all left now."

Rachelle turned toward Claude. "Isn't Vanessa's thing barbiturates?"

He shrugged. "Hell if I know."

Rachelle covered her mouth. "Gosh, you don't suppose *she* knocked Herb off?"

"She was at Bertie's party that night," Mary Liz said. "At the estate."

Claude snickered. "Yeah, figure that one. Who knew Bertie had it in him?"

"But why would Vanessa want Glidden dead?" Sasha asked.

"Who knows?" Rachelle said, shrugging. "Secrets, secrets, secrets, everybody wanted Herb dead and yet none of us know why. None of us *girls*, that is." She looked at Randolph. "Maybe the weak link in the chain will break someday and we will find out."

"Fuck off, Shelley," Randolph said.

"Watch the mouth," Charles Kahn said sharply.

"Watch the wife!" Randolph advised him.

By the time the dessert dishes were taken away, Isabel Lemieux had stormed out of the ballroom—insulted by her husband—and Randolph Vandergilden had fallen backward in his chair to the floor. (Mary Liz suspected that Rachelle may have done something to expedite the latter.)

It was just a nightmare. Mary Liz had never before seen such drunken bitchiness and animosity between "old friends." There was fear in this group, and years of anger and resentment, to say nothing of simmering suspicions and outright accusations.

Wendy reappeared as they were all moving outside to the terrace for dancing. Although the orchestra was excellent and the tent beautiful—with such notable cardboard couples as Fred Astaire and Ginger Rogers, and Gene Kelly and Leslie Caron dancing around them—nobody of their group wanted to stay, least of all Mary Liz, but they had to, for Aunt Nancy's sake. And so she danced with Jake, danced with Bertie and even danced with Julius, suffering his hand slipping down to her derriere because she knew that slapping it away would only embarrass Jeanine.

What a group.

When they were finally allowed to leave, at nearly one o'clock, the conversation in the limo was almost nil. Finally Wendy said, "We'll meet in the morning?"

"Ten?" Mary Liz said. "At your house?" She handed her clutch purse to Wendy. "According to our table, everybody has some kind of motive for killing Glidden."

"Like what?"

"No one will say," Mary Liz said, "but they all look at each other like they know what everybody else's motive might be. The men, that is. I honestly don't think the women cared about him one way or the other."

"I got the impression there might have been some kind of blackmail going on," Jake said.

Mary Liz agreed. Wendy had rewound the recorder in her own pocketbook, listened to it, fiddled more with it, listened again, was satisfied and then handed it to Mary Liz when the limo stopped in front of the cottage to drop her off. "You might want to listen to the next ten minutes or so of this. Then drop it off tomorrow with me, okay?"

They said their good-nights and Mary Liz went inside. A few minutes later, stripped down to her robe, she went outside to the yard to listen to the tape. This part of the tape was during dinner; Mary Liz could hear the silverware against the china.

JULIUS: "Yes, it's official now, it was murder." Pause. "I'm supposed to talk to the police tomorrow. Can you imagine? They think I could be a suspect!"
BERTIE: "I would imagine you'd be the prime suspect."
NANCY: "Bertie."
JEANINE: "Well, he's right, I suppose. To have Herb gone certainly helps secure Julius's position—"
BERTIE: "In suing my mother?"
JULIUS: "That Schyler Preston's still at the top of the list for me. Herb's dead and he's gone the next day and no one knows where the hell he is."
BUCK: "Oh, crap, Julius. The man's away for a few weeks, that's all."
JULIUS: "You're just embarrassed because you've been boarding a murderer."
BERTIE: "Better to board one than to be married to one, eh, Jeanine?"
NANCY: "*Enough!*" Pause. "Tell us about the foundation's office, won't you?"

The conversation drifted on aimlessly after that, and after Mary Liz heard Jeanine tell everyone at the table that Michael Anderson of the *Times Book Review* was sitting at the next table, and she wanted them all to look at the shameful shenanigans a certain young novelist was trying to pull in an attempt to seduce him—"Look at her! Well, I suppose that's one way to get reviewed, isn't it?" (gales of laughter)—Mary Liz got bored and turned off the tape recorder.

The only thing interesting to her on the tape was Buck's dogged determination to speak up for Sky.

Interesting.

Sky and Buck, Sky and Buck. What could the connection be? Nobody could tell her it was simply golf. Not now.

24

On Sunday morning Mary Liz went over to the guest house to talk to Wendy. Only when she knocked on the door did she notice there was a car in the driveway, a forest green Alpha Romeo.

"Hi," Wendy said.

"Interesting tape," Mary Liz said, handing the recorder to her. "Thanks for sharing it. Listen, do you have five minutes?"

"I was just going up to see Nancy," Vanessa Buckley said, appearing from behind Wendy. "Hello, Mary Liz. You looked sensational last night."

"Thank you. Needless to say, you did, too. You always do."

Vanessa beamed. "Wendy, I'll see you later. Thanks again for calming me down last night." She excused herself, and started up to the Big House.

Mary Liz watched Wendy watch her. When Wendy turned back to her, Mary Liz said, "She's a lot more clearheaded today." She couldn't help it. She had to say it. Didn't Wendy know Vanessa was on pills or something? Last night, Rachelle said barbiturates.

Barbiturates. Maybe Buck had taken some from her and he and Randolph and Claude had killed Glidden that night.

"Yes," was all that Wendy said softly, leading her inside.

They sat down. "This won't take long," Mary Liz said. "But there's something I wanted to tell you before I left. The other night, when you and Bertie were in the library, late, talking, I was there in the hall. I came up from the Safe Room and I was going to say hi, but I stopped when I overheard you ask Bertie if he had murdered Glidden."

Wendy nodded once, her expression unreadable.

"And I also heard him say that if he told you, you had to swear you'd never tell me what set him off that night." She paused. "And I also heard you refuse to make that promise," she said. "Thank you."

"You're welcome. The one thing I know is," Wendy said, "it had to be something Mrs. Hoffman told him. He had just come from the Big House, to check on her, and he was livid."

"I wish you'd find out what it was while I'm gone," Mary Liz said. "And I wish you would tell me when I get back."

"I couldn't do that," Wendy said. "Bertie's not only my employer, he's my friend."

"Well, let's put it this way, then—find out what it is, and if you think it's something I need to know, you'll consider telling me. Or at least let me try to force it out of you." She was smiling, but longing to know whatever it was.

"I'll see what I can do."

"Fine. Thanks. One more thing," Mary Liz said. "About my trip to Europe. The itinerary I gave Nancy—" She hesitated. "Let me put it this way, I'm not just going to Amsterdam. I've got some other business to do. Something concerning Glidden, I'm pretty sure. And I really need someone who's very smart and very fast on her feet to make some calls for me and act as my assistant."

"What do I do first?" Wendy asked.

A car service picked Mary Liz up in the afternoon to take her to JFK Airport for Europe. A well-traveled veteran who believed strongly in the virtues of walking and sleeping comfortably, she wore khakis, a blouse and blazer, and cross-trainers. As they approached the entrances into the airport complex, Mary Liz directed the driver to Aer Lingus.

"It says on the order you're flying overseas on American," the driver said, handing her his form.

And, indeed, Mary Liz had a ticket to Amsterdam on that airline, only she had no intention of using it.

"No, I need Aer Lingus, please," she told him.

Inside the terminal, Mary Liz waited in the ticket line and when she reached the desk, asked if there were any seats on the next flight to Dublin. Only in first class, the ticket agent said. Tourist was packed with tour groups.

First class. What a sacrifice.

Mary Liz paid for her one-way ticket in cash.

Whoever was bugging her phone already knew she had purchased a ticket on the American flight. By the time anyone could know she hadn't actually taken it, she hoped her business in Dublin would be over.

The only surprise for Mary Liz was how enormous the Aer Lingus plane turned out to be. In tourist, she was told, the plane sat nine across—two, five in the middle and two—and had a wingspan so long, the ends had to be angled up to stabilize them. The whole world, it seemed, wanted to go to Ireland. (Who could blame them?) And since with every travel group at the gate there appeared to be at least one priest or nun, Mary Liz knew she need not worry, there would be far better protection for this plane than any FAA safety regulation could possibly provide.

She was tired. She had been up most of the night before, making notes and trying to think things out. Mary Liz was one of those travelers who couldn't care less what people thought as she transformed herself from an attractive young woman into a sleep-seeking freak, complete with blinders, inflatable neck-pillow and earplugs. She had slept on airplanes, trains and cars in this gear; she had slept in airports, hotel lobbies and hospital waiting rooms. She was a person to whom sleep was a precious commodity. Walk, Eat, Sleep, the WES method of traveling and living to survive it.

So there she was on her flight overseas, blue neck-pillow inflated, green spongy earplugs in her ears and black blinders over her eyes, the two elastic straps binding her hair down, making it look like straw in a whisk broom.

Who the heck cared. She was asleep.

The sun was rising over the Emerald Isle and Mary Liz's breath was taken away as they circled over Dublin. The land, for miles and miles, was the deepest green she had ever seen in her life. Deepest greens. And the Irish Sea, sparkling various shades of blue, was rolling in on dramatically rugged and rocky shores. The city itself seemed small and low to the ground, stretching north and south, with a host of suburban areas just outside it. And then, farther out, nothing but wild beauty.

When they landed, 6:00 a.m. Ireland time (1:00 a.m. in New York), it didn't seem as though anybody else was at the airport. There were a couple of Midway planes sitting near the terminal, but no other planes were landing or taking off, and there were no trucks or tarmac hustle bustle like outside every other airport she had ever visited. No, at this airport, while taxiing in, all she saw was a stone wall alongside the runway and a couple of cows casually glancing over at the massive plane as it rolled by. Her luggage came quickly and she was speedily checked through customs. She was assigned a cab and the drive into Dublin, traveling south, thrilled her. There was no other word for it. A complete and utter sucker for eighteenth-century architecture, she had her fill when the cabdriver took her the scenic route through the city. It was only six forty-five in the morning and the traffic was light.

"It was the war, you see," the driver explained. "People forget that the English were building in Dooblin too in the eighteenth century, but durin' the war, you know, World War II, the Germans bombed London terribly. Thank the Almighty, we weren't even touched here, not by bombers. And there, right there, you see? Irish Parliament, once the home of the Duke and Duchess of Leinster. Just as they built it in 1745. Almost. You in America used the blueprints for that house to build the White House. Look it oop when you get home and see if what I'm saying isn't true. It was burnt down, your White House, the first one, look it oop.

"Aye, that is Trinity College. All the tourists come here. Particularly down the road there, in Grafton Street, where all the fancy shops are. Don't be going shopping there, go up on O'Connell, the way we came down, and find yourself a bargain. Yes, 'tis a beautiful schoool, but you know, they wouldn't let a Catholic go there until the 1930s, so it wasn't such a beautiful schoool to us all. But now it's a proper university, and the people with the brain can go. It's not like it was—we're all equal down here in Dooblin. Although I still be driving a cab and all the Anglos be still sittin' up on the hill, so to speak." He looked at her in the rearview mirror. "Don't be lookin' at me foony now. I must be talking to an Anglo." He chuckled. "I thought maybe you were one of my nice, rrrich Catholic relatives from New York."

Whatever the cabdriver's religion and politics were, he knew his Anglo-Irish eighteenth-century architecture, and when he dropped Mary Liz off at her hotel, the Shelbourne on Saint Stephen's Green (which was actually a tremendous residential square, whose massive park inside, the driver told her, offered not only beauty, but free concerts every Tuesday at lunchtime), she was very grateful. She wouldn't have time to see anything else. She tipped him handsomely and wished him good luck. He shook her hand with both of his. "You're ah nice girrrl. We want more Americans like you spending your mooney here. You're a beauty and a blessing. God bless ye."

Mary Liz was dumbstruck by the beauty of Saint Stephen's Green in this urban setting. She stood there while the porter held her bag, waiting for her while she looked across the corner to see the beginning of eighteenth-century town houses, neat and sparkling in red Georgian brick, white woodwork, massive windows and grand staircases up to the front doors. The front doors were massive, with elaborate brass knockers and door handles, each door painted a different bright color than its neighbor: red, blue, yellow, green…

"Lovely, isn't it?" the porter asked. "You must be from America. Are you from Noo York?"

"No, Chicago."

"Ach, well, 'tis all the same, isn't it, in America? That's why you all come here. We have everything, you know, and everything is beautiful, even our children." He gestured to a young mother walking by, a baby in a stroller, a little boy and little girl walking hand in hand beside her. All four had blue eyes, pale complexions and blond hair, the fairer version of the map of Ireland on their round faces.

"Follow me, won't you? You have an early check-in, I'm hoping. You'll be needing a nice hot bath and a nap before you start your day."

The Shelbourne was not eighteenth-century, but nineteenth, a Victorian vision of splendor. "The Shelbourne was where the Constitution was written," the porter told her. "Right upstairs. If you ask, I'm sure they'll let you peek at the suite."

The Shelbourne was also a very expensive hotel, perhaps the most expensive in Dublin, but its prices were far better than luxury hotels in New York, and wildly more reasonable than London's. It was formal but friendly, luxurious but had a comfortable—though rich—lived-in feel. The staff was warm and friendly and clearly determined to please. Her room was to die for. The double bed had a canopy over it. Two wingback chairs were settled comfortably around a tea table by the window overlooking the Green. The carpet was thick and soft, the wallpaper and wood moldings elegant. In the bathroom the plumbing was modern, but the bathtub itself an antique, an enormous old iron tub on feet, and next to it, there was a heated towel rack. The toilet was in a closet off the bath.

Mary Liz started the water in the tub and turned down her bed. A nap was in order. A bath and a nap.

At 2:27, Mary Liz walked briskly up the stairs of a magnificent eighteenth-century town house on Northumberland Road. She was in southeast Dublin, an area called Ballsridge, which appeared to Mary Liz to be a well-to-do town within the city. She touched the wrought-iron railing as she went up (she was in heels now), and rang the bell for Dunlau Gunney. She was buzzed in and walked into a very impressive waiting room, where Mary Liz explained her business to the pretty young woman behind the mahogany desk, who, in turn, motioned for Mary Liz to take a seat in any one of the plush antique chairs or settees, and offered her a cup of tea.

It turned out the tea needed to be brought in to the office of a firm partner, Mr. Geoffrey Brown, where Mary Liz was taken to see the youngish-looking man. "Ah, a Rachelle Zaratan suit," was the first thing out of his mouth.

"You know your clothes, Mr. Brown," Mary Liz complimented him. She bet he knew a lot of other things, too.

They shook hands and chatted a bit about the building; it had been the home of a maiden niece of the second duke of Leinster, he explained. This had been her sitting room; did she see how the doors opened onto the balcony that overlooked the back garden? Mary Liz walked out on the balcony and smiled at the abundance of flowers.

Then they got down to business.

"Your assistant said that you are in charge of a court-ordered inventory of the estate of someone named Alfred Hoffman," Mr. Brown said. "As I told her, I will tell you—we have never had a client of that name."

"I realize that," Mary Liz said, having not known this at all until this very moment, "but Alfred Hoffman was the founder, chairman and owner of Howland Films, the studio in Los Angeles."

Mr. Brown's expression remained impassive.

"And, as you know, Herbert Glidden, who did the financing of Howland films, was a client of yours."

"No," Mr. Brown said.

"Well, he was a customer, let's put it that way," Mary Liz said. "You represented a client, or clients, who made an investment in those movies."

He simply sat there, not confirming or denying it, waiting for her to continue.

"The reason I'm here," Mary Liz explained, "is there has been some confusion about the estate, including Howland Films, confusion which Herb was working with me to clear up. But then, unfortunately, he recently passed away in a swimming accident."

"I understand he was murdered," Geoffrey Brown said.

Mary Liz blinked. Bingo. They had done business with Glidden. But why had Alfred jotted down the firm's name? To be a client himself? Or to check on Glidden's investors?

"I wouldn't know about that," Mary Liz lied. "My concern is whether or not Howland Films can continue to have a business relationship with you. In particular, I want to discuss with you the financing of the movie they're shooting in the fall, the one starring Sasha Reinhart. Herb gave me the impression that you had at least one client lined up to invest— I'm sorry, is there something wrong?"

Geoffrey Brown's face had grown very dark during this last gambit of hers. "This meeting is over, Ms. Scott," he said, standing up. "I don't know what game you're playing at, but our firm has no interest in doing business with you."

"But—"

"We have never invested in a movie, not ever," he snapped. "You're lying and I don't know why and I have no reason to want to know. Good day, Miss Scott." He escaped out a side door and closed it behind him.

Didn't invest in the movies, eh? What then? Ah! She had an idea.

The receptionist was standing in the doorway. "Miss Scott? This way, please."

Mary Liz had half a notion to cause a commotion, but opted for congeniality instead. "Thank you. Let me ask you something, do you know what designer made this suit?"

The receptionist started to say something but stopped. "No," she said.

Mary Liz checked out of the Shelbourne and flew out of Dublin on Midway over to Amsterdam. She had been to this city before, and felt renewed by *its* terribly romantic eighteenth-century buildings (very different from Ireland's), to say nothing of the cobbled streets, footbridges and hundreds of canals. When she reached the Grand Hotel Krasnapolsky, where she had stayed while visiting on business before, she found a message waiting that Bill Pfeiffer had called.

In New York it was only about four in the afternoon, so she called him back at his office.

"All set for your meeting tomorrow?" he asked her.

Tomorrow she was to meet with the film and video company that Alfred Hoffman had co-owned with Bernard Braxer.

"Yes, I think so. And your package arrived. The papers look great." And then she laughed. "Thanks for the little cheat sheet on lawyer's terms in Dutch."

"If they give you any grief, Mary Liz, you just start yelling those at them."

"Not a problem."

She was dying to say something to him about Claire. Actually, she was dying to find out how he felt about Claire, if maybe there was a chance of something real working out between them.

"Call me as soon as you get out of the meeting," Bill said.

She promised she would, hung up, got ready for bed and knocked out for ten straight hours.

"How do you do?" the chief financial officer of Dag Gisteren said happily. "We were so terribly sad about the deaths of Mr. Hoffman and Mr. Braxer, and I'm very sorry I never met the gentlemen."

"How long have you been here?" Mary Liz asked him.

"Twenty-one years, since the company began."

This guy didn't look like any CEO she knew. He looked more like a sixty-year-old organ grinder out of costume, dressed at the moment in blue jeans, boots, T-shirt and blue blazer. He had an earring in his left ear.

Mary Liz smiled and added, "I certainly appreciate your expediency in preparing for my arrival."

"I have a complete set of financial records for you to take back, but I am here to explain everything to you firsthand. I have been assured by your assistant that you are aware of the sensitivity of the situation, and why such confidentiality has been a necessity."

Sensitivity of the situation?

"In addition to the records," Mary Liz said, "I need a list of the actual projects, every film, every video, complete with a profit-and-loss and royalty history. I would also like a complete list of your vendors."

He nodded. "It has already been done." He stood up. "We have prepared a conference room, complete with screening monitor, so you can review our current inventory."

Mary Liz got up and followed him down a hall. The walls were wood-paneled and the floor concrete. This town house was the strangest film studio she had ever been to. He stopped, and with a big smile, opened a door and stood there, holding it open for her.

Mary Liz walked into the conference room, surprised by the number of videotape boxes that were piled up against the far wall.

The CEO walked over and picked one up from the top of the pile and held it up. "This one is our current big seller, *Ingrid's Penis Day.*" He grinned. "Get it? *Ingrid's Penis Day?* Instead of *Independence Day?* Beautiful alien women invade earth to find the men with the biggest penises—including the president of the United States. It's very funny, very hot. This is the English version—over there you'll find the German, French, Swedish, Italian and Spanish product." He handed her the video. "By the way, our distribution in South America is going through the roof. You'll be very pleased."

Oh, Alfred, Mary Liz thought, reaching for a chair to sit down.

"It's a *what?*" Bill Pfeiffer nearly shrieked from his apartment in New York. "Why didn't that information turn up in our research?"

"Well, the laws are different here, Bill," Mary Liz said, not able to stop smiling. It was kind of funny. Not what she'd have to tell Aunt Nancy when she got back to the States, but after all the filth and obscenity she had seen today, the only thing she *could* do was laugh. Who had sex the way these people did, anyway? What man had a fourteen-inch penis? Or skinny women with watermelons for breasts? According to the videos, everybody did!

"Dag Gisteren isn't the name the stuff is marketed under. The name they go by is something like Big Cock and Tits—" She completely broke up at this, having to wipe tears from her eyes when she finished. "I'm sorry, I wrote down the name and it's something like that—" She started laughing again. "Oh, gosh, and the guy wanted me to take back all these samples, and of course, I freaked, visualizing myself being arrested at customs. I mean, Bill, you gotta see some of this stuff. It's unbelievable."

He was laughing now, too. "Sure, anytime."

"Good," she told him, "because he's shipping all the stuff to your office."

After getting off the phone, Mary Liz hurried to her next appointment, pulling her suitcase along with her. She had told Bill she was going to spend a day in Amsterdam before traveling on to Paris, which was true—sort of. She'd spend *this* day in Amsterdam.

Eeghlenburger Commodities Brokers had a very impressive building near the city center. Clearly these folks made big money. Mary Liz went into the reception area to announce herself, and she was shown into the office of a lovely young blue-eyed blonde who was cordial—that is, until Mary Liz brought up Herbert Glidden's name. At that, the woman frowned, and then politely but firmly told Mary Liz she must be mistaken, Eeghlenburger had never been involved with movies in any manner, shape or form.

"Are you sure?" Mary Liz asked.

"We never handle investments in entertainment companies," she said.

Mary Liz drew out of her briefcase the profile she had gotten on Eeghlenburger. "Let's see," she said, flipping through the pages, hoping to intimidate the woman a bit, "you did underwrite a television studio not long ago."

"It was a production center for an all-news network."

Mary Liz met her eye. "And you don't classify that as entertainment?"

"No."

"What about this string of radio stations in the American Southwest?"

"I wouldn't know about those," she said, sounding angry.

"And the bond issue for the playhouse renovation right here in Amsterdam?" Mary Liz looked up at her. "Don't tell me, let me guess—they only read the news in the theater, so it's not considered entertainment."

"I find your tone insulting, Miss—" She looked down at a piece of paper. "Miss Scott."

"And I find your presentation positively paranoid, Miss—" Mary Liz looked down at the papers in her hand "—Breda. Tell me what your investors *do* invest in."

"Commodities. Livestock. Metals. Grains. What do you think? Commodities!"

"And you're trying to tell me you've never dealt with Herbert Glidden?"

The woman glowered over her. "I'm trying to tell you to leave."

Mary Liz stood up. "Grapes. Now there's a thought." She looked at the woman. "Grapes? Wine, perhaps?"

The woman said nothing and Mary Liz moved to the door. "By the way," she added, opening the office door and turning around, "you do know that Herbert Glidden was murdered, don't you? Ah! I see. Then I suppose you have good reason to be scared. If I were you, I would be, too, Miss—" she looked down at the paper in her hand again "—Breda."

Dragging her suitcase behind her, Mary Liz boarded a tram to reach Amsterdam's train station. She sorely regretted not being able to stay. Understanding how to ride the long eight-foot-wide trams that snaked through the city had been an achievement on her first visit. She wanted to stop thinking about clothes and grapes and money and murder, and stay on to walk the canals and bridges and browse and shop, and stop at a café and have a sandwich and beer. She wanted to go to the flower market and the home where Anne Frank had been hidden during the war, and she wanted, most of all, to be in love with Sky, holding hands under the lights of the tall town houses, walking, drinking in the city and maybe taking a nighttime cruise through the canals.

She should place a bet. Schyler Preston or Stephen Pembroke. Which was it?

She bought a ticket and boarded a train for Brussels.

It was late when she reached the city of Brussels and Mary Liz was too tired to trust her sense of direction on the Metro. She hailed a cab that took her to Le Dix-septième, in central Brussels, a small hotel she had stayed in once. She went out for dinner (having, of all things, Indian food) and took a stroll in the Grand Place before sacking out at the hotel. The next morning she went to Banque de Veurne where, the receptionist confirmed, she was expected. Unfortunately, her reputation must have somehow preceded her, because she never got past a vice president (with two security guards) in the building lobby, who informed her in brisk English that she was not affiliated with any company they knew of and that the bank had no business with her.

"But I am affiliated with Howland Films," she told him.

"Not according to Howland Films, *madame*," the vice president told her.

"Did you talk to the owner?"

"No, *madame*, there is no owner at present. The matter is in dispute."

"Who did you talk to?"

"I am sufficiently satisfied you have no legitimate business here."

"And am I supposed to be sufficiently satisfied that you run a legitimate bank, *monsieur?*" she asked him, losing her temper. "And that you wish for me to cause you great trouble? Because, trust me, *monsieur,* I am about to. Your liaison with the American, Herbert Glidden, will cause you great trouble."

"I have no idea what you are talking about," he said, waving the security guards on. "Show her out."

Mary Liz was burning with anger. "Good luck with the auditors, pal." She grabbed the strap of her briefcase and rolled out of the bank.

Darn. She'd never got to ask him about architecture or magazines or country clubs.

Back to the train station and on to Paris.

After Mary Liz's train arrived at Gare du Nord, she took a cab to the Hotel Lutetia, an old favorite of hers from her days of doing deals for Reston, Kellaher. It was on the Boulevard Raspail, and had been built in 1910, a luxury hotel similar in feel to the Plaza, though much more intimate and quiet. This evening she needed to think, and so she took a long, luxurious bath, wrapped herself in the robe she requested, ordered a room-service dinner from the most excellent Le Paris restaurant downstairs and called Wendy in the States.

"The suspect list for Herb's murder may have to go international," Mary Liz told her. "Something's definitely big-time strange about how he raised money, or where he got it from, and who he was giving it to under what conditions. I think Alfred knew that, too—or was finding that out."

"So Bertie could be right," Wendy said. "His father's death might not have been an accident."

Mary Liz could hear Sky's voice echoing in her head, pleading with her to back off anything that had to do with Glidden. Well, too late now. "How's Bertie?" she asked.

"Not great," Wendy admitted. "The police want to arrest him as Glidden's murderer."

At 10:00 a.m. the next morning, Mary Liz was at the appointed apartment door to meet with one of the people who, for years, Alfred Hoffman had been handsomely paying under the heading Miscellaneous European Expenses and through a maze of fictitious corporations.

The woman who answered the door, Yvonne Bonet, invited her in. Happily, she was fluent in English. She was an extremely pleasant woman of fifty or so. "I am afraid I am confused about your business here," she told Mary Liz.

Mary Liz explained she was representing the estate of Alfred Hoffman—and the woman looked utterly baffled. Mary Liz said his name again, Alfred Hoffman.

Nothing.

"I'm sorry," the woman said, shrugging.

"The source of your monthly income?" Mary Liz asked

The woman shook her head. "I have a pension, from Cinema Seis, that is all. It is the pension of my dead husband."

Cinema Seis. Right. The fictitious company that actually issued the checks to this woman.

"I'm very sorry to hear about your husband," Mary Liz said.

"Thank you," the woman said, nodding.

"May I ask you when it was he passed away?"

"May of 1987," she answered.

That checked out with when the payments had started.

"He was killed while they were making a movie," she explained. "My husband was a caterer. There was an accident on the set and it caused a propane tank, which my husband used to keep food warm, to explode. It burned him very badly, and the next day he died."

"I see," Mary Liz said as she pulled out a pad. "Would you mind if I took some notes?"

"I'm not sure what the accident was," Mary Liz told Bill Pfeiffer from a telephone kiosk, "and I'm not sure we want to know. I think we ought to just leave the woman in peace and let her have the pension."

"We have to check it out, Mary Liz," Bill said, "but I'll do it. Let me talk to Howland Films and see if they have a record of it."

"I wouldn't go too deep," she warned him. "If Alfred felt obligated to pay her out of his own pocket, instead of through Howland, it might be something—"

"He was probably just being a good guy," Bill said. "Helping out a widow."

"You mean, to assuage his guilt over his porno house?"

"Mary Liz, he didn't make the pornography himself."

"Tell that to Aunt Nancy when the time comes, will you?"

* * *

Next stop (off the radar), to see Jacques Gorce, the independent investment banker. She called to confirm her appointment. Surprisingly, his secretary said not only was she expected, but Mr. Gorce would like to serve her lunch while she was there.

Hmm.

She was shown into his office where, he explained, he ate lunch every day, at his desk, a habit he had picked up from his years on Wall Street. "Very un-French, don't you agree?"

"But very reassuring to the client, no doubt," she said, smiling.

In contrast with the others noted in Alfred's diary to whom she had spoken, Gorce was very open. After she explained her position, that of inventorying the Hoffman estate, and the confusion there was at Howland about certain financial arrangements between Herbert Glidden and the company, Gorce couldn't have been more helpful.

"Oh, yes," Jacques said. "I knew Herb Glidden very well. I've known him for years. But I'm afraid there has been some misunderstanding. I have never had a client invest in Howland Films, not through Herb, or anyone else."

"Never?"

He shook his head.

"But you knew Herb."

"As I said, very well. And I did one deal with him, oh, maybe five years ago."

Mary Liz cocked her head. "Really? Could I ask you what kind of deal it was?"

"It's no secret, it was in all the papers, here and in America. My clients financed Claude and Isabel Lemieux's purchase of the American edition of *Je Ne Sais Quoi.*"

Mary Liz beamed. "I see."

Elienne Bresseau led Mary Liz through to the back room of the dress shop where she worked. They seated themselves around a small tea table where the employees took their break. Elienne, a lovely young woman in her twenties, was very happy to talk to her. Until, that is, Mary Liz had to tell her that Alfred Hoffman had died in a plane crash. Elienne cried a little.

"Oh, poor man," she said, wiping her eyes with the Kleenex Mary Liz offered her. "He was the kindest man I ever knew."

Huh?

"He support me and my son since the day Marc is born." She gestured to the shop. "I work here to keep busy, while Marc is in school. But thank you to Mr. Hoffman, I don't need the money." Suddenly she looked timid. "Now he is dead, does it mean it will stop?"

"No, no," Mary Liz quickly assured her, briefly touching Elienne's hand. "He's made lifetime provisions for you, and your son will be provided for until the age of eighteen, at which time he will come into a trust fund to pay for his education. And then, at the age of thirty, there will be another lump sum for him to spend as he wishes."

"Oh, sweet, generous man," she said, smiling sadly. "He told me this, but I did not know for sure."

"Um," Mary Liz faltered, "you are aware that Mr. Hoffman was married?"

"Oh, yes!"

"And that he had children?"

"Oh, yes."

Mary Liz was trying to find a tactful way to ask about her son, Marc, if he was Alfred's, or what the story was.

"May I ask you, Elienne, when the last time you saw him was?"

"Mr. Hoffman?" she asked. "But I've never seen him. A Mr. Braxer came to me before Marc was born and said Mr. Hoffman wanted to make sure we were all right. I thought it was going to be just one payment to get rid of me, but Mr. Braxer said no, Mr. Hoffman wanted to make right, and make sure we were looked after."

"And you receive a check every month?"

"Yes, from the studio. Cinema Seis." Elienne looked worried. "Have I upset you in some way? If I have, I am sorry—"

"Me? No, not at all. I was just thinking. I'm a little confused about why Mr. Hoffman wanted to look after you."

Well, there, she had said it.

"Because that bad man worked for him," she said, her eyes narrowing. "Mr. Hoffman heard what that man did and he wanted to help me. Because that man—" She had practically spat out the last, and was so angry she couldn't go on.

Mary Liz waited.

Elienne looked at her. "He raped me! My little Marc, he is a blessing, yes, but at the time—" She looked to the heavens, gesturing. "I was lost, I was—it was very terrible."

"The man who raped you, he worked for Mr. Hoffman?"

She bared her teeth in a snarl. "And it was only by luck I found out who he was. And when I tried to contact him, in the States, he said I was crazy and made the story up!"

"I'm so sorry," Mary Liz murmured.

"Herbert Glidden," she hissed, clenching her fist. "I will never forget!"

Mary Liz took in a breath. "Herbert Glidden, yes, now I see." She shifted a little in her chair. "Elienne, may I ask you, do you happen to have a picture of your son with you?"

"Herbert Glidden!" Bill Pfeiffer cried. "How could that be?"

"Well, wait—there's more." Mary Liz sighed into the telephone. She was in the airport, waiting to board her flight back to JFK on American. "She'd no sooner finished telling me how he had attacked her, and raped her—"

"*Raped?* How old was she?"

"Fifteen."

"Fifteen? God!"

She knew he must be thinking of his daughter, Jenny.

"But that's not all, Bill. Hold on to your seat." Mary Liz turned her back to the man who had arrived at the next telephone. "She showed me a picture of Marc—and I'm telling you, Bill, the kid is the spitting image of Alfred Hoffman."

25

The flight from Paris was mercifully unremarkable and Mary Liz used the time to review all that she had learned.

One, Glidden had found investors through Dunlau Gunney in Dublin, and not for movies; and something had also gone down between him and Eeghlenburger in Amsterdam and Banque de Veurne in Brussels.

Two, Glidden had definitely brokered money through Jacques Gorce in Paris for Claude and Isabel Lemieux to buy the American edition of *Je Ne Sais Quoi*.

Three, because of number two, she suspected more than ever that Glidden may have arranged financing for others in the East Hampton poker group. It was the only thing that made sense of why the men had simultaneously loathed, feared and tolerated Herb.

Alfred Hoffman had written down all four names of the financial firms—Dunlau Gunney, Eeghlenburger, Banque de Veurne and Jacques Gorce—and was intending to investigate. Or something. Had he finally had enough of Glidden? Three weeks later, Alfred died in a plane crash.

Mary Liz remembered Sky's warning again, about staying away from anything that had to do with Glidden, and she was developing more than just a glimmer of who—or what—Sky might be. Of course, she could be horribly wrong about Sky on all counts, but she didn't think so.

Back to her list of what she knew.

One, Alfred Hoffman had been a pornographer.

Two, Alfred Hoffman had felt guilty about the death of a man on his set.

Three, Alfred Hoffman had been a rapist.

It was dusk when they landed at JFK, and Mary Liz took her time making her way to the baggage area, stopping at the ladies' room to wash her face, reapply a little makeup and brush her hair, and stopping at a water fountain for a long drink of water. She got her bag and went on to customs, reading in line to pass the time. When she was finally checked through, Mary Liz was surprised to see a driver in the waiting area holding a cardboard sign up over his head that read M. L. SCOTT. He was patiently wandering the outskirts of the crowd. Mary Liz went over to him. "Who are you looking for?"

He was a heavyset guy in his forties, dressed in gray slacks and a blue blazer and white shirt. He quickly looked at a piece of paper he drew out of his jacket pocket and carefully said, "Mare-ree Liz Scott." He looked up at her hopefully. When she didn't say anything, but didn't move away, either, he read from the card, "Meesus Nan-cee Hoff-man ordered a car to pick you up."

Mary Liz smiled. "How nice. Great. Well, I'm Mary Liz. You're going to take me out to Long Island?"

"East-Hamp-ton," he said, his English stumbling through his Eastern European accent.

"And you know the way?"

"Yes!" he said enthusiastically. "No problem. I have di-rec-tions. And radio! In car." He fumbled into his pockets again, withdrawing something and handing it to her. "My card. Madam."

Executive Car & Chauffeur

Leo Kracztsky
at your service
1274 Industrial Drive Patchogue, LI
516-555-8989

"You like my dri-ving, you call me again—o-kay?"

Mary Liz had to smile. Knowing that everyone's ancestors had to have hustled the same way when they first arrived in America, it was impossible not to admire his spirit. He'd make it. He'd get ahead. His family would have a good life.

Mary Liz handed her bag to Leo, and he effortlessly carried it over to the inspector. Mary Liz showed her claim check and they were waved through. Leo's car was outside (several inspectors began yelling at him about leaving it there), a late-model black Lincoln Town Car. He put her bag in the trunk, unlocked the doors, ushered her into the back seat, jumped in the front seat and threw the sign propped against the windshield—#63 Executive Car & Chauffeur—on the floor, locked the doors and started them on their way.

They chatted for a while about the car itself. Leo owned it.

Well, his family owned it. They all had put in money. He liked working for himself. She thought it was a nice car? He cleaned and washed it every day, rain or shine. The dispatcher service was pretty good. Charged a lot. So many papers in America! Give us this fee, give us this tax, let the commission rob you blind, money, money, money! Yes, bad, but not like home! Russia. Yes. A wife. Two children. Two born here, one four, a boy, one two, a boy. No, mother still in Russia. She won't come.

Mary Liz settled down in the back seat, shoulder harness comfortably on, flicked on the reading light and opened the *New York Post* Leo gave her to scan the closing prices of the day's markets.

Even at close to nine o'clock, traffic was bad around JFK. "Six-seven-eight very bad," Leo told her. "That is why I was late. Everything near L-I-E is a mess. Total mess." At any hour on a Friday night in summer, the Long Island Expressway was a legendary nightmare. "I know way to get around all this," he promised, turning off 678 onto the Rockaway Expressway. "I show you how good a driver I am!"

Mary Liz gratefully left the driving to him and returned to the paper.

The traffic let up and they sped ahead, the overhead expressway lights rhythmically moving light across the car interior. Mary Liz glanced at the dashboard; there was a gauge with the outdoor temperature: eighty-one degrees. Leo was going about sixty-five. Good. He was going to swing under and around the traffic and get her home sooner.

It was pleasant in the car; it smelled vaguely of English Leather aftershave. She turned to her horoscope and it said to keep her wits about romance, and that finances could put on a dazzling display.

She looked out the window. They crossed a bridge over an inlet and bounced hard over a pothole. There was so much water around JFK—around New York City, for that matter. This whole stretch of New York and Long Island had nature's every blessing, and at night it looked so ideally clean. In the daylight, she knew, it was a very different matter.

They hit another pothole. Leo was still going sixty-five, it was still eighty-one degrees outside, but their direction was changing, the expressway taking a deep bend to the right, which she thought was west. "Don't we have to keep going east, Leo?"

"Just this little part, then we swing around. No traffic," he assured her.

They were bouncing along in the left lane, weaving when necessary to pass the cars that were only going about fifty. They bounced over another bridge and Mary Liz said, "Leo, are you sure you've got this right? There's a sign for the Cross Bay Veteran Bridge and that would take us north back to the airport. I think we needed to take a left back there somewhere."

"I know where I'm going," he said, racing off an exit for Far Rockaway.

"Why don't we just stop at a gas station and make sure?" Mary Liz suggested. "I could use a soda, anyway. I'll buy you one."

"No, not yet. Later," he said, gunning the engine and shooting out just before the light changed.

"Hey, Leo," Mary Liz said a moment later, "you can slow down. I'm not that much in a hurry. You nearly hit that kid on the corner."

Leo didn't say anything. Mary Liz leaned forward. "Did you hear what I said?"

"Sorry. Just have to go over here," Leo said, gesturing off to somewhere. "Fast shortcut." They were on a two-lane road now, passing low storefront-type buildings, garages and warehouses.

When Leo crossed the solid yellow lines to pass a car, Mary Liz had had it. Mr. Russia needed a driving lesson and Mary Liz needed to live. She undid her seat belt and slid her briefcase strap over her head so that it crossed her chest. At the next light, she was getting out. She waited as they roared and bounced and braked and accelerated along the road, every light seeming to be green. Finally they hit a red light, thankfully right next to an open gas station. When they stopped, Mary Liz opened the door.

Or tried to.

The door handle didn't pop the lock.

She tried to pull up the metal lock-post in the door; it wouldn't come up. She pulled the door handle again. Nothing.

"What you do?" he asked, turning around.

"Leo, open the door. I have to go to the bathroom."

"When we get there," he said, gesturing off to nowhere again.

Then she used the line she knew every driver feared. "Leo, I'm going to be sick—I'm going to throw up! Unlock the door!"

He didn't. Instead, he floored it and ran the light. Mary Liz threw herself forward over the front seat. "Stop this car, immediately! Dammit, I mean it!"

"Sit back," he said, and Mary Liz watched in astonishment as his right hand came up brandishing a tire iron, which he proceeded to heft in front of her face. "Get back!" he barked. "Be quiet!"

Oh my God, she thought, falling back into her seat. *This guy's going to rape me. He's taking me somewhere to rape me!*

He took a screeching left just then, and a block later, a screeching right, and then another left. Now they were on some sort of dimly lit access road into some sort of docking and warehouse complex.

She had to do something. Now. Before it was too late.

She lunged to get the tire iron and he slammed on the brakes and backhanded the tire iron into her face. A blinding pain cracked through the bridge of her nose, and she fell back, grabbing her face. When she looked up, blood was streaming down over her hands and onto her chest, the car had sped up again and now Leo was waving a gun.

Then, suddenly, there was the flash of car lights and the roar of an engine and an old station wagon came screeching out from behind a building and across the road in front of them. Leo slammed on the brakes and spun the wheel, but the Lincoln still caught the right end of the station wagon at about thirty miles an hour. Mary Liz had braced herself in time and closed her eyes before impact, which was a good thing since the windshield of the Lincoln burst, showering the inside of the car with safety glass. There was a hearty crash and then the grind of metal on metal as the Lincoln took out most of the end of the station wagon. A second after impact, Mary Liz heard the locks pop up on all the car doors. She didn't hesitate, but opened her door and ran to the closest building, a brick storehouse of some kind. She ran behind it and kept running and stumbling on, trying to find her way back to the main road.

By this point, blood was coursing down the back of her throat, making her periodically half gag and she told herself she could not faint, she could not be sick, she was going to make it to that road and find help.

She came out between two buildings and saw a small guardhouse lit up about three hundred yards away. It was in the direction of the docks, though, and Mary Liz would not go back there. The thought of being stationary anywhere right now made her panic. Not with that gun-toting maniac around. She ran on, heading toward what she prayed was north, toward where a main road must be. Finally she saw what she hoped was a streetlight between two buildings and headed for that. It *was* a streetlight. On a street. A dark deserted street with that sole streetlight. She was thoroughly turned around now, but took a right on the road, hoping this direction was east, back in the direction they had come. Her mind was a blank now, she couldn't pretend she knew where she was. All that seemed familiar was the tangy smell of saltwater that seemed to permeate everything.

She kept going, keeping close to buildings and bins and storage units, hiding, watching for cars. Finally she could see headlights coming quickly down the road. Better yet, there were flashing lights on it! Unfortunately it—which turned out to be a blue-and-white police car—screeched into a dramatic turn about a hundred yards ahead of her, and disappeared.

Then she heard a siren and she saw more flashing lights. Maybe they were coming because of the car accident. Thank God. She began to jog up the street, knowing she was nearing the end of her energy, if not consciousness. It was an ambulance and a police car coming. Mary Liz ran into the street, frantically waving her arms. "Help!" she cried. "Please help me!"

The ambulance turned into the dockyards, but the police car shot ahead to stop in front of her. Two officers jumped out, a man and a woman.

Tears mingling with blood, Mary Liz stumbled toward them.

IV

26

The police officers applied cold packs to Mary Liz's face while speeding her to the emergency room. They had already radioed in the assault and a description of the assailant. When they reached the hospital, Mary Liz heard a voice over the radio say that if the victim was able—after being treated—they were to bring her immediately to the station.

The police officers went into the hospital pushing their authority; this was a priority, the victim was needed at the station immediately. *If the victim is able,* Mary Liz replayed in her head. *Did you guys forget that part?*

She was zoomed into an examination area where she was cleaned up by a nurse, x-rayed, and then a doctor rushed in, pronounced her nose broken, packed it with gauze, put a big X of adhesive tape over it, told her she had a big bump on her forehead but no concussion, lots of bruises but no internal bleeding, gave her some codeine for the pain and sent her off with the officers back to the station.

At the precinct, a detective introduced himself to her as Marty Hearn, and told her he had her suitcase from the back of the Lincoln. He had Mary Liz sit in a chair next to his desk, asking her questions and typing stuff into a computer. First, however, he let her call Wendy in East Hampton.

The officers who had rescued her wandered over to talk to colleagues; other cops were working at their desks; there was some lady screaming and crying in the corner; a man in handcuffs was loudly demanding to talk to his lawyer. Evidently, hot and humid Friday nights in summer were swinging times for lawlessness.

"We didn't find anyone else from the accident," the detective told her. "Both drivers were gone. There was only a night security guard, and he didn't even know about the crash."

"Who called it in?"

"A guy on a cellular phone. That's all we've got." He tapped his Bic pen on the pad of notes next to the computer screen. "What's very strange, Miss Scott, is that not only was the limo reported stolen in Flushing yesterday, and both the name of the driver and the car company are fictitious, but the plates of the station wagon that crashed into you are registered to someone who's been dead for two years and the vehicle identification number is not registered anywhere, anyhow." He glanced at the computer screen in front of him, hit a key and looked back at her. "Weird."

She shrugged, feeling new pain in her neck.

"Miss Scott—"

"Call me Mary Liz, please. Miss Scott sounds like I'm under arrest."

"Mary Liz," the detective said, leaning forward to read his notes again. "He doesn't seem to have said anything of a sexual nature to you."

"No, he didn't. Quite frankly, the sexual assault idea only came to mind because of that incident a few weeks ago I read about—a cabby driving a woman passenger to a deserted place in Queens to rape her."

He looked her straight in the eye. "Can you think of any possible reason why this man—or anybody—would want to snatch you at the airport?" While she was trying to think, well aware her mind was not working yet, still in shock, he said, "You said you had come in from Europe, from Paris. Did you have any unusual business incidents, or unusual occurrences there?" He furrowed his forehead, trying to force her to concentrate. "Did anyone give you a package to take back to the States? An envelope? Anything at all?"

She shook her head. "No."

"Now think carefully. Was your luggage out of your sight anytime today?"

"No, I don't think so."

"Any maid in your hotel room while you were packing? Did you leave the suitcase at the hotel while you were out?"

"No. I checked out and took my bag with me to my appointments. I wanted to catch the earliest flight I could back to New York."

"Did you leave your bag anywhere during your appointments? In a waiting room? Or check it at a restaurant?"

She shook her head, aware of yet another new pain in her shoulder. "No."

"So you were with your bag until you checked it at the airport."

"Yes." She took a breath. "You're thinking I was carrying something in my bag and that's what Leo—or whatever his name was—was after. Like drugs or gems or something." She thought again.

"No. My bag was never out of my sight. At least, not until I checked it at Orly." She frowned. "But if he just wanted the bag, why not just take it from me at the airport?"

The detective frowned, too. "Think, Mary Liz. There must be some other reason why someone wanted you picked up."

"Well," she said, thinking of what she should have thought of in the first place but hadn't (because it was too awful), "I suppose it's possible someone wanted to throw a scare into me."

His eyes brightened immediately. "Tell me about that."

"I'm afraid I don't know who, exactly, or why exactly, either, but on my trip, I was raising some questions about overseas money that had come into the United States as investments—money they know I know could be suspect."

"Raising questions with who?" he asked.

"Legitimate financial companies," she said. "At least on the surface. An investment banking firm, a commodities brokerage, a commercial bank and an independent investment banker. It's complicated, but the bottom line is, either someone at one of those companies, or one of the clients those firms represent, might have wanted to scare me. To shut me up and make me stop snooping."

"That's got to be why *he* was there," the detective said victoriously, jumping out of his chair and running off somewhere with notepad in hand.

He who?

Detective Hearn was gone for over a half hour, leaving Mary Liz sitting there. The policewoman who had rescued her came over and offered her something to drink; Mary Liz accepted some water. About five minutes later, Wendy and Jake came bursting into the squad room, spotted Mary Liz and hurried over.

"Oh my God," Wendy declared, bending on one knee to look at Mary Liz's face.

"I told you he broke my nose," Mary Liz said.

"In how many places?" Jake asked.

"Just one, the doctor said. The bridge."

"You're bruising all the way down to your chin," Wendy said. "My God, Mary Liz, you look as though—"

"Don't tell me," she protested. "I haven't looked and I don't want to hear. I just want to get through this and get out of here. By the way, thanks for coming." She started then. "You didn't leave Nancy alone, did you?"

"Bertie's with her," Jake said.

"She's going to have a stroke when she sees me like this," Mary Liz groaned. "You didn't tell her, did you?"

"No, I thought it better not to," Wendy said.

"Good," Mary Liz said. "Maybe I'll look a little better tomorrow."

From the look Wendy and Jake gave each other, she knew this would not be the case.

"Anyway," Mary Liz continued, gesturing to the detective's empty chair, "his first theory was that I must be a drug smuggler or something and Leo wanted my suitcase."

"You told me he was going to rape you."

"Oh. Well, that was only my theory. The detective doesn't seem to think so. Now we're working on theory two, that I must have upset somebody in Europe enough that they wanted to throw a scare into me."

"I told you this whole thing was dangerous," Jake said to Wendy.

"Did you tell the detective, Mary Liz," Wendy said, "that Herb Glidden was recently murdered? And that you're mixed up in the estate of another man with whom Glidden did business, who may also have been murdered?"

She tried to smile but couldn't. One side of her mouth was numb. "No. I was saving that up for possibility number three."

Jake looked around. "Which one is he?"

"He's gone off somewhere," Mary Liz said. "I'm hoping when he gets back, he'll explain what's going on. I get the distinct feeling he has an idea who the driver was."

They waited around a bit, not speaking. Then Wendy leaned over. "So did you find out what that studio's worth in Holland?"

Mary Liz looked at her miserably. "You had to remind me, didn't you?"

"Problems?"

"You have no idea. I don't even know where to begin." Mary Liz sighed. She looked up. The police officer had come back with a pitcher of water and was refilling her glass. She was very grateful. The pain medication made her thirsty, although it couldn't be working too well since her whole body was beginning to throb.

"We should get you in to see a plastic surgeon," Jake said.

"Oh, my nose is broken, what difference does it make? It either sets in line or it doesn't. Either way, with the mess the cartilage is in, I'm going to have surgery somewhere along the line, anyway."

Mary Liz watched as the detective came back into the squad room. He went over to the officers who had rescued Mary Liz and talked to them. Then the three of them came over. Mary Liz introduced Wendy and Jake.

"If you don't mind," the detective said, "I'd like your friends to wait outside for a few minutes."

"You can talk in front of them," Mary Liz said.

"We'll talk first," he said, "and then we'll see. All right?"

Mary Liz nodded and Wendy and Jake reluctantly left the squad room.

The detective handed Mary Liz a thick manila folder full of loose pictures. "Could you please go through these pictures and tell me if any one of them looks like your man? The man who called himself Leo?"

Most of the pictures looked vaguely like Leo: men with oval faces, fair skin, in their forties, rough complexions, blue eyes. But the identification was a snap. "This is Leo," she said, pulling his photo and tossing it on the desk.

"Wow," one of the officers said.

She looked up. "Can you believe I told him I *admired* him for all his hard work as an immigrant in this country?" She looked at the detective. "So who is he? Is he even really Russian?"

"Oh, he's Russian, all right," the detective said, writing something down on the back of the photo. Then both police officers initialed whatever he had written. Then Detective Hearn picked up the phone and punched in a couple of numbers. "Positive ID," he said into the handset. "She picked him out of thirty photos."

Moments later a very tall woman, dressed in a pantsuit, came striding into the squad room. She was introduced to Mary Liz as Debbie Cole, an agent with the FBI. She shook hands with Mary Liz, looked at the group and said, "I think we need to move somewhere a little quieter and have a chat." The group followed her down the hall to an interrogation room, where they all settled around a table. Detective Hearn turned on a tape recorder, and clearly stated the day and time and each of their names.

"The driver that you knew as Leo," the agent began, "his real name is Ivor Vrensk and he belongs to an organized crime ring based in Brooklyn—Brighton Beach."

"You mean, like the Mafia?"

"Like the Mafia, but definitely Russian, and definitely more violent," she said. "What we need to find out from you, Ms. Scott, is why a Russian gang would be interested in you. From what you've told Detective Hearn, you believe it might have something to do with overseas investments in this country, which you had just been raising questions about in Europe."

"Yes."

"Can you explain?"

And so, for the next two and half hours, Mary Liz—given fruit, water, a sandwich and more codeine to keep going—explained how she had come to East Hampton to discreetly inventory the estate of the dead producer, Alfred Hoffman, and how she had crossed paths with the financier, Herbert Glidden, who had bankrolled a number of his films.

"Crossed paths how?" the agent wanted to know.

"He wanted to hire me," she explained. "Probably as an attempt to bribe me to stop the inventory of the estate and switch to his side and help him win his case for control over Howland Films."

"And why did you say he wanted Howland Films?"

"I'm not entirely sure. I used to think he just wanted to insure that he would continue to be the only money man for the studio, but now I'm beginning to wonder if he wanted to make sure that no one would—or could—ever trace things back to the primary movie investors, discovering exactly who they were. Or are."

"Why would he want to prevent that?"

"I don't think the money was clean," she said.

Detective Hearn sighed. "Ah, Hollywood."

"New York's no better," Mary Liz said quickly. "It's everywhere, Detective."

"Where is Glidden now?" the FBI agent asked.

"Someone recently murdered him."

"The floater in East Hampton a couple of weeks ago," the detective reminded her.

The New York City law enforcement officers sat back in their chairs to consider this, while the FBI agent, who Mary Liz had come to call Agent Debbie in her mind, seemed not surprised in the least and pushed on, "If Glidden had nothing to do with the estate, why were you raising questions about Glidden and the investors on your trip?"

"Well, first of all, I simply wanted to know. The man was a nightmare, which brings me to the second and most important reason—

Alfred Hoffman's son, Bertie, was never convinced his father's plane crash was an accident. And I wanted to know if there was a link—his crash, Glidden, the overseas investors and maybe even Glidden's murder."

"So you went over to take on international organized crime all by yourself," the agent said.

"No, I went to explore some assets of the Hoffman estate, and since I was over there, I paid a call on some of the institutions I thought might have invested in some Howland Films projects through Glidden. Now I don't think the projects were confined to Howland movies. I think Glidden was financing other businesses, too."

"Where did you get the names of these overseas investment firms?" Agent Debbie asked.

"Well, that's a long story, too. The long and short of it is that Alfred Hoffman himself had jotted down the names of these four firms in his business diary—with no annotations, nothing—and then was dead within the month."

"Summing up as simply as you possibly can," Agent Debbie said, "what do you think Herbert Glidden was doing that could have cost him his life?"

"Or mine," Mary Liz said absently.

"Ms. Scott?"

She tried to stay alert.

"I asked you what you thought Herbert Glidden was doing."

"Moving money into the United States on behalf of organized crime—money laundering."

The FBI agent was nodding. She looked at her watch. "We've got a lot of ground to cover, Ms. Scott, and you've obviously been through a lot. Where are you staying tonight? Would you like us to put you up in a hotel?"

"I want to go back to East Hampton," she said. "My friends will take me. Could we possibly continue this out there?"

"No problem," Agent Debbie told her, standing up. "As a matter of fact, we'll send someone out with you to keep an eye on things." She turned to Detective Hearn. "You better talk to her friends, make sure they know. We don't want to scare them."

Mary Liz gave a sad, tired little laugh. "I'm not sure we can be any more scared."

Detective Hearn leaned forward slightly. "I'm afraid they want to do a whole lot more than just scare you, Mary Liz. That's why it is so important you do exactly as Agent Cole tells you." He paused.

"Why? What do you think he was supposed to do?"

"Ivor Vrensk, the man you identified," Detective Hearn said, "is a hit man. No joke. By profession. We believe he was sent to kill you. And dump your body. That's why he was taking you to the docks."

27

Mary Liz remembered nothing after climbing in the back of the Range Rover. When she awakened, it was to find herself in her bedroom at the cottage, drapes closed against daylight, central air on, the clock swearing it was 2:10. She closed her eyes. Her head throbbed, her body ached. What day was it? she wondered. How much of it had been a dream? She tried to open her eyes again. And gingerly she tried to sit up.

"Darlin'," a familiar voice murmured. A figure rose from the chair and hurried over to the bed. "Poor child," her Aunt Nancy said, sitting on the edge of the bed and leaning over her but not touching her. "What have they done to you?"

"I'm going to be fine," she managed to croak out. "Really."

Something wet was on her arm. She looked down; it was Ashley, looking up at her, gently licking her arm as if afraid to hurt her if she did anything more.

The dog was probably right.

"She wanted to see you," Nancy said. "Every time I let her out today, she made a beeline for your door."

Mary Liz rubbed the dog's nose.

"Two FBI agents have been here all day." Nancy smiled. "I get the distinct impression, Mary Liz, they think you're the greatest thing since sliced bread."

"So it *did* happen." She closed her eyes, thinking the pain in her head was going to kill her.

"Yes, darlin', it sure did. And the estate is under guard to prove it."

Mary Liz got her eyes open again. "Really?"

"FBI, dear. Top-drawer for our girl." Her brow furrowed slightly. "Mary Liz, I have to let your parents know something."

"No, let me call them. Later. I promise I will."

Nancy sighed. "Are we through yet, darlin'? Is the inventory done? Can I send you somewhere to rest?"

Mary Liz couldn't even nod; her neck was like a block of concrete with shoots of pain radiating from it. "I just need to finalize the numbers, write the summary and the inventory is done," she said. "But I'd like to stay on for a bit, if that's okay with you. We'll go over everything in a few days, all right?" Just the thought of what she had to tell her godmother gave Mary Liz a blinding shot of pain between the eyes. She had to close them.

Aunt Nancy, your beloved husband was an international pornographer. Aunt Nancy, your husband was a rapist— (Strike that; she wouldn't tell her that part. Nor would she reveal that her husband was, in Mary Liz's book, a child molester.)

Aunt Nancy, your husband has another son, and has done right by him, except his son thinks his father was Herbert Glidden.

Mary Liz opened her eyes again, wishing they would focus properly. She wondered if the blurriness had something to do with the pain in her head. "Excuse me, but I need to visit the bathroom."

"Let me help you."

"It's okay, Aunt Nancy, I can go by myself. I'm just stiff."

Stiff, ha. She was dying.

But she did manage to get up and walk to the door. And she did manage to ask her godmother if she could make her some tea and put some yogurt in a bowl on the breakfast bar for her. Anxious to do something, Nancy hurried off.

Mary Liz crept down the hall to the bathroom, turned on the light and closed the door behind her. Her hands were shaking slightly from who only knew what; she reached for the codeine bottle on the sink and fumbled as she got two out and then ran a glass of water to take them with. Closing her eyes, she swallowed the painkillers. Then she opened her eyes.

And saw herself full face in the mirror.

Good God.

It look as though someone had forced an oversize golf ball under her skin between her eyebrows. The "white" of her left eye was bloodred. Black-and-violet pouches sagged under her eyes, swollen with blood, which then gave way to streaks of deep red and purple and finally black down in her cheeks, looking as though it were slowly dripping into her chin. And then there was the slightly dirty-looking X of adhesive tape that held a bandage over her nose, and then from inside, the crusty brown packing.

Gingerly she tried to take out the gauze packing in her nose. It was caked with blood and was completely disgusting. Piece by piece she pulled it out. Her nose did not start bleeding again, thank

God. Now she only felt like gagging because clumps of something were suddenly running down the back of her throat.

She coughed something up into the sink.

Blood.

She ran the water to get it down the drain and clean the sink. Then she rinsed her mouth. Then she rinsed it again. And then she sipped more water. Then she gargled with Listerine.

And then she sat down on the john and started to cry.

When Mary Liz had pulled herself together enough to leave the bathroom, she put on her terry-cloth robe and walked into the living room. There she was somewhat dismayed to find a man sitting cross-legged on her living-room floor with what looked like a variety of little electronic gizmos.

"Did Liam send you?" she asked. "Are you debugging my house?"

The man turned around. "Oh, hi," he said cheerfully. "You must be Miss Scott."

"Unless you know other people who look like this," Mary Liz said.

"Believe it or not, I've looked like that. And believe it or not, in a couple days you'll start looking like yourself again." He nodded vigorously. "Really. Oh, and Mrs. Hoffman put out something for you to eat and said she'll be back. My supervisor will be here soon to talk to you. I'm Agent Travers, FBI." He reached into his back pocket.

"That's all right, don't get up, I believe you," Mary Liz said, moving on toward the breakfast bar. The world was not focusing the way it should and it made her nervous. "But you might tell me what's the status of the cottage—am I still bugged or what?"

"It's clean now. So is your phone, computer and fax."

"And did you find out who's been listening?"

"My supervisor will be here in a moment."

"Come on," she said, sliding onto a stool. "Look at me. Look at what I've been through. You can at least tell me that much."

He hesitated and then said, "Yes."

"My security guy said it was at least two, maybe three different parties."

He hesitated again, looked at the door and then whispered,

"Yes." Then he made a sign like an umpire makes when a runner slides into a base and is safe.

No more.

God bless Aunt Nancy, for she had not only left the yogurt and a pot of tea and honey and milk out, but the new issue of *Vanity Fair* as well, as if this were like any other day and Mary Liz might be interested. This little touch, for some reason, made her feel better.

The codeine was starting to work; she forced herself to eat some yogurt so her stomach wouldn't be upset from the drug. She tried to turn her head to see what the FBI agent was doing, but her neck wouldn't cooperate, so she gave up and stared straight ahead, out the kitchen window over the sink.

In about ten minutes, someone came bounding into the house. Mary Liz didn't bother to try to turn around. She knew the attempt would be hopeless.

"Ms. Scott!" a cheerful voice said, and Mary Liz knew it was Debbie Cole, aka Agent Debbie, from the police station the night before. The agent walked around the breakfast bar, saw Mary Liz's face and openly flinched. "Yow. You really got it, didn't you?"

"Yeah," Mary Liz said sulkily, wishing Agent Debbie would stop staring at her. Now that she knew what she looked like, she didn't want anyone to see her.

"Ms. Scott, as much as we regret what happened to you last night—and we really, really do—because of your misadventure we, and another federal law enforcement agency, have been given a vital new connection in a major case. And I mean *major*."

"What kind of case?"

The agent's face took on that sudden blank expression that so many of these law enforcement people had lapsed into with Mary Liz within the last twenty-four hours. "As soon as we get clearance, you'll be the first to know."

Mary Liz leaned forward slightly. "Do I look like I'm in any shape to run around telling everybody?"

She only smiled. "I'm sorry, Ms. Scott."

"Please stop with the Ms. Scott. You make me feel like I'm in trouble. Mary Liz."

The agent nodded.

"Just tell me this," Mary Liz said. "Does this *major* case of yours have to do with money laundering?"

Agent Debbie got that blank expression again.

"I'm going to take that as a yes," Mary Liz decided.

The agent smiled slightly.

"Are they the ones who bugged my house?"

"I'm sorry—I can't comment on that. Not yet."

"Are *you* the ones who bugged my house? I understand I had two, maybe three audiences."

"I'm sorry, Ms.—Mary Liz—but I can't comment on that, either, right now."

"How 'bout something new on my old friend Leo, the hardworking immigrant murderer for hire?"

"He's not for hire. That is his function in the organization."

"So you haven't found him," Mary Liz surmised. She sipped her tea. It was cold now, and she wasn't feeling so hot, either.

"Mary Liz," Agent Debbie said, "I know you've been through a lot, but it's very, very important we go over some things."

"Sure, okay."

"Mrs. Hoffman has already turned all the Howland Films files in her basement over to us."

Mary Liz panicked for a second, but then remembered there wasn't anything in them that could compromise the Hoffman estate—or the Hoffmans themselves.

Agent Debbie dragged a stool around to sit opposite Mary Liz at the breakfast bar. While the agent taped the conversation and took notes, Mary Liz talked and talked, spelling the name of the investment banking firm she had visited in Dublin, the commodities brokerage in Amsterdam, the bank in Brussels and the independent investment banker in Paris. She spelled the names of the people she saw and told the agent everything they had said to her when she had visited their offices. She told her about the investment banker in Paris who said Glidden had never handled any movie investments for him, but that he had, however, through Glidden, underwritten Claude and Isabel Lemieux's purchase of the American edition of *Je Ne Sais Quoi* five years ago. Mary Liz told her how strange it was that Claude had made a big show of disliking Herbert Glidden over the years, when, it turned out, he had every reason, in Mary Liz's opinion, to be extremely grateful to him.

She also told her about the other members of the poker group—Henry MacClendon, Randolph Vandergilden, Buck Buckley and Charles Kahn—and the fact she suspected Glidden had found investment money for them, too.

She told her everything she knew about Glidden, from his business to his son to his agoraphobic wife, to every conversation she could remember ever having with him. She told her about his lying around town, telling everyone that she was working for him, and throwing everyone into a tiz. She told Agent Debbie everything that could be relevant to the FBI's interest in the movement of any international moneys, and she pointed out where any of this information coincided with Alfred Hoffman's death, or possible motives for the murder of Herbert Glidden.

Mary Liz wished she hadn't promised to take the agent into the office now to photocopy Alfred's diary entry and other relevant notes and papers she had. She was pressing her luck badly and was starting to lose focus.

"One thing, before we go into the office," Agent Debbie said, getting that blank expression again. "Agent Travers tells me that a couple hundred photographs, papers and manila files have been very recently burned in your fireplace."

"You're kind of a sneak, Agent Travers, aren't you?" Mary Liz called, thinking, *Didn't they have to have some kind of warrant to be doing this kind of snooping in her house?* Cooperating with the authorities was one thing, causing her Aunt Nancy even further pain over her dead husband was another. No way she was coming forth with Alfred's "collection."

"Agent Travers is outside," Agent Debbie told Mary Liz.

Good grief, she couldn't turn around, she couldn't see straight, she couldn't even *hear* properly. The guy had gone outside.

"As I was saying," Agent Debbie said, scanning her notes, "over two hundred photographs were burnt."

"Two hundred seventy-six, if you want to be exact," Mary Liz said.

Agent Debbie made a note and looked up. "Do you want to tell me about it? About why you first shredded two hundred seventy-six files and photographs and *then* burned them?"

"All I can tell you," Mary Liz said, sighing, wishing she could rub her eyes, but knowing she couldn't, "is that they had absolutely nothing to do with anything we're talking about."

"Not good enough, I'm afraid."

Mary Liz looked at her. "So what if someone had some dirty pictures tucked away? Why does his widow need to know?"

"Pornography?" the agent persisted.

"Just some dirty pictures that have nothing to do with anything," Mary Liz said. "I swear, I would have kept them if I thought they had the slightest relevance to anything—except embarrassing the widow."

Agent Debbie did not look convinced, but made a note. "Okay, let's move on, then. What I'd like to see now are the papers you mentioned, and that diary. And then, I promise, we'll leave you alone so you can get some rest."

"Sure, okay," Mary Liz said, sliding gingerly down off the stool. "Follow me."

"I can't tell you how much we appreciate your efforts," the agent said. "You've been fantastic."

The room was starting to look strange. "It's my pleasure," Mary Liz said, and she was going to say something about how gratifying it was to see the feds catch on to a twisted trail of funny money, that in the world of high finance it would be considered a freak occurrence, but then the room suddenly started to get light, kind of yellow, and then there was a roaring in Mary Liz's ears, and the yellow light turned to gray and...

"Hello, my precious, dearest, darlin' baby angel," a voice whispered.

It could only be one person. Her mother. Mary Liz struggled to open her eyes. It was Mom. Hanging over her, smiling, but with two big tears rolling down her face.

"Hi," Mary Liz managed to say.

"Hi, babe," a voice whispered from the other side.

"Dad," she murmured, wanting to smile. No go. Her whole body felt incredibly heavy. She wondered what her parents were doing here and wanted to ask, Wasn't her college graduation next week?

But was she in school? She couldn't remember and she couldn't keep her eyes open...

Mary Liz's eyes flew open.

It was daylight. And she could see. Clearly.

She didn't have to sit up; she was already cranked up, in a hospital bed.

Where on earth was she?

"Mary Liz," a voice whispered hopefully from slightly behind her. A shadow fell across her bed and then there he was. Sky. Smiling. Looking pale and haggard and worried. And with a huge gash across his forehead that required stitches. But he was smiling. At her. "Thank God," he whispered.

"What happened to your head?"

"What happened to *your* head?" he asked her.

Mary Liz raised her hand and made a fist. "I oughtta slug you."

"I don't blame you," he whispered. "But please don't make me go. I've been so worried about you." He reached for the bell cord to ring for the nurse.

It was three in the afternoon on Sunday. She had been out for almost twenty-four hours, during which they'd shot X rays again, because when she had passed out at the cottage, she had crashed down headfirst to the floor. The verdict was excellent, though, Sky told her, it was only a slight concussion, and otherwise just chronic fatigue in the aftermath of severe physical and mental shock.

The nurse came in, beaming. "Sleeping Beauty has awakened." And then she cringed, as though she had said something terribly inappropriate.

She had. The memory of what her face had looked like came back to Mary Liz in a wave of sadness.

"How do you feel?" the nurse continued, coming over to check her pulse and take her temperature.

"I'm starving and thirsty," Mary Liz reported.

"Wonderful. Then I can take you off this. How about some water?"

"How about a Coca-Cola?" Mary Liz said, watching the nurse disconnect an IV. She hadn't even noticed the needle taped into her arm. "When I was a child, I was always allowed to have a Coke when I was sick."

"I think I can rustle up one of those," the nurse said, glancing at her again. "You really do look good. It's amazing. When they brought you in yesterday, you were pretty out of it."

"Please stop looking at me," Mary Liz begged Sky.

"I'm just so relieved, Mary Liz."

To the nurse, she asked, "Any chance I can get out of here?"

"Tomorrow, maybe," the nurse said. "The doctors want to keep an eye on you for at least one more night." She had taken the needle out of Mary Liz's arm and pushed the IV apparatus back out of the way. "Okay, let me go and call your parents and tell them you're awake. And I'll try to find you that Coke." She left, leaving the two of them alone again.

"Please stop looking at me," Mary Liz repeated, suddenly starting to cry. She felt so hideous, so happy, so awful, all at the same time.

"It's okay, it's okay," Sky murmured, trying to hold her a little.

"Everything hurts," she whimpered. "I feel so helpless, so ugly and ill."

"You've had a very serious injury, Mary Liz," he said softly. "But a plastic surgeon's already been here, a friend of your Aunt Nancy's, and she says you're going to come out of this looking like yourself. There's nothing broken but your nose, and the knot on your forehead's already going down, and the purple parts are starting to turn bluish green, which means it's healing—"

"I'm turning blue-green, oh, what a relief," she said, suddenly starting to laugh. She felt so strange, crying, laughing, all every which way, slightly giddy and mildly hysterical.

"It's your nervous system, darling," Sky said. "You can't help this part. It's part of the healing process."

Darling.

"But I don't even know who you are," she said, closing her eyes. "One day you're Schyler Preston, the next, Stephen Pembroke."

There was a decisive pause. "Who told you that?"

"Does it matter?" she said, eyes still closed.

"Actually, it does. Very much."

She opened her eyes. He was serious. "Herb Glidden gave Aunt Nancy a photocopy of a page out of a yearbook. It had your picture and the name Stephen Pembroke under it. It said you received a law degree."

He was staring at the wall, thinking. She shook his hand to get his attention. He was silent, though, for almost a minute more. Then he hung his head. "So he found out."

"That you were Stephen Pembroke?"

Sky raised his head. "No. I mean that Glidden ran a check on me and he found out exactly what I wanted him to find out—that I was a lawyer, Stephen Pembroke, and that I was probably trying to seduce you because I was working for Braxer & Braxer, trying to find out what you knew about the Hoffman estate."

"Well?"

"Well what?"

"Is it true?"

He frowned. "Of course it's not true!"

"Well, it's not as if you've explained a damn thing to me, Sky."

"The most important things, yes, I have," he said softly.

"Sky," she said, tightening her grip on his hand. "You have to tell me who you are."

He smiled, leaned to kiss her lightly on the side of the head and, leaning close to her face, whispered, "I am Schyler Preston. But yes, I do have a law degree. And no, I don't teach school—but I do coach a Little League team in the spring." He paused. "I did my best to warn you, Mary Liz, without telling you what I was doing here."

"Why couldn't you tell me?"

"Because I still didn't know if you were implicated."

"Implicated in what?"

"In the case I'm working on. All I could do was warn you off Glidden—and even by doing that, I was breaking the rules."

"Whose rules?"

He sighed. "Mary Liz, even if you weren't actively participating in Glidden's activities, he still might have been using you in some way. And that's what I came here for this summer, to observe, to track, to report—to figure out how Glidden's operation works and how to get as many of the fish in the net as possible."

Her eyes were starting to tear, not out of emotion, but fatigue. "Are you FBI?"

He shook his head.

"CIA?"

He smiled. No.

"DEA?"

"No."

"What's left?" she asked him.

"Federal prosecutor," he told her.

"Oh." She closed her eyes. "Buck's made some sort of a deal with you, hasn't he? You've got something on him, that's why you're at his house, isn't it?"

"I can't say any more. As it is, as of now, my life's in your hands, Mary Liz." He paused. "Which, under the circumstances, seems only fair."

She opened her eyes. "I didn't know federal prosecutors went undercover."

"They usually don't." He grinned. "Not all of them are as good a golfer as I am."

"What would you have done if you had found out I was a crook?"

"I didn't believe you could be. Ever."

"But what if I had been? Isn't there a rule about sleeping with the enemy?"

He didn't speak for a moment. "I want to marry you. I know, it's too soon to say something like that, and believe me, I'm not a rash kind of guy, but in your case, somehow I've known from the start that you're the person I've come through everything to find."

She closed her eyes again. "You certainly have a colorful way of avoiding the point."

"Here we go," the nurse said gaily, coming in with an icy can of Coca-Cola, a cup of ice, a banana and some strawberry yogurt. "See what progress you can make with this. Dinner's in a couple of hours."

"I'll bring you dinner," Sky said. "Anything you want."

Mary Liz cracked the tab on the Coke and poured some out. "Cheeseburger, French fries, chocolate shake from McDonald's," she said without hesitation.

"Done," he told her.

"Your mother and father are coming right over," the nurse said, walking back to the door. "They should be here soon."

"They're at some friends of your Aunt Nancy's here in Southampton," Sky explained.

She looked at him. "Did you meet them?"

"Yes." He smiled. "We spent several hours together this morning. You know what they say, before you marry the daughter, meet the mother to see what you're getting into in the years ahead." He grinned. "Your mother's extremely attractive, may I add. A real Southern belle and wonderful lady."

Mary Liz was trying to ignore this marriage talk. He was talking nonsense. They had only known each other a couple of months. "What about my father?"

"Oh...well, *he* was pretty scary. He wanted to know who the heck I was and what my connection was to you—"

She laughed, making her head hurt.

"I told him, 'My name is Schyler Mark Preston, I'm thirty-five years old, born in Boston, Massachusetts, Congregationalist, undergraduate degree from Middlebury College. My mom is a schoolteacher and my father is a retired oil-company executive. I own a three-bedroom cottage in Virginia, an old Mercedes, and have some savings and investments. I've fallen hopelessly in love with your daughter and have been trying to make her fall hopelessly in love with me so that in a year or two we can get married.'" He grinned. "So you know what your dad says?"

She imitated her father's voice. "Don't you have a job?"

He was amazed. "How did you know?"

"I know my father," she said, laughing. "So what did you tell him?"

"I told him that yes, indeed, I had a job, which I would sit down with him and properly explain later."

"So you didn't tell him."

He shook his head and leaned close. "I can't, darling. You're the only one who knows. And it has to stay that way awhile."

She looked into his eyes, wondering how on earth he could look so lovingly at someone whose face would be frightening even on Halloween. "Where were you? When I talked to you?"

"Holland."

"Really? I was just there."

He nodded. "I know."

She would have squinted her eyes if she could. "Did you see me?"

He nodded.

"And in Brussels?"

"Someone else did."

"In Dublin?"

"No one did. By the time I knew you were there, you were already on the way to Amsterdam."

"And what about Paris?"

"I was there."

"You followed me?"

"I was watching out for you."

"You were spying on me."

"Whatever," he said, settling it. "And I was on your flight back to New York. In tourist." He lowered his head. "And I will never forgive myself." He raised his head to look at her again. "We just didn't get it, Mary Liz. It wasn't until Vrensk turned off the expressway and headed deeper into Queens that we realized— And by that time—" He sighed. "I'm the one responsible for you getting so banged up like this."

"I'm responsible for me being banged up like this," Mary Liz said, reaching to touch the side of his face. "I started the panic with whoever these people are. It must be some gang. But who banged you up?"

"I slammed it on the frame of a car door," he said. "Some limo hit the back of my station wagon."

She stared at him. "That was you? In the station wagon?"

"I had to stop him," Sky explained. "I didn't know where the hell he was going until the very end."

"And then where did he go?"

Sky grimaced. "There's a reason why they keep prosecutors off the field. He shot me and split."

"Shot you?"

He pointed to his thigh. "Now we match. He didn't do any damage, he just scared the hell out of me."

"But the police said no one was there when they reached the accident."

"No one was," Sky confirmed. "I called them and then went off to try and find you. But damn, lady, you move fast when you want to."

Mary Liz smiled, her eyes closing, drowsiness washing over her. Sky squeezed her hand.

She was safe. She would sleep.

28

Mary Liz was released from Southampton Hospital Monday morning and was taken to the Big House. Under Nancy's orders, she was put in Denver's room, a palatial bedroom looking out on the ocean, complete with dressing room and bath. Tucked into the queen-size bed, looking out from her puffed-up pillows to the ocean, Mary Liz felt like mistress of the manor. On the floor next to the bed was Ashley, snoozing.

"I like the cut of his jib," her father said. The French doors to the balcony were open and he was sitting in a chair getting the fresh air, doing the *Times* crossword puzzle.

"Whose jib?" Mary Liz asked. "Is Bertie out there sailing?"

Her father looked at her as though she were a geek. "Schyler's."

"Oh," she said. He meant he liked the cut of Schyler's character, the way he carried himself.

"The only concern I have is his reluctance to discuss his job," he said, standing up and coming over to sit on her bedside. "And you haven't known him very long, Mary Liz, and he already says he wants to marry you."

"He's got good taste, what can I tell you?" she said.

He wasn't buying it. "I wish you would come home."

"We've discussed this, Dad. And the answer is no. Not yet. I've got police protection, I've got Sky and Wendy and Jake and Bertie, I'll be fine. Besides, I've got to sit down with Aunt Nancy and tell her about what I've found out."

Her father sighed, looking down to his lap. "I don't envy you, babe. And I really appreciate you doing it. Somehow, I think it will be easier for her to hear it from you."

There was a quiet knock on the door and then it opened. "Angel?" her mother said, popping her head in. "Claire's here—a friend of Nancy's? She's downstairs with Bill Pfeiffer. They wanted to come up and say hi. Is that all right? You're not too tired?"

"No, I'm fine, Mom. Send them up."

Her father stood up. "So you think Bill did a good job?"

"Very good job," she confirmed. "He's drawing up the final report on the holding companies."

The knock on the door came and Claire swept in with a big basket of flowers from her garden. "You don't look so bad to me," she said, kissing the top of Mary Liz's head.

"I'm a lot better," Mary Liz said.

"And you'll be your gorgeous self again soon," Bill said, coming over to stand next to the bed. "Thank God you're all right. I couldn't believe it when Claire told me what happened." Then he turned. "Hello there, old man," he hailed her father, and the two met in the middle of the room, shook hands heartily and moved out to the balcony to talk.

"You gave everybody quite a scare," Claire said quietly, easing down on the edge of the bed. All Claire knew, like everybody else (except Sky, Bertie, Wendy and Jake), was that she'd been the victim of an attempted sexual assault. "Have they caught him yet?"

"Not yet."

"Nancy's offering a fifty-thousand-dollar reward."

"Gosh, maybe I'll go find him." Mary Liz's smile still wasn't working very well. She looked over at the men outside. "So how is that going?"

Claire beamed and said, "Wonderfully. Absolutely wonderfully. He is an extraordinary man." She was blushing a little. Fifty-two and blushing. She was in it, all right, head over heels.

They didn't stay long, but shortly after Claire and Bill left, the FBI was announced, Agent Debbie and Agent Travers, and her father had to leave because they needed to have yet another one of their chats.

Ashley, the dog, watched their every move.

They were here today, Agent Debbie explained, to tell her they had gotten everything they needed to know from Mary Liz, and they probably wouldn't be talking to her again. At least not for some time, or until the case was concluded, whichever came first. But Mary Liz wasn't to worry; they would be providing protection for her as long as it took for them to catch Ivor Vrensk.

"Wait a minute," Mary Liz said, sitting up. "There's no way you're walking out of my life without telling me who was bugging my house."

The agent took a moment to think. "What I can tell you, Mary Liz, is that three different parties were listening in. One was Herbert Glidden."

"I knew it," she said. "What about Braxer & Braxer?"

Agent Debbie shook her head. "No."

"No?" Mary Liz would have frowned if she could. "Who were the other two?"

Agent Debbie glanced over at Agent Travers and then looked back at Mary Liz. "For the moment, it's best you don't know who the third party was. It's for your own protection. But I can tell you—and actually I came to tell you this—that the second party was us. The FBI."

"*What?*" Mary Liz yelled, losing her temper. "I asked you if you had before. Why didn't you tell me?"

Ashley jumped up, shaking her tags, looking back and forth between Mary Liz and the agents, as if waiting for the word to attack them.

"It was by court order, all clear and legal. There was strong evidence, Ms. Scott, that indicated you might be participating in federal crimes."

"Oh, really? And now you won't tell me who the third party was—presumably the people who *are* participating in federal crimes!"

"I'm sorry," the agent said lamely.

"You can tell me about the dead guy, Glidden, but you can't tell me about the alive guys—the ones who are trying to kill me?"

"I'm sorry," Agent Debbie said yet again.

That was it, positively *it*. "Get out of here!" Mary Liz shouted.

Ashley jumped up on the bed in front of Mary Liz and started barking at the FBI agents.

The agents looked at each other and started for the door. Agent Debbie turned around. "I'm very sorry. And we are extremely grateful to you—"

"Get out of here!" Mary Liz yelled again. Ashley was barking her head off, dancing around on the bed, threatening to charge them at any moment.

The door opened, and her father and Jake were standing there. Mary Liz flew out of bed and across the room. "Out! Out! All of you! Leave me alone!" And then she slammed the door and locked it. And then she went back to the bed, curled around a pillow and started to cry.

Participating in federal crimes.

Idiots.

The dog was still barking her head off.

No, Mary Liz thought, painkillers did not bring out the best in her.

29

Over the subsequent days, Mary Liz slowly healed. Her parents reluctantly returned to Winnetka. Aunt Nancy had to go to Los Angeles to meet with Julius and the lawyers, accountants and board of directors of Howland Films, but Mary Liz still had plenty of visitors while her godmother was away: Claire, Jeanine Hoffman, Vanessa Buckley and even Isabel Lemieux stopped by to loan her a machine that allowed her to play bridge by herself (although Mary Liz couldn't imagine why anyone would want to). Wendy, Bertie and Jake were in constant attendance (Bertie had her as a captive audience for windsurfing because she could watch him from the window), and Sky was there in his every free moment. Sasha came over daily with all kinds of dreadful-smelling lotions, health foods, crystals and other magical healing objects, and Mary Liz was very touched when one afternoon the diva asked her, almost shyly, if she would like it if she sang her a lullaby.

Rachelle Zaratan came out from Manhattan on Friday, and she and Sasha and Wendy and Mary Liz played Trivial Pursuit Saturday night into the wee hours of the morning, the three nonpatients getting tanked on the gallons of fruity sangria that Sasha had Riff drag over.

Sky was back living in the garage apartment at the Buckleys' and went to the country club mornings, but disappeared to some unknown place around noon, usually to reappear at Mary Liz's side sometime in the evening. She never asked what he had been doing; that was their deal.

Word was out around town, incidentally, Vanessa Buckley told Mary Liz: the investment banker and the teacher-golf ringer were in love.

The really big news that first week, however, was that the authorities had dropped their investigation of Bertie as a suspect in the murder of Herbert Glidden. Yes, the police had witnesses who confirmed that Bertie had stormed off the estate that fateful Saturday night, in search of Glidden; yes, they had witnesses who confirmed that Bertie had been raging he would fix Glidden for good; yes, Bertie had a motive to kill Glidden; yes, there had been witnesses who had seen Bertie at the marina after midnight, taking out the launch; and yes, Glidden had been found dead in the ocean the next morning. But, Wendy explained to Mary Liz, it was all circumstantial, there was no hard evidence; no one had found the object that had been used to strike Glidden over the head, nor had any drug paraphernalia been found.

"And what did they say Bertie's motive was?" Mary Liz asked her.

Wendy looked faintly stricken by this question.

"Oh," Mary Liz said, "so you did find out, didn't you? What Aunt Nancy told Bertie that night that made him so angry."

Wendy sighed, bit her lip and nodded.

"Look, Wendy, I know more horrible stuff about Alfred Hoffman than anyone could possibly believe. So if Bertie thinks I would be in any way surprised at anything concerning his father, or Glidden—"

"It's not about his father," Wendy said.

Mary Liz studied her face. "It's about Aunt Nancy then."

She nodded. "Bertie said Glidden had come over to emotionally torture his mother, to lord something over her and make her beg him to stay quiet."

"About?"

Wendy shook her head. "It has nothing to do with the estate, Mary Liz. It had nothing to do with Alfred, or with Glidden."

"But it has to do with me," Mary Liz said. "I overheard Bertie say so."

"Then you'll have to talk to Mrs. Hoffman about it."

They both knew Nancy was still in California.

"Mary Liz, I've got some errands to run," Wendy began, edging toward the door.

"Oh no you don't!" Mary Liz declared. In a moment, she was up and blocking the door. She was feeling much better at this point, but her face was still far from ready for public consumption. She grabbed Wendy by the arm and sat her down in a chair. "You're going to tell me."

"I can't!" Wendy wailed.

Mary Liz threw open the bedroom door and yelled, "Bertie!" down the hall of the Big House.

"What?" came his voice a few seconds later. "I'm eating a sandwich!"

"I need you!" she yelled.

Within a minute, Bertie and Jake were standing in the bedroom. Bertie was in trunks and flip-flops, Jake in jeans and a work shirt. "What's up?"

Mary Liz closed the door. "I'm not handing over the inventory of the estate until you tell me what your mother told you the night Glidden was murdered—what got you so upset that you went to find him."

Bertie's head swung in Wendy's direction. She held out her hands, as if to indicate she couldn't help it.

"I'm serious, Bertie," Mary Liz said. "Because I have a right to know—don't I? It has something to do with me, doesn't it? Something you've sworn Wendy to secrecy about."

Bertie looked at Wendy again, and then to Jake. Jake shrugged, looking helpless, as well. Bertie turned back to Mary Liz. His expression was very sad. "I don't want to hurt you," he said softly. "And there's no need for it. I swear."

"That's my decision, Bertie, and I've made it. Anything Glidden told your mother that is connected to me, I must know what it is."

Bertie looked as though someone was holding a knife to his throat. "But it would kill Mother if she knew you knew. She'll never be able to face you again. And it will break her heart if you hate her."

"Hate her?" For the life of her, Mary Liz could not imagine what this could be about.

He nodded. When Mary Liz looked at Wendy, she nodded. Even Jake looked morose at this point, evidently resigned with the others that Mary Liz was making a big mistake by pursuing this.

Bertie swallowed. "He threatened Mother he was going to tell you about something that happened a long, long time ago."

Mary Liz waited.

"That had to do with your parents."

Her heart started to pound.

"Mother would have done just about anything for him not to tell you." Bertie paused. "Mother is extremely fond of you. And you know how she feels about your mother, how long they've been friends."

Mary Liz took a sharp breath. "Tell me."

He didn't want to, but he said it. "Mother fell in love with your father."

Thud. Someone had just slugged Mary Liz in the stomach, or that was how it felt.

She blinked. "Are you trying to tell me they had an affair?"

"It was over twenty years ago, Mary Liz," he said hastily. "And your mother threw your father out."

Mary Liz knew exactly when it had been, too, during the time her father had been commuting to California to work on the Getty trust. And Mother must have thrown him out that summer, when Mary Liz was twelve. Her parents had explained to Mary Liz and the boys that he had to go away for a while, a long time, to do some special work. And then Mom had taken them up to the summerhouse in Canada for the whole summer. Dad had called, but had never come up. But then when they had returned to Winnetka, around Labor Day, Dad had been there. And had been there, with their mother, ever since.

"Mother was hysterical," Bertie said. "Most of all she didn't want you to think badly of your father. She blamed the whole thing on herself, that it had been a hard time in your parents' marriage—"

It had been. Her brother had been ill with spinal meningitis for almost the entire year before, and, ironically, when he started getting well again, her parents had started arguing a lot and then her father had taken on the Getty trust.

That night, when Sky took her for a walk along the beach with Ashley, Mary Liz told him the whole story. And she cried a little, and talked out loud, trying to rationalize her feelings, trying to make sense of it. It was going to take her a while to fully process this news.

Yes, Sky agreed.

And she wasn't sure if she would ever acknowledge to her parents that she knew about it. That Dad had had an affair with Mother's best friend!

It was twenty years ago, he reminded her. And her parents had a wonderful marriage now, didn't they?

That wasn't the point. The point was, they had always pretended to be model parents.

Then, Sky asked, *weren't* they model parents? So good at parenting they protected their children from what had happened? And had worked it out between themselves and had gone on together, as a couple, as two parents whose commitment to each other and their children and their family was the most important thing in the world to them? Giving no cause for the children to worry?

It was beginning to dawn on Mary Liz the level of admiration she owed her mother.

Yes, Sky said.

She and Sky walked and walked. And she talked, and then she cried a little again, too.

The next day, Mary Liz moved back down to the cottage from the Big House, and Sky moved in with her. And since Nancy was still away, so did the dog.

Facing what she must before her godmother returned, Mary Liz worked on her presentation of Alfred's hidden "assets." Sky had settled in unobtrusively, and as she learned how, the first few nights, to sleep with him, Mary Liz felt a sense of quiet elation that was new to her. To truly sleep with him. Who preferred which side; how long he could hold her before she had to turn over; who liked how many covers and on and on. They did not make love. She was healing, he said. There was plenty of time ahead, there needn't be any rush.

This guy had to be from Mars.

It was too good to be true, she thought. But then, she wasn't the only one who felt as if she had been blessed with a miracle this summer. Claire and Bill Pfeiffer were getting serious and Claire had said something one day that let Mary Liz know they were sleeping together. They *were* making love, Mary Liz was sure. You could tell just by looking at Claire.

Jeanine Hoffman came over to the estate every day to play tennis and always dropped by to say hello. While Jeanine might really be concerned for her recovery, Mary Liz was quite positive that Jeanine was checking to make sure Mary Liz hadn't heard about anything going on out at Howland Films. When were Julius and Nancy coming back? she kept asking. I don't know, Mary Liz kept saying.

Julius hadn't been in East Hampton since the night of the Alfred Hoffman Memorial Dinner Dance. For that matter, Charles Kahn, Rachelle's husband, hadn't been, either. He was on some kind of cross-country spot check on the store placement of her clothing line. Nor was Claude Lemieux around. He was in France by himself, visiting his mother, whom Isabel detested. Randolph Vandergilden was in the Napa Valley for some kind of vine auction and had delayed his return. Mary Liz had no idea where Henry MacClendon was, but she had heard no mention of him being around, either.

Buck Buckley was the only one of Alfred's poker group who had stayed in East Hampton since Glidden's murder. Interesting.

"Do you suppose Nancy knows about Bertie?" Sky asked Mary Liz. After repeated reassurances, Sky had finally convinced her she could go out in public and not scare people, and he had taken her to East Hampton Point as a trial run. The freedom was delicious and so was the food. She had only been off the estate to see the doctor in Southampton.

"I don't even know if *I* know about Bertie," Mary Liz declared. "Everybody just carries on and pretends they don't see anything. Even Wendy hasn't said anything to me about him and Jake, and I haven't had the nerve to ask."

"I like Jake. He's a good man."

Mary Liz put her knife and fork down on the edge of her plate. "Surely Aunt Nancy can't still think Wendy is Bertie's girlfriend."

"She sees what she wants to see," Sky said, biting into his steak.

"I'm going to talk to him about it," she decided. "He's got to tell his mother. This is ridiculous. The only chance this family has is to get rid of all these secrets."

Sky raised an eyebrow. "Secrets?"

She couldn't and wouldn't air the family laundry, not even to Sky. Of course, given the wiretapping, the FBI could have already told him about the possibility of Hoffman having a son in France—they would have heard her and Bill discussing it—but she'd be damned if she'd acknowledge that, or the pornography studio, to anyone but Aunt Nancy. *She* would have to make the really hard decisions.

"Well," Mary Liz said, "a secret like that. He's thirty years old, for crying out loud."

"And what's with the daughter?" Sky asked her.

"Denver? She's shooting that TV series out in L.A."

"But she's never here."

Mary Liz shrugged. "She's working."

"Claire says she hasn't been here for three years."

"Really?"

"Yeah. I saw Claire at the club today. She and Bill played nine holes. He's on vacation this week."

"I wonder if they'll get married," Mary Liz said.

Sky looked at her.

"What?"

"Claire and Bill?" he said, as if this was a very strange idea.

"Yes. What's wrong with that? I don't mean get married any time soon, I meant down the road."

"Oh," Sky said, putting down his knife and fork.

"Oh, no," she said. "Don't tell me you're one of those guys who sees something wrong with the man being younger."

"Heck, no," Sky assured her, looking down at his plate. It wasn't until nearly a minute later, though, Mary Liz noticed, that he picked up his fork to resume eating.

30

On Saturday morning, Mary Liz was excited. Even she could see that she no longer looked like a freak, and today she was going out on the town with Sky and the gang. The "white" of her right eye had completely drained and was truly white again; the area around her eyes was no longer swollen; and all that horrible black to purple to blue to green to yellow in her face had faded. All that she had left was a knot about the size of a quarter over her eyebrow, and a bump and slight horizontal swelling on the bridge of her nose. She was very pale, though, because the plastic surgeon insisted she wear a large hat to shield the sun from her nose until the break had fully healed.

In the meantime, Sky had gone off to the club this morning and she had printed out the hard copy of the official Hoffman-estate inventory to review. And even if she did have to say it herself, the report was terrific. It was clear, it was concise and it was graphically pleasing. Each detailed entry had dates, addresses, phone numbers, account numbers, plus final dollar amounts that Mary Liz knew were accurate. Officially speaking, after all "known" assets and debits were listed, the estate of Alfred Hoffman was worth $191,650,000 before taxes.

In Mary Liz's unofficial addendum, which she had not attached to this report, the estate had an additional seventeen million dollars coming from his secret half-ownership in the Dutch pornography studio; and a one-million, four-hundred-thousand-dollar stash in Europe, from which Cinema Seis checks were issued to the widow of the French film worker, to Alfred's unclaimed son, and that son's mother.

The way his will read, roughly sixty-five percent of Alfred's liquid and semiliquid assets were given to his wife, Nancy (a little over $124,500,000 from the "clean" estate alone); fifteen percent to Julius (over $28,700,000); five percent, each, in trusts for Julius's two young children (over $9,500,000); and five percent outright to both son, Bertram, and daughter, Denver (over $9,500,000 each), who, upon their mother's death, would receive another ten percent (another

$12,500,000 plus). And so, of that sixty-five percent of the liquid and semiliquid assets in the estate he had left in Nancy's care, she was largely free to do what she wished with over eighty-six million dollars after taxes. And what Aunt Nancy planned to do, Mary Liz knew, was to funnel forty million dollars into the Alfred Hoffman Memorial Foundation.

In East Hampton circles, this was not the biggest fortune around, not by a long shot. There were more than a few takeover artists and Wall Street wizards around town who could manage a fifty- to hundred-million-dollar donation to secure a high social position on an institutional board in the city, like, for example, the Metropolitan Museum of Art.

Under the right management, however, a forty-million-dollar endowment could have a life in perpetuity. And if Nancy's own investments did well, no doubt she would settle more on the foundation upon her death. The point was, Nancy Hoffman was determined to use her husband's talent, hard work and good fortune to bring better fortune to those in need. It might be in the form of a living stipend for a research scientist working on a cure for lupus or cystic fibrosis; it might be a lump-sum donation to a community job-placement center; it might be allocations for child-care programs; it might be summer camp for an inner-city child; whatever, Nancy Hoffman was determined that her husband's death would make an ongoing contribution to *life.*

Well, this was all well and fine—unless, that is, the Hoffmans chose to acknowledge ownership of the pornography studio in Amsterdam. The scandal would be too much for the media to pass up. And the Hoffmans' lawyers, Mary Liz knew, would want to do this, acknowledge the pornography house so that they could prove Braxer & Braxer had sought to steal it, which would then hasten a dismissal of the firm's claims against the estate. Besides, the pornography studio would add an extra seventeen million dollars to the estate, translating into over $7,500,000 more for Nancy; over $2,500,000 for Julius; $850,000 extra for each of his kids; $850,000 each up front for Bertie and Denver, with the promise of another $1,700,000 down the road.

Nancy would have a tough time going up against Julius and the children, Mary Liz imagined. That is, of course, providing she chose to tell them about the pornography studio in the first place.

And then there was the issue of Marc Bresseau, who, Mary Liz was sure, would prove to be Alfred's biological son. If the Hoffmans acknowledged his existence—and came forward in goodwill to tell the child who his real father was—it meant risking being forced, in court, to reallocate the other children's inheritances. Alfred had quite pointedly intended his children to each get fifteen percent of his money—Julius, Denver and Bertie each ultimately receiving $28,700,000 plus—but the courts might well decide it should be shared four ways, including the other son, thus reducing each American child's inheritance to $21,500,000 plus, and making little Marc an overnight multimillionaire. There was also the risk of the four flesh-and-blood children banding together to contest the percentage left to Nancy.

On the other hand, the Hoffmans could first "buy" the son's rights to the estate—that is, offer him big money to sign those rights away before telling him what they were, what his true status was in the world. They could just use a million of the overseas fund to do it with.

Or, the Hoffmans might choose to leave things exactly as they were.

Mary Liz longed to get her talk with Aunt Nancy over with. Let *her* think it over, let her consult whoever she needed to consult, let her decide which version of a written report she wanted, and to whom she wished to show it.

Someone knocked on the front door of the cottage and Ashley started barking, charging out of the office and down the hall. Hushing her, Mary Liz made her way to the front door.

"Do you have a minute?"

It was Wendy, looking uncharacteristically disheveled and upset.

"Of course. Come in. I was just going to make some coffee."

"No, no thanks," Wendy said unsteadily, making her way in. She sat down in one of the wingback chairs and Mary Liz continued to the kitchen to make the coffee. Wendy didn't say anything for a while, so Mary Liz just chatted inanely about the weather—would it remain sunny for the polo match today, or would it be cloudy, or hot and humid....

"I need to talk to somebody," Wendy finally said.

She looked so miserable, Mary Liz had to stop what she was doing and come back in and sit down.

"There's something I need to tell you," Wendy said. She gave an ironic laugh. "Otherwise, how will you know why I'm upset?"

When another minute had passed and Wendy had yet to say anything, but sat there wiping her eyes with a tissue, Mary Liz said, "If it's about the relationship you've been having, Wendy, it's okay. I know about it."

The tissue stopped in midair.

"And that whatever your preference is—" Mary Liz shrugged "—that's no big deal."

Wendy's hand dropped into her lap. "How?"

"How did I know?"

Wendy nodded.

"I accidentally saw you. Together. You and Vanessa."

She thought Wendy was going to die of embarrassment. The formerly cool, calm and collected young woman was hiding her face in her hands. But then Mary Liz had made it sound a lot less embarrassing than it had been (Golly! What had been left to the imagination? First on the beach and then in the kitchen!), and kept telling her that it didn't matter to her at all—that she had gay friends, for heaven's sake.

Wendy finally came around. "Well, none of it matters anymore anyway, because she announced this morning she's in love with some advertising guy. She doesn't love Buck and she doesn't love me."

"Did she stay over last night?"

"Yes."

Mary Liz frowned. "You mean, Vanessa came over and slept with you last night and then told you this morning she's in love with someone else?"

Wendy nodded.

"Well, that was smart, wasn't it? Get the sex first and then tell you," Mary Liz muttered, getting up. "I guess she hadn't taken her morning handful of pills yet." Her mean-spirited sarcasm sounded horrible even to her, but she didn't care. Vanessa Buckley had hurt her friend. "On the other hand, maybe before she took those pills she had one lucid moment where she could see what a horrible thing she was doing to you."

Wendy looked at first shocked and then crushed.

Mary Liz softened up immediately.

"And that's probably it," Mary Liz added gently, coming over to kneel by Wendy's chair. "That she realized if she truly cared for you, she had to let you go. That she had no right to play on your feelings, to pull you down to her level. Surely you don't think you were the first, Wendy?"

Tears started to fall from Wendy's eyes and she did not even bother to wipe them away. "The first woman."

"I know you care about her," Mary Liz said (although she wondered how anyone could truly care about someone as utterly at sea as Vanessa Buckley, no matter how rich or attractive she might be), "but, Wendy, you know, I hope, that it isn't true that she's in love with someone else, because right now Vanessa's incapable of *any* reliable feeling."

"She's a pill addict, I know, but I can't help it!" Wendy suddenly burst out, burying her face in her hands again.

Who would have thought it? A smart, attractive, eminently capable woman like Wendy chasing after a drug-addicted four-times-married woman who had no history of being gay.

Mary Liz had always hoped that gay women were smarter than heterosexual women, because Mary Liz felt that their lives were going to be harder anyway, and what woman needed any more grief? But straight, gay, indifferent, so many women, it seemed, got hooked, in their romantic lives, on trouble. When she herself had realized that Ken was not the man she thought he was, and was, in fact, maybe even a glorified sexual con man, it still had taken her months to face up to it. That it was quite possible that Ken had been *incapable* of caring for her beyond a certain level. Even then, losing him had felt like death, particularly since she had left Jim—and ultimately lost Jim for what turned out to be a mere fling for Ken.

Now, of course, she knew it had been the best thing that had ever happened to her.

And too, of course, right now she felt the best thing that had ever happened to her was finding Sky. (They had sort of slipped and made love for hours last night.) But although she thought she might be really and truly falling in love with Sky, only time would tell. The sexual attraction, the intellectual attraction, the longing to touch him, to have him look adoringly at her—all of that was superficial, she knew, all part of that dizzying passion of the first six months of any love affair.

And it was a different kind of love affair she felt ready for, an affair of love with one man that would last for years and years, that would ebb and flow, flame up and die down, flame up and die down, over and over.

And her every instinct told her Sky wanted that, too. With her.

There was something to be said for life experience.

She looked at Wendy, sitting there in the chair, sobbing into her hands because a drug-addicted, straight woman she had been sleeping with for six weeks had dumped her.

The woman needed a wake-up call. Wendy was so very lucky to be out of it!

Mary Liz excused herself, promising to return in a minute or two, and went back into her office.

Okay. No bugs in here anymore.

She looked up a number on her Rolodex and dialed. "Lucy? Hi, it's Mary Liz... Yep. In East Hampton. I know, I'm sorry, but it's been really crazy—but I'm calling now!" A laugh. "Look, I know it's last-minute, but I've got the most incredibly smart and attractive woman here who's in desperate need of meeting at least one great gal... You *are?*... Well, I'm sorry for her, but I'm not for Wendy's sake. That's my friend—Wendy. No, listen, Lucy, I don't mean just attractive, I'm talking early thirties, bright, talented, drop-dead debutante beautiful... What do you mean, can she pay her light bill? Yes, of course she can pay her light bill! She's a private detective... No, a real one. Very exclusive, actually, usually works for high society... Yes. She went to Brown... What do you mean, 'What's the matter with her then if she's single?' *I'm single!*" A sigh. "Boy, are you hard to please...."

Ten minutes later, Mary Liz emerged from the back hall with a piece of paper in hand. "You and I, my friend," she announced, "are going into the city tonight."

"Thanks, but no thanks, Mary Liz," Wendy said. "I just want to crawl into bed and stay there for the rest of my life."

"Well," Mary Liz said, throwing herself down on the couch, one hand behind her head, "you can't. We have a dinner date."

Shortly after Wendy departed, Bertie appeared at Mary Liz's front door. "Wendy told me you know about her."

"Come in," Mary Liz offered.

"No—this will only take a minute." He smiled. "I guess I just wanted to know if you knew about me, too."

"Why don't you tell me, Bertie," she suggested. "After all, we're friends, aren't we?"

"I hope so," he said. "Well, I'm gay, Mary Liz. But please don't tell Mother. It will upset her dreadfully."

"You don't think she suspects?"

"Well—" he faltered. "Why would she?"

"Because she's your mother."

"Ah. I see."

"Consider telling her, Bertie. Please. Just consider it."

He looked at her for a full moment. "You think," he finally said, "I haven't been for the past fifteen years?"

At noon Mary Liz was dressed in what she hoped Sky would enjoy looking at as much as she enjoyed wearing it: a simple, sleeveless white cotton dress with a blue sash around the waist, tied in the back with a bow, white sandals and a large white straw hat with another blue ribbon around that. The year before, she had gone to the August races in Saratoga Springs with her mother, and Mom had bought Mary Liz the outfit as her concept of proper summer horsey attire. Mary Liz loved the feel of it, and felt extremely feminine and pretty in the outfit, but she also worried it might be a little bit too Southern-belle for a woman from Chicago.

She heard Sky's step on the porch and went to the door. He covered his mouth with one hand for a moment, blinking. "Wow," he finally said. He met her eyes. "You look so utterly beautiful, darling." He smiled. "We'll have to go to the derby. Clearly you're made for this, my love."

"I'm not sure it's right for polo," she said, a little embarrassed, kissing him on the cheek.

He took her in his arms and kissed her properly, a long, searching kiss, and her body responded, big-time, a shot of desire running straight down to—well, there.

He came up for air. "We've got to go. We promised Bertie."

"And if we didn't go," Mary Liz said, "what would we do?"

He smiled. "You're a bad girl, Mary Elizabeth Scott."

She put her arms around his neck. "Just so you get it—I want to be positively *evil* right now." And then *she* kissed him this time.

The horn of the Range Rover was blowing outside. That would be Bertie and the others.

They smiled at each other a little sheepishly, smoothing their clothes. Then he offered her his arm and they went outside.

Since Aunt Nancy was still in Los Angeles, Bertie had the windfall of a box for eight at the Hamptons Cup polo tournament at Two Trees Stable in Water Mill. As her first big venture into public, Mary

Liz was ecstatic. She had been to a few polo matches before because Ken actually played, and she thought it was one of the most exciting sports she had ever seen.

The box was at the top of the temporary stands, practical from the viewpoint of watching the match, as well as safer since they only had to watch other spectators get clobbered by the ball. They climbed the stairs to the top and found Claire, Bill and Jeanine Hoffman already there.

Mary Liz sat down next to Bill. "I finished the inventory this morning," she said. "Dotted every 'i' and crossed every 't.'"

"But you didn't include the other, right?"

"No. I'll wait until the decisions are made."

He nodded. "I think that's wise. When's she coming back?"

"Tonight, I think. I hope."

"Me, too," he said. "I'd like to put my stamp on things and turn it over to your father as soon as possible."

"Hey," Sky said, leaning forward past Mary Liz to look at Bill, "that was a pretty handy-dandy little game of golf you played the other day. I told Buck he should encourage you to play there."

"On scholarship, I hope." Bill laughed. "I don't have a million dollars."

"I don't, either, Bill. I told you," Claire said, "Buck just signs me in as his guest once in a while. And Sky's right. When he goes back to Virginia, Buck's going to need another ringer."

The first match was about to begin and they all settled back in their seats. Sky took Mary Liz's hand firmly in his own and rested them together on his knee.

The opening celebrity match was kind of stupid, Mary Liz thought. Besides mugging for the cameras, the actors and local millionaires didn't seem overly coordinated. They had learned the game, yes, and they had practiced, yes, and they had fine muscles and the finest ponies and equipment, but they lacked the grace and finesse that Mary Liz had come to love in the sport. Her interest drifted and she checked out the stands. With her big floppy hat and sunglasses, she felt comfortable staring at whoever she wished without being detected—Christie Brinkley was over there, looking great—and she wondered if all the other women in big hats and sunglasses were doing the same as she was, spying on others.

She saw that Henry MacClendon and his young wife, Cindy, were sitting in a box to their left. She looked thin already and Mary

Liz wondered how she was doing it, if she was starving herself and exercising, or had she had herself wrapped or what. At any rate, she looked good. But Henry sure looked old sitting beside her in the sunlight. Mary Liz thought of the night he had come over to Claire's and she almost felt sorry for him. His life had to be a lot different now. No fawning over him anymore.

Claire, on the other hand, was looking radiantly accustomed to romance. And Bill was looking pretty good himself. Like a rooster.

She looked around for Sasha and Rachelle. She thought they would have been there. Sasha had said something about it the other day. She did see Riff down in the crowd by the fence, and he spotted her and they exchanged waves. For a moment she wondered if Sasha's bodyguard was on loan—for her.

The first real polo match began and Mary Liz was quickly enthralled, not caring about anything except how very, very happy she was. Happy to be alive, happy to be holding hands with Sky, happy to be with friends, happy that her whole life lay ahead of her.

31

It had gotten very hot and humid at the polo matches that afternoon and Mary Liz was forced to start all over again this evening to get ready for her trip into New York: shower, wash hair, apply new makeup, adorn new getup.

"It'll be fine, Sky," Mary Liz insisted, giving a last brush of her hair. "Bertie's driving us in, we'll have dinner with Lucy, have a few drinks and come home. I told you—" she turned around "—you're welcome to come. Though I'm not sure it's quite your thing."

Sky's reaction to her announcement of her little adventure tonight was priceless. "Oh," he had said when she explained she was taking Wendy to a women's bar in the city to introduce her to an old friend of hers. Another single gay woman. And then a second later, he said, "*Oh.*" A second later, "Wendy?" When Mary Liz had nodded, yes, he'd shrugged and said, "Oh," again.

"Jake would come with us," Mary Liz continued, "but somebody's got to pick up Aunt Nancy at the airport."

"Bertie's not—I mean, he can't go into that bar with you, can he?"

"He can if he wants to," she said, sliding her arms around his neck. "It's a free country. But he'll be next door in the *men's* bar." She kissed him. "Seriously, if I felt nervous at all about going, I'd be the first to tell you. So go and play poker at the club with the guys, guy."

"You better tell that agent you're going."

"The agent" was any of the three FBI agents who were keeping round-the-clock surveillance on the estate.

"I think Bertie told him, but I'll make sure." Mary Liz had a sudden chill. It had never occurred to her to worry about being a target in the city. How would anyone know she was there? Still, Sky was right. Better to play it safe.

Wendy was standing outside on the porch of the guest house at six sharp. She was in jeans, beige clogs, a white halter top, carrying a beige linen blazer over her arm. She looked like a goddess, frankly, with her tan, hair streaked by the sun, blue eyes and those long, sleek arms and legs. Her friend Lucy was in for quite a jolt. Standing next to Wendy, Mary Liz felt shorter, heavier and positively matronly in her khakis, blouse and Topsiders.

They climbed into the Range Rover, Wendy up front with Bertie, and they were off. A few minutes later, Bertie turned off Route 27 onto Airport Road and Mary Liz figured it was a shortcut of some kind. It wasn't. It was simply the way to the airport.

"Bertie, you didn't," Wendy said as they approached it. "It's such a waste of money."

"But Mary Liz has never gone," he said. "Everyone should do it at least once."

"We're not flying are we?" Mary Liz asked.

"I hope you're not scared of heights," Wendy said as Bertie turned into the parking lot, "because that—" she pointed "—is what we're going in."

Oh, my, Mary Liz thought. A four-person, glass-bubbled helicopter. No, she wasn't scared of heights, but she was scared of dying and if anything went wrong with a helicopter, they just dropped out of the sky, didn't they? And they all died.

"You'll love it, Mary Liz, I guarantee it," Bertie promised happily, hopping out of the car. "You're going to see the coastline of Long Island by sunset."

"Does that mean if the motor stops, we drop into the water?" Mary Liz asked nervously, fumbling to get out of the car.

"Well, yes, actually," Bertie said. "Which is why it's much safer, so don't worry."

"'Don't worry,' he says," she said out of the side of her mouth.

"It actually is quite wonderful, Mary Liz," Wendy said to her. "After the first ten minutes or so, I think you'll enjoy it. It is beautiful and it feels safe, and there's no wind tonight, and we'll be on the east side of Manhattan within an hour."

"How are we coming home?" Mary Liz asked as they walked toward the terminal. "Or should I buy a parachute while we're there?"

"I've got a car picking us up," Bertie said. "There won't be any traffic tonight."

"Wait a minute," Mary Liz said. "What about my FBI guy?"

"It's all arranged," Bertie said. "They'll be posted outside the restaurant to keep an eye on things."

Bertie went in to sign some papers and then waved the women to follow him over the tarmac to the helicopter pad. There was a figure coming from the other way, holding a garment bag over one shoulder with one hand and pulling a suitcase on rollers with the other. Bertie was waving. "Hey, Charles! Did you just fly in?"

It was Charles Kahn. "Finally get to go home!" he declared. "Been on the road for weeks on a spot-check tour for Rachelle." The men stopped to talk and the women drew up behind Bertie. When Charles saw it was Mary Liz, his expression immediately turned to one of sympathy. "I was so sorry to hear about what happened. You look good, though. Rachelle told me it was pretty bad, but that you were really quite the trouper."

"Thank you," she said. She hated being reminded of it.

"Did they catch the guy?"

"Not yet."

"Well, I don't know what I could do, but if there is anything, please let me know."

"Thanks."

He was nodding, sympathetic still, and turned to Wendy. "So what are you guys up to?"

"We're flying to Manhattan for dinner," she said.

"In the copter?" Charles asked Bertie, turning around to look at it.

"Yeah."

"Where to? East River? By the Water Club?"

"Yeah."

Charles looked at his watch. "You'll be there in no time." He looked at the women. "First time?"

"I've been," Wendy said.

"It's my first time," Mary Liz said, "and I'm not sure, but I think I'm scared to death."

"Oh, you'll love it," Charles assured her. "Rachelle didn't even want to look at my plane after riding in one of those. Oh, hey," he said, glancing at his watch again, "I've got to hustle. Rachelle has something on tonight."

"The Cajun supper at the beach," Bertie said. "It's a good party."

"Oh, right," Charles said, nodding to the ladies and picking up the suitcase strap again. "You guys have fun. You'll like landing. You'll feel like Trump."

The helicopter engine was fired up and the gigantic blades began to whirl and Mary Liz thought she might faint before getting near it. She dutifully followed Wendy, however, into the back seat. Bertie sat in front of her and closed his door. Immediately it was a lot quieter. "Larry, I want you to meet my friend Mary Liz Scott. Mary Liz, Larry Johnson. Great pilot. Larry, this is Mary Liz's first time going up."

"You're in for a treat," Larry promised her. "It's perfect flying weather tonight. Did you bring a camera?"

"No."

"Here you go." He handed her a disposable camera, with a zoom, that had a roll of film with thirty-six exposures. "For first-timers, you relax a lot sooner if you concentrate on taking some pictures. So if you get nervous, look through that viewfinder."

"Can I take a picture of you now?" Mary Liz sort of half joked. She was terrified.

Wendy strapped her into the safety harness.

"A life jacket is under your seat," Larry said. "And an air-sickness bag behind my seat."

She wondered how many people had been forced to use either one. Then she wondered why there weren't any smelling salts back here.

"Sit back, relax," Larry called, handling the controls, "and take some pictures. Next stop, Manhattan."

Within moments they were rising from the ground with a kind of ease and grace Mary Liz had never imagined. It was like magic, like being Peter Pan, some invisible string pulling them straight up from the earth. It wasn't dizzying at all. In fact, it felt rather exhilarating. She could see the airport grow smaller and then they were gone, sweeping over Route 27, over trees and fields and houses and then, suddenly, they were over the Atlantic Ocean and she was looking at the coastline of Long Island.

It was one of the most beautiful sights she had seen in her life.

To heck with the camera. Nothing could capture what her eyes were taking in.

The sun was setting behind Manhattan as they came around to the East River. The sun was orangy red, and the sky above and beyond was pink and red and violet for miles. The city's buildings, straight and tall, were almost in silhouette, and Mary Liz, for the fifteenth time, wished Sky was here to see it, too.

Sky. Good name. The feelings were not terribly dissimilar, looking at Sky and looking at this sky, her heart and spirit lightened with a combination of wonderment and joy.

The ride ended far too soon, although when Mary Liz tried to climb out onto the helipad, she found her legs buckling and she nearly fell. Bertie caught her arm and steadied her. Then he gave her a big hug and said she was a totally great gal, did she know that?

Mary Liz thanked Larry profusely and thought maybe if she were the pilot she would feel a little less tense. Like driving a car. (Was there anything worse than being a passenger with a bad driver? Yes. Being a passenger with a bad pilot.)

The helipad was right next to the Water Club, the famous restaurant built on a barge, and they had no problem getting a cab since many were stopping to drop people off for dinner. The cab ride was short, north on the FDR, exit and west on Forty-ninth Street.

"I bet that's the FBI tail," Bertie said, turning around. "That Crown Victoria's been with us since the helipad."

"You really are quite the celebrity these days," Wendy joked.

"Thanks, but no thanks." Mary Liz turned around, trying to see the car Bertie was talking about.

"It's back a couple of cars now," he said.

They headed north on Third Avenue, and east on Fifty-eighth Street for all of fifty feet, where they got out. "We're early," Wendy said, "so we might as well go into Julie's for a drink."

"So you know this place?" Mary Liz asked her on the sidewalk as Bertie paid the driver.

Wendy smiled. "Yes. Of course I do. It's rather famous, actually, for attracting the best-looking women from around the world."

"Such modesty," Bertie observed.

"And where is the Town House Restaurant?" Mary Liz asked.

"Just down the street," Bertie said. "And down a little farther is the Town House Bar—for men—where I'm going after dinner, when you guys come back here."

"Come on," Wendy said, waving Mary Liz on. "It's early yet, it'll be quiet."

Following Wendy, Mary Liz looked over her shoulder. "Are you coming?"

"Sure," Bertie said.

The entrance to the bar was discreet. It was a wood-paneled entranceway, with a door on the side. On the front there was a small window, shade drawn behind it, that said in an elegant script, Julie's. Wendy led the way. As she opened the outer door, Mary Liz immediately felt cool air, smelled cigarette smoke and heard music. She saw a coatroom. They turned the corner and Mary Liz marveled. It was not a large place, but ahead of them was a beautiful mahogany bar, U-shaped, with comfortably cushioned stools, and beyond that, a kind of large living room with low tables and covered armchairs, and banquettes built into the walls. There was thick wall-to-wall carpeting on the floor and the walls were covered in what looked to Mary Liz to be an expensive French paper. At the end of the room was a piano. In the corner, a CD jukebox. Hanging from the walls were portraits of famous women who were presumably...

Egad, Mary Liz thought. *Am I ever out of this loop.*

Every woman sitting at the bar, it seemed, turned to look at them as they entered. Mary Liz smiled tentatively and every woman smiled back. She wondered if this meant they thought she was attracted to them, and then thought she was being stupid.

"Let's get a table in the back," Wendy said, moving them along.

The female bartender, extremely attractive, smiled and said hello.

As they walked past the bar, behind them, Mary Liz saw that built into the wall, was a high-definition color TV. The sound was off, but closed captions running along the bottom of the screen were narrating the Yankee game in progress.

Neat.

It was dark and lovely and cool and calm, and the smoke wasn't too bad. (As an ex-smoker, Mary Liz was perhaps hypersensitive to it.) She liked the place very much. At the moment, it seemed just like a neighborhood place—strike that, more like a friend's lovely large living room—where one could just stop in for a drink when she felt the need for companionship. Mary Liz certainly didn't feel as though she was in danger of being hit on.

Twice in her life she had been openly propositioned by women. The first time had been by her roommate when she was a freshman in college, who, getting loaded before the Christmas break, confessed to Mary Liz she was in love with her. It had been tricky; while Mary Liz genuinely loved the girl as her friend—and they were best friends—she didn't have sexual feelings toward her. In the end, the next semester, they changed roommates, and when the girl had gotten involved with someone else, who was gay, they had resumed their close friendship.

That girl had been Lucy, the woman they were meeting tonight.

The second time had been shortly after Mary Liz's thirtieth birthday. She had been working on a bond issue for a small chain of TV stations out West. The woman who had been assigned to take her on a tour of the stations, a week-long endeavor, had been very helpful. The last night, however, when she asked Mary Liz to have dinner with her, Mary Liz thought her radar had detected something. The woman was about forty, sweet-looking, a little overweight, with short hair and a crisply tailored skirt and jacket. Mary Liz had assumed she was gay; it wasn't anything specific, it was just the woman's way in general.

At any rate, Mary Liz expected the same behavior from the women she did business with as from the men: do business, become friendly, maybe, but never cross the line by making a sexual or romantic overture. What happened that night at dinner was not sexual or even romantic, not by a long shot, but it was very upsetting since the woman arrived at dinner drunk, had more drinks at the table and then started crying and carrying on that of course Mary Liz didn't find her attractive because she was pathetic and no good and on and on. It got so bad that Mary Liz finally had to get her out of the restaurant and take her home in a cab—a ride in which Mary Liz was trapped in the back seat for a half hour, alternately listening to this woman sob and pushing her off as she lunged to try to kiss her.

It was horrible.

The next day, the woman left an apology on Mary Liz's voice mail in Chicago. Mary Liz just wanted to forget the whole thing and never see her again, but another part of her said no, she couldn't let it go without saying something. And so she did.

"Thank you for your apology," she'd told the woman over the phone. "And you needn't worry, it will go no further. In fact, the whole incident is forgotten."

"Thank you," the woman practically whispered.

"Except for one thing," Mary Liz added. "You've got a drinking problem."

Silence.

"So don't confuse the issues. There's nothing wrong with being who you are, or having the orientation you do, but don't kid yourself—there is something *very* wrong with your drinking and you need help."

"Fuck you," the formerly meek and apologetic woman had said, hanging up on her.

A young and very attractive blond waitress came over to take their drink order. Amstel Lite for Wendy, a draft for Bertie, a glass of Chardonnay for Mary Liz. When the waitress came back with their drinks, Mary Liz paid for the round.

"So, what do you think?" Wendy asked.

"I think it's wonderful," Mary Liz said.

The women there were all ages, all sizes and shapes. There was a group of three elegantly dressed black women at a table in the corner; there were two women, obviously in love, tucked away in another, holding hands; there was a very large white woman at the bar who looked, well, pretty masculine; the woman sitting next to her was about forty and extremely feminine, with a long blond ponytail and tasteful jewelry; other women at the bar were attractive, all ages, all kinds of dress. Some in denim. Some in silk. Some in cotton. Just women. Cool.

"It's quiet because so many go to the country on the weekends in the summer," Wendy explained. "The patrons tend to do very well, and a lot of them work here, in midtown. The other bars are all down in the village."

That's where Mary Liz always thought gay bars were, Greenwich Village, not here in midtown Manhattan, not right around the corner from Bloomingdale's.

As soon as Wendy got up to use one of the bathrooms, Bertie said, "Thank God you got her out of the house. That damn Vanessa will be back tonight, you know. She'll get high as a kite and come sneaking back."

"I was wondering what you thought about it," Mary Liz said.

"Are you kidding? Mary Liz, I warned her and warned her as soon as I saw Vanessa lay her eyes on her. I swear I could see the wheels turning in Vanessa's little brain, '*Ah-ha!* A novelty! What fun!' And then after it started— I've been begging Wendy to break it off before Vanessa hurt her, which I knew she would. It was only a matter of time."

Before Mary Liz could steer the conversation back around to Bertie's situation, how much did he think his mother knew of *his* romantic life, Wendy came back and announced it was time to move next door.

As soon as Lucy bounded into the Town House Restaurant, Mary Liz knew this had been a good idea. She and Wendy and Bertie stood up at their table, and her former roommate gave her a tremendous hug, shook hands with Bertie and then positively beamed at Wendy, holding her hand out to her. Wendy smiled and shook it.

Bertie snuck a wink at Mary Liz.

The Town House Restaurant was owned and operated by gay men, although there were at least three tables of women eating there, too. It had a very sophisticated and gracious feel, with a decor not far from that of a Victorian gentleman's club.

Lucy sat between Wendy and Bertie, and across from Mary Liz. What Mary Liz had feared might be a slightly awkward dinner turned out to be two straight hours of talking and laughing and eating as the three from Long Island tried to explain to Lucy what they had been doing all summer without telling her too much about anything.

"Let me get this straight," Lucy said to Wendy. "You're a private investigator, hired by Bertie, but now you're a family friend."

"Well, sort of."

"And Bertie, you...?"

"I am no longer a suspected murderer."

"I see. And Mary Liz? Bertie's mother is your godmother, and since you just quit your job— And by the way, why didn't I hear about that? Why didn't you write me?"

Mary Liz sighed. "I just wanted the whole thing to go away."

"You and I have a lot of catching up to do," Lucy said, "but tonight I get to talk to your friend," and returned her attention to Wendy.

After dinner, Bertie went to the Town House Bar, agreeing to meet Mary Liz and Wendy in front of Julie's at one o'clock. The car would be there to pick them up. "And I *know* the driver, Mary Liz, so don't get in, ladies, until I get there."

The women went next door to Julie's and the place was jumping now, packed with women laughing and dancing and carrying on. Mary Liz followed Wendy and Lucy, squeezing past the women at the bar and finding herself in the middle of an undefined dance floor. Wendy found a place for them to stand in the corner. Their waitress made her way over and took their orders. As soon as the drinks arrived, though, Lucy took Wendy out on the dance floor to gyrate to an En Vogue song.

Mary Liz felt kind of stupid standing there with three beers sitting in front of her on the piano. She felt the way she had at her first dance in seventh grade, when her best friend had a boyfriend and she didn't, and she had stood on the sidelines watching. Later, of course, she had danced, but not with the boy she wanted to (actually, that was her best friend's boyfriend), but with a boy she otherwise would have dreaded.

And, like that night so many years ago, another such merciful person was coming over to her. She was wearing black leather pants, a white sports bra and had a ring through her forehead. "Dance?" she said to Mary Liz.

She didn't know what to say. She didn't want to hurt the woman's feelings, but she certainly didn't want to dance with her, either. But—oh, heck, she couldn't say no (the woman would think she thought she was some kind of freak, which, actually, Mary Liz did), and Mary Liz went out on the dance floor.

Wendy and Lucy laughed when they saw her. Especially when Mary Liz's partner seemed to sink into a highly expressive dance world all her own and paid absolutely no attention to Mary Liz as a partner. She had closed her eyes and was kind of jerking around, slowly, although the music was fast and furious.

The song ended, Mary Liz said, "Thanks!" and ran to get her beer and take a vacant chair. The next song was a slow dance; NO WAY.

Everyone moved off the dance floor except Wendy and Lucy, who were looking at each other, debating whether to go on dancing or not. And then they drew together, Lucy sliding her arms up around Wendy's neck (for Wendy was the taller), and they slowly started moving around, not terribly close, but not very far away, either.

There was something definitely erotic about these two. The way they moved, the way they smiled, looking at each other, just going slowly around and around, not minding or caring they were the only ones dancing. Others were watching them, too. And for good reason. They were the most stunning women in the bar and it was not hard to imagine what these two would be like in bed: graceful, intertwined, beautiful.

A low whistle came from behind Mary Liz. "Are those babes hot or what?" a voice asked and a group broke out in laughter.

Mary Liz decided she needed some air. This was getting more than a wee bit uncomfortable for her now.

She met Wendy and Lucy on the way out and said she was just going out for a breather and would be back.

Outside, it was surprisingly quiet. But then the light on Third Avenue changed and cars started zooming past her on their way to the Queensborough Bridge. Mary Liz walked down Fifty-eighth Street a few steps, looking in the window of an Indian restaurant, shoving her hands in her pockets and then smiling at a middle-aged couple as they passed—but they didn't even see her. Ah, New York.

It was a quarter to one. She strolled all the way down the block until she saw a brownstone that said Town House Bar. There was a bouncer at the door, talking to two young men.

She turned around and started back up Fifty-eighth Street. She stopped to look in the window of a closed interior design shop and heard a sudden screech of brakes. She turned around and saw a car coming up on the sidewalk. She jumped back in the doorway of a brownstone, wondering if it wasn't the same Crown Victoria that Bertie said the FBI had been following them in from the helipad earlier. But then a man jumped out the passenger side and Mary Liz thought, *God! It's that guy Leo!*, and then a second car came up on the curb, hitting Leo and sending him crashing to the sidewalk.

By now Mary Liz had backed herself up against the door of the brownstone. Leo was on the ground groaning and the doors flew open on the second car and a man and a woman got out, holding guns over their doors and screaming for everyone to freeze, *they* were FBI.

The female agent made her way around to the driver's-side door of the first car. There was a shot and Mary Liz dropped into a crouch against the door, holding her hands over her head. There was another shot; someone yelled and Mary Liz heard footsteps. She dared to look up; the female FBI agent was standing with a gun at the head of the driver of the Crown Victoria and Leo was gone, being chased up the street by the other agent. A police siren sounded and then there was a yell from up the street and then, *blam! blam!* there were two more shots. Seconds later, two New York City police cars came screeching to a stop on Fifty-eighth Street.

"Officer down, officer down!" someone was yelling. "Suspect's been shot, as well—"

Mary Liz got up and tentatively moved toward the street. A cop was now cuffing the guy the agent had pinned in the Crown Victoria, but otherwise all the attention was now up the block. Mary Liz hurried toward Julie's, outside of which a crowd had gathered on the curb. The crowd parted as the second FBI agent from the car, the man, was led out and over to a police car; he was clutching his lower arm, which was bleeding profusely. It was Agent Travers.

Then Mary Liz heard Wendy's voice somewhere in the crowd, "Look, I have a license to carry it. I'm a private investigator and I'm on a case and I have every reason to believe this man is a professional assassin who tried to kill my client before."

"That's right, she is," Mary Liz heard another familiar voice say. "Take the cuffs off her, but keep her gun." It was Agent Debbie from the FBI. She took Mary Liz's arm and pulled her into the crowd. Wendy was standing there; a police officer had pushed up her pant leg to take something off her that looked like a garter. Mary Liz realized it was a gun holster for the tiny pistol she saw another officer holding in a plastic bag.

"Mary Liz Scott," Agent Debbie said, pointing down to the man who was writhing on the sidewalk, clutching a shattered knee. "Do you recognize this man?"

"Hey, Leo," Mary Liz said. "Nice to see you again. How 'bout going for a ride?"

32

"Why do they say *I* shot him and print my name, but Mary Liz remains 'an unidentified client'?" Wendy wanted to know Monday morning, tossing the *New York Post* down on the kitchen table and picking up the *Daily News.*

"Presumably, to keep her alive," Bertie said.

"Who would ever think of Chicago as a safe place?" Mary Liz said to no one in particular, tossing the *New York Times,* and getting up for more coffee. They were in the guest house, lingering over breakfast. Mary Liz had come over because Sky had to leave early this morning and he didn't want her to be alone. Not quite yet. "It will be over soon, now, darling, I promise."

Still, even after Mary Liz had escaped the second attempted kidnapping—or murder, who knew?—the authorities had told her next to nothing. They had been dragged down to a station house in Manhattan for hours and when Sky showed up at seven the next morning to pick them up, he had made each of the three retrace every conversation, every moment, everything that had happened to them from the time they had left the polo grounds in Water Mill to the time of the attempted snatch.

Finally, Wendy had turned to Mary Liz in the back seat and said, "This guy's no simple schoolteacher, is he?"

"Nothing about being a teacher is simple," Mary Liz said, settling in her seat and closing her eyes. "Go to sleep."

Sky was the only one who told them anything at all. That, indeed, as they'd figured out amongst themselves, the Crown Victoria following them from the helipad had not been the FBI. It was, in fact, Ivor Vrensk, aka Leo—the man who had snatched Mary Liz from JFK—and a partner. "Thank God the feds were watching the restaurant and Julie's," Sky said. "And thank God Vrensk didn't make his move until you got to Fifty-eighth Street."

The burning question now was, how did Vrensk know Mary Liz would be landing there at the helipad when she herself had thought they'd be driving in?

"Shit, don't look at me like that!" Bertie had yelled at Sky. "I would no more hurt Mary Liz than Mother!"

Wendy, ever since, had been bugging Mary Liz about who the heck Sky was, but Mary Liz refused to concede anything. Not yet. She had given him her word.

Back in the kitchen, Wendy glanced up at Mary Liz as she rose from the table. "Anything in the *Times?*"

"There's a little piece in the B section you'll like. They quote one of the cops saying, 'She's a private eye with the looks of a fashion model and the aim of Annie Oakley.' I turned down the page."

"You know," Wendy said, rustling the paper, "I once had a client who fired me because he said I'd never shoot anyone. He said I was too softhearted. I'm going to send him copies of these articles."

"Might as well," Bertie said, "because I think your cover as an idle high-society debutante is a bit compromised now. Mercenary soldier may be more in line."

Mary Liz turned around, sipping her coffee, leaning back against the counter. "Wendy, have you been carrying a gun all this time?"

"After the airport thing." She smiled at Bertie and imitated his deep voice. "Listen, from here on in, you have only one job—to protect Mary Liz. You're her bodyguard."

Someone was knocking on the front door of the guest house. Then they heard it open, and then footsteps across the living room. Sky appeared in the doorway. "Not the greatest security measures around here, are there?"

"Depends on your point of view," Wendy said, continuing to read the paper while pulling back her robe to expose a holster over her nightgown with a big black gun in it."

"Wendy!"

"You can't have it both ways, Mary Liz. You either want to live or you want to die."

Sky came over to kiss Mary Liz hello. She offered him coffee, which he accepted, but insisted on getting it himself. He came back to the table and sat down, looking across the table at Bertie. "I need you to do something, Bertie. And it's probably going to take some doing. But I need you to do it, and I can't explain why, except to say that if you will do it, it's very likely that all of this—everything that's happened this summer—will be settled and over and will never touch any of you again."

"He really is a most remarkable teacher," Wendy commented to Mary Liz.

"Wendy," Sky started to say.

"Yes?"

"A week. That's what I need. And then I will explain everything. I swear."

"Like who the hell you are? I ran a check on you and came up with some financial lawyer named Stephen Pembroke. You're not some sort of a spy for Braxer & Braxer, are you?"

"That's what Glidden was supposed to find and think if he checked Sky out," Mary Liz explained. "But he's not." She looked to Sky. "Are you?"

He smiled. "No," he said, shaking his head. He turned to Bertie. "What I need for you to do—and Wendy, Mary Liz, anything you can do to help, please do it." He slid a piece of paper across the table. "Somehow you've got to get all these people together at the Big House. Within a week. All together at the same time. No more, no less than who is on the list."

Bertie scanned it. "It would have to be on the weekend. Half these people aren't here during the week."

"Then get them here next weekend," Sky said. "But it has to be before Monday."

"Why Monday?" Mary Liz said.

"Something's coming down," was all he'd say.

"The only person who could swing getting them here is Mother." Bertie looked up at the ceiling, thinking.

"We'd have to get Julius back from L.A...." he continued. "Saturday's the Artists' and Writers' Softball Game, Saturday evening there's that Broadway Cares ballet, Saturday night the children's clinic dinner, the Caswells' dinner dance and the Ann Hampton Callaway concert. Sunday there's something on during the day, I think the Little Flower reception for homeless children, and there's some kind of tea dance, too, but..." He looked at Sky. "A brunch on Sunday, earlyish, say, eleven, is possible."

"Fine," Sky said.

"But it will take all of Mother's wile and cunning to get them here. And you've got Denver on this list. What on earth could we say it's for?" He looked to Mary Liz. "What do I tell *Mother* it's for?"

"Let's see the list," Wendy said, pulling the paper over and sharing it with Mary Liz.

Vanessa Buckley
Sinclair "Buck" Buckley
Riff Cahill
Bertram Hoffman
Denver Hoffman
Jeanine Hoffman
Julius Hoffman
Nancy Hoffman
Charles Kahn
Claude Lemieux
Isabel Lemieux
Claire MacClendon
Henry MacClendon
Wendy Mitchell
Jake O'Leary
William Pfeiffer
Schyler Preston
Sasha Reinhart
Mary Liz Scott
Randolph Vandergilden
Rachelle Zaratan

"This is everyone who went to the fireworks at the Simpsons' beach that night," Mary Liz observed.

"Denver wasn't there," Bertie pointed out.

Wendy looked at Sky. "Who the hell *are* you? *What* are you?"

Sky held up his finger. "One week."

Wendy frowned at Mary Liz. "And you sleep with this guy?"

Mary Liz smiled. "Yep."

"Trusting soul."

Her smile expanded. "Yep."

Any animosity Mary Liz had felt toward her godmother because of Nancy's dalliance with her father two decades earlier was gone. Aunt Nancy was so emotionally exhausted by all that had gone on, that when Mary Liz went with Bertie to talk to her about the infamous brunch, she wondered if she would ever be able to bring herself to tell her about Alfred's son in Paris, or the pornography studio in Amsterdam.

"Mother, all I can tell you is this," Bertie said. "If you can get these people here, I believe it will be the last of all the unpleasantness that has happened this summer."

Aunt Nancy looked too weary to believe or disbelieve him.

"We have this brunch, Mother," Bertie urged her, "and life can go back to normal."

His mother looked back down at the list. "Then I'll get them here," she said.

V

33

All the leaves had to be added to the dining-room table to accommodate the brunch guests. It was a stinker of a hot August day, so humid one couldn't be sure if it would be officially classified as sunny or hazy, and there was not a breath of air, not even from the ocean, which was as flat and glassy as a lake. All the windows and doors of the Big House were shut today and the central air-conditioning was on.

In the dining room, though, it was so pleasant as to be exhilarating. Aunt Nancy sat at the head of the great table with Bertie at the opposite end, and nine people sat on one side of the table, ten on the other. There were three centerpieces of flowers (from the cutting garden), a white linen tablecloth, peach-colored linen napkins and the "luncheon silver," which (Mary Liz had learned over the summer) was not nearly as heavy as the dinner silver (the stems not as thick and the knives nowhere near as long).

Help was brought in, one woman and one man, whom Mary Liz immediately suspected were not in the serving business at all, since no hostess on the level of Nancy Hoffman would ever have a woman who served from the right, and a man who always spilled a little while pouring the water, orange juice, white wine, Bloody Marys and mimosas that were being offered.

It was the first time Mary Liz had met Denver Hoffman, the twenty-five-year-old actress. She was blond, blue-eyed and anorexic. She was also so superficially nice, Mary Liz was sure she had to be a lousy actress. But so what? Her mother controlled the studio that produced her TV show, and the show had an ensemble group of five actors who could carry the hit show regardless of how good or bad an actress she was.

What surprised Mary Liz was how obvious it was that Denver and Bertie did not get along. They were tolerating each other, but there were constant hints of resentment on both sides. In comparison, Bertie and Julius seemed positively brotherly today.

Yes, they were all here. Julius had come back from Los Angeles because Nancy told him his fate at the studio depended on it. The

Buckleys were here simply because Nancy asked them to come. (Vanessa had scarcely taken her eyes off Wendy the entire time she'd been there.) Getting the Lemieuxes had not been difficult, either, because Claude had returned from France. Charles and Rachelle were delighted to come, too. Claire and Bill were eager to accept, delighted to be considered "a couple." Randolph Vandergilden was happy to go anywhere there was free booze and food. Sasha was happy to come next door, but was perhaps a little surprised that her bodyguard was also on the guest list.

Henry MacClendon had been a little tricky to get there, since Sky had been adamant that his new wife, Cindy, *not* be present, but Nancy had made something up and he was there—a little angry, perhaps, at having to sit and watch his ex-wife with a younger man, but he was there. And, of course, Mary Liz and Sky and Wendy and Jake were all present, the latter of whom made a very special point of greeting Randolph Vandergilden and Isabel Lemieux.

So, there they all were, eating and drinking and chatting as if it was the most normal of brunches in the most normal of upper-class East Hampton homes. They ate eggs Benedict, eggs Florentine, fruit salad, muffins and granola, and although she was nervous, Mary Liz found herself eating a lot. She also had a Bloody Mary to calm down, and then turned around to ask the waiter for coffee to perk up.

At some unseen signal, Aunt Nancy cleared her throat and looked expectantly around the table. The conversations quieted and then ceased altogether.

"I'm very grateful to all of you for coming today on such short notice," she began.

"You always give at least six weeks' notice, Nance," Randolph said. "That social secretary of yours always calls first and then, presto, an invitation appears in the mail the next day. Not even a mailgram this time!"

Aunt Nancy smiled slightly. She was nervous, Mary Liz could tell, and she wondered what Sky had said to Aunt Nancy in his private little meeting with her this morning. Mary Liz and Wendy and Bertie had also met with him separately to prep for the direction Sky wanted the conversation at the gathering to go.

"I have brought us all together for a very important reason," Aunt Nancy said, looking at each person around the table in succession: Bill Pfeiffer, sitting to her left, and then Claire, Julius, Wendy,

Charles Kahn, Mary Liz, Henry MacClendon, Vanessa Buckley, Claude Lemieux, and at the end, Bertie, and then back up the table at Jeanine, Jake, Rachelle, Denver, Sky, Isabel, Randolph, Sasha, Buck Buckley and Riff Cahill. "One of us killed Herb Glidden and I want to know who it is."

Dead silence. And then Denver started to giggle. "Good God, Mother, you sound like Angela Lansbury."

"I'm serious, Denver."

"Well, I didn't do it, Mother, I was three thousand miles away."

Nancy turned to her right. "And what about you, Mr. Cahill? Where were you?"

"Me? I was asleep."

"No, you weren't, Riff," Sasha said. "You were playing Hearts with me and Rachelle. Remember? It was after the fireworks."

"Conducting your own private fireworks, no doubt," Randolph said, guffawing.

"You're revolting," Rachelle told him. Then she turned to Nancy. "Charles left for Pittsburgh that night, remember? So I stayed over at Sasha's." She looked across the table at Vanessa while continuing, "Frankly there was too much noise coming from the guest house next-door to sleep." Down the table to Sasha, "If you rent that house again, Sash, you've got to get air-conditioning so you can close the windows at night if you have to."

Denver turned to her brother. "I was under the impression you murdered Uncle Herb."

Bertie made a face. "*Uncle* Herb? You're sick, Denver."

"*Me? I'm* sick?" Denver said. "You're the textbook case. Where's that waiter? I want another mimosa." Denver's anorexia apparently didn't apply to alcohol. She had drunk several drinks already.

Bertie turned to his right. "So where were you the night of the murder, Claude?"

"Drunk," Claude said. "With Buck and Randy. Down at the marina. Remember? We were the ones who told the cops we saw you go out on the boat."

"Oh, right," Bertie said. "I'd forgotten to thank you."

"Well, we had to tell them the truth," Buck spoke up from his side of the table. "And they found out you didn't do it, so what's the problem?"

"What were you doing at the marina?" Vanessa asked her husband.

"He wasn't fucking you, that's for sure," Randolph retorted.

"Hey!" Buck said sharply.

"Leave it, Buck," Vanessa said, sipping her white wine. "He's not worth paying attention to."

"And where were you, Vanessa?" Nancy said.

"I was here, at Bertie's party."

"Only, Bertie wasn't at his party," Claude pointed out. "He was at the marina."

"But Wendy was," Vanessa said.

"So I heard," Rachelle said, when Vanessa looked at her. "You *were* pretty loud, Vanessa."

The way Rachelle said it created a wave of understanding and eyes widened all the way around the table. Particularly Aunt Nancy's, whose eyes hadn't stopped blinking yet.

Randolph was staring at Wendy. "You're a—"

"Don't say a goddamn word," Henry MacClendon said, shutting him up.

"Thank you, Henry," Claire said, looking down the table at him. "I was about to say the same thing. Anyway," she said, addressing Bertie, "I went home after the fireworks and Bill came with me. We talked until almost four in the morning."

"Talked," Randolph said, coughing over his drink.

"Talked," Bill Pfeiffer told Randolph, setting him straight.

"Well, let's see, then," Bertie said. "That leaves Julius—"

"I was home with Jeanine," he said quickly. "And while we're on the subject, why the hell did everybody keep saying to the cops that we were the last people seen with Herb? At the fireworks?" He glared around the table. "We didn't even *see* Herb at the fireworks!"

"What?" Wendy said. "But everybody said—"

"Yeah, everybody said, that's the problem. We didn't see Herb at all that night!"

"That's right," Jeanine said, backing him up. "We didn't go to the ARF benefit. We had flown up to see the children at camp and only got back in time for the fireworks."

There was a moment of silence.

"What about you, Mary Liz?" Bertie said. "Where were you?"

"Yeah," Randolph said. "You were the one who was working for Herb."

Mary Liz looked across the table. "I was not working for him."

"He told me you were."

Sasha gave Randolph an irritable poke with her elbow. "Get with the program, will you? He told everyone that, but it wasn't true."

"How was I supposed to know?" the vintner said.

"Go to Hazleton, already." The diva looked over at Mary Liz and, with a hint of a smile, said, "So, where were you, Mary Liz?" as if she already knew the answer—and she did, because Mary Liz had later confided in her about it. About how Sky's fiancée, Kate, had died seven years ago, the whole nine yards, including her decision to start sleeping with him.

"I was home, in the cottage," Mary Liz said. "With Sky."

"I'm sorry, but that's not true," Vanessa said. "Sky dropped me off here and then went home."

"And came back," Sky said.

"So where was your car?"

"Up the road."

"Why?"

"Stop it, Vanessa," Buck said.

"No, Buck, I want to know. You've been letting this guy walk all over you this summer. Why did you sneak back here?"

"To kill Herb, no doubt," Randolph said. "Snuck out, clubbed him over the head and threw him in the ocean."

"Goddess almighty," Sasha said, turning to Randolph. "I will *pay* for your stay at Hazleton."

"You came back to spy on me, didn't you?" Vanessa demanded. "For Buck."

Sky shook his head. "No."

"He snuck back because he's discreet," Wendy finally said from her end of the table. "He didn't want the whole world to know Mary Liz's business."

"Yes, he is certainly discreet," Claude said. "So discreet that he completely vanished after the murder."

"I told you," Buck said, "he had a family emergency."

Claude lofted an eyebrow at Buck. "So many people have told me so many things lately, I'm having trouble keeping everyone's story straight."

Buck shot Claude a look, but didn't say anything.

"Mother," Denver said impatiently, "can I go now? This is boring."

"Sit still, Denver," her mother said.

"Oh my God, she listened," Bertie said in wonder.

Denver made a face at him. "I get an extra million in my inheritance for coming today. What do you get?"

"Oh, Mother," Bertie groaned, "you didn't."

"I should have made it two million to come back into this house," Denver added. Mary Liz was genuinely shocked. This was hardly the sweet younger sister people had told her about. She obviously hated Bertie, and seemed to despise her mother, as well.

"So, Jake," Bertie said, moving on. "Where were you when Herb was murdered?"

"Oh, for crying out loud!" Denver declared, throwing her napkin down on the table in disgust. "You make me sick, Bertie. How can you even have that—*person* sitting here at the table!"

Bertie ignored her, waiting for Jake's answer.

"I was here," Jake said. "To make sure the party didn't get out of hand."

"Mother," Denver said warningly, "you *better* make it two million. Waiter, refill. And can you please check the glasses of the guests? Or are they expected to wait on themselves?"

The waiter fumbled a bit, but picked the mimosa pitcher off the buffet table and made his way over to her.

"You can hit me again with that, too," Randolph told him.

The waiter looked as though he would like to.

"And what about you, Wendy?" Bertie said. "Where were you?"

Wendy didn't bat an eye. "I was with Vanessa. Like she said."

Rachelle snickered.

Bertie quickly pressed on, turning to his right. "And you, Isabel?"

"I was at home. In bed," she said.

"Tragically alone, no doubt," Randolph added.

Isabel looked at him with cool disdain. Then looked at the waiter. "Wine, please."

"Well, then, that's all of us, isn't it?" Julius said, dropping his hands to the edge of the table as if getting ready to leave. "None of us murdered Herb. Can I go back to California now?"

Denver's head snapped to attention. "What flight are you taking?"

"No, wait," Sky said loudly. Everybody froze. He looked at Nancy. "And where were you, Mrs. Hoffman?"

For a moment, Nancy didn't answer, but only studied her water glass, turning it 'round and 'round by the crystal stem. Then she looked up. "I was at Herb's."

There was a gasp from someone at the table.

"And as I told the police from the beginning," Nancy continued, "Alex and I—Herb's son—we waited up until almost three for him to come home." She swallowed. "He never did."

"You never told me that, Mother," Bertie said.

"There's a *lot* Mother hasn't told you," Denver promised him, drinking away.

"When was the last time Alex saw his father?" Mary Liz asked.

"When he dropped him off at the ARF benefit," Nancy answered.

"We saw him there," Mary Liz confirmed. She looked at Jeanine Hoffman across the table. "And you're absolutely sure you didn't see him at the fireworks?"

"Yes—I'm—sure," Jeanine said, clearly exasperated. "And I don't know how that idea got started in the first place. We hadn't seen Herb all weekend."

"Somebody told us he was sitting with you," Mary Liz said, squinting, trying to remember.

"I remember looking for him," Claire said. "And someone saying he was there somewhere."

"Sitting with the Hoffmans," Mary Liz added.

"It wasn't me," Nancy said.

There was silence at the table again.

"Well," Claire continued, "does anyone remember who Herb was with at the animal parade?"

"He was with me for a while," Claude volunteered.

"And me," Randolph said.

"I saw him," Charles said. "And so did Rachelle. And Sasha."

"I talked with him," Buck said.

"Me, too," Bertie said. "And so did Wendy and Jake."

"I saw him," Riff, Sasha's bodyguard, said, as well. "But I didn't talk to him."

"Did anyone see who he left with?" Mary Liz asked.

Silence.

"I know Alex drove him there," Nancy said. "He told me he had dropped him off because Herb said he didn't want to drive after drinking—and he felt like drinking that night."

"Yeah, he was drinking," Buck said. "Once in a blue moon he'd let go, and that was going to be the night. In fact, I could have sworn his death was accidental. I've seen him get messed up before."

"On booze," Mary Liz said.

"And pills, too, occasionally," Sasha spoke up. "I've seen him take amphetamines when he was working."

"But this was barbiturates," Mary Liz said.

At this reminder, all heads swung in Vanessa's direction.

"Oh, go fuck yourselves," she muttered, finishing her Bloody Mary. "And even if it were any of your business, I already told the police someone ripped off one of my prescriptions in the medicine cabinet during a dinner Buck and I had in June. And by the way, they *are* prescribed for me. By a doctor. They're medicine."

Rachelle laughed.

"So," Wendy said, speaking up, "Herb Glidden went to the ARF benefit, but no one saw him leave."

Silence. They all looked at each other.

"So someone must have gotten to him there," Sky said. "At the benefit."

He paused, looking around. "The question is, what motive did anyone have to want him dead?" He looked at Mary Liz. "Any theories?"

"Oh, I've got a lot of theories," Mary Liz said. "Starting with business."

"The only one who did business with him was Julius," Jeanine said, "and we, I told you, weren't there."

"Julius could have hired someone to knock him off," Buck offered.

"Thanks, pal," Julius said.

"Julius is the last person who wanted Glidden dead!" Jeanine snapped.

"Why do you say that?" Sky asked her.

"Because Julius and Herb were working together to get Howland Films back."

Ah-ha. So they had been working together to get the studio.

"I knew it!" Bertie cried. "You are such a scumbag, Julius—"

"I'm sorry, darling," Jeanine said to her husband, "but you can't let them drag you into this. Besides, you'll get Howland Films fair and square. You never needed Herb—"

"Actually," Mary Liz said, interrupting Jeanine and indicating to the waiter she'd like more coffee, "when I said business, I was thinking more along the lines of the kind of business you did with Herbert Glidden." She was looking down the table at Randolph Vandergilden. "I'm speaking to you."

The vintner's head jerked in her direction. "You're speaking to me about what?"

"About the business dealings you had with Herbert Glidden."

"What the hell are you talking about?" he said angrily.

"I'm talking about the ownership of the winery."

"My investors own most of it, so what?" he demanded.

"So Herbert Glidden found you those investors, Randolph, didn't he? Through the Eeghlenburger commodities brokerage in Amsterdam." All was silent at the table. No one moved. "The only problem was, Glidden didn't tell you until after you took the money and spent it who, exactly, the investors were that he had lined up through Eeghlenburger, and what a rough bunch they were. So rough, in fact, that unless the winery did business exactly the way they suggested, very bad things could happen to you. And thus, even though the wine you make is, well, shall we say, 'unusual,' there's a Dutch importer who buys eighty percent of your wine, isn't there? At three point two times the price of a *good* wine?"

Randolph didn't say anything. He was sweating, looking at one of the centerpieces.

"But don't feel bad, Randolph," Mary Liz continued, "because Glidden got to Claude, too. You guys should have been better friends. You should have talked to each other."

"What?" Claude said. "You're crazy. Isabel and I own the American edition of *Je Ne Sais Quoi*, we don't work for anyone. Everyone works for us!"

"You don't really work for yourself, do you, Claude?" Mary Liz asked him. "Tell us, how did you get the twenty-nine million to buy the rights and launch the magazine here in the States?" She raised a hand to stop him from answering. "Jacques Gorce, the independent investment banker in Paris. He told me himself."

"That's no secret," Claude said, looking around the table. "In fact, we promoted the fact, he's highly reputable."

"But Herb Glidden set up the deal for you, didn't he? And only after you had finished celebrating the deal and were gloating to your wife that you were no longer under her father's thumb, that's when you found out you were under an even bigger thumb. A very threatening thumb. Glidden explained to you how the accounting was going to work with your repayment schedule, and about how there was going to be a constant movement of moneys circling from the United States to France and then back to the States, because the magazine was going to continue to borrow money and pay it back. And when you objected, he explained who some of your investors actually were, whose money it was you had gladly taken, and you got very scared." She looked sympathetic. "And for good reason."

Mary Liz shifted in her seat to look down the table at Charles Kahn. "I think you got the worst deal of everybody, Charles. I know you genuinely only wanted to make Rachelle's clothing line a success. I know you would have done anything not to have someone else buy her company and take her national. You two had dreamed and planned of owning it and running the empire yourselves. And so, when Herbert Glidden set you up with the Irish investment banking firm, Dunlau Gunney, who said they not only had investors who would be willing to finance you nationally, but insisted that you go *inter*national, how could you resist?"

Charles finished his Bloody Mary and didn't look at his wife.

"And then when it was all done, and Herb came to you to explain who your actual investors were, and Herb explained how Rachelle Zaratan Clothing would be perpetually moving millions of dollars around the world, that organized crime would be using your wife's talent and success—"

"This can't be true," Rachelle said quietly, looking at her husband. "Charles."

He wouldn't look at her.

"He can't say anything, Rachelle, because he loves you," Mary Liz said. "And he feels as though he betrayed you. He didn't get into the mess on purpose, none of the poker group did. Glidden was one clever fellow." She turned to her left. "Isn't that true, Henry?"

"No," Claire said sharply. "I don't believe it. I was there, dammit, I was there! Henry's work was taking off. Everyone was trying to finance him to go national, to open offices across the country, he didn't need Glidden—he didn't even like him!"

"But he went with the investors who wanted to open offices in six cities around the world," Mary Liz finished. "Investors who made payments through Banque de Veurne in Brussels. And so the offices of Henry MacClendon Architects, were opened in London, Paris, Brussels, Geneva, São Paulo and Moscow."

"São Paulo?" Sasha asked.

"Brazil," Mary Liz announced.

"So *what?*" Claire demanded.

"So after the deal was done and the offices were created," Mary

Liz said, "Herb had a little chat with Henry. He explained how the accounting would work, how money would flow from country to country in the form of invoices, payments and overhead. How Henry could only use certain contractors and suppliers—"

"What is it that you're trying to say?" Rachelle finally exploded. "That all of us are crooks?"

"No," Mary Liz said quietly, "but that you were all taken in by a master. For years Glidden had only financed Howland movies, getting the funds Alfred needed to make it a major studio. His only condition to Alfred was that every production be in some way partially produced overseas, using his list of preferred unions, work groups, production centers and suppliers. The only problem was, Alfred didn't realize—or didn't want to realize—that he was being used to move massive amounts of illegal money into the U.S. and, even if a movie bombed, and the studio couldn't repay the whole investment, the investors still always got at least partial repayment in clean money, plus clean business and income through the overseas production businesses they had created to accommodate Howland and other American studios."

"So he really was a money launderer," Sasha said in awe.

"For years," Mary Liz said. "And then when he wished to expand, to stop this one deal/one film approach, he approached a group of, shall we call them, 'organized investors,' who represented a number of illegal money sources and had the perfect financial terrain to hide literally billions of dollars, because they were operating within a system that answered to essentially no one. The Russian banks.

"And so," Mary Liz continued, "Glidden threw his lot in with them, and was guaranteed a never-ending source of venture capital, made available through a network of established financial institutions in stable European countries. And so, when he decided to branch out six years ago, he approached the most likely takers he knew." She looked meaningfully around the table. "Henry, Claude, Randolph, Charles. And yes, of course, you, too, Buck."

"Dad must have known something," Julius said.

"Only when some of his old friends began to approach him," Mary Liz said. "About Glidden. About the money he had raised for their ventures." Mary Liz paused. "And not long after, Alfred died in the plane crash." She looked around the table. "Convenient, wouldn't you say?"

"It was an accident," Sasha said.

There was an exaggerated sigh. "I had a feeling, oh dear husband of mine," Vanessa said, "that if all your friends got taken in by old Herb, that even smart old you wouldn't escape his clutches, either. He found all the money for you to start up East End, didn't he?"

"Hey, but listen," he said, leaning forward in his chair, "it was a fabulous deal. I got the financing, I built a grade A country club with a top-flight course—come on, you guys have to admit it, it's a hell of a club. Okay, yes, later, Herb let me in on who my investors were and what I was going to have to do. But you know what? Regardless of what even happens now, I don't regret a minute of it, because I built that club and it *is* a great club. And without Herb I never would have gotten the chance to build it, because none of you ever thought I could do it."

"True," his wife acknowledged. She looked at Mary Liz. "What's the twist on the club?"

"Those foreign members who pay a million dollars to drop by once a year."

"I knew those Japs were too good to be true," Vanessa said.

"For your information," Buck told his wife, "the Japanese members are the only ones who are legit. It's all those suave Brits and Germans you're so damn fond of who're bogus."

"Then it's a miracle you weren't caught before, dearest," Vanessa said, "because there is nothing suave about them."

Buck turned to address Nancy. "But I swear to you, Nancy, I did not kill Herb."

"I didn't kill Herb, either," Randolph said.

"Well, I didn't kill him," Henry announced.

"And *I* didn't kill him," Charles said.

"Wait a minute, Charles," Claude Lemieux said, "but I think you might have."

All eyes swept to Claude.

"You and Herb went to look at your plane and he never came back."

"What are you talking about?" Charles said. "Herb went to work on his plane when I came back for dinner."

"But Herb wanted to party all night," Claude said. He looked to Buck, who nodded in agreement. "But after the parade, he went off with you and disappeared."

"No one picked him up from the benefit," Mary Liz said.

"No one took him to the fireworks," Bertie said.

"And he never came home," Nancy said.

"You took him to your plane, Charles," Claude said, "and fifteen minutes later, you came back. Alone."

"This is nonsense," Rachelle said. "Don't trust the French, that's what my father always said and he was right. World War II should have taught us something, Charles—certainly about Claude."

"Rachelle," Sasha began.

"Don't Rachelle me," she snapped at her friend. To the group, "Charles may have shown Herb his plane, but he came right back and had dinner, and then he and Sasha and me went to the fireworks. And right after the fireworks, I drove Charles to the airport and we stood right there, on the tarmac, and watched him board his plane and take off."

"With Herb in it," Henry said.

"Herb was not on the plane," Rachelle insisted. "Was he, Sasha?"

The diva nodded. "That's right, he wasn't on it."

"I didn't say he was *conscious*," Henry said.

"Oh, fine, Henry," Charles said. "I expect this kind of crap from Claude, to try to pin it all on me, but not from you. I didn't kill Herb. I wasn't even here when he died! Check the airport in Pittsburgh. I was there."

Sky cleared his throat. "You were in Pittsburgh, but not all night."

"That's not true," Charles said. "I landed about midnight. Check the flight log."

"Someone did," Sky said. "And it's true, you did file a flight plan and you did fly to Pittsburgh, and you did land at midnight, and your plane was there all night."

"So what's your fucking problem?" Charles demanded.

"My problem is *you* weren't in Pittsburgh. You were flying back to Long Island in your friend Hal Porter's Cessna with Herbert Glidden."

"This is ridiculous," Charles said.

"It's not ridiculous," Sky said, "it's gruesome. How well you planned it. On the way to the benefit, in front of Rachelle, you called on your car phone to file your flight plan to Pittsburgh. You attended the benefit, lured Glidden to look at something in your plane, slugged him over the head with a socket wrench and then shot him full of enough dope to nearly kill him. You covered him with a tarp, locked the plane and then waltzed back to the benefit to eat dinner. You didn't even stop to wash your hands."

Mary Liz was horrified.

"You accompanied your wife and Sasha to the fireworks and, when asked, said you saw Glidden there with the Hoffmans. On the other side of the beach. After the fireworks, the ladies dropped you off at the airport and watched you climb into your plane, get clearance and take off. You landed in Pittsburgh shortly after midnight and parked your plane next to Hal Porter's Cessna."

Rachelle's expression was turning to one of shock. White, chalky shock.

"You had called Porter on Friday at his office and asked him if you could borrow his plane Saturday night," Sky said, "because you wanted to double back to the Island to see a woman Rachelle was becoming suspicious about. He said sure. So you called ahead to Pittsburgh to file a flight plan in Porter's name. When you landed in Pittsburgh Saturday night, you parked next to Porter's Cessna, moved Glidden's body over to it, stripped him to his shorts, put the tarp over the passenger seat and propped him up against the door of the passenger's seat. At this point, he was barely alive. Then you took off again, this time as Hal Porter, on your way for a short visit to MacArthur Airport on Long Island.

"Only you took a little detour over East Hampton, didn't you? Got your bearings, slowed the plane, put it on autopilot for a few seconds while you reached over to open the passenger door and push Glidden's body out."

Sky paused. "You did a good job. He drowned and the current took him right in to the Hoffmans' beach."

Charles's eyes had lowered.

"Then you tossed the syringe and the wrench into the ocean, landed at MacArthur briefly, cleaned out your friend's plane—wrapping the tarp in one bunch of newspapers and Glidden's clothes in another—refueled, got clearance to take off and flew back to Pittsburgh. You moved the newspaper bundles back into your plane and went to a hotel and went to bed. In the morning, you flew to Chicago, where you dumped the tarp in an airport trash bin. As for Glidden's clothes, you waited until you reached Indianapolis the next day, where you stuffed them into a Dumpster outside a downtown Burger King."

The table was silent for several moments.

Charles turned to look at Nancy. "But I didn't have anything to do with Alfred's death. I swear."

"I know you didn't," she said quietly.

"No one killed Alfred," Claude said impatiently. "The official report said it was an accident."

"No, actually," Nancy said, "that's not true. Herb had Alfred killed."

Sky leaned forward. "How do you know that, Mrs. Hoffman?"

She met his eyes for several moments. And then Aunt Nancy took a breath and fell back in her chair. "Because I begged him to."

"I knew it!" Denver screamed. "I knew it!"

Nancy seemed to come back from whatever faraway place she had been, to frown at her daughter. "Your father was evil, Denver. He had to be stopped."

"He was not evil!" Denver yelled. "He was kind and gentle and loving and never should have been stuck being married to a bitch like you!"

"Shut up, Denver," Bertie said.

"You shut up, you stupid faggot! What do you know?"

"Denver!" Mary Liz said sharply, forgetting herself.

Denver turned to Mary Liz. "Don't think I don't know who you are! You're India Reynolds's daughter, Mother's dear roommate from school. Well, how dear was she, really, do you think, since Mother went ahead and fucked your father? Did you know that? Because Daddy did and it broke his heart and if he ever did do anything wrong, it was because she destroyed him! Cheated on him and destroyed him!"

Mary Liz sat forward, folding her hands on the edge of the table, trying to keep her voice even. "I am well aware of the fact that my father and your mother had a love affair. The operative word, though, I think, is *love,* something your father apparently couldn't comprehend." Her voice wavered a little on the next. "Because I know my mother knew the meaning of the word, since she did her best to forgive my father twenty years ago—and then they worked very hard to go on together. And they continue to."

"While *your* father, Denver," Claire said suddenly, "turned into a monster. Of course he may have always been that, I don't know. I was only clued in five and a half years ago. And I do know that I came very close to killing him myself when I discovered what he was."

Henry was staring down the table at his ex-wife in horror. "Why? What did he do?"

"Forget it, Henry," Claire said. "I handled it. And he's dead now, so no one I love need ever be afraid of him anymore, thank God."

"Shut up, shut up, shut up!" Denver screamed, standing up and holding her hands over her ears. "You're all lying!"

Jeanine stood up and went to Denver, putting her hands on her shoulders. "I'm sorry, Denver."

Denver dropped her hands, looking at her half-sister-in-law.

"You have to know." Jeanine pushed Denver back down into the chair and held her there, while looking to her husband. "Tell her, Julius."

He looked very grave. "Denver—I loved him, too. I thought he was the greatest man in the world when I was growing up." He shook his head, looking pained. "But Dad had a lot of problems. He did stuff— He did some very terrible things, sexual things." He cleared his throat. "To girls." He looked to Bertie. "That's what we fought about, me and Dad. That's what caused our falling-out."

So Julius did have some values, after all, Mary Liz thought.

"I didn't know, Denver," Nancy was saying to her daughter. "I swear to you, I had no idea what your father was up to until Claire told me. And then I couldn't ignore it. And once I was looking for it, that kind of behavior—" Her eyes welled up. "I confronted him, threatened him, and he went for help."

"But why did you stay with him, Mother?" Bertie said. "How could you?"

"Because he was your father and he did—as I said, he went into treatment. It wasn't your fault, or Denver's, who your parents were, and you deserved the chance to get your father back. The man he had been."

"So what happened?" Mary Liz asked.

It was as though Nancy was aging in front of their eyes. "It happened again. When we got home from Ireland." She glanced at Claire. "A neighbor's thirteen-year-old daughter. And Alfred was trying to buy the parents off." She looked to Sky. "So I went to Herb and I told him I was through, what did I have to do to see Alfred dead. He told me to give him five hundred thousand for expenses and it would be done. I gave him the money and the moment I heard that Alfred's plane had crashed and he was dead—I'm sorry, Denver, Bertie, but it was the greatest relief of my life. The tragedy was that innocent people died with him."

"I'm glad you've said it, Mrs. Hoffman," Sky said, "because your children had a right to know."

Denver pushed Jeanine's hand off her and stood up again. She was shaking from head to foot. Sky grabbed her arm and gave it a little shake. "Denver, listen to me," he said. "Your mother was not responsible for your father's death. She thought she was, and Herbert Glidden wanted her to go on thinking she was."

"But she told him to do it," Denver said, starting to cry.

"Yes," Sky said, "but listen to me! The FBI and FAA have reinvestigated the crash, and they have reexamined every piece of that plane. The crash *was* an accident. It is an absolute certainty. No human being could have rigged that plane for the freak mechanical failure that occurred."

Nancy Hoffman shocked everyone at the table when she let out a bitter little laugh and sat back in her chair again. "Oh my God. Well, I'll give Herb that—by cracky, he was right clever up to the very end."

Denver fled the table and ran out the back of the house.

"So I guess I'm to be charged with something," Nancy said to Sky.

"I just can't believe it, Mother," Bertie said from his end of the table. "You should have come to me."

"And asked you to murder your father? I mean, really, darlin'." Aunt Nancy's good humor seemed to have been restored now that she knew she had not been responsible for the crash. She turned to Sky. "What now?"

Sky ignored Nancy's question, and addressed Charles Kahn. "When you flew home from your last business trip, Charles, you saw Mary Liz, Bertie and Wendy at the airport, didn't you?"

Charles looked first to his wife and then to Sky. And nodded.

"And then you used your car phone to call someone. To check in. And you happened to mention that you saw them."

When Charles wouldn't answer, Sky said, "And you told this person that Mary Liz was going into Manhattan by helicopter, didn't you? And that she'd be landing at the helipad next to the Water Club."

Still Charles didn't say anything.

"And this person you told, Charles, this was the same person who forced you to kill Herbert Glidden, wasn't it?"

Something close to a gleam of hope seemed to appear in Charles's eyes.

"Because this person had been sent to replace Glidden, hadn't he? And had orders to get rid of him because Glidden was calling too much attention to himself, was getting far too sloppy in his deals. Nor did they *want* Glidden to own Howland Films and use it as his own laundry. Glidden was becoming wildly unstable, even you could see that, and given the mess he had made of your life—and what he was lording over your head, Charles—you thought you had nothing to lose if you agreed to kill him. In fact, it seemed like you had everything to gain."

"No," Charles said quietly, finally looking at Sky. "That wasn't why I did it. It was because they threatened to hurt Rachelle." He swallowed. "And she had never done anything. To anyone. Ever." He smiled slightly to himself, then, eyes misting over, he turned to Mary Liz. "She works too much, doesn't she?"

"We'll protect her, Charles," Sky said. "But you have to name the person who threatened to harm your wife. You have to name the person who forced you to kill Glidden. You have to name the person you called after you saw Mary Liz at the airport."

"Charles—" This came from Rachelle. "I will be fine," she said quietly. Tears were streaming down her face. "You must tell him."

He looked miserable. "But they'll get you, Rachelle."

"They *won't* get her," Sasha said sharply. "Look at me, Charles, I've got every kook and weirdo in the world stalking me and I'm still alive." Then more gently, "I will teach her how to live. There are ways of keeping safe. But you have to come clean. Goddess in the sky, what jury could blame you for murdering Glidden when you had mobsters threatening to kill Rachelle?"

Sky reached into his back pocket, took something out and tossed it across to Charles. It was a billfold of some kind. Charles opened it. And nodded.

Sky spoke. "As a special prosecutor for the United States government, I give you my word, we will do everything in our power to protect your wife, and I have every reason to believe we can and will do so successfully. And as we speak, every major player in this international money laundry is being taken into custody. Here and in eighteen other countries. There is only one other person I need from you, Charles. The person responsible for the murder of Herbert Glidden. The person responsible for the near death of Mary Liz Scott, not once, but twice."

They did not have long to wait.

By the time Charles had said his name, Bill Pfeiffer had risen from his chair, holding a gun to Claire's head, making her stand up with him.

Sasha screamed.

"Don't move, any of you. Waiter, facedown on the floor. Waitress, same to you. *Now.*" The couple complied. "Agent Cahill," Bill said abruptly to Riff—but not without a smile—"and you, Preston, on the floor. Facedown. Make a move and Claire's dead."

While they did as he said, Mary Liz said, "You son of a bitch, Bill, you were the one who bugged my house. That security expert of yours did it, didn't he? When he installed the system?"

"Shut up," Bill said. "Wendy—on the floor, facedown. *Move!* Mary Liz, get the housekeeper out here."

Mary Liz reluctantly went into the kitchen and brought Delores back in the dining room with her.

Bill had moved around the table and was exchanging Claire for Sasha as a hostage. When he dragged the diva back around the table with him, from the floor Sky said, "You don't want to do this, Bill."

"Shut up!" he commanded, firing a bullet into the floor right next to Sky, making everyone react. The gun placed at the side of her head, Sasha was trying to keep her head up, but was sobbing.

"Mary Liz," he barked, "get a pillow off the couch in the living room and bring it in here. Move!" She moved, grabbing a pillow and hurrying back. "Buck, frisk the five on the floor. Start with the small of their backs. I want everything on them. Guns, wallets, everything. Hurry up! Mary Liz, unzip the casing and pull out the stuffing—fast." She did. "Now go over there and have Buck put everything in it." She moved over. "Faster, Buck!

"Wait!" Pfeiffer cried to Buck a second later. "Put the handcuffs and the keys on the sideboard. Charles, get over there and open those handcuffs."

By the end of the frisking, there were four sets of handcuffs and keys on the sideboard, and several wallets, two wire-sets, three badges, four IDs and six handguns in the pillowcase Mary Liz was holding. Once Charles unlocked all the handcuffs and returned to the table, Pfeiffer had Mary Liz put all the keys in the pillowcase, too, and hand it over to him. Then he had her handcuff Riff's wrist to the policewoman's ankle, her other ankle to the policeman's wrist, and handcuff Sky's wrist to the handcuffs between the two police officers (the waitress and waiter), and simply handcuffed Wendy's hands behind her back.

"Sasha," Pfeiffer said then, moving her out of the dining room toward the front door, "as long as no one stops us, I won't have to shoot you. If I have to, I promise I'll try to shoot you in the larynx so you'll have a chance to live, but I'm afraid the voice will have to go." He was holding her very close to him and now she was too scared to even cry. "Hear me, people? I suggest you wait until I've let Ms. Reinhart go before you try to get me. After I let her go, you can shoot at me all you want. That's fair."

And he was out the front door, Sasha's plea for mercy the last sound they heard.

34

The two FBI agents watching the property, Debbie Cole and Agent Travers, were dutifully aghast at how far awry the end of brunch had gone. There had been absolutely no record of Bill Pfeiffer ever possessing a weapon of any kind, of being involved in any kind of violence (except, of course, ordering the murder of Herbert Glidden) or ever having been in the service. And yet the man had produced a gun, traded hostages to get a superstar, incapacitated four law enforcement people ("Riff is an FBI agent?" Mary Liz asked again, amazed) and one private investigator, and succeeded in dragging Sasha Reinhart through the hedges to her house next-door.

Within fifteen minutes, a SWAT team had landed on the beach by helicopter and the entire road was blocked off by East Hampton and the New York State police. No one inside Sasha's house would answer the phone. The authorities didn't have a clue where in the house the gunman and the hostage might be.

Once the authorities cut the handcuffs off the police officers in the Big House, their colleagues tried to help them save face by allowing them to arrest Charles Kahn and take him away. The authorities then ordered everyone to evacuate the estate. Sky instructed Mary Liz to wait at the Buckleys' for his call.

The phone call didn't come until six hours later. By that time Buck had explained to Mary Liz that last winter Sky had contacted him, warning that he was about to hand down an indictment for his arrest on the charge of laundering money for an organized-crime group. Buck had agreed to turn state's evidence, and provide a cover for Sky so he could infiltrate the East Hampton social scene over the summer.

"Oh, Buck," Vanessa fretted. "Why didn't you tell me?"

"And implicate you?" He shook his head. "We've got a lot of problems, Nessa, but even you didn't deserve this."

"I take it that's some kind of reconciliatory note," Vanessa said, walking over to the big leather armchair where he was sitting. "Now that you're going up the river, you want me to help paddle in the other direction." She sat down on the arm of the chair, looking at him with something close to fondness. She picked up his hand and held it. "It is a first-rate club, Buck. You built an institution."

The phone rang and Mary Liz flicked on the portable phone that had been sitting in her lap. "Hello?"

"We lost him," Sky said. "Can you friggin' believe it? We sat out here for four hours, not knowing where the hell they were in the house, whether he had hurt her. Finally the SWAT guys send someone in and he's gone. Cleared out. Vanished. Poof! *Gone.*"

"What about Sasha?" Mary Liz said quickly.

"She's fine. I'm sorry, I should have told you that, first thing. We found her upstairs, tied up, stashed way back in the bottom of a closet. Actually, Mary Liz, could you come over here now? To Sasha's? She's pretty badly shaken up and I know you'd be a comfort to her."

"Of course," Mary Liz said. "I'm on my way. But Buck wants to talk to you."

When Mary Liz arrived at Sasha's, she found the property still crawling with police, most of whom, Sky told her, were moving out, since they had just received a sighting of William Pfeiffer in Brighton Beach, Brooklyn. "Please just calm Sasha down," he said. "She's got tons of protection here, she's absolutely safe."

"Where are you going?"

"Into New York. I've got to see this thing through." Uncharacteristically, he then let out a string of curses. "I can't believe he got away."

"Go get him, Sky," she said, kissing him on the cheek. "And please, be careful."

He hugged her and told her not to wait up.

Mary Liz got clearance to go into the diva's house.

Poor Sasha was a basket case. After rummaging aimlessly through all her herbs and crystals and blue algae and the like, she looked gratefully to Mary Liz when she said perhaps a brandy was in order, and then proceeded into her living room to take a huge swig of Napoleon right out of the bottle. After prying the diva's fingers off the bottle (she was shaking, still, poor soul), Mary Liz gave her a small snifter to carry around with her for the rest of the night. She made Sasha sit on her bedroom floor with her and meditate—"I am safe in the love of God"—for fifteen minutes; made her come down and eat dinner (refried rice and vegetables and warm, buttered bread); put her in a hot bath, then put her in bed, where Mary Liz read *Pride and Prejudice* to her until she fell asleep. Then she kissed Sasha on the forehead, turned out all but the bathroom light and crept downstairs to sign out with the police.

It was still warm and humid outside, even now, at eleven. All the outside lights were on at the manor, each casting fuzzy rings of light. She cut through the hedge and went to the guest house to check in with Wendy.

"Do you know that silly bitch Denver heard everything from out back," Wendy ranted, "and didn't even call the police? She just sat out there, hoping Pfeiffer would shoot everybody."

"Where's she now?"

"At Julius and Jeanine's, thank God. Bertie's up with his mother and that lawyer. The police are coming to arrest Nancy in the morning. The lawyer thinks they'll be able to get her out on bond, though, tomorrow, too."

"I'm sure Sky will be able to help somehow," Mary Liz said.

"I hope so. I dread to think what will happen to Bertie if he loses her."

"Actually," Mary Liz said, "I'm beginning to think that might be the best thing for him."

As Mary Liz walked back down to the cottage, she wondered how Rachelle Zaratan was doing. It must have been quite a shock to find out her husband and partner of over twenty years was capable of cold-blooded murder.

She'd call Rachelle in the morning.

There was a note on the door for her to call Bertie at the Big House. She unlocked the door and went in, punching in the security code to turn off the alarm. She switched on some lights, went in to use the bathroom and then came back out to the kitchen to pour herself a glass of wine and call Bertie.

"They're arresting Mother tomorrow at ten o'clock," he told her.

"Wendy told me."

"I was wondering if you could come up for breakfast at eight-thirty. I think Mother wants to thank you for what you said in front of Denver this morning. About—you know."

"Her and my father," Mary Liz said. "Tell Aunt Nancy I'd be delighted to have breakfast with her." Weird, wasn't it, arrest by appointment?

She played the messages on her answering machine and called her parents to tell them she was fine, she'd tell them all about it in the morning.

Then she flopped down in the living room with her glass of wine and flicked through the stations. Oh, wow, there was Sasha's house—and the Big House—video taken today by helicopter. And Bill's picture.

Bill Pfeiffer. Who the heck would have ever believed it? To think he was the same man she had seen with his little girl, to think he was the man who had so brightened the life of Claire MacClendon—

Poor Claire.

She flicked off the TV, brought her glass to the kitchen and then went back to her bedroom to change. She had thought she might try to wait up for Sky, but there was no way. She was exhausted. She pulled the curtains closed over the windows and then went to the closet to slide open one of the doors.

And found Bill Pfeiffer standing there pointing a gun at her. She didn't scream, but did jump back, heart in her throat.

"Sorry, Mary Liz, but I'm afraid I need your help," he said, looking around and then stepping out. "Change the sandals for sneakers and get your car keys."

"I can't believe this," she muttered, feeling more annoyed at having the hell scared out of her than anything else. This was Bill, for heaven's sake, the guy she had liked and had been working with for the past couple of months. The idea he would actually kill her seemed very remote. She wouldn't argue. She would do as he said, but she did push past him to get her sneakers. "How the hell did you get in here?"

"My security guy. He gave me the pass code you chose and made a couple of keys to the cottage for me."

Good God. That meant Bill had had hours to himself in here today, to eat, freshen up, and, she noticed, change into some of Sky's clothes—blue jeans and a white polo shirt. Mary Liz yanked on her sneakers and started tying them. When she straightened up, she said, "I really feel like biffing you one, you know. Maybe it would be worth getting shot dead, just to hit you once for Claire."

Pfeiffer actually laughed. "Just like a woman to think the most serious trespass concerns dating her friend."

"And your little girl, Bill, my God, how could you get into this? You've destroyed Jenny's life!"

Before she knew what was happening, Pfeiffer had struck her on the side of the face with the butt of his gun, sending her spinning back into the wall. "Shut up, Mary Liz, we're leaving. Next time, it'll be the bridge of your nose."

She wasn't bleeding, but she would get another one of those eggs under her skin on her forehead, she knew. The thought of him hitting her on the bridge of her nose, though, made her cringe. The break was still so tender.

"Where are we going?"

"Shut up. Not a *word,* Mary Liz. We're going outside and getting into your car."

And that's what they did. Mary Liz looked around, wondering where all the law enforcement people were. Over at Sasha's, probably. But surely someone must be watching the Big House, to make sure Aunt Nancy didn't go anywhere. But then, they'd be watching the Big House, not down here, in the darkness, where she and Bill were getting into her car.

"Put the top down," he ordered.

She did.

"Now start her up and head for 27. If we're stopped, you call me Sky. Or I will shoot whoever stops us in the face."

They put on their seat belts and Bill put his arm along the back of Mary Liz's seat, holding his gun under a newspaper in his lap. She noticed, only then, that he had slipped on the spare set of Sky's glasses. They drove out of the driveway and turned right, past Sasha's driveway. No one stopped them; in fact, the officers at the end of Sasha's driveway waved back at Bill when he waved.

Now what?

She headed for 27, where he directed her to turn east. They drove for nearly forty-five minutes, branching off on the Old Montauk Highway along the coast, in complete silence, until he told her to slow down, and then, to turn down a gravel driveway that sloped down toward the ocean. There was a small house. And a dock. And at the dock, a long tubular boat. A cigarette, Mary Liz thought they were called. A racing boat.

They got out of the car and Pfeiffer walked her to the dock. A man was sitting in the driver's seat. The two men nodded. "Get in, Mary Liz," Pfeiffer told her.

"Come on, Bill, just leave me here."

The man on board stood up and came over to hold out his hand.

Resigned, she took it and climbed aboard. The pilot started the boat, a loud two-engine roar, and Bill looked around, cast off the lines and then jumped aboard, too. The pilot reversed the boat from the dock and turned around, and then shot them ahead toward open water. They did not have their lights on.

The occasional lights twinkling on shore grew distant. The boat was perhaps two miles out when the pilot stopped it, letting the engines idle. He switched on a dashboard lamp.

Mary Liz swallowed. "Don't be a fool, Bill, and murder me, too."

"I'm no fool," Bill said, waiting as the pilot rummaged around in a tack box. He brought out an orange life preserver. "Some would say I've got a soft spot for you, Mary Liz. Put it on."

She complied.

"We're two miles out," Pfeiffer told her. "The water's sixty-two degrees. You keep swimming and you'll get in fine. Now, off with you."

She looked out at the darkness, at the endlessly dark water, and shivered. But he was offering her her life. She put one foot up on the side of the boat and turned. "Well, thanks for finishing the inventory."

Pfeiffer stuck out his hand.

"You've got to be kidding," she told him.

He dropped his hand. "Tell Claire my feelings were genuine," he said quietly.

"You've got to be kidding," she said again.

"No. Goodbye, Mary Liz," he said as the pilot helped her up to stand on the side. "We won't be seeing each other again."

Mary Liz jumped, thinking, *Oh, hell, he's probably going to shoot me now.* The water splashed cold and salty, but she resurfaced quickly because of the life preserver. Now she was a great target. But instead of being shot, she saw Pfeiffer wait until the boat had drifted safely away from her before giving the signal and the pilot flicked off the lamp, gunned the engines and the cigarette boat went flying out to open waters.

Mary Liz was left bobbing in the darkness. She took a deep breath, turned to select a target light on shore and began the long swim in.

35

Three days later, on Wednesday, Mary Liz was talking to her father on the telephone. "Believe it, Dad," Mary Liz said, "because it's true. They think he was airlifted by helicopter from the boat and taken to Logan, where he boarded a plane to Iceland and hopped a Russian freighter or something."

Sky came into the kitchen.

"His daughter was grabbed in Central Park yesterday and they can't find her now, either."

Sky opened the dryer and took out the clothes in it.

"Sky says they recruited him when he was living in London. They had something on him—some sort of illegal transaction... Heck, yes! They paid him a bloody fortune! But Bill's wife left him, anyway. Listen, Dad, I'll tell you all about it later," she promised. "Sky's getting ready to leave now." Pause. "I will. I love you, too. Bye-bye." She hung up the phone. "Dad sends you not only his best, but his highest regards."

"For what?" Sky muttered, untangling some socks. "Screwing up a two-year investigation?"

"One guy, Sky," she said, going over to him and sliding her arms around his waist. "And you'll get him. Sooner or later, you'll get him." She released him to help sort some clothes. "This is the last load. Is there anything else I can do?"

"You've done far too much, as it is," he said, throwing a piece of clothing back down and taking her hands. "Do you have any idea how much I love you?"

"I think so," she said, eyes shining.

He kissed her. "I've to get going, darling. When are you taking off?"

"Couple of hours, then it's back to Chicago to open my mail."

"And then?"

"And then, my love," she murmured, kissing him, sliding her arms up around his neck, "I rendezvous with a certain gentleman I know who has a cottage and an old Mercedes in Virginia."

* * *

After Sky left for Washington, Mary Liz walked up to the guest house. Bertie and Wendy were nowhere to be found, but the Range Rover was still in the driveway so she knew they must be around somewhere.

She found them sitting in the cabana, sipping beers in their bathing suits, Wendy lying on the couch, Bertie on the floor against the kitchenette refrigerator. Mary Liz marched right over, took the beer out of Bertie's hand and poured it down the sink.

"Hey!"

Mary Liz looked at her watch. "In one hour you've got one of Dad's partners coming here to review the records of the estate with you."

"With me?"

"Yes, with you. So I want you showered and changed and looking dignified, got it? I'll start you off in the meeting, but then you're taking over. And after that, everyone's going to be coming to you."

He looked utterly confused and slowly stood up.

"You're going to be signing some papers, Bertie," she told him, "that are going to make you the coexecutor—with my father—of the estate."

"Me?" He sounded scared.

Mary Liz nodded. "And I know of no better choice. *You* are the patriarch of the family now, Bertie. It's up to *you* to reestablish the Hoffman name. My father will help you, Bertie, and I know you'll do an excellent job."

Bertie smiled and then suddenly threw his arms around Mary Liz, giving her a tremendous hug and lifting her off the ground. She laughed and laughed; he refused to put her down, making her wonder if maybe she had lost some weight this summer. Finally, he plopped her down. "You've got to promise I can talk to you."

"Anytime," she promised. "And listen, something else." She kicked her head in Wendy's direction. "You and Jake set a good example for her, okay? Show her what a really good relationship is like."

Instantly Wendy's and Bertie's mouths fell open. "What are you talking about?" Bertie cried. He held up a defending hand. "Not that it's not a nice thought—believe me, it's not as if I'd never thought about it."

Wendy was screaming with laughter on the couch. "I can't believe it! This is too good! Oh, Bertie, *do* set a good example for me!"

Mary Liz looked back and forth between them. Finally she pleaded, "What? What? Let me in on it, what's the joke?"

"It's no joke, Mary Liz," Bertie told her, laughing. "It's reality. You've got it all wrong. Jake doesn't belong to me, he belongs to *Mother*."

The housekeeper let her in and Mary Liz went upstairs to Sasha's bedroom suite. The diva was amidst a flurry of clothes that were lying on every uncovered surface of the room. Outside, on the balcony, a man was surveying the water with a pair of binoculars. "Hi," Sasha said, looking up as she pressed some clothes into a suitcase.

"Hi," Mary Liz said. She looked around the room. "This is so sad."

"Yes, well, Rachelle's a mess and so I'm moving into Manhattan with her for a while. She can't stay here, not with all the publicity, but she can't just leave Charles in jail, either." She kicked her head toward the balcony. "That's the new guy, Jeff." She blew a strand of hair off her face. "An FBI agent in my house all this time, I still can't believe it. I knew Riff was too slim."

"How do you think I feel knowing that he bugged my house for the FBI?" Mary Liz said. "I mean, how many bugs does a wired house make?"

"Isn't that like a knock-knock joke?" the diva asked before returning to her original line of thought. "And, you know, it turns out Riff's married. You'd think if they were sending someone undercover around here, they'd send someone who could *go* under the covers, if you know what I mean. Don't you agree?"

"Oh, Sasha, I'm going to miss you," Mary Liz said, going over to hug the diva.

She was going to miss them all.

"Well, *don't* worry about me," Claire MacClendon said rather crossly, yanking out another weed from her garden, "because I'm fine. I'm just sick of people trying to talk to me about it."

"Get it straight, Claire," Mary Liz said rather crossly back. "I *don't* worry about you. You're a gifted, beautiful woman who only needed to be reminded of that."

"Stop it, Mary Liz," Claire muttered. "You're being a complete and total ass." She sat back on her haunches, pulled her gloves off and threw them on the ground. "You know nothing about what it's like to be fifty-two." She got up to her feet. "When you get to be my age, you'll know what I'm talking about."

"I do know that he cared for you."

Claire stopped in her tracks, looking at her, and didn't say anything.

"And I know that Bill Pfeiffer loved and cared for Jenny more than anything else in this world, and I know he exposed Jenny to you, let her get to know you, care for you, look forward to seeing you, letting her hope that you'd be a part of her Poppy's life and make him happy—because he wanted you as a part of his life, too."

Claire had started to cry. Mary Liz went over and put her arms around her. "My God, Mary Liz," she said, sobbing, "he's practically a murderer."

"Aunt Nancy?" Mary Liz said softly at the door. Ashley came trotting over and licked her hand.

On Monday her godmother had been arrested, arraigned, and released on bail, all by late afternoon. She was now standing at the open French door, looking out at the ocean. She turned around.

"I wanted to tell you that you're going to be very proud of Bertie," Mary Liz said. "I've just left him with the new attorney, and he's doing just fine. He and Dad are going to talk almost every day, and I will be calling in, too, but he's a fast learner and I think you can trust he will handle everything very well."

"Dear, dear, darlin' Mary Liz." Her godmother sighed, crossing her arms over her chest. "How ever will we thank you for all you've done?" Her eyes were tearing. "You are a very generous and loving young woman, and I will always remember how kind you were to me, even when you knew about what happened so very long ago."

"Well, I think it takes a pretty generous and loving person to do what you're doing with little Marc in Paris."

"Dear God in heaven!" Nancy declared. "It's the least we can do."

When her godmother had made this decision yesterday—after they had sat down to go over the estate inventory—to inform Marc's mother of his true father's identity, Mary Liz briefly struggled but then quickly reversed herself on another decision. She had given a list to Aunt Nancy of every underage girl she had found a file on in Alfred's collection, along with whatever information there had been to find them. What her godmother now did with that list was up to her, but Mary Liz had a feeling some sort of compensation might be coming the victims' way.

"This house is mine," Nancy said, raising her head to look at Mary Liz, "and I'm going to sell it. I also have some money tucked away and I can live very nicely on that. The foundation will go on, but I think we'll change the name. To simply, the Hoffman Fund. Perhaps that way, it will give Bertie and Denver and Julius greater incentive to support it."

"You sound as though you're not going to be here."

"I'm probably going to have to go to jail for a while. Eventually. Conspiracy to commit murder. Think of it, Mary Liz, had Alfred's plane only crashed a minute before I gave Herb the money..." She shrugged and said, "Oh, well, I'm sure we'll sort it out. But I will tell you, Mary Liz, Alfred's dead and Herb is dead and I can't help but feel the world is a better place for it."

Mary Liz didn't—couldn't—say anything.

Her godmother drew herself up. "Which brings me to something I wish to give you, Mary Liz."

"That's not necessary, Aunt Nancy. I— You've already given so much to the charities I mentioned."

"No, darlin'," her godmother said, taking a step forward. "This is something special—just for you. I don't suppose you'd have any room left in that sporty car of yours, would you? For a not-so-little dog who worships you?"

Mary Liz's heart stopped. "Oh, no, Aunt Nancy, no—don't do that to yourself, please, there's no need—"

"I can't take her with me," she said softly, looking down at Ashley, who was lying at Mary Liz's feet. "She loves you, Mary Liz." She looked up. "We all do."

Epilogue

Charles Kahn was the only member of the East End Country Club who went to prison. (That is, the only club member who was also a member of Alfred Hoffman's poker group.)

Due to the extraordinary lengths Buck Buckley had gone to turn state's evidence and provide Sky Preston with the means to investigate the multiple money-laundering operations created by Herbert Glidden, he was granted a full pardon. He had to give up the country club, though, and the new board elected to return the million-dollar tuition paid by every non-American member living overseas and revoke their memberships. (The Japanese members fought this, though, and are still members.)

Three days after learning what a mess her husband had gotten into with Glidden, Vanessa Buckley finally admitted that *she* was a mess and committed herself to a ten-week drug and alcohol rehabilitation program at a hospital in Rhode Island. She has remained sober (and somber, a lot of people say), and she and Buck are considering starting over in North Carolina.

Claude and Isabel Lemieux forfeited their ownership of *Je Ne Sais Quoi* and returned to France, where Claude once again works for Isabel's father.

Randolph Vandergilden has cirrhosis of the liver and is still drinking. He has retired in East Hampton.

When the scandal concerning his firm's role as an international money laundry broke out, Henry MacClendon's wife, Cindy Claydon, left him and filed for divorce. Henry let her have the divorce, but has won daily access to his son, and Henry has retired to divide his time between Manhattan and East Hampton to do it.

People were at first shocked when they saw Henry and Claire together around town, but as the months passed, it became clear that the MacClendons—after all that had happened—still had intense feelings for each other. And Claire has come to make a very big fuss over Henry's son, caring for him and talking about him and showing off pictures of him as if he were her own.

A remarriage of the MacClendons wouldn't surprise anyone now.

Denver Hoffman was hospitalized for a suicide attempt, but is back working on her TV series.

Bertie appointed his stepbrother, Julius Hoffman, chairman of Howland Films. Jeanine Hoffman is still busy in her role of Beverly Hills wife, mother and homemaker, and has made admirable attempts in persuading Denver to get the help she needs to sort herself out. In fact, most Sunday mornings Denver can be found playing tennis at Julius and Jeanine's house and having breakfast with the whole family.

Sasha Reinhart is a bigger star than ever, but is a less lonely one since Rachelle agreed to move into one of the four houses on her Malibu compound. "You can deal with the lawyers in New York, or here on the beach," was the line Rachelle said had convinced her. Sasha went ahead and made her movie with Howland Films and it looks as though it might be a hit. While filming some scenes in Texas, Sasha struck up a friendship with a cowboy extra who has since become her constant companion in the tabloids.

As for Nancy Hoffman, she served six months in a California county jail and is now living in the old Bailey homestead in Georgia. Delores is there with her, and so is Jake.

Nancy directed that Alfred's estate be redivided among his children so as to include young Marc Bresseau, who turned out to be a perfect DNA match with Alfred. She made up the difference to the three older children out of her own share.

Bertie Hoffman moved into a Manhattan apartment and is finishing an MBA degree at New York University. There are no secrets concerning his life anymore, and he is openly seeing a doctor, Matthew, who is an internist.

Bertie often sees Wendy Mitchell in town, and a couple of times they have cross-double-dated for events, such as the Cancer Ball, Wendy attending on Bertie's arm, her girlfriend, Lucy, on Matthew's.

People in Washington, D.C., are begging Sky Preston to use his high profile in the Russian Laundry Case to run for office. He has absolutely no interest in doing that. Besides, it will be years before the prosecution of the Russian Laundry is finished, and Sky is determined to stick around to personally handle the inevitable appeals of the more powerful fish caught in the net.

The biggest disappointment of his career, however, is that William Pfeiffer has yet to be found. And neither has Jenny, Pfeiffer's daughter.

As for Mary Liz, she gleefully admitted to friends and family that she had lost her mind—"And good riddance if my past was the only kind of life my mind could conceive of for me to live!"—she had sublet her apartment in Chicago, sold the Camry and driven Ashley and herself to Virginia in the LeBaron. It was to be a trial run.

The Chicago apartment is now on the market.

Mary Liz and Sky have had some lulus of arguments, just as she always suspected they would (God, he was stubborn about certain things), but their life together has otherwise been amazingly smooth. Sometimes they even get a little spooked by it, how it sometimes feels as though they met each other in the middle of a lifetime of love instead of at the beginning.

"Well, maybe we're just both worn-out the same way," Mary Liz would say, sighing and smiling and nuzzling his neck.

To no one's surprise, Mary Liz is wearing an engagement ring and the couple has set a wedding date. The only real surprise for anyone occurred at Reston, Kellaher, when it was announced in the *Wall Street Journal* that Mary Elizabeth Scott, their former partner, had been hired in Washington as a special investigations consultant to the Department of the U.S. Treasury.

A lot of people on Wall Street, that day, went out to have a drink at lunch.